Previous working book cover and poster design. Copyright Jerome Matiyas, 2013

The Epic Adventures of Mekonnen:
(The Mekonnen Epic® Series)
Book One:

MEKONNEN
The Warrior Of Light
(Part 1 of 2)

2nd edition

By
Jerome Matiyas

This book is dedicated to
Almaz and Enku.

*"I see a book coming out of you! Yes, its so profound!
And you are a prolific writer. The way you articulate and the
way God uses you is profound!"*

Prophesied by Pastor D. L. Scott, August 20, 2017.

Scripture quotations are from King James Version and Amplified Parallel Bible, copyright 1995 by
The Zondervan Corporation; Good News Bible with Deuterocanonicals/Apocrypha, copyright 1979 by
American Bible Society; Amharic Bibles (KJV), copyright 1980 by Bible Society of Ethiopia; The New
Testament in Amharic and English, Copyright 1962, 1994 by United Bible Societies.The Interlinear NIV
Hebrew-English Old Testament, 1987, by J.R. Kohnlenberger III. Deuterocanonical/apocryphal quotations
are from 1 Enoch, 2004, by G.W.E. Nickelsburg, and James C. VanderKam; The Book of Jasher, 1840
edition, by unknown ancient authors; The Book of Jubilees (The Apocalypse of Moses), copyright 2006,
Trans. by Joseph B. Lumpkin.

ᐸማን፡ህልወ፡ሥላሴሆሙ፡ነአምን፡ ፡ከ፡ኪሩቤል፡ወሱራፌል፡ያወርጉ፡ኮቴ፡ስ

When Darkness descends
upon a kingdom,
a warrior must rise up
to restore the Light.

WWW.MEKONNENEPIC.COM
Ellicott City, MD, USA

Table of Contents

MEKONNEN: The Warrior of Light (Part 1)

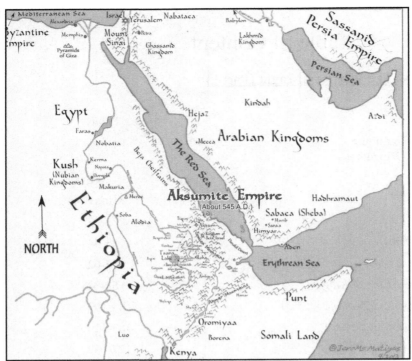

The world of MEKONNEN EPIC®, Book 1.
In the 6th century, between 540 to about 560 A.D. Showing the Empires and Kingdoms of the Realms of Earth around the Red Sea.

Foreword

By Theodros Tadese, PhD

T he book is written in superbly imaginative language which expressed inventions, thoughts, passions and insights. It is highly narrative in the way it expressed life, and the heroic adventure of MEKONNEN – the core subject matter of the novel which excites deep interest in those that read it.

The writer and artist, Jerome Matiyas, managed to approach and expressed the entire novel with a strong emotion and feelings of which the personalities and characters of the novel were highly integrated with circumstantial historical events and episodes in the respective places and sites of the Aksumite kingdom and its civilizations. Furthermore, his choice of exact defining terminologies inserted in various parts and aspects of the texts is quite suitable and indicates the writer's knowledge of the culture from which the entire novel was based.

The people that inhabited the kingdom are personified by those characters and individuals throughout the novel. The Kingdom of Aksum epitomized a nation of great power with the relics and the wonders of the obelisks and stele that are still in place in present day Aksum, located in the northern province of Tigray, in Ethiopia. The novel illustrates how this ancient city could be ravaged by the evil Armies of Darkness only to be saved by the Sword of Light from the young warrior Mekonnen. The story also shows the treat of the evil forces spreading to the neighboring communities and nations in the region as Mekonnen must learn to befriend people of various cultures and languages throughout Ethiopia, Eritrea and the rest of the Horn of Africa. The story encourages unity and comradery among people of neighboring cultures, who must band together to fight evil forces that are not from this Earthly realm.

The novel emphatically denotes the power and personality of the writer with great importance attached to the subject matter with the illustrations and depictions of the great empire of Aksum, for a more graphic and visual demonstration of the action and adventure taking place. Most of the illustrations, more than 120 of them, were done by Jerome Matiyas himself, in the modern styles shown in American and Japanese comic books and animated features. It is in this part of the world where the warrior and keeper of Light resides and is in control. Again, it is here where the mythology and the reality combined were discovered, as they have existed for millennia to this day, and combined to offer an imaginative narration of the novel.

The book has a potential for great drama given the personalities and characters with whom it is associated, and the virtues and values of the characters have been elegantly personified and allegorically represented.

The book, as a novel, encompasses historical realities with its associated myths by depicting the past and current culture of traditional customs, spirituality and belief systems. The warrior represented by Mekonnen, indeed portrayed, the reality of the past in its historic time and civilization-The Aksumite kingdom. The novel in its representation illustrates with pictorials and caricatures the past and present people, their patriotism and gallantry to which respect, humility, morality and not to mention their strong belief system is a part of.

The book is well conceived, written, and illustrated in a manner that mixes reality and mythology as integral part of the traditions and customs. In this overarching culture of society emerges a patriotic individual—Mekonnen—who embarks on fighting the evil and the darkness of the day to bring about the light by his belief system and moral virtue placed on him. Such story is inherent and manifests in the folklores of the society from past to present day Ethiopia and Horn of Africa.

I highly recommend this novel to those who love and enjoy reading history, traditions and cultures. In particular, this novel will be an ideal read to the youth who can find this it as a model to learn and to take courage in the pursuit of righteousness and truth in the face of all the evil that ravages the good of society. Only in such confrontation of the evil with the bravery and courage of individuals the world will be a better place.

Professor Theodros Tadese, PhD
Anatomy and Physiology
Northern Virginia, USA
5/18/2020

Jerome Matiyas

Preface

When I was growing up I loved comic books. My favorites were Conan the Barbarian, created by Robert E. Howard (1906 - 1936), and the various Batman titles, created by Bob Kane (1915 - 1998). I really enjoyed Conan's epic adventures with sword in hand and bravery in his heart, venturing into exotic yet extremely perilous locations, in an ancient Earth. A world littered with gleaming kingdoms and savage regions crawling with deadly men, women, and beasts of all shapes and sizes. The artwork from world-class painters and illustrators like Ernie Chan, John Buscema, and Frank Frazetta were very energetic and captivating, and the stories written by Roy Thomas and Barry Windsor-Smith were well crafted in Victorian English style that sounded classy to me.

Then there were the Batman comic books I really enjoyed because Batman himself was so mysterious, brooding, intelligent, yet very agile, and strong. He was and still is one of the most psychologically complex characters in all comic books and movies for the past 20 years or so. These are two out of many great comic books and graphic novel titles that influenced me through the years and made me want to create my own comics or graphic novels.

Then there were the Fantasy, Sword & Sandal, and Sword & Sorcery movies that I really loved that fueled my imagination and thirst for epic adventure in exotic locations, ancient and faraway places, with mythological creatures and eclectic people. Fantasy films like *Lord of the Rings* (Ralph Bakshi's 1978 animated version), *Willow*, the *Labyrinth* and *The Dark Crystal* come to mind. Sword and Sandal epics like *Ben-Hur* (1959), *The Ten Commandments* (1956) and *Spartacus* (1960), and the Sword & Sorcery epics like *Clash of the Titans* (1981) and *Excalibur* (1981) were important to my humble upbringing as a young lad passing time with my younger brother Joel in the twin island Republic of Trinidad and Tobago.

At an early age I grew to love drawing, and redrawing our favorite superheroes was one of the ways my brother and I learned how to draw and understand proportions and human anatomy. So eventually, I decided I wanted to create my own comic books and graphic novels. One of my classmates in secondary school, Mergil Rosales, used to intrigue and entertain everyone by drawing comic book versions of popular sci-fi movies like *Predator*, *Cyborg*, and *Aliens*. So, I was inspired to attempt to do the same, but I would always start one but never got to finish my comic books. Other classmates also tried with varying degrees of success, but Mergil was the only one I remember that was the best and did it consistently.

Fast forward a few years to my late teens and I decided to be a born-again Christian and became very involved in my local church that I grew up in since I was a toddler. The messages I always listened to preached by my pastor Rev. Clinton Providence, gradually became more real and life changing to me. I accepted the Lord Jesus Christ, the Son of God the Father, who died on the cross for my sins, and the sins of all mankind, as a sacrifice, so that I would not have to live or die in my sins anymore. He sent the Holy Spirit to live with me and communicate with me forever. As profound and simple as this may sound for those who may or may not believe or understand this, I took this new way of life very seriously.

So, after this, I decided I still wanted to create comic books and graphic novels, but this time I wanted my stories and adventures to be spiritual and portray a positive or Christian message of deliverance and salvation. But still be adventurous and exciting like *Conan the Barbarian*, *Ben-Hur*, and *Lord of the Rings*.

But then I realized, most of my favorite heroes in movies, comic books, and TV, did not look like me, a brown skin, curly haired boy of mostly African and some European descent in my ancestry. Most of my favorite heroes were of White European descent. But because of what I was thought in school: that Caribbean and American people of African descent were descendants of slaves; and what I saw in the news on T.V.: Like famine in Ethiopia and Somalia in the early 1980s. All I saw on Television were dry, barren lands with skinny children with swollen bellies. Then I saw in movies, natives in African jungles, living primitive lives, only wearing loin clothes and abiding in straw huts. Even though these may be true at some points in time, in certain regions for certain people, that is not the whole story for a whole continent of billions of people for thousands of years. Africa is huge continent with a vast variety of people, cultures, history, civilizations, empires and natural resources.

So I began thinking to myself, if I want to create a hero that was as brave and adventurous as Conan and Ben-Hur, wielding a powerful sword and wear flashing armor like King Arthur in *Excalibur*, and venture through fantastical lands and face mythological beasts like Bilbo, Frodo, and Aragon in the Hobbit and Lord of the Rings novels, but he was of African descent? Where should my hero come from? What should be his background that could positively represent Africa and Africans, still be connected to the biblical stories and historical events, and still convey a spiritual message for all people of all races? This is what I seriously thought about between age 18 and 20 years old.

My answer came from four sources: 1) Pastor Providence's sermons about Africans mentioned in the Bible, 2) Bible verses mentioning Ethiopia and Cush/Kush, 3) Bible verses about the Armor of God for Spiritual warfare, and 4) Emperor Haile Selassie I, who is venerated by the Rastafarians and in

Jerome Matiyas

Reggae music.

To explain the first: In his Sunday morning sermons sometimes, Pastor Providence would preach to the congregation about God's love for all races, including Africans, as opposed to the way people of African descent were portrayed as being called sub-humans and primitive during the Trans-Atlantic Slave Trade from the 17th to the 19th century. He would occasionally mention the Ethiopian Eunuch who was on his way back to his kingdom, probably the Meroe Kingdom in Nubia, now known as North Sudan, reading the Book of the prophet Isaiah in his chariot. Then the apostle Philip ran to the chariot, explained the meaning of the scripture to the Eunuch and then baptized him in water as a new believer in Jesus Christ. This is written in the Book of Acts 8: 26 – 39. Other sermons that stuck with me is from Numbers chapter 12 when Moses married an Ethiopian/ Kushite woman. Miriam and Aaron came against their brother Moses for his new wife, but God struck Miriam with leprosy until she repented and was put in quarantine for seven days. These verses and several others our Pastor Providence used to encourage us to love all people because the God of the Universe loves all mankind.

These sermons connected naturally with my second source, my own studying and research of the Bible, leading to Psalms 68:31, "Princes shall come out of Egypt; Ethiopia shall soon stretch out her hands to God." And in Genesis 2: 13, Ethiopia being one of the first regions mentioned in the creation of the Earth and Eden, although in the original Hebrew Torah it is called Kush, which means "black" (or it is possible the word Kush became synonymous with a person having dark skin). Then there is an account in 2 Kings 19:9; Isaiah 37:9, which is rarely spoken of, but confirmed in historical secular records, when King Tarhaqa of Ethiopia/Kush assisted King Hezekiah of Israel in fighting off the invading Assyrian army lead by King Sennacharib.

Thirdly, the description of the Armor of God in Ephesians 6: 10 – 18 became one of my favorite verses. It triggered imagery in my mind about the ancient and medieval fighting action I enjoyed reading and watching in Conan comic books and movies like Ben-Hur, Excalibur, and Lord of the Rings. I thought to myself if I created a comic book hero he should somehow have to acquire the parts of the Armor of God to battle against evil principalities and powers in the spiritual realms, not fighting against flesh and blood of mankind. This concept is expounded in Isaiah 59:17 and in Hebrews 4:12, about the "Word of God being quick and powerful, sharper than any two-edged sword…" added to my fascination with the spiritual Armor of God as a plot device for an epic story.

Fourth and lastly, I began to ask myself: So, who is this Emperor Haile Selassie I've been hearing about for most of my life? Why do they always sing about him in Reggae and Dancehall songs, and the Rastafarians call him

be of Judah," and "Jah, Rastafari!", titles I attributed only to
"Lion of the one who died on a cross for our sins and resurrected on the
Jesus Chr why do they say he was descended from the Queen of Sheba
third d mon? Is this true? Is modern-day Ethiopian really that special
and here the Queen of Sheba came from? Was he the first Rasta?
a "Ras" or "dreadlocks" like his followers do? I had a lot of
about this person who I heard of and saw portraits and paintings of
life but never knew who he really was. So, I did my own research,
ing through articles in our family collection of The Encyclopedia
ica, then I went to my town's public library in downtown Arima. I
the librarian to show me books about Ethiopia, Haile Selassie, etc. I
d my notebook and pen and was ready to gather knowledge. One of the
first things that struck me was Emperor Haile Selassie did not himself have
long Rasta locks like his followers do. Then I learned his title was Ras Tafari,
Ras meaning "Duke" of sorts, which is where the term Rastafari came from.
Mind you, I did not notice his father's name was Makonnen at this time, I
learned this fact several years later after I decided to name my character
Mekonnen.

So, then I began to focus more on ancient Ethiopia and Eritrea and
zoomed in on Aksum, a great kingdom that become an empire, and once
ruled much of the Horn of African and the Southern Arabian Peninsula which
was known as Sabaea, or Sheba. The empire lasted for hundreds of years,
and the kings believed and claimed they were descended from King Solomon
and the Queen of Sheba. Their legendary son Menelik was the first king of
Aksum after his mother's reign, and the Ethiopians claim to have possession
of the Ark of the Covenant in Aksum to this day. I was intrigued and kept
on reading and writing notes. Then I read it is one of the first kingdoms, and
first African nations, to accept Christianity as a state religion since about
330 AD when the Syrian monk Saint Frumentius converted the King Ezana
to the faith. And to this day it is still a Christian nation, and the Solomonic
monarchy continued until the death of the last Emperor, Haile Selassie I, in
1975. I read all this and was sold.

I thought, "This is it! My comic book hero should come from the
Kingdom of Aksum. He's going to come from a bright and prosperous
kingdom of gold and incense, where the Ark of the Covenant resides, and the
people and kings are connected to the Bible, the Israelites, the Ethiopians/
Kushites, and King Solomon. And my character will have on the Armor of
God to battle evil creatures, and demons like Conan and Aragon did. Except,
my story will be a spiritual one about the power of God instead of fighting
against flesh and blood. Kind of like *Pilgrim's Progress* by John Bunyan
(1628 - 1688), but more rooted in history, and hopefully, more exciting."

It all seemed like the perfect fit and launching pad for a story, and I
believe I was right. Little did I know my journey to get one book complete

and published would take so long. For a long time, I did not ha
to a list of authentic Ethiopian names to choose from so I used the *ess*
Martigon, borrowing it from Val Kilmer's warrior character in the
adventure movie, *Willow*, Madmartigon. I finally found the name M
Makonnen while searching online around the year 2000 when I was in
college. I like the sound of the name and the meaning: "An Elite Person
Commander" was the definition given on the website. I did not know it w
the name of Ras Tafari's/Emperor Haile Selassie's father, Ras Makonnen.
found out years later while doing more research.

Through the years my experiences and adventures in writing, researching, planning and illustrating The Epic Adventures of Mekonnen (The Mekonnen Epic Series) has been rewarding, challenging, sometimes frustrating and quite profound. It has transformed my life to becoming fully graphed into the Ethiopian community and lifestyle. My original plans to make it into a graphic novel series gradually transformed into being traditional novels with illustrations sprinkled throughout the chapters (sometimes called caption novels). In the process of researching and putting the historical, mythological, legendary and spiritual information together, plus crafting a story around it, it was easier to just write out the whole story as a novel. Producing a comic book or graphic novel is a whole different process and skill set to craft satisfactory, which I was not able to fit into my schedule. I would still like to collaborate with a reputable company or studio to make Mekonnen into a graphic novel, animated series or movies in the future. Ironically, it seems I finally figured out how to draw comic book panels after completing this more than 350 plus pages of the novel you're reading right now.

These are the series of events in a nutshell that inspired and sparked the making of this book and the forthcoming series of novels in the Epic Adventures of Mekonnen. There is much more I can write concerning my journey and inspiration for creating this work but it will take up too much space. I may explain more in the introduction of the second part of this story. I hope and pray you enjoy the story and illustrations and that you will be intrigued, informed, and inspired.

Acknowledgements

I would like to thank and give credit to these people who have helped and encouraged me through the years to make this book, and the ones to come. First, I need to thank God – Egziabeher Amlak – the Creator of the Universe for life and giving me the vision and inspiration to create this book. I thank my parents James and Joycelyn for always encouraging me to use the gifts the Lord has blessed me with to follow my dreams and do the best in whatever I put my hands and heart to. I thank my brother Joel Edward for always encouraging me with affirming words, wacky jokes, and smiley faces in text messages ☺.

I thank Israel Endalkachew, one of my first Ethiopian friends, and who was instrumental in introducing me to the larger Habesha community in the Baltimore, DC and Virginia area. Big thanks to Seifu Haile Selassie for introducing to the Ethiopian Orthodox Church in DC which opened me to the remnants of ancient rituals, processions, music, and culture for the first time. Also, it was my first exposure to the Ge'ez language which was very helpful to me to use in my art in the early days when I restarted this project in 2006-2007.

I thank Claire Dorsey for volunteering to be a proofreader when you were available and your encouragement to press on. Thanks to Kamau Sennaar for the encouragement and insight and lending me your Interlinear Hebrew-English Old Testament. Very helpful! I thank Celina Stewart, Toni Milden, Tom Henry, Sandy Jackson and Brooke Barber for the encouragement and supporting me by purchasing items from my online store that featured prints of my artwork. I thank Hawani Tessema for encouraging me often and urging me to display my artwork in the back of the church after services when I first started attending in 2012. I thank Aibesse Tessema for assisting me in my tent that one time when I displayed my art for the Annual Ethiopian Festival in 2013. Thanks to my Pastor Paulos Hanfere of Overflow City Church (and Next Generation Ministries before that) for being my spiritual leader, encourager and a friend for the past four to five years we've known each other since I started coming around to DC. I thank Pastor Abel Araya of JGA Ministries for encouraging words and prayers in all seasons of life. I thank Eyerusalem Feleke for helping me understand the sentence and word structure for the parts of the Armor of God as written in the Amharic Bible. Thanks to Mahilet Moges for helping me understand the different styles of traditional Ethiopian and Eritrean clothing.

I thank Awale Abdi for the tons of great information and history of Horn of Africa people and culture and the many beautiful commonalities among us you shared with me through emails.

Betty Amare, my birthday twin sister! Thank you for allowing me to draw you as the likeness of my character Nuhamin. God bless you forever.

Saba Fassil, thank you for your patience! You waited five years for me to render a drawing of you as Nigist Saba – The Queen of Sheba. It's finally done! By now it should be a masterpiece!

These guys have become like brothers to me through the almost ten years: Gedion Mulat, K.B. Megersa, and Motuma Sima. Thank you and your families, for being a part of my life. All the time we spent together, the meals, weddings, sleepovers, holidays and many events we're celebrated together. Yerusalem Work, the poet and author, thanks you for your creative and caring heart. Samuel Getahun the artist and Frenchman, thanks for the encouragement and the Wacom tablet. To Nathanael Terefe, thanks buddy

Jerome Matiyas

for the moral support and Friday night calls. Thanks, Sammy Belay for attempting to predict and declare how much I can make selling my books, even when I insist that making money was never my motivation but just to create art with the talents God gave me. Michael Knight, thanks for praying for me and all of us, and encouraging me to pray more. I thought I was praying enough at the time, but I probably wasn't. Now I believe I am.

Shout out to Yared Tadese for looking out and introducing me to young talented up-and-coming artists in church. Thanks to Yonatan Tsehai, Samuel Zelleke, Yoni Rosario and Zema Meseretu for reading the first draft and your honest feedback.

To Barbara Makeda Blake-Hannah and her son Makonnen Blake-Hannah in Jamaica, I thank you two so much for finding me online and constantly follow my work in progress through the years and the continued encouragement and support for this passion project. It's no coincidence Makonnen looks like my character Mekonnen. Before you found me, I already drew him in your likeness without knowing it.

I must thank Nevin Govan for his consulting and advice on the architecture and perspective drawing of the Ta'akha Mariam Palace, which was once the royal palace for the Aksumite royalty in Tigray, Aksum, Northern Ethiopia. I thank Kandie Dellie for the little online collaboration we did years ago when we advertised each other's websites and online store. I thank Bishop William Hawthorne for encouragement and seeing the bigger vision and potential for the Mekonnen Epic series.

A special thanks to Prophetess Kelly Crews and her team at Kelly Crews Publishing for proofing and editing my first novel.

I thank Cherrie Woods, Public Relations Consultant, for her helpful advice and tips on effective publishing, designing and marketing a novel. I thank CreateSpace.com and Kindle Direct Publishing for the opportunities to self-publish my first novel, and hopefully won't be the last.

To the Ethiopian and Eritrean communities of Maryland, DC, and Virginia (DMV), USA, and around the world, I thank you all for your support, encouragement and inspiration.

Jerome Matiyas
3/2019, Maryland, USA
www.mekonnenepic.com

Also from **MEKONNEN EPIC®** Productions

The First MEKONNEN EPIC Comic Book.
28 pages of epic storytelling in vibrant colors!

Story, artwork and color by Jerome Matiyas.
Color and consulting by Nicholas Carrington.
Feature poem by Yerusalem Work.

Get it at mekonnenepic.square.site
or selected bookstores.

MEKONNEN EPIC® is supported
in part by the Maryland State
Arts Council (msac.org)

MEKONNEN: THE WARRIOR OF LIGHT

Prologue

Ezekiel 1:4-28; 10:1-14
Daniel 10:5-6
Revelation 1:13-16; 4:2-9

ANCIENT DAYS, ANCIENT CONFLICT
JEROME MATIYAS © 2018

Jerome Matiyas

PROLOGUE

FOR EONS the Armies of Light have been at war with the

Mysteries of Darkness as they struggle for power and reign over the various Realms, Kingdoms, and Dimensions in the Universe. Now the Realms of Earth are caught in the midst of this ancient struggle, and the fate of all creation hangs in the balance.

Malakot: The Almighty Creator, The Elect One, and the Breath of Life.
As it is written in the sacred Oracles of old, inscribed on the golden tablets by the Malakim and Erelim that are in the Highest Realms of *Shamayim*, then handed down as holy writ to the first enlightened ones in the Realms of Earth: In the beginning was the Ultimate, Ever-existing Almighty One, Ancient of Days in whom dwells the living Word, in whom and from whom illumines light and essence of love, righteousness, peace, joy and life everlasting. The Almighty Everlasting One abides in the highest places of the Kingdom Realms of Lights, with his heavenly hosts worshiping and ministering unto him, continually.

This is a mystery, for everything was created by and through the living Word, who existed from the beginning in the Almighty One, yet the Word has manifested physically and was beheld as the Elect One, the Anointed One, the *Mashiach (Messiah)*, who will stand and rule over the Kingdom Realms of Earth in peace and righteousness. And those that have been found worthy and meek, obedient, righteous and *Yashar*, which is to walk the Upright way, will be redeemed and shall rule with the Elect One, forever.

On the highest mountain, in the highest realm of pure beaming Light,

The Ancient of Days, On the Great Throne of Glory. Jerome Matiyas © 2016

in the seventh level of Shamayim is the enthroned Almighty One, Lord of Lights, in his brilliance and splendor, a being of light, wind and fire, not to be perceived as mankind with flesh and blood yet still a real living, tangible being of intelligence, knowledge, love, compassion, justice, righteousness, and holiness.

In the beginning, the Almighty One, *Elohim*, enthroned between a pair of mighty Cherubim, who bow with outstretched wings before him. The Supreme Being with multiple attributes, through the living Word that manifests tangibly and by his *Ruach*, which is the breath of life that proceeded out before Him like a flame of cleansing fire. Out of His igneous breath, the sound of the Almighty's voice resonated throughout the universe as he declared,

"Let There Be Light!"

And there was light.[1]

Mesqalon: Affair of the Hosts of Shamayim.
In His presences are the highest-ranking creatures of his creation: the *Chayot HaKodesh*, which are the four Living Creatures who worship around the throne, having the body of a four-legged beast with multiple wings and multiple heads, and many eyes. They are a dreadful sight for the average

1 *Genesis 1:3, John 1:1, Book of Adam and Eve*

man of the Earthly realm to behold but are the purest and holiest of heavenly creatures, praising and worshiping the Almighty *Elohim* continually in his presence. As it has been recorded by the ancient scribes, the faces of the four creatures are in the likeness of a lion, an ox, a man and an eagle respectively.

The *Chayot HaKodesh* is followed by the seven *Sar Malakim*—Arch-Angels—that stand in the presence of the Lord of Host, in the midst of a crystal-clear sea of glass, and engulfed in the *Shekinak* clouds of glory, consuming pillars of fires of sanctification and brilliant light of innumerable colors that the eyes of man only see as the colors of the earthly rainbow. The most famous of the seven to mankind are Miykael, Gabriel, Uriel and Raphael, each corresponding somewhat to the Four Living Creatures, the four cardinal points and many other *quartos* in the universe. The other three *Sar Mal'akim* are Reuel, Sariel, and Remiel.

In the midst of those creatures are the *Ophanim,* which are spinning wheels with eyes and intelligences, what some may call the Almighty's *Merkabah* or Chariot. Their hierarchy and order vary depending on the scribe and oracle that recorded these things.

Then there are the *Serafim*, the Burning Ones, engulfed in flames within and without, in the appearance of men or eagles, bearing multiple wings ranging from one to three pairs of wings. Some earthly cultures know them as the Phoenix of old legends.

Next in order are the *Cherabim,* the Mighty Ones, of various kinds and forms similar to the *Chayot HaKodesh*, having the body of a four-legged beast with the head of a lion, an ox, an eagle or a man, having wings of one to four pairs. They fly to and fro from one end of *Shamayim* to another in service of the Almighty One, the Ancient of Days.

There are the *Hashmallim,* which are glowing amber, *Erelim;* or the Valiant Ones, with strong faces like lions. Then the *Bene Elohim,* which are the Sons of God, of which some oracles describe as being the same as or similar to the *Malakim,* that look like men at first impression but are much more glorious in apparel and powerful in strength.

Next are the *Ishim*, the manlike beings who look very much like *Ishim-Adam* of Earth, are probably the same or a few levels lower than the *Malakim,* and *Bene Elohim,* since through the eyes of mortal man they look alike and intermingle with men unnoticed until they reveal themselves by demonstrating miraculous acts.

Helel: The Expanding Cherub.

Now, it has been recorded in the ancient Oracles that besides the *Cherubim* pair and the *Chayyot* quad, there was another creature even more glorious and splendid than all the hosts of Shamayim can declare. He expanded even over the two Cherubim who bow with outstretched wings. This creature's

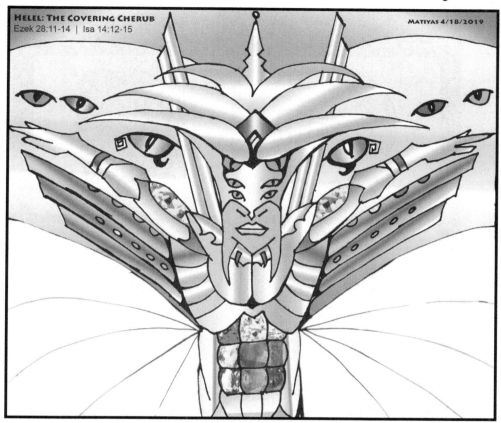

HELEL: THE COVERING CHERUB
Ezek 28:11-14 | Isa 14:12-15

MATIYAS 4/18/2019

name was deciphered to be *Helel-kherub-mimshak[2]-hashak*, which translates to "Helel[3], the expanding cherub who covers." His title *Helel* translates to "Brightness" and later interpreted in earlier oracles as "Morning Star," attesting to his glorious illumination of brilliant light that shone forth from his being as he sheltered over the magnificence of the Almighty One, Elohim.

Helel was a magnificent creature, with massive wingspans stretching with awesome form and beauty, and a breastplate decked and bejeweled with every precious jewel and stone imaginable, reflecting light into a kaleidoscope of colors throughout all the highest realms of Shamayim. The likeness of sardius, topaz, diamond, beryl, onyx, jasper, sapphire, emerald, carbuncle, and gold decorated his body in a mosaic of elaborate patterns. Organic pipes and rhythmic timbrels were fitted into his body to emanate the most beautifully melodic tunes that flow from the Almighty himself. And pure cleansing fire burned within him and projected out of his mouth on cue

---

2 *This is the only instance the Hebrew word Mimshak is used in the Torah which is more accurately translated 'expanding' (see Ezekiel 28:14). Most modern translations use the word 'anointed', which differs from the true Hebrew word for 'anointed', Meshiach or Messiah.*

3 *The Hebrew word Helel, meaning 'Brightness', 'Light bringing' or 'Morning star', is translated into Greek as 'Lucifer' in Isaiah 14:12.*

Jerome Matiyas

THE FOUR

ARCH-ANGELS

Clockwise from top left: The Arch Angels Miykael, Gabriel, Uriel and Raphael. Character illustrations for the Epic Adventures of Mekonnen. Copyright © 2019 by JeroMe Matiyas

with the heavenly choirs. Indeed, he leds the choirs, and they harmonized gloriously. All creatures beheld him and saw that he was beautiful. Even then his appearance was like that of what the Sons of Adam and the Malakim called a *Nakhash*, a dragon, or a winged serpent. But back then, eons ago, everything the Almighty One created was still good and pure. Until something went wrong, and iniquity was discovered in the *Nakhash*.

The Conspiracy of the Nakhash.
As the tale has already been told and written down in the ancient scrolls, it was pride that first got into the heart of *Helel* the *Nakhash*, when he thought he was perfect enough to ascend to the zenith of *Mount Tsion*, the glorious mountain of Elohim – which is the highest peak among the seven bejeweled mountains in the Realms of Shamayim – and to dethrone and usurp the reign of the Almighty One and His Elect. The details are limited and have been lost through the millennia, but there was a process that built up to the first seeds of pride and rebellion in the Nakhash to the gathering to himself Malakim, Cherubim, Serafim, Erelim and other ranks of beings to join him in celestial mutiny. For he declared, as it is written,

The Warrior of Light, Part 1   7

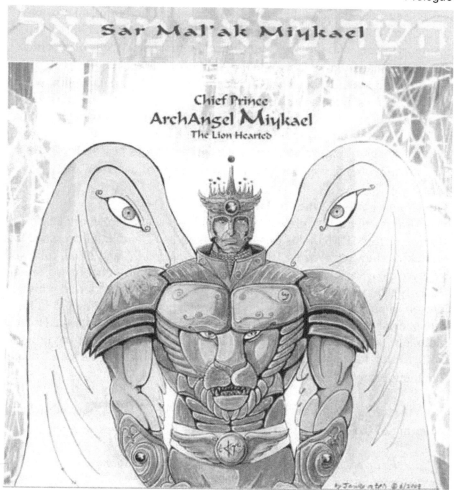

"I shall ascend into Shamayim; I will exalt my throne above the Stars of Elohim. I will sit upon the Mountain of the congregation, in the side of the north." (Isaiah 14:13)

And he went on further to declare boastfully,

"I will ascend above the heights of the clouds; I will be like the most High!" (Isaiah 14:14)

And those that he gathered onto himself roared and cheered till the inner light within them faded into outer darkness, casting a black shadow in the Realms of Shamayim.

It is suspected that at the forefront were other Cherubim and creatures that resembles the Nakhash's 'reptilian' features, those resembling dragons, lizards, serpents, and the like. Thus, were the first black seeds of rebellion planted in Shamayim to assemble the Armies of Darkness.

What a dark and dismal time it became in that age in Shamayim, when one of *Elohim*'s greatest creatures whom he created in love from fire and light and precious stones, and appointed him reign over his own Dominion. Yet still, *Helel* became discontent with his rank and decided to spark a mutiny and rallied an army in an attempt to storm the precious pearlescent gates of Shamayim with many elaborate celestial weapons of cosmic warfare.

The Congregation of the Declaration.
The Almighty One, though just, and merciful, is also a protector and a warrior. Before HIM are his trusted Mal'akim that stand in his presence: Sar Mal'akim, the Arch-Angels *Miykael, Gabriel, Raphael,* and *Uriel,* followed by myriads of various creatures of the heavenly realms gather in and around His holy tabernacle. *Elohim*, the all existent one already conferred within himself to prepare Miykael as Chief Commander of his Armies and fit him with special armor and weapons forged in the sacred fires under the Highest Mountain, which is *Mount Tsion*, and to lead the Armies of Shamayim into battle to stop this attack from the Nakhash, formerly known as *Helel*, and his rebellious Army of Darkness.

From then on it was formally declared by the Chief Mal'ak Sar Gabriel at a gathering of the congregation in Shamayim,

> *"Hear ye, all creatures of the seven Realms of Shamayim! As announced by the Almighty One who created us all, and now inscribed on golden tablets to be written forever. The Nakhash must no longer be addressed as Helel, for that title has been stripped from him. He has now made himself HaSatan, The Adversary. So, from henceforth, that shall be his new name and title! All praise and honor and glory to the Almighty One!"*

Arch-Angel Miykael and The Whole Armour of the Almighty One.
Therefore, Miykael's splendid robes of purest white were replaced for a solid silver and golden suit of armor complete with a magnificent Shield and a flaming Sword. Ministering Mal'akim gather around Sar Miykael to assist in putting on each part of this mighty armor. One by one, two by two, the Mal'akim approach Sar Miykael to deliver and fasten an article of war armor onto his celestial body.

Each piece of armor was given a name and anointed by the Almighty One himself through His Word and *Ruach* —The Spirit.

As Sar Miykael stands upon a translucent marble-like platform, two Mal'akim walk towards him, carrying a hefty golden article between them with the head of a mighty fierce lion engraved on the front of it. It was the *Breastplate of Righteousness,* fastened onto his chest and back to protect his heart and inner soul from being pierced, shielding his heart from unrighteous contempt and pride.

As the first two left the platform, another Mal'ak approached with a golden object in his hands. It was the *Helmet of Salvation,* placed upon his crown, to protect his head and ears from negative sounds and lies from the enemy.

Another Mal'ak appeared on the platform to slip on *The Belt and Guard of Truth* which was precious and must be protected at all cost. Gold and silver-cladded gloves were also fitting on his hands as sturdy gauntlets.

Two Mal'akim approached, each holding one part of a pair of ornately engraved articles to secure Miykael's feet and legs all the way up to his shins and knees. It was the *Shoes of Peace*, which will allow *Sar Miykael* to be ready and steady and to stand firm in heated battles, steadfast for the *Yashar Sodi*—the Upright Ways— of Shamayim.

Another Mal'ak approached with a large, round disc embedded with twelve precious round stones of varying types, sparkling with the brilliance of twelve different colors of light. It was the *Shield of Faith,* prepared to quench any fiery spears or flaming breath from the Nachash and his hordes.

The last Mal'ak walked up to Sar Miykael with a long, broad and mighty sword in its blue and gold sheath. Miykael grabbed the sword's handle and held the powerful flashing weapon aloft with the blade upwards as a bolt of lightning struck the blade, then trickled down all the parts of the whole armor from the helmet on his head to the boots on his feet, surging divine power throughout his whole body. It was granted unto Sar Miykael to wield this *Sword of the Spirit* of *Elohim*, to slice through any adversary, of spirit, wind, fire, metallic substance and precious stone, and all that is impure;

Lastly and most importantly to complete the whole armor, it was Sar Miykael's continued dedication, faithfulness and *Prayer* to the Almighty One as he knelt on one knee in the Lords inner court and declared:

> *"Almighty Elohim, creator of the universe, I pray thee always to remind me, even after this battle to always stay connected to Thee, the source. Never to let pride, darkness and evil creep into my own heart. I pray that through the Word and Ruach thou hast given me strength and agility to wrestle with and disarm the Nakhach and his Armies of Darkness that now come quickly this way. Use me and thine multitude of*

*hosts of Malakim, Serafim, and Erelim who have remained
faithful to Thee, two-thirds of all thine hosts in Shamayim, as
beacons of power, justice and light. Empower us to be Thine
righteous swords, hammers, arrows and spears. In thy name
and honour only. Amen."*

Angelic Battlefield

On that note, the trumpets of war sounded as Sar Miykael lead Shamayim's
Warriors of Light to be armed and assembled into army ranks until the
enormous pearly gates were swung open. From without the open gates, they
saw a horde of Darkness approaching from the lower realms of *Shamayim*
where they were gathered lead by a loud noise as the sound of music that has
been distorted and mangled, coming from the ornate wind pipes propelled by
the massive, flapping wings of the Nakhach. Where beauty once emanated,
now instead it spewed out a black cloud of smoke, advancing like a swarm of
wasps.

The Warriors of Light and the Armies of Darkness clashed with an
immense, violent explosion, rocking the very foundations of the universe,
shaking it to the very core of creation. The battle went on for ages, though
records said not the duration of time for they existed outside of earthly time
as mankind understands to count it, but as it is written in the holy tablets in
Shamayim and by scribes in the ancient oracles and scrolls,

*"And there was war in Shamayim and Miykael, and his
Malakim fought against the Dragon, and the Dragon fought
and his Malakim, and lost the battle, and neither was there
any more place for him in Shamayim.*
*And the Great Dragon was cast out, that old Nakhash, called
the Devil, and Satan, which deceived the whole world, he was
cast out into the Earth, and his Malakim were also cast with
him."* (Revelation 12: 7-9)

And the Nakhash, now titled *HaSatan*, and his Armies of Darkness were
defeated in this Great War, but they were not totally annihilated. At least not
yet. Until the appointed time has come. For it was the power and love of the
Almighty One, His love and promise of life and mercy that spared Him from
destroying the Nakhash instantly. Instead, the Almighty One had a master
plan. A plan to provide a sacrifice, yet He kept it hidden from the Enemy, but
gradually revealed more of the Promise to His followers, the *Yashurun*, the
Righteous Ones, throughout the ages, from generation to generation.

A New Era.

When the *Nakhash* and his subjects were displaced and their Dominion destroyed, this caused the realms in the universe to be changed and shifted from the balance of what was known before. Therefore, some of the realms were destroyed and left null and void, just sludge of earth and water mingled together, and left in darkness for ages.

Then Elohim, the Almighty One creator of the worlds in the universe, who resides outside of time and space as we know it, stood back and aloft, looked into the dark void and began to speak the *Word*,

"Let there be Light!"

And the Word illumined forth, and there was Light.
And in the Light, the Almighty began to form the realm of Earth, just outside of the seven higher Realms of Shamayim, in 6 days of His time and era. The waters and the creatures in them. The land masses and the creatures in them. The air and the creatures in them. The plants and trees and the fruits and seeds that bare in them.

His crowning jewel, from the dust of the Earth, he forged *Ish* and *Isha*, man and woman, after his own image. Clothed in light, love and the innocence within. He called them *Adam* and *Hawah*.

Declaration of War: Light.
Alas, the Almighty One arose up before his heavenly hosts and declared:

> *This Word I declare to you,*
> *All creatures of mine heavenly Hosts.*
> *A decree I declare to thee, mine victorious Army*
> *First and foremost,*
> *Be yea clothed in Righteousness!*
> *For it is precious and pure as light unfold*
> *It shall guard thine heart from spears of Darkness.*
> *As a Breastplate of purest gold.*
>
> *In like fashion*
> *Behold the belt of Truth*
> *Treasured for Words of life and compassion*
> *From the soul bears much fruit.*
>
> *Secure thine Helmet as unto Salvation*
> *Protect thine head and shawl*
> *From evil thoughts and contemplation*

Against the great and imminent fall.

Calling mine Heavenly Warrior Angelos
Thine feet are ready and steady
Stand firm in the time of chaos
With courage go forth into realms of the enemy

With mighty Shield of Faith, broad and sure
The Almighty One shall prevail
Against the Nakhash, I have declared war
Spears and daggers consumed to no avail.

Behold the Alpha Sword of the Spirit and flame
Flashing double edge in my Name
Slicing through bone from marrow,
Soul from spirit, Light from shadow
The Omega ultimate pledge proclaim.[4]

Blessed and courageous are they who conquer and overcome the
Darkness with the everlasting Light.

Declaration of War: Darkness.

Out of the dark and miry abyss from whence the defeated Armies of
Darkness had been cast, the *Nakhash* exhorts a boastful decree:

O, Great and Mighty One of Army Hosts
Thou hast prevailed against me and mine army.
Yet from out of the Darkness we shall reemerge
To challenge thine sovereign decree!

With swords and spears
We shall counter-attack
When thine warriors converge on us
With savagery, we will fight back

With battle axes and hammers
The Beautiful Gates we will tear down
And when we storm the glorious temple
I shall take the throne and have thy crown

---

4   *This poem is inspired by and draws references to Ephesians 6:13-18, Isaiah 59:17 and Hebrews 4:12.*

Out of the Darkness,
I will consume the Light
Fire and brimstone I will spew out of my depths
And burn to ashes all beauty in sight

I shall ascend into Araboth[5]
And usurp the Great White Throne
Then all the Realms of Shamayim
I shall rule as my very own.

The Almighty One discerned the vain thoughts of the *Nakhash* and declared:

Malevolent statements from the one I reject
But thou knowest not the majesty in my Elect
And the Light that is destined to reflect.

Thus is my order, This is my decree
Between Armies of Darkness and Warriors of Light
There will always be enmity.

Alas, the *Nakhash* glared with resentment into the heavenly realms and materialized himself into the new Earth where he saw the first Ish and Isha whom the Almighty One created in his own image. Adam and Hawah. Dwelling peacefully with all the creatures of land, air, and sea in a luscious garden called Eden.

Behold, in this garden the vile serpent saw the Tree of Knowledge of Good and Evil and dwelt in it as he waited patiently for the right moment to strike with a vengeance. First, with a venomous scheme of deceit.

~ End of Prologue ~

---

5 *In some ancient Jewish teachings, Araboth is the seventh and highest level of the heavenly realms where the Almighty Creator God resides on His Throne. The seven realms from the lowest to highest are: Shamayim (Vilon), Raqia, Shehaqim, Zebul, Mahon, Mechon, and Araboth. (Spelling varies for all names.)*

Arch Angel Miykael, #2

Jerome Matiyas © 3/15/2018

Arch Angel Uriel
Jerome Matiyas © 2009

Arch Angel Gabriel
Jerome Matiyas © 2009

Arch Angel Raphael
Jerome Matiyas © 2009

Jerome Matiyas

The Elect One
Ultimate Warrior King
Revelation 1: 13-16
Revelation 19: 11-16

Revelation 19: 11-13

11. And I saw heaven opened, and behold, a white horse appeared? And The One Who was riding it is called Faithful and True, and He passes judgment and waged war in righteousness.

12. His eyes blazed like a flame of fire, and on His head are many kingly crowns; and He has a title inscribed which He alone knows.

13. He is dressed in a robe dyed by "dipping in blood, and the title by which He is called The Word of God.

Jerome Matiyas © 5/5/2011

Revelation 1: 13-16

13. And in the midst of the lampstands one like the Son of Man, clothed with a robe which reached to His feet and with a girdle of gold about His breast.

14. His head and his hair were white like wool and as white as snow; and his eyes were as a flame of fire;

15. His feet glowed like burnished bronze as it is refined in a furnace, and His voice was like the sound of many waters.

16. And in His right hand He held seven stars, and from His mouth there came forth a sharp two-edged sword, and His face was like the sun shining in full power at midday.

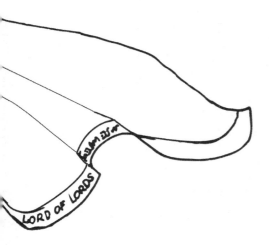

Revelation 19: 15-16

15. From His mouth goes forth a sharp sword with which He can smite the nations; and He will shepherd them with a staff of iron. He will tread the winepress of the fierceness of the wrath of Almighty God.

16. And on His garment and on His thigh He has a name inscribed, King of Kings and Lord of Lords!

The Seven Realms of Shamayim

(7) Araboth

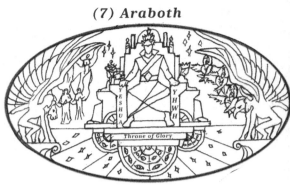

Psalms 68:4 - *Him who rides upon the heavens (arabah) by his name YAH...*
Rev 4:2-9 - *a throne was set heaven, one sat on the throne*
Ezek 1:4-28 - *The four living creatures*
Isaiah 6:2 - *the seraphim*
Enoch 46:1-3; 71:6-17 - *the Head of Days, Son of Man*
Enoch 25:2-3 - *The Lord on His Throne*

Duet 26: 15 - *Look down from thy holy habitation (ma'ohn), from heaven.*
Jude 6 - *the angels that kept not...*
2 Peter 2:4 - *...cast them to hell, into chain of darkness...*
Enoch 18:10 - *Imprisoned watchers*

(5) Machon

(3) Shehaqim

Psalms 77:17 - *the skies (shakh'aqim) sent out a sound...*
Isaiah 45:8 - *let the skies pour down righteousness*
2 Corinth 12:2 - *caught up to the 3rd heaven*

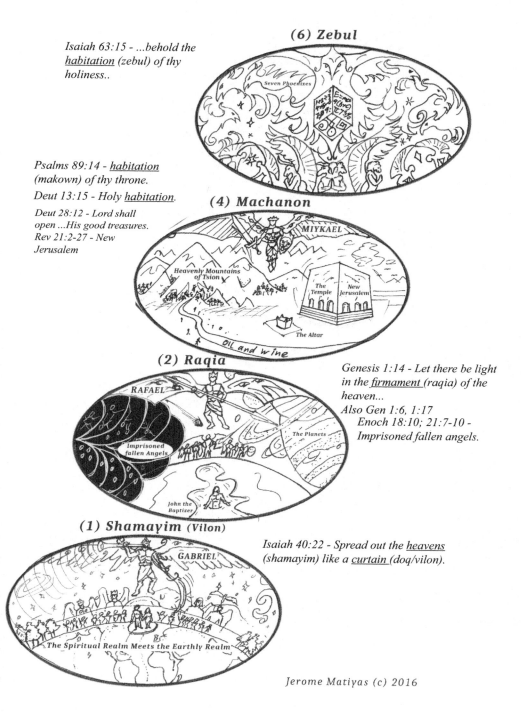

(6) Zebul

Isaiah 63:15 - ...behold the _habitation_ (zebul) of thy holiness..

Seven Phoenixes

Psalms 89:14 - _habitation_ (makown) of thy throne.

Deut 13:15 - Holy _habitation_.

Deut 28:12 - Lord shall open ...His good treasures.

Rev 21:2-27 - New Jerusalem

(4) Machanon

MIYKAEL

Heavenly Mountains of Tsion

The Temple   New Jerusalem

The Altar

Oil and wine

(2) Raqia

Genesis 1:14 - Let there be light in the _firmament_ (raqia) of the heaven...

Also Gen 1:6, 1:17

Enoch 18:10; 21:7-10 - Imprisoned fallen angels.

RAFAEL

Imprisoned fallen Angels

The Planets

John the Baptizer

(1) Shamayim (Vilon)

Isaiah 40:22 - Spread out the _heavens_ (shamayim) like a _curtain_ (doq/vilon).

GABRIEL

The Spiritual Realm Meets the Earthly Realm

Jerome Matiyas (c) 2016

Chapter 1

Chapter 1

Timkat

(Epiphany)

A young man ran as fast as he can! He darted through a moonlit forest at full speed because his life depended on it. Barefoot and bruised all over his body, with ripped clothing that was once white linen but became soiled with patches of green and brown from plants and dirt, mingled in his own sweat and blood.

> *"My life is in your hand, Egziabeher! Rescue me from those who hunt me down relentlessly!"*

This was the young man's desperate prayer, loosely quoting a verse from one of the beloved sections of the sacred oracles known as *Dawit Mezmur* (The Psalms of David, chapter 31, verse 15), is all he can remember right now.

For those who hunted him down were savage creatures. Maybe demons from the pit of Hell. More than a dozen of them had the appearance of tall men in white robes and hoods over their heads, but they have no faces. The skin of their faces, arms and legs were darker than the blackest night. Their eyes glowed red under those head coverings. They were armed with all manner of weapons: swords, daggers, scimitars, spears, bows, and arrows. They have killed and wounded many of his warrior comrades already. Now arrows and lances whizzed by this lone running warrior who proved to be an elusive moving target, dodging and ducking behind trees.

Just as terrifying were the dog-like creatures with the hooded ones, that were more like hounds from hell. As large as lions and leopards, but much more ravenous, with dark, murky colored fur, red eyes, and long, vicious teeth. They snarled and howled like no animal he had ever heard in the land or seas. The wound on the young man's left arm was from being bitten by one of those savage beasts earlier, but he had no time to feel pain. Just ran for his life.

Oh, how life had transformed from beauty into terror in a short space of time. Just a few days ago he was fulfilling his duties as a guard for the Kingdom of Aksum in Aksum City to the north, along with his comrades.

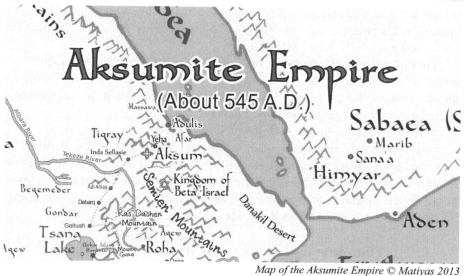

Map of the Aksumite Empire © Matiyas 2013

Oh, the smell of incense and spices that filled the air. The sound of church bells ringing, maidens singing and children laughing. The sight of priests and deacons in radiant robes and garments more colorful than a rainbow, in processions through the streets. And the streets of gold he walked after the *Hade*, the Emperor, threw handfuls of coins and gold nuggets into the crowd. It was one of the sacred annual celebrations of the Kingdom called *Timkat* when people came from far and wide to participate. How he took all that beauty and splendor for granted.

He lost his weapon earlier in the mountains, a sword of the royal guards of Aksum with a golden hilt. He grabbed up a sturdy stick from a tree branch, hoping it would suffice if one of the creatures caught up to him and got near enough to cause harm.

Still, the most surprising weapon he had on him that he never expected to harness such potency is the mysterious golden belt around his waist. It was a gift given to him two days earlier when he was about to leave a meeting in the Hade's palace. A mysterious young man approached him with a formal salutation and handed it to him, claiming it was a gift from "The King of Kings." It seemed whenever he was in great danger or calls out to the Almighty One for intervention, a bright, blinding flash of light emanated from the belt itself, temporarily blinding his pursuers. There was no logical explanation for this phenomenon, but it has saved the runner's life at least three times already.

He knew he was in the south-western end of the great mountain range of the land called the Samen, but he had no idea what direction he is running nor the distance to the nearest town or village. There was a river nearby, for he smelt the water. A little closer and he heard that it's a waterfall. "Which

Jerome Matiyas

one of the waterfalls was it?" he thought as arrows flew by his head. "It cannot be Tis Issat falls. I expected it to be bigger. Must be one of the smaller, uncharted waterfalls. Must get closer."

He ran closer to the sound of rushing waters until he came to a ledge where he saw the waterfall. In a second all that came to mind was to jump into it to escape his pursuers. "I would rather drown in this waterfall than be ripped apart by these creatures." he declared.

Without further ado, the young warrior ran then leapt off the edge, making a swan dive into the cascading waters, falling head first with arms stretched up, vertically aligned to the magnificent wall of waters. As he free fell his life flashed through his mind. He remembered the rich beauty of his home city and thought back to the moments before all this happened. Before his life changed, and darkness descended upon the kingdom.

Four days earlier. Aksum City, circa 545 A.D.

It all began in the highlands of an ancient land in the Horn of Africa, nestled in the mountains like a multi-hued, sparkling jewel near the Erythrean Sea (Red Sea), there flourished the Kingdom of Aksum. A great city in all its splendor and glory, Aksum was situated in the northern parts in the land of *Habeshinya* (Abyssinia), and south of what the Greeks called Ethiopia. As the source of the great Nile River, this land has been a mystery and a myth to the Greeks and Romans for centuries, and which the Egyptians revered for millennia and dare not provoke its inhabitants. Here reigned a succession of kings who declared themselves *"Negusa Negast"* which means King of Kings and *"ZaYihuda Anbessa"* which translates from the official Aksumite language of Ge'ez to The Lion of Judah.

This title eluded to the monarch's belief in possessing divine kinship and succession to the glorious and holy King of Kings and Lord of Lords, the risen and ascended redeemer, *Iyesus Kristos* – Jesus Christ. The very same *Iyesus Krestos* who was proclaimed the Son of the Almighty Creator, conceived of and born of a young *Salap Miriam Betelehema Yihuda* – Virgin Mary in Bethlehem of Judea – about 540 years earlier, crucified on a rugged cross, died and arose from the grave in three days, then ascended up into *Samayat* – The Heavens – and gave spiritual gifts to mankind who ever believed in him. It is a kinship they trace through legendary descendants of the controversial union between the ancient Israelite King Solomon, son of King Dawit, and the famous Queen of Sheba, Nigist Makeda, who traveled a great distance to learn of Solomon's wisdom and riches. It was a union that conceived Aksum's first mythical King, Negus Menelik.

It was the 11th day in the month of *Ter* (January 19th in the Gregorian calendar) about 545 A.D. in the Aksumite calendar. The Aksumites were preparing for *Timkat*, a brilliant three-day festival celebrating the occasion

MEKONNEN AND AFEWORQ ON GUARD DUTY
AS THREE GIRLS WALK BY.
JEROME MATIYAS © 2019

when Yohannes the Baptizer reluctantly performed the sacred ritual of submerging dedicated believers in a body of water upon the Lord *Iyesus Kristos* in the Jordan River in Judea more than 500 years earlier. It was a significant event that formally introduced the foretold *ZaEgziabeher Ebn*, the Son of God, to the world.

All citizens of the surrounding cities and towns, the shepherds, merchants and artisans, the priests, monks and clergy of all churches and monasteries, all royalty and nobles in the palaces and castles, prepared in great anticipation for one of the most colorful and splendid ceremonies of the year. All the King's noblemen and guards also prepared in their own ways and according to their responsibilities. They awoke before sunrise to bathe and perfume themselves and dress in their distinct uniforms. The *Qasisan* (the Priests) dressed in full regalia of splendid ceremonial robes of velvet and fine satin and swung bronze censers as sweet incense smoke billowed into the air. Guards and warriors, in full garb and armed with swords, shields, spear, bows, and arrows, were all poised, distinguished and ready for battle. The musicians in the king's court began to quietly play arranged music on the *kirar, begenna, washint, sistras,* and *masenko*, allowing the sounds resonate through the halls, and permeate the souls of all who can hear as well as those who could hear but could feel it.

Ethiopian Orthodox priests in a procession carrying a tabot.
Photo © Matiyas 2007.

Imperial Majesties.

Ella Ameda II, officially titled *Gabra Masqal*, son of the honorable *Ella Atzbeha* also known as Emperor Kabel, was the reigning *Negusa Negast*, and Nigist Semret[1], his wife, the Empress and First Lady of the land, officially titled *Nigisa Nigist*, Queen of Kings. Together, the Imperial couple arose early in the morning and went to separate rooms with their maids and servants to assist with preparations. Over white cotton garments both the king and queen donned black *kaba* capes embroidered with gold patterns around the neck and extended to the shoulders and front hems. Two servants then draped over the king's shoulders a magnificent royal-purple robe, decorated with golden, fanciful embroidery patterns of geometric shapes and cross motifs. His Imperial Majesty (HIM) is presented with rings for his fingers, strapped sandals, a lion-head scepter, and finally his bejeweled golden crown. The King and Queen both stepped out of their changing quarters wearing matching regalia. They greeted each other with kisses on the cheeks — right, left then right again — they proceeded down the hallways to the throne room for breakfast in the company of two servants and four guards. The aroma of sweet-smelling incense and frankincense mingled with food permeated the corridors and hallways.

---

1 *Historically, the name of the queen was not known at this time. I use the name Semret, which means "Unity". Originally, I thought of using "Azeb" from Ethiopian legend and popular girl name today in Ethiopia and Eritrea.*

A Particular Warrior.

While the royal family prepared, so did the royal guards in their quarters. Hundreds of guards of various ranks and distinctions. There were chief warriors of higher ranks, experienced captains and sergeants and young foot soldiers and royal guards all according to their assignments and ranks. It was an honor for a young man to be considered worthy to become a warrior and defend the King and his country in the name of *Egziabeher Amlak,* Almighty Creator, God of gods. Enforce the law, defend the faith and execute judgment justly and truthfully.

One such young man, in the prime of his youth, is Mekonnen, son of deceased senior warrior Sofaniyas GabraTsion, just six months shy of being 27 years of age, serving as king's guard and warrior since he was 20 years old. Young, fresh, bright-eyed and ready to take on the world, Mekonnen Sofaniyas GabraTsion was skilled in sword fighting, spear throwing, and archery. He performed hand to hand combat without weapons, in martial arts fighting styles similar to those of ancient Egypt, Nubia, and Meroe. He practiced with his friends and fellow warriors every day except the Lord's day, on Sunday, when the whole Aksumite Kingdom attended church services.

Mekonnen stood at approximately 4 cubits tall (6 feet)[2], medium built and muscular like most warriors would be, particularly in the shoulders, arms and upper chest area. Black curly hair like sheep's wool frames his medium brown face, a handsome face it is. His noticeable eyebrows sheltered lively brown eyes, divided by a high nose ridge that forms a bridge from his round and wide forehead down to a nose shaped like an arrowhead pointing downward, rounded at the tip with elliptical nostrils. He had the typical, distinctive features of most inhabitants native to this part of Northeast Africa, where the land, people, and culture of the various Kushite peoples were in close proximity to the land, people and culture of those of the Shemites of Sabaea[3] and Arabia across the Reed Sea to the east, and the Puntites to the southeast in the Horn of Africa. Historically, and in popular legends, Hebrews from the land of Israel and Canaan were known to have journeyed into Kush and Habeshinya and settled here since about 2000 to 1000 BC adding significantly to the genealogy, culture, customs, dietary laws and belief systems of the people, including that of the royal family and monarchy.

That day, the first day of *Timkat*, Mekonnen put on his loose fitting but comfortable off-white trousers fitted short-sleeved shirt of the same color with vertical ribbed ridges from shoulder to biceps. He fastened his brown leather belt with a bronze lion head for a buckle, with two sheaths, one for

---

2 *The Aksumites probably used the Greek Cubit which was about 18.3 inches. The Aksumites used Greek letters on their coins and did trading/business with the Byzantine Empire.*
3 *Sheba, across the Red Sea in present day Yemen. Also, historically known as Sabaea.*

a long sword and another for a 6-inch dagger fastened to the waist. He wore a robe of baboon's fur on his shoulders, covering his back and forming a flower shape, narrowing as it came down the front. The older Warriors wore more colorful robes and baboon fur headpieces. Mekonnen strapped on his sandals wrapped a white turban around his head and grabbed his 2 cubits long spear in his right hand and his metal shield which is a cubit in diameter, geometrically studded with small dome-shaped nubs near the curved edges in his left hand. He wore a decorative, one-inch armband around his right biceps, not a requirement but just for personal style. All the men in Mekonnen's rank wore matching warrior apparel and marched out together as one unit, ready to protect the King and Queen and celebrate Timkat.

"*Salāma! Anta sannay?*, — Peace! Are you well?" Mekonnen addressed his fellow guard, Afeworq.

"*Bāḥā, ana ba-sannay*! — Greetings, I am doing well!" Afeworq replied. "Nice morning isn't it?

Mekonnen: "Yes it sure is, *Egziabeher* is gracious to give us fine weather, this morning. But I think it could rain later this evening."

Afeworq: "Rain? No, don't say that. It will be sunny all day, I hope. It is not even rainy season."

Mekonnen: "I only say that because of yesterday. It seemed *Egziabeher,* and the *Nakhash*[4] were fighting each other, sun, then rain, then sun. Then sun and rain at the same time."

Afeworq: "U-wa, I remember. Then there was a beautiful rainbow in the south over the Samen Mountains."

Afeworq mused as he motioned with his outstretched right arm to the highlands of *Tigray* to the north-west and Mount *Ras Dashen,* the highest point of the Samen Mountains, in the southern highlands of the Amhara region. As he turned around to face Mekonnen, Mekonnen's eyes widened, and he exclaimed jokingly,

"Oh, but look, the rainbow is still there!"

Afeworq swung his head around to view the highlands again, "Huh, where?"

Mekonnen playfully tapped Afeworq on the back of his head,

"*Tapp!*"

Afeworq quickly realized the joke and punched Mekonnen on the arm with equal playfulness, then they both had a good laugh at themselves.

"…but this is a new day, Mo'kay, my brother, let us eat." Said Afeworq and the two companions follow the rest of the guards to the breakfast-hall tables.

These two were very familiar with each other as they grew up together. In fact, people noticed that they resembled each other in appearance and that is because they were near kinsmen, cousins, in fact, their fathers being

---

4 The serpent, the devil.

brothers. Although many Abyssinians of the Aksumite Kingdom resembled each other even if they may not been close blood relatives, yet many were related in some way, having large families and marrying within their close-knit towns and communities. Even strangers recognized the unique facial features of the inhabitants of Aksum, a mixture of various ethnic groups, of *Khamite* and *Shemite* influences in genealogy, culture, and speech. The Arabians across the Red Sea to the east called them *Habeshat*, thus naming the country *Habeshinya* (Abyssinia), land of the mixed people.

The Splendor of Aksum.

The City of Aksum was a center of attraction at this time of year. It was a city situated between two verdant mountains that were among a vast mountain range system that extended for thousands of miles beyond the boundaries of the Empire. A city arrayed with magnificent palaces, castles and church cathedrals of fine architecture in authentic Aksumite style that suggest combined influences from local Kushite and Shemite cultures, with Mediterranean and Sabaean elements: A unique style identified by semi-circular arches over doorways; crescent shapes atop obelisks and chiseled out of walls that represent the rising sun; Coptic style crosses called *Masqals* illustrated and carved in walls; square shaped beams at the four corners of real and false windows and doors; and mural paintings depicting people, angels and the Godhead with large almond shaped eyes and oval-shaped heads amidst grand biblical and historical events.

The Royal Palace sits upon a platform of steps and has four high towers each adorned with a brazen unicorn as if protruding out from the towers, elegantly formed with fine craftsmanship, frozen in a dramatic trotting pose standing 20 cubits high, each facing in one of four directions, north-east, north-west, south-east and south-west. In the center is a dome shape with balconies around it and a Coptic cross at the very top. Reports of these four shiny unicorns galloping out of the four towers have reached as far as Rome in Europa[5] and is even written in the journals of the Egyptian monk, Cosmas Indicopleustes[6].

The hundreds of towering Aksumite stelaes were impressive structures to behold, surpassing even the ones in Egypt. The underground passage ways, tombs, and rock hewn caverns were still a mystery to most Aksumites. People from far and wide came to the glorious city either to celebrate, trade or obverse. Indians, Arabians, Egyptians, Sabaeans, Himyarites, Nubians, Hebrews, Judeans, Chinese from the far-east, and even Greeks, Romans, Turks, Anatolians and Syrians were all expected to converge into Aksum and other Ethiopian cities to intermingle with the locals. Some foreigners take advantage of the season to do buying and trading with those who would

---

5 Europe
6 Christian Topography of Cosmas Indicopleutes.

Jerome Matiyas

need wares, clothing, satin, lace, spices, frankincense and materials needed for festival preparations. They themselves were hoping to return to their respective countries with large shares of Abyssinian gold, bronze, ivory spices, myrrh, exotic animals and birds and much more, not to mention mint Aksumite coins for business and souvenirs.

By this time of morning people were caravanning on foot, donkey, camel or horseback according to their social status and whatever one can afford. Some nobles, officials, and various royal and priestly individuals came in chariots and carriages drawn by handsome horses and tremendous African elephants fitted with beautiful harnesses decorated with gold and silver fabric and colorful precious stones. Chariots drawn by the elephants were a grant spectacle and leave the little children awestruck from the enormous size and motion of the whole thing. Followed by the giraffes, zebras, lions, leopards and exotic horses that were paraded in the main streets of Aksum for a grand spectacle.

A Warrior's Introspection.

Sometime later Mekonnen and Afeworq were at their post near the king's palace. Mekonnen is and has been thinking deeply about his life and state of being for some time. Questions have been swimming in his mind like, "What is the purpose in life," "What is my destiny," "Who is *Egziabeher* and is he real?", "And why were we put in this world, to labour, suffer and cry in pain?" So, he turned to Afeworq and said,

"You know Afey; I've been thinking, about life and such. Like the future and destiny. What about you, do you think about the future?" Afeworq glanced at Mekonnen and wondered about his cousin's sudden cogitativeness.

"Yes, I think about the future, I don't worry about it because I know exactly what I want to accomplish in this life. In the right time, *Egziabeher* will provide and show me the way. What's wrong, thinking about a girl. Thinking about finding a wife Mo'kay? Start a family?" Afeworq smiled as he made fun with Mekonnen.

"Well, yes but, not that. I mean eventually, I hope to marry someday but more than that, like what is this life for? We eat, sleep, fight, play *genna*, celebrate festivals and protect the *tabots*, Ark of the Covenant and the Emperor. But what else is there to live for?"

"Well, to protect and to serve one's country and honor your family and fellow man is to serve *Egzio*. Is it not written in the holy scriptures to *'Love your neighbor as you love yourself.'* And *'Do to others as you will have them do to you.'* "

"Well yes, this is what the priests read to us in church. But how do I know that's what it says for myself? I've just been thinking."

They stood in silence for about a minute observing the crowds gathering

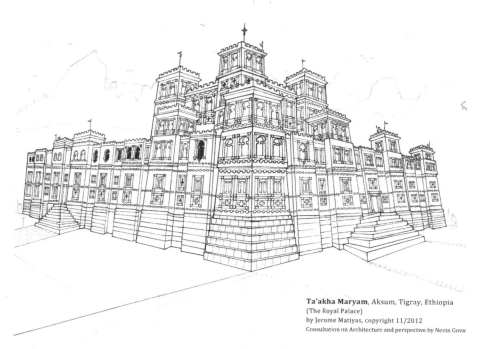

Ta'akha Maryam, Aksum, Tigray, Ethiopia
(The Royal Palace)
by Jerome Matiyas, copyright 11/2012
Consultation on Architecture and perspective by Nevin Govas

and young women dressed in blue dresses and red crosses stitched to the front, singing church songs and clapping with high praises.

Then Mekonnen said to Afeworq, "You know, the other day I wrote a song."

"Oh really, you write songs now? I did not know you can sing."

"Well, No, I don't really sing, but I write songs and poems sometimes."

"Hmm, Mekonnen the Psalmist! That is interesting. How does it go?"

"I do not want to sing it now, well, maybe I will just recite a few verses. It begins:

Oh, Aksum, Kingdom of great splendor,
And magnificence among other kingdoms.
Kingdom of high steles and glorious palaces
Perched upon high mountains, like a nestled dove
For all the nations to see
Your fame has gone abroad, How God has blessed you
With magnificence and Glory of the Kings of old
Upon your throne is the seat of King Dawit
The throne of the son of the wisest King of Zion
Within you resides King Solomon's abundance
And the most Holiest of Holies,

The Ark of the Covenant.

Wisdom and glory abounds but where is your heart and soul?
Do you have a heart and soul?
Do I have a heart and soul?
Are my beauty and splendor in my outward appearance
In what I see?
Or in what is within me?
My heart cries out, my soul thirsts to be filled
Fill me with peace, and contentment.
I pray thee not for power and glory
I pray thee, for wisdom and understanding
And let me be all that I could be.

That's it."

Afeworq paused for a moment then replied,

"That was deep my friend. I like it! you should put it to music. Let one of the court musicians help you."

"No, I do not want to do that yet, it is a rather personal verse, straight from the heart."

"Which is why others should hear it. Oh wait, Look over there."

Six young Abyssinian girls were approaching their way, very beautiful, shapely with petite figures and doe-eyed glances, dressed all in white covered from head to ankles with embroidered *masqal* crosses at the top, center, and front of their dresses. Three of them wore round brass disks along their hair lines at the top of their foreheads, framing their faces. They all seemed to have near flawless complexions, ranging in shades from amber to dark brown. Their heads were covered with blue and white *shemmas*, which could not hide their lovely smiles as they walk pass two handsome guards that were Mekonnen and Afeworq, blushing and smiling with a softly spoken,

"Selam." As they kept walking by, giggling amongst themselves.

"Selam!" The two young warriors replied, sticking their chests out and tucking stomachs in with a little more effort than usual. When the young ladies were a good distance away from them, Afeworki said,

"You see Mekonnen; there are many lovely maidens in Aksum. You can have someone in your family arrange to set you up with one if you like."

With a smirk on his lips Mekonnen replied, "Well, actually I was speaking to one of those maidens yesterday. You didn't even know."

"Oh, really?! I didn't even see you two! You see, you already have a head start!"

Mekonnen smiled and thought to himself that Afeworq's suggestion may be a good idea.

Afeworq drew closer to Mekonnen, "So which one was it you were speaking to?"

"None of your business. I am not telling you." Mekonnen rebounds.

"*Hawey*! Come on tell me! I bet it was the one on the far left. Or the one in the middle with the blue shemma!"

Processions.

The sun was a little higher in the sky, and the King and his Queen began to come out of the royal palace with royal guards before and behind them, marching out in time and formation in perfect rhythm. The palace priests followed in beautiful, kaleidoscopic colors holding the holy tabots above their heads. Musicians followed them playing on their instruments and singing praises to *Egzio* and his son *Iyesus Krestos*. Warrior guards and foot soldier like Mekonnen stood at the outskirts of the platform and palace and upon high walls and low among the people, on the alert for crowd control, suspicious behaviors or the very rare sudden attacks. The palace was elevated by many steps, at the top is the wide platform where the King and all his 50 guards and 24 priests now stood looking down at the sea of people, most dressed in all white like earth-bound angels, the faithful citizens of Aksum, Abyssinia and strangers from the uttermost parts of the earth, bow down low to honor the *Hade* (Emperor), *Gabra Masqal*. The tops of *tabots* could be seen from the palace as priests from other provinces and towns in the kingdom came to celebrate with the royal family. Not all the priests from far away districts were able to go to the capital city of Aksum, but the ones that were at close proximity and reasonable distances do made an effort to march up to the King's palace.

Bahetawi in the Midst.

Also scattered randomly among the crowds were hermit-monks called *Bahetawi* who were not affiliated with a particular house of worship but were still considered to be holy men, respected and revered as much as local priests and bishops. They emerged from their solitude in the wilderness and caves they choose to make their homes during major festivals and sacred ceremonies to observe and intermingle with the crowds, giving advice, exhortations, counsel and prophetic words to those who will receive it. They looked like some of the monks or priests, wearing brightly colored robes and head wraps with Coptic crosses and emblems of the *Virgin Mariam with Iyesus* the child, or *Qeddus Giorgis* on horseback slaying a dragon hanging from chains around their necks, holding up a staff or cross in hand. But what usually set them apart was the sign of the Nazarite vow, as described in *Orit Zahwəlqw* (the Book of Numbers, chapter 6), the fourth book of the *Orit* written by Muse the Law Giver (the first eight books of the Old Testament, the five books written by Moses), as they sport long locks of hair, in varying length and thickness depending on the amount of time that passed since the Bahetawi had started his extended walk and talk with the Almighty Creator of the universe, *Egziabeher Amlak.*

Mystery of the Tabots and Priesthood.

As for the history and significance of the *tabots*, the fabled Ark of the Covenant and the whole *Timkat* festival with the processional of priests and musicians through the streets? The story behind it was fascinating and complex. But most of the common folk of Aksum were able to explain to any stranger in a few sentences at least. They would tell them that the *tabots* carried by the priests on their heads wrapped in cloth were the actual, or copies, of the stone tablets engraved with the 10 commandments that the biblical Muse received from Yahweh, the Great *I AM*, The God of the children of Israel. That the tablets were usually stored in the mysterious but powerful Ark of the Covenant, an object in the shape of a rectangular box with a golden lid on top ornamented with 2 cherubim facing each other as the I Am instructed Moses and the children to Israel to build while they wandered in the wilderness after escaping from being slaves in Egypt. It was between the cherubim that Yahweh, the Great I AM, came down as a great Light to commune with the Children of Israel, and by His power embodied in the Ark, they were able to level cities like Jericho, defeat their enemies and established the kingdom by King Dawit and King Solomon.

They would also tell a stranger that the priests were Levites, descendants of the Moses' brother Aaron, who came from Jerusalem with the Ark of the Covenant during the time of King Solomon of Israel. As for how the Ark of the Covenant and Levites and sons of Aaron made their way to Aksum was another profound mystery. The fact was that not even in the sacred oracles and chronicles of the Kings of Israel and Yihuda was it mentioned what happened to the Ark of the Covenant, sometimes called the Ark of Zion and Holy Zion. It seemed to have just disappeared from the pages of the sacred scriptures and history.

But to the Askumites, people of Habeshinya and particularly the royal family it was not a mystery as to what happened to the Ark of Zion, for they claim to have it sealed and protected right there within a church sanctuary called *Qedus Mariam Tsion* (St Mary of Zion) right there in the City of Aksum. Mekonnen has not seen the Ark of Zion himself, for only an assigned monk and a chosen few were allowed to see it, but he had been assigned to guard the sanctuary several times. Though he had heard stories that in earlier times before he was born they did bring out the Ark of Zion in processions through the streets for all to see on special occasions.

TSADKAN:
THE NINE RIGHTEOUS ONES
JEROME MATIYAS © 3/1/2019

Tsadkan: The Righteous Ones. From Left to Right: Abba Aftse, Abba Gerima (Yeshaq), Abba Guba, Abba Liqanos, Abba Pantelewon, Abba Aregawi ZeMikael (Libanos),Abba Sehma, Abba Yem'ata, and Abba Alef.

The Nine Righteous Ones.

Mekonnen looked about the city and saw the streets and alley-ways teeming with people, from near and far. It was always a glorious site to behold. After the king's exited and the citizen's and visitors bowed, a lot a chattering ensued. Then two musicians, one at the far right and one at the far left of the platform, took three steps forward, stopped, turned slightly and 45 degrees, one on the left to the left, and the other on the right to the right, each raise a horn to the lips then blew in unison:

"Tutooooot, tutoot, TuToooooooooooooot!!"

At the sound of the horns, the crowds quieted their murmurings then gradually stopped talking because they knew the King was about to speak. Emperor Gabra Masqal stepped forward then began in a loud voice:

"Greetings and blessing to my people of Aksum, in the name of Yesus Kristos!

Greetings to all visitors and strangers from afar, Selam, Peace be with you! I, *Negus Gabra Masqal* of Aksum and Abyssinia greet and welcome you all to celebrate in our wonderful festival of *Timkat*, venerating the baptism of our Lord *Iyesus Kristos*. We shall now proceed as we follow the lead of the royal priests through the main streets to the cathedrals, the field of great stelae and then to the water at Queen of Sheba's Bath where the waters will be blessed tonight.

All praise to the father *Egziabeher Amlak* and the son *Iyesus Kristos* on this glorious day. I salute and thank our friends and allies from the four corners of the earth for being here with us. I salute and recognize the Nine Saints – *Tsadkan* – (The Righteous Ones) that have recently encouraged the Kingdom of Aksum to translate the Holy Scriptures from Greek to our own language of Ge'ez. What a glorious blessing that is to bring the Words of Life to our priest who impart it to our own people to understand and be saved. Praise be to *Egziabeher Amlak*, his son *Iyesus Kristos* and the *Manfas Qeddus* (Holy Spirit). Amen. We give honor to the *Holy Virgin Mariam* for the grace given onto her to bring The Son of God into the world. We shall now have a reading by one of the Nine Saints, Abuna Aregari"

When the King said *"Abuna Aregari"* the crowds began to jostle a bit, and some tried to press forward to get a better look at one of the legendary *Abunas* from the Mediterranean regions who contributed to the spiritual knowledge and culture of the people of Axum. Out comes *Abuna Aregari* from among the other priests and begins to read from the Holy Scirptures in Book of Mattewos (Matt 3:13-17) about Iyesus' baptism in the Jordan River by Yohannes the Baptizer. He read the verse twice, first in Greek, then in Ge'ez,

"Then Iyesus came from Galilee to the Jordan to be baptized by Yohannes. But Yohannes tried to stop him, saying 'I need to be baptized by you, and do you come to me.' Iyesus replied, 'Let it be so now, it is proper for us to do this to fulfill all righteousness." Then Yohannes consented.

As soon as Iyesus was baptized, he went up out of the water. At that moment heaven was opened, and he saw the Spirit of Egziabeher descending like a dove and lighting on him. And a voice from heaven said, This is my Son Whom I love; with him, I am well pleased."

At the end of the reading, the crowd resounded, "Amen!", Then the musicians began playing, and the royal priesthood lifted their tabots, which were covered by decorated clothes, above their heads and proceed slowly down the palace steps. Some of the women in the crowd began ululations,

"Elelelelelele Eelelelelelelel...!" and singing, dancing and clapping commenced.

Suspicious Visitors.

Meanwhile, among the crowds of Aksumites and foreigners, there were strange figures lurking around in the shadows and alleyways in this city. They blended in quite effectively with the masses alright, staffs in hand, wearing all white garments with hoods and shamas like everyone else, but their hoods were hemmed with intricate designs that seemed familiar at a glance, but at close inspection, they were not. Strange symbols were hidden within their embroidered hems and tattooed onto their hands and feet. There were about eight or nine of them, probably more, the average height of men, dispersed among the crowds. Looking, watching, waiting, and signaling to each other. What for? Nobody knew who they were or where they came from. Nobody really noticed them, unless someone accidentally bumped into one of them and sensed an uneasy feeling within the soul.

They blended in, but still seemed suspicious. Spies from another country or province, scouting the land and kingdom? A strange cult seeking new converts? Rumors and stories traveled that cults, sects, and isms sprouted up quite often in the Egyptian city of Alexandria and caused all kinds of riots and unrest. Or were they strange beings from another dimension or realm, just observing human mortals like they've been doing since before the Great Deluge until Almighty Egziabeher saved only Noah and his family in the Ark? Perhaps self-made monks and holy men.

Or perhaps scouts from Beta Israel – The House of Israel – an ancient people descended from tribes of Israelites that intermarried with local Agew speaking peoples. They lived by the laws and precepts of the five Holy Oracles written by Muse (Moses), and refused to convert to the religion on the Aksumite kingdom when Negus Ezana declared it in 330 AD, the new covenant and teachings of *Iyesus Krestos*. Therefore, they were called *Falashas* since they were exiled from the kingdom of Aksum. Since then the two kingdoms had been in conflict with each other for more than 200 years, with the occasional peace treaties in effect.

Though it could not be proven, The House of Israel may have been venturing out from their own kingdom to the south of Aksum in the Simien Mountains and north of *Tsana Hayk* – Lake Tsana – by orders from Negus Phenias to plan another surprise attack. Nobody knew. Few noticed them. Whoever they were, their hoods casted a perpetual shadow over their faces, so it was never revealed, even in broad daylight.

Priestly Procession.

The *Qasisan* (priests) walked single file with the *tabots*, which were covered in brightly colored satin cloths, over their heads. They were followed by the deacons, behind, then acolytes and the musicians lead by the chief of Aksumite's sacred music, Yared the Deacon and his skilled musicians of the royal court. Singing and dancing, like Negus Dawit[7] in the streets of Aksum, commenced as they all headed towards the Queen of Sheba's bath place.

They sang a Psalm of Dawit (Ps 150):

Praise you the Lord Egziabeher in His sanctuary,
Praise him in his mighty heavens.
Praise him for his acts of power.
Praise him for his surpassing greatness.

---

7 King David from the Kingdom of Israel.

Jerome Matiyas

Praise him with the sound of the trumpet,
Praise him with the harp and lyre,
Praise him with tambourine and dancing,
Praise him with the strings and flute,
Praise him with the clashing cymbals,
Praise him with resounding cymbals.
Let everything that has breath praise the Lord.

A Captain's Orders.

Mekonnen said to Afeworq as they stood together shoulder to shoulder,

"After this long day, I would love to have *injera* and *wot*, then play a game of *genna*. What about you Afey?"

"I will race you first to the field to play *genna*!" Afeworq replied with a grin on his face.

Mekonnen boasted, "You want to compete against me, you loser?! You know I will run faster than you!

"*Iyasseh*! No Way! I will Not lose, you turtle!" Afeworq replies, the two began chuckling louder than they should on duty.

As they laugh, a figure lurks and approaches the two from behind. It is a man, tall and with a serious scowl on his face, framed with an impressive headpiece of baboon's fur that looks like a lion's mane. This person raises both his hands to the sides of Mekonnen's and Afeworq's heads and smack them hard on the ears, causing the duo's puffy-haired heads to knock together. "*Tonkks!*"

They stopped laughing immediately and turn around to see their angry captain, Negus Mulualem, glaring at them.

"Stop laughing like hyenas and behave your selves in the presence of the Emperor! You two should know better!"

Captain Mulualem scuffed at the young men, with his brilliantly colored robe over his shoulders and back revealing his authority and seniority as one of the head Captain of the Royal Guards.

Rubbing their aching heads, Mekonnen and Afeworq bowed and nodded several times, as they apologized repeatedly,

"We are sorry, Egzi Negus Mulualem, *yikrai-ta, yikrai-ta.*"

Captain Mulualem gestured roughly with hands pointing in opposite directions,

"You, Mekonnen, over there! And you Afeworq, way over there! And don't even look at each other. Look at the Negusa Negus, and the crowds like you were supposed to!"

The young duo moved from each other immediately at Captain Mulualem's command, knowing their full punishment could be worst or still pending.

"*U-wa, Egzi.* Yes, Lord." And they were off.

When Captain Mulualem was gone from sight the two glanced at each other from afar and nodded and smiled, acknowledging their plan to meet later still.

But not too far away, one of the strange, dark hooded ones looked on at the scenario that just transpired among the three men. He was taking notes of positions and movements of all the guards and warriors as if to plan some sort of malignant mischief or deadly attack. His other shadowy companions were doing the same lurking motions throughout the city of Aksum. Watching. Strolling the streets. Emerging out of shadows and corners. Appearing atop buildings and high structures. Waiting. They observed everything.

Matiyas © 2013

Qedus Tsion, St. Mary of Tsion Cathedral in Aksum.
The resting place of the Ark of the Covenant and tablets.
Here they are alleged to reside since after the reign of King Solomon of the Kingdom of Israel and the destruction of the temple in Jerusalem.

Jerome Matiyas

© Matiyas 2013

Jerome Matiyas

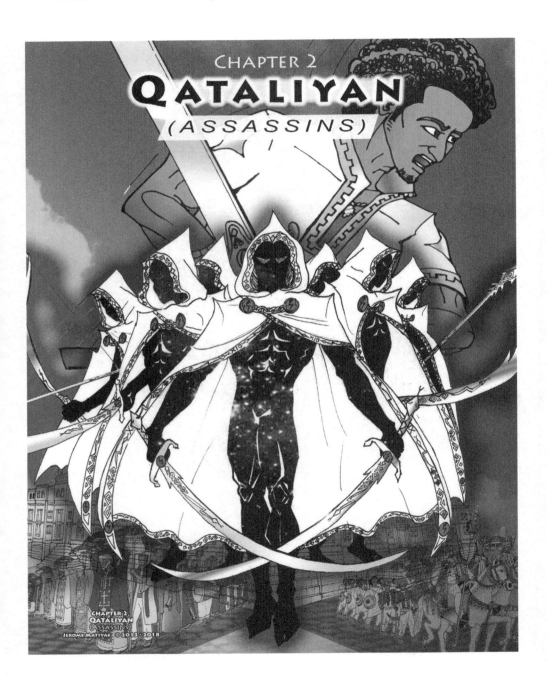

Chapter 2

Chapter 2

Qataliyan

(Assassins)

The streets were enlivened as crowds of people hustle and bustle in the metropolis of Aksum, in the midst of the vibrant *Timkat* festival. Commander in Chiefs tried to instate some order and control by dispatching their regiments on foot and on horseback to clear the way for the Emperor's procession to march through the streets on the way to The Queen of Sheba's Bath Basin called *Mai Shum*.

Meanwhile, a little boy, about five years old, was running and playing in the streets with his friends when suddenly he accidentally bumped into the leg of a stranger and falls to the dusty ground. The little one sprung back up happily with a bright smile on his face and immediately he was polite as his mommy taught him and bowed and said, *"Aytehazeley, Yikrai-ta Egzi!"*[1] which translates to: "I'm Sorry, Excuse me, my Lord!" The boy looked up at the stranger's face only to see darkness framed by a white hood. The mysterious hooded stranger turned to look down at the little one and let out a menacing hiss as his eyes glowed crimson in the darkness under the hood. Immediately the child was terrified at the sight and ran off with a shriek to find his mother. He found her not far away talking with three of her young lady friends and jumped into her arms shouting *"Emm, Emm!"* which is "Mommy, Mommy!" in Ge'ez. Then he whispered in her ears, *"Emm,* that man, he hissed at me, and his eyes are red."

The mother asked, "Which man?"

The boy pointed in the direction from where he encountered the strange man, but he was gone. She figured her son was just imagining things as little boys sometimes do, thought nothing of the matter, turned to her friends and said, "My boy Nati thought he saw a monster or something. He will be alright, probably just tired or hungry." Then they casually went on their way, but the little boy was still cowering in his mother's arms, looking over her shoulder at the stranger man with the evil glare, now lurked next to a fruit vendor cart.

---

[1] I want to use Ge'ez here but I don't know the language well yet so I used Tigrinya. Tigrinya and Tigre are supposed to be closer to Ge'ez than Amharic.

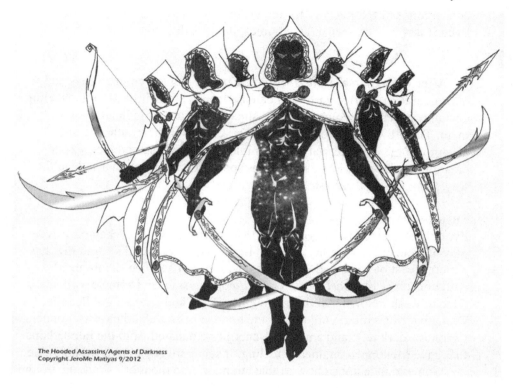

The Hooded Assassins/Agents of Darkness
Copyright JeroMe Matiyas 9/2012

The Cloaked Ones.

They had no idea that there were many sinister men with white hoods pulled over their heads dispersed among the people in the streets and alleyways. But they were organized and grouped into positions that only they knew as planned amongst themselves. And nobody really noticed them blended with the crowd; they could even pass for holy monks who dress and similarly cover their heads. Except for the unique patterns in the hems of their hoods and overalls, and that strange symbol, a black lightning shape inside of a red circle. This emblem was embroidered in the front of and below the collar and tattooed on the back of their hands and on their feet.

None of the warrior guards noticed anything strange at first, not even Mekonnen and Afeworq. Soon the sound of music was heard coming from a distance, and minstrels and psalmists in white can be seem coming from a distance with various instruments playing as they lead the procession for the *Timkat* festival. As music and frankincense fills the air, here they came on their way as priests in beautifully colored garments and robes with tassels on the fringes, surrounding the one carrying the *tabot* on his head. Vibrant parasols held up above him and other priests, bishops, and also the "*Tzadakan*" the Righteous Ones of sacred legend, all combined to make this scene look like blossoming flowers in a field. What a beautiful and enchanting sight, especially for the visitors who have never seen it before. Even if it was been seen a dozen times, it was still a grand spectacle to behold.

Afterwards, horses trotted with their proud looking commanders and head guards in warrior garb with baboon manes on their heads and dazzling costumes of vibrant colors, swords, shields, and lances in hands riding them. The crowd gazed on in awe and reverence of their authority and accomplishments. Afterwards, the animal trainers presented their exotic creatures on leashes. First, some lions sporting large black manes lead the way, then baboons and ostriches.

Suspicion Arises.
Everything seemed to be going well, Mekonnen reckoned. They may even play a game of jousting later that night. Perhaps sit around a camp fire, have a merry feast of fruits and vegetables, with *injera* and *beg* (lamb meat) with hot spices like *berbere* and *mitmita* on the side, and some excellent wine to wash it down. All those thoughts of fun and relaxation filled the young warrior's mind until one of the hooded ones walked pass Mekonnen. Coldness, darkness, and a negative energies emanated from the hooded one that gave Mekonnen an uneasy feeling. It sent chills up and down his spine.

"Something is not right with that stranger." He thought, "Walking around like that, sneaking and light-footed. Why is he looking around like that, Scoping out the area?"

"Psst, Afeworq?" Mekonnen whispers to his cousin, with eyes still fixed on his suspect,

"Look, something is not right with that fellow. Wait here."

"I see him." Afeworq affirmed.

Mekonnen drew closer into the crowd with eyes focused on his prey who was quickly engulfed by the sea of people. Just then, Mekonnen spotted another hooded one nearby who looked conspicuous. And it looked like he picked up a signal from the first hood he was following. Mekonnen became keener and more observant. His heart rate accelerated yet he remained calm and focused. Then, upon the left on a roof top, another mysterious hood acted suspiciously. Another hooded person walked by, and Mekonnen looked at him intently, but this one was different. This one did not look and act suspiciously, and he can see his face. Normal sunlight revealed this ones face and the patterns on the hem were less distinctive like the suspects. Might just be a monk, so he lets him walk by. Mekonnen could really notice the utter darkness under the hoods that were suspect and can even see the difference in the patterns on the clothing from the other common people and that strange symbol they have on the front of their clothes, a crooked line within a red

Mekonnen running
with Sword in Aksum
Mattyas @ 1/28/2018

circle. Afeworq spotted another hooded suspect upon a high wall, stooping down and peering over in the distance beyond the procession of the *tabot* and the animals.

Just then the distinct sound of a particular animal gave Mekonnen and Afeworq an idea of what the hood on the high wall was looking at in the distance. The trumpet-like cry of a great elephant rang out in the distance, a sound that was a familiar hint for the Aksumites as to who was approaching. It was the Emperor Gabra Masqal and his Queen, Her Majesty Nigist Semret seatted on thrones on top a platform, drawn by four huge African elephants. Alongside the platform were about seven or eight other members of the royal family riding on horseback and in golden chariots. The crowd around

Mekonnen and Afeworq became restless and excited at the sound of the elephants as their large heads and ivory tusks were be seen in the distances down the cobbled street.

Royal Procession.

"Oh look, the Emperor and Empress are coming. The Negus and Nigist are coming!" was the buzz in the crowd as some tried to position themselves in a spot in order to get a good view of Ella Gabra Masqal and his royal family. Guards tried their best to control the crowds to make way on the street. Mekonnen motioned to two guards to be on the alert for suspicious activity.

The King's procession drew nearer. So close, the rough textures and creases in the elephants' dark brown skin became noticeable. Two in the front and two behind those, harnessed with thick ropes and leather straps connected to the platform on wheels. The elephants were adorned with decorative garments on their heads and backs, speckled with gold and pearl beads with golden tassels. On the backs of each of the behemoth creatures were riders seated in fancy saddles guiding them in the right direction. Even the elephants' tusks were capped with round golden stubs of fine décor. Behind the creatures was the golden chariot, which was more like a platform on wheels, that they drew carefully and steadily as their trainers and riders would allow them.

Within the chariot sat His Majesty Negus Gabra Masqal also known as Ella Amida, son of the great and famous Ella Abreha, the former Negus Kaleb, who gave up his crown to live a monastic life. He stood and waved in his glorious regalia that was just as colorful as the priestly garments but more bejeweled and ornamented. From the crown of his head to the sole of his feet, Ella Gabra Masqal was an ornamented sight to behold: His golden crown quite high in several layers with golden streamers hanging down, fluttering as they reflected the natural sunlight. His collar, armlets and multitude of bracelets and rings all of fine, pure gold. Even his kilt was of pure gold on linen cloth. His chest wrapped in straps embroidered with pearls. Guards were on the platform with the Negus, but he was still pretty much dangerously open and an easy target. Normally the Negus would also be holding a gilded shield and a lance, but this time he chose to just hold up his lance in a vertical position with spear pointing upwards.

Mekonnen tried not to look conspicuous, doing his best not to let the suspects know that he and Afeworq were on their trails. He couldn't help but notice how unprotected the Emperor was, with just two guards at lower levels at his side and few others on the platform. The warrior determined that was not enough. And the ones present were not alert enough to what may be about to take place.

Suddenly, it happened. Mekonnen's cover was lost. The cloaked ones noticed Mekonnen on their trail and signaled to each other. The first suspect was out of sight, and Mekonnen became nervous. The Negus was still an open target, and his guards were not paying attention. Mekonnen leapt up upon a fruit vendor's table to spot them again, causing many lemons, leaks, and melons to fall to the cobbled ground. He scanned the crowd ecstatically, left, right, up and down. He spotted one! Now he knew what they were trying to do. Afeworq saw Mekonnen on the table and moved in closer but did not notice a hooded one approaching him from behind, eyes glowing red in the darkness.

Mekonnen saw clearly what was going to happen. At a distance, a cloaked one appeared behind a palace guard on a ledge and stabbed him in the back, taking his spear as the guard collapsed to the ground. Adrenaline rushed in, and a bolt of energy hit Mekonnen, as he leapt from off the table with spear in one hand and a round shield in the other, he darted out towards the King, shouting,

"Alert, Shield the King!!"

Intended Target.

The King's guards were now alert but confused, not really sure from which direction the impending attack was coming, but they positioned themselves to encircle the Emperor and the Empress, shields, and spears up. The crowd was now startled and concerned, some duck down their head or lay low, others gasp with mouths open, looking in multiple directions. A few women and young girls grabbed on to each other or onto their little ones. Seeing Mekonnen run frantically towards the King's chariot, the hooded one who stabbed the guard on the ledge now holds the spear and positions himself to throw it, angling its sharp pointed spear head towards the Emperor, Negus Gabra Masqal. The king's guards could not see the would-be assassin because the sun was directly behind him. But Mekonnen saw him clearly enough from his angle. Now the hooded assassin leaned back, aimed, heaved and then thrusted forward and released, sending the spear sailing through the air, headed straight for the intended target, the Negus.

The hood behind Afeworq began to pull out a sword from under his cloak, but before he could pull the blade all the way out of its sheath, Afeworq heard the sound of a blade dragging against surface and sensed the foul presents. He swung around and hits the hood on the side of its head with the spear shaft and thrusts the blade and shaft through its chest, as quick as two second. Afeworq yanked the spear out of his attacker and watched him fall to the dusty ground, dead, then kept on moving, looking for more suspicious ones.

Meanwhile, Mekonnen ran frantically towards the Negus' aid from the right, determined to save His Majesty from the flying spear that was aimed for Negus Gabra Masqal's torso. Whichever got to the Negus first determined

His Majesty's fate. Life or Death. Mekonnen, just a few steps away, leapt with shield in right hand, and became almost horizontal in mid-air in front of the Negus, just in time for the deadly spear to strike Mekonnen's shield instead of Royal flesh.

"Craaacksh!!" the sharp head of the spear penetrated Mekonnen's shield and missed his arm by an inch. But Mekonnen's flight carried the spear away from His Majesty and Her Majesty the Nigist Semret, sending Mekonnen and spear tumbling to the ground on the left side of the royal platform, rolling over about three times.

By the time Mekonnen leapt up to his feet a little bruised and dusty, the King and Queen were surrounded by guards, deacons, and priests. The elephants got stirred up by the commotion but were still under control by the trainers and riders.

Rain of Arrows.

A cry went out to be alert and seize suspected *Qataliyan* – Assassins – in their midst. By that time Afeworq was at Mekonnen's side checking to see if he was okay and said,

"Come on! We must catch the rest of them! I already took one down."

"Yes, lets go!" Mekonnen replied then turned toward the king's platform and asked the guards, "How is the Emperor, and the Empress? Are they safe? Are they well?!"

"Yes, His Majesty and the Nigist are unharmed!" Was the reply. But as the guard spoke, arrows began whizzing by, landing on the platform, and even striking two of the elephants on the left. Arrows were being fired from the general direction of where the spear was launched. The two elephants cried out like loud trumpets in a panic as they attempted to move away from the rain of arrows that just barely penetrated the surface of the thick skin but caused enough pain to be irritable. The other two elephants did not move, causing them to bump into each other and jolted the platform, which caused a few guards and priests to fall off. The crowd panicked, screamed and ran in many directions. One of the elephants in the front on the right stumbled and crashed into a building, destroying the façade with the impact. No one seemed to be hurt in that accident. Mekonnen and the rest of the guards realized they needed to cut the elephants loose into the streets of Aksum otherwise they would drag the platform with the King and Queen still on top of it, placing them in danger of being severely injured or even killed.

"Quick! Cut the elephants' ropes! Hurry!" one to the guards commanded, as two other guards quickly dealt two to three hacks at the thick ropes until they broke free.

The elephants cried out loud, "Whhaaaahhh!" and lifted their trunks in the air. One of them reared up on its hind legs causing people nearby to panic and shout to get out of the way as the elephants stormed down the street.

Now the city was in utter chaos.

Mekonnen looked up in the direction the Qatali's spear and arrows were coming from and exclaimed,

"That cursed beast. Afey, let's get them before they escape into the wilderness!"

And off they ran, hoping to capture the hooded one who threw the spear that almost impaled the Emperor.

Meanwhile, the other hooded ones scattered into different directions trying to hide amongst the panicking citizens of Aksum. It was possible they may have a plan to meet and regroup in different locations. Some of the royal guards went after them and confronted some of the suspects in sword fights. Subduing and capturing these agile and elusive hooded Qataliyan dead or alive proved to be very difficult.

More arrows were released and flew into the air then came down and struck several guards as civilians got caught in the crossfire. It was as if they came to start a war and take over the venerated city of Aksum. But the royal guards and warriors would not allow such actions to persist.

The Aksumite royal palace as described by Egyptian Monk and traveler Cosmas Indicopleustes.

Ark of Tsion Barricade.

Immediately the royal army brought out their own artillery of archers and marks men, with traditional bows and crossbows ready for action. Commanders Mulualem, Telemarkos, and Alazar, the war hero, shouted orders to their royal guards,

"Warriors of Aksum!! Assume your positions to form the Ark of Tsion Barricade! Now! Now! Nowwww!!"

They quickly organized their warriors and mercenaries to form special barricades in the main streets and alleyways that lead up to the holy chapel *Qedus Mariam Tsion* that housed the Holy Ark of the Covenant. These barricades involved creating several layers of defenses one behind another in order to make it very difficult, or even impossible, to penetrate and get at the Ark of the Covenant that was claimed to be kept in this chapel within the city of Aksum. There was already one monk in the holy chapel who had been chosen since the age of 7 years to protect and keep the Ark of the Covenant for his whole life, accompanied by armed guards surrounding the chapel outer gate, day and night. The barricade formation began at the top of the street with a row of 10 swordsmen standing side by side in the front, completely blocking the path, enforced behind by 2 rows of spearmen poised side by side. Followed by four warriors on horseback wielding swords and lances. And 4 of the finest archers on horseback. Lastly, two

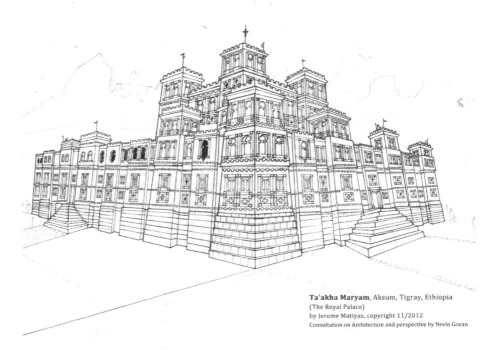

Ta'akha Maryam, Aksum, Tigray, Ethiopia
(The Royal Palace)
by Jerome Matiyas, copyright 11/2012
Consultation on Architecture and perspective by Nevin Govan

elephants mounted by warriors armed with swords, daggers, lances and bows, and arrows. With practiced precision these tightly knit barricades were put together just as they had been done it several times in times of peace and war since the days of Negus Ezana more than 200 years earlier ago.[2]

In Pursuit.

The archers answered the adversaries' rain of arrows with their own, striking down eight of the hooded ones. The others decided to flee rather than continue with their attack. Foot soldiers went after them, but they were gone almost instantly as if they had disappeared into the shadows.

They then looked at the bodies of the cloaked *Qataliyan* they struck down, but instead of the usual human carcasses they expected to see, they beheld a strange, ghastly sight.

Meanwhile, Mekonnen and Afeworq mounted up on brown Arabia horses of the royal guard to pursue the other hooded attackers who headed south for the wilderness towards the Samen Mountains. They rode through the crowded cobbled streets of Aksum; this section with white and beige colored buildings of occupations and trades, workers of arts and crafts, and smiths of iron and precious stones, and vapors of sweet perfumes, enchanting incenses, and hot streams all mingled together in the warm atmosphere. Everyone tried to get out of the way of these warriors on steeds in hot pursuit of those who threatened the safety of the Kingdom, who dared attempt to strike down Aksum's *Negust Negusa*, The King of Kings.

"What a pity." Mekonnen thought to himself. Right near the tail end of the glorious three-day Timkat festival. At that time the citizens and visitors of Aksum would be preparing to gather for great banquet feasts, followed by praises, singing, dancing, music, jousting and other forms of merry making. The festival would continue after this brief episode of chaos subsided, but at this moment, civilians and strangers retreated indoors, and in the shade, until it was safe to come out again. The show must go on.

Warrior Comrades in Action.

As Mekonnen and Afeworq rode on to the southern ends of Aksumite territory in hot pursuit of the Qataliyan, they were joined by five more royal guards on horseback. They converged from different directions, from various streets onto the same path with Mekonnen and Afeworq. Valiant warriors they were, all quite acquainted with the two kinsmen. Their names were Endal, Gedion, Biniyam, Kale'ab, Endubis, and Nezana. Endal rode up beside Mekonnen and saluted,

---

2 I made up this military formation in my head that seems plausible after studying a few books of battle formations like Warfare in the Classical World by John Warry (1995) and hints for medieval and fantasy movies that depict ancient warfare.

"Selamta, my brother! Let us catch these wretched dogs and show them we don't welcome *qataliyan* here, okay!"

Mekonnen replied with zeal, "*U-wa*, Yes, my warrior! For Aksum, for Negus Gabra Masqal!"

And in unison, the seven warriors belt out ululations with glistening swords and spears raised up in the air,

"Elelelelelelelelele!!"

As the cloaked strangers took flight, they showed themselves to be as wise and cunning as serpents. A few stopped running and blended in with the crowd; others stole horses and headed for the Samen mountains in the south and to the mountains in the north. The warriors assumed these villains may have a special place in the forest and hills where they met and regrouped themselves to plan another attack.

As the warriors rode onward, a cloaked assassin leapt out of the second story window of one of the buildings along the way, right above Biniyam, alias Bini, as he rode by. Like a creature from the wild, cloaked villain lets out a ghastly snarl with sword drawn above his head, intending to strike down Bini. But the warrior was quick, as he thrusted the point of his spear into the hooded thing as it came down on him. The impaled body slams onto Bini, throwing him off balance and lose control of his horse for a moment, but he pushes off the limp body and regained control.

Gedion, alias Gedi, was armed with a big, 4-foot-tall bow and arrows and while riding his horse was able to draw, aim, release and strike down one of the villains who ran ahead on foot. Another one leapt out from another window onto the back of Kale'ab's horse, grabbing on to him from behind with one hand and drawing a dagger with the other, ready to slit the warrior's throat. But Kale'ab, alias Kebi, was able to grab onto the arm with the dagger quickly and uses his elbow to hit his attacker hard in the ribs.

One, two, three, four times Kebi thrusts his elbow backwards into the torso of his assailant, but he still wrestles with him. Then the warrior reaches for his curved sword and thrusts the blade into the stomach of his attacker as he then clenched, lost his grip on Kebi, as the body grew lifeless and slided off into the street, and got trampled by the horses behind ridden by the other warrior companions, Nezan, Bini and Gedi. Mekonnen and Afeworq still galloped in the lead.

Eventually the seven caught up with four more Qataliyan who were ahead of them on stolen horses. Mekonnen, Afeworq and Endal were in front and charge on at accelerated speed, urging on their steeds to go faster, "Hyaaah, Hyaaah!" Passersby and camel riders tried to get out of the way of the galloping madness of royal court guards on horseback in hot pursuit of hooded beings of unknown origins.

Deadly Arrows.

Then one of the villains spun around quickly to ride backward and face his pursuant, drew back his bow string and fired two arrows in quick successions. One arrow missed and hit no one, the other arrow whizzes by Mekonnen's left ear as he shifts slightly to the right, but it hit Endubis – alias Endi – , who was just behind him, in his left shoulder.

"Ahyy!" cried Endi, wincing in pain. Endal fired back two arrows piercing one villain in the back. Another hood flipped around on his horse and rode backwards like the first one and fired off two arrows, and hits Afeworq with one in the chest and the other his horse in the upper right shoulder by its neck. Afeworq cried out and his horse wined in pain but still kept on riding forward. Mekonnen noticed his cousin's injury and calls out to him, "Afey! Are you, okay?! Hold on my brother, hold on there!"

"I'm fine…" Afeworq assured Mekonnen but unconvincingly for the obvious look of pain in his face.

More arrows were fired by the hooded ones, and this time Nezan was hit in the thigh, and Endi and his horse were hit again, but this time his horse was badly injured in the front leg, sending both horse and rider tumbling down onto the street of tiled flat stones which was at a slight decline at this point. Endi was hurt badly and unconscious on the ground, bleeding from his head and body, his horse neighing and wreathing on the hard ground. Nezan was going to continue onward but stopped and went back to help his fallen companion.

Mekonnen roses up on his horse from a sitting position to a standing posture, with his spear in right hand, aimed and launches it forward, impaling the second cloaked archer in the face, straight into the darkness under the hood. As the hooded rider fell off his horse with the spear in his face, his leg was caught in the horse's stirrup causing the body to hang over and drag on the left side of the horse, and pulled the steed in that direction as it lost balance and tumbled over, tripping three of the four other horses ridden by hooded villains. This incident started a chain reaction, creating a massive tumbling heap of men and horses, with Mekonnen, Afey and Endal got tangled up in the heap and fell over as well. But as they fell, Afeworq got another arrow in the torso, which pierced some vital organs. Bini and Gedi managed to escape this massive tumble in the streets of lower south Aksum, but they both turned back to assist their friends, unwittingly leaving one villain to escape down the cobbled streets to the south towards the Samen Mountains.

Fallen Warriors.

Both men and horses attempted to raise themselves up from the collision, whipping out swords and daggers from sheaths. Mekonnen, though bruised and in pain, was the first to rise, followed by Endal and Afeworq, though he his wounded and bleeding with two arrows in his torso, was determined and ready to fight with sharp, curve swords in hand. One of the villains managed to get back up on his stolen horse and rode off speedily down another side street. His two remaining hooded companions were ready to attack the Aksumite warriors with glistening swords in hands.

Mekonnen clashed swords with one of them while the other battled with Afeworq who barely seemed to be able to defend himself, as he lost a lot of blood and his strength was failing him.

"Afeworq! Hey Endal, help him!" exclaimed Mekonnen as he battled his opponent in sword play. Endal lounged at Afeworq's opponent and swiped with his sword but missed and got a hard kick to the chest from this tall villain who was about 6 cubits high. With the impact, Endal lifted off the ground slightly and tumbled back down to the ground.

Mekonnen prevailed over his opponent first by jump kicking him with both feet to the chest, then slashed off its right arm at the elbow that held the sword, then off with its hooded head with a swift move of skillful swordsmanship. Afeworq was not so fortunate; his cloaked opponent stabbed him in the stomach. But with one last move and ounce of strength left in him, Afeworq was able to stab upward with his sword through the villain's chin with the blade coming out the top of his hooded head.

"Afeworq, No!" screamed Mekonnen and ran to his cousin's aide, now collapsed to the ground next to his felled horse. Mekonnen pushes off his cousin's killer and finishes it off by chopping off its head. Then grabbed Afeworq in his arms, Endal looked on in sadness a few yards away.

"Afeworq, come on stay with me, you will be alright!"

"I'm sorry Mekonnen, I...don't think I'm going to make it this time. It is my time to go. Pray that Egziabeher will find me worthy to enter into *Samayat*."

"Oh, Afey my brother! I should have been there to save you! Forgive me."

"No, it is not your fault. All... in Egziabeher's plan. All in...his...his will."

Tears began to well up in Mekonnen's eyes. He pleaded,

"No, I'm sorry...I...!"

"Goodbye, Mo'kay my...brother. See you in *Samaya*t."

Then Afeworq breathed his last breath and gave up the ghost. Gone from this life to the Realms of Samayat, the abode of the great *Egziabeher*, and His faithful *Mal'ekt* and *Qeddusan* – Angels and Holy Ones.

Mekonnen leaned over in sadness and cried. Endal bows his head down mournfully. The sky began to become overcast with low gray clouds like they were full of rain. Just then Endal noticed something strange and ghastly with the dead bodies of the hooded ones. They became shriveled and chard looking. Not only that but where their limbs were severed, black snakes slithered out of them.

Gedi approached them on foot and exclaims loudly, "Mo'kay look out, Snakes!"

"What sort of vile sorcery is this?!" Mekonnen retorts as they both began to hack off the heads of the slithering creatures hastily. While swiping at the vipers, the rain began to fall.

"There, I think we got them all, Mekonnen. The snakes I mean, I think we got them all," said Endal as he looked down the ally way and street where the other two hooded villains escaped. He looked up at the dark gray clouds, as the sky cried rain drops upon his face.

Mekonnen, on his knees, still holding Afeworq, looks up into the same sky, the rain first mingled with then washed away his tears, he whispers,

"Why *Egzi Hawey* – Oh Lord. Why did this evil come upon us."

There was no reply but the rains came down heavier, some nebulous clouds to the south illumined with flashes of lightning. Curious bystanders converged around the four warriors, but they kept their distance. Two middle-aged women drew closer to assist the warriors with the body of Afeworq, but Mekonnen insists on picking up his cousin's limp body in his arms and carried him back up the cobbled street by himself.

Back in Aksum city a woman searched and called out for her child who got separated from her amongst all the madness earlier that evening.

"Natanael! Natiii! Where are you Nati? It is time to go home now! Nati?!

It was the same young woman whose son bumped into one of the hooded Qataliyan. The same boy, Natanael was his name, his mother called him Nati, who saw the darkness under the hood and glowing red, evil eyes, then ran to his mommy for safety. Now, this same boy appeared to be missing, nowhere to be seem. Apparently, he's unable to respond to his mother. Perhaps hiding somewhere in a corner to escape the chaos, perhaps hiding under a market food stall. Perhaps he was with family or friends. Perhaps he was lost or stolen, or even worst.

Yet in the midst, amongst the crowd of citizens of Aksum and strangers and merchants from far and wide, there lurked a mysterious individual, a hooded creature, who seemed like a normal man on the outside, but on the inside bore a dark soul. As black as night and as deep as the Bottomless Pit. Venom seethed through its veins. Slithering and peeking like a viper with eyes glowing red in the shadows, seeking another opportunity to strike.

The thing maneuvered its way through the crowds and detours southwards towards the Samen wilderness and mountains, hoisted a medium sized bag over its left shoulder like a sack of potatoes. There was something in the sack that moved and squirmed. Muffled sounds and faint cries came from the sack. It was difficult to decipher what might be in there, whether an animal, creature, person or thing. Nobody noticed. Nobody knew. It was little Nati bounded in ropes inside that sack.

*Mékonnen in Aksum
ready for battle.
Matiyas © 2009*

Mekonnen running into battle.
Matiyas © 2009

CHAPTER 3
NEGUSA NAGAST
(KING of KINGS)

CHAPTER 3, KING OF KINGS
JEROME MATIYAS © 2013 - 2018

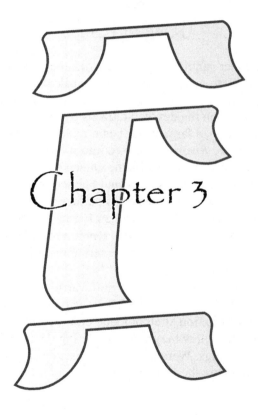

Chapter 3

Chapter 3

Negusa Nagast

(King of Kings)

That night, under candlelight and lanterns, the citizens of Aksum were relatively back to normal, though a bit shaken up by the commotion that took place earlier. As the *Timkat* festival wound down with the sprinkling of waters upon the devoted citizens by the *Qasisan* to baptize them in at the *Mai Shum*, a large water basin replenished by tributaries flowing from the *Tekeze River* that flowed into it from the south and west of Aksum city. A reservoir believed to be the Queen of Sheba's own bath place, now believed to be sacred waters, holy and blessed by the priests and utilized to baptize devout believers who wished to partake in the same experience, to be anointed by the Spirit of God as when Iyesus Krestos was baptized by Yohannes in the *Yordanos Wehiz* – Jordan River – more than 500 years ago. Great feasts were prepared, and diverse entertainment in music, games, and dances livened up the city streets.

But the royal palace with the priests and warriors was not quite back to normal as they mourned the loss of fellow warriors, despite the victory over the sudden assassination attempt made on the *Negusa Nagast* Gabra Masqal earlier that day. Now they were pondering the true origins of those mysterious hooded beings. Were they men, beasts or phantoms? What was their motive for attacking the Emperor? And would they expect them to return for a second attack?

That night the Emperor Gabra Masqal summoned an audience in his royal court of the throne room. The glorious throne room with large pillars of finely crafted engravings and bejeweled with all manner of precious stones. Seven steps lead up to Emperor's and Empress' throne with stone cut statues of lions seated on the sides of each step, very much like the throne room of Negus Solomon as recorded in the history books and the ancient oracles that are written about the Kingdoms of Israel and Yihuda (Judah). There were

J. Matiyas © 2013

**Hade Gabra Masqal, Emperor of the Aksumite Empire,
circa 543 - 560 AD.**

© Jerome Matiyas

also real male lions with their impressive, dark-colored manes, near and around the Negusa Nagast, quietly prowled, lounged and licked themselves occasionally, as HIS majesty sat on his throne.

Seated next to and on the right side of the Emperor, his wife, the Nigist Semret[1]. On smaller thrones behind them were his younger brothers all addressed as Negus in the kingdom. Seated to the right of Nigist Semret and slightly behind from the oldest to the youngest: Negus Gabaz, Negus Ioel, and Negus Hataz. While to the left of Hade Gabra Masqal sat the youngest brothers under the age of 20: Negus Gersem and Negus Armah being about 12 years old[2].

Standing with the royal family on the platform were twelve royal guards with spears and round shields in hands, decked in brightly colored robes and head pieces of gelada baboon fur. Off to the side of the royal platform was a young man seated on a chair behind a small table with paper parchments, a feather pen and a small vial of ink in front of him. He was a scribe and the Negus' personal amanuensis. Occasionally the Negus would have a scribe write down all that was said and done at special gatherings, so he could have the notes for his personal records or for the history books and chronicles. This seemed to be one of those pivotal occasions His Imperial Majesty fancied a record of the unusual events that happened earlier. Mekonnen had seen this scribe before but could not remember his name at that moment.

The Negus arose from his throne to address his subjects, lifted his scepter and declared,

"Selamta, in the name of our Lord, Egzi Iyesus Krestos, Son of Egziabeher Amlak, Negusa Aksum, Negusa Meder. Amen."

The audience in the court bowed down low and replied in unison,

"Amen!"

Mekonnen stood with his fellow young warriors, Endal, Gedion, Kale'ab, Motuma, Biniyam, Nezana and a wounded and bandaged Endubis. Senior warriors in colorful uniforms and lion manes on their heads stood behind the younger ones. Many more were outside guarding the palace and patrolling the city streets.

The Emperor continued, "I must thank my royal guards and army of valiant warriors for protecting the Nigist and me today in the… assassination attempt."

The Emperor hesitated to mention what transpired earlier as it dawned on himself how close he came to be a dead Emperor. He paused, trying his best not to show any sign of fear and concern to his subjects. He swallowed, then continued.

---

1 *The name of the queen of Aksum was not recorded so I used the name Semret which means Unity.*

2 *According to history and records these were the real names of Kings of Aksum after Gabra Masqal, but their ages were not known.*

"You are true heroes and patriots. I mourn the loss of warriors who have fallen in the line of duty. Great honor and compensation will be granted to each one of them and their families."

All the warriors remained standing at attention. Mekonnen was in formation, but the sorrow could still be seen in his face at the loss of Afeworq his kinsman. Gabra Masqal arose and walked towards Mekonnen, and with true concern he said,

"I greatly regret your loss; I understand he was your kinsman. You have my deepest sympathies. And my greatest gratitude for saving my life. You are a true *Mastatsabe ZaAskum* – Aksumite Warrior – risking your own life to save thine Negus."

Mekonnen bowed down on his hands and knees, "*Egziabeher Amlak abarek, Negusa Nagast.*"

"*Egziabeher abarek*, my son. Some of your other comrades have also fallen. *Salamawi nafas* – Peace be onto their souls – as Krestos welcomes them to the paradise of *Samayat.*"

Gabra Masqal gently placed his right hand on Mekonnen's head. Mekonnen then made a request.

"*Germawi Hawey* – Your Majesty, Hade Gabra Masqal! I ask your permission to go from your presence and seek out the villains that that tried to kill you and escaped into the mountains. I will bring them to justice and rid the Kingdom of evil."

"My dear fellow, the culprits will be pursued, but now you may go to your home and rest. I temporarily relieve you of your duties for your bravery and your loss." Said the King intently. Mekonnen insists,

"I would prefer not to wallow in my grief, Your Majesty, but to serve my country and the King, and bring the guilty ones to justice swiftly, Your Highness."

The Emperor replied,

"I see. I greatly admire your zeal, but we must not be hasty until we know who and what we are up against. We do not know if it is an army or a small sect. Or a rogue faction from within the Kingdom."

One Commander named Alazar Berhane who was well known throughout the land as being a war hero after successful expeditions in Sabaea and Himyar across the Red Sea shares his observation that may prove to be invaluable information,

"Excuse me, Your Majesty, Lords, and Commanders but may I add that the *Qataliyan* – assassins – bare a symbol on their clothing. At a glance, it looks like the letter *nähas* "ጓ", (the letter "n" in *fidel*, the Ge'ez/Ethiopic alphabet), inside of a red circle. At closer inspection, the *nähas* looks like the very meaning of the letter, a literal snake! Having an arrow-shaped head and forked tongue. In any case, this tells me they are an organized group with sinister affiliations. Trained to fight, for sure."

Another senior guard replied with concern in his voice,

"Do you think they can be the people of *Beta Israel*? You know, the ones we call *'Falashas'*?"

Another replied, "No, maybe not. The way these strange men moved, and fight is not like them. Neither is the make of their weapons."

A third guard added, "The strange markings and symbols embroidered on their clothing do not look like theirs either. A warrior brought in some samples of the robes and hoods they left behind after…"

A fourth guard interrupted, "They don't change into snakes either!"

Some of the other guards and warriors who were not aware of that bit of detail gasp in surprise and exclaimed together,

"Snakes!!"

Even Negus Gabra Masqal cringed at the thought.

The fourth guard continued, "Yes, didn't you see, some of their carcasses became snakes?"

"Some kind of *Asmat*! – Sorcery! It may be the snake cult of old *Waynaba* is rising up again."

Another senior guard added, "Waynaba? Wasn't that great *Zendo*, that great Serpent slain by Angbo the Sheban/Sabaean more than a thousand years ago?"

Another guard added,

"Yes, Negus Angbo, the father of Mekeda, the *Nigist Saba* (Queen of Sheba), did slay Waynaba the great Nakhash Zendo, the Snake Dragon, a long time ago. But you never know, his spirit must be coming back, probably summoned by an *Ma'anseb* – an evil Sorcerer!"

And so, they went back and forth on the topic until the conversation turned into an argument as unsupported theories and wild speculations emerged. The Emperor finally had enough,

"*Hrai*, Okay, that's enough! Let us not begin speculating here. We need more solid evidence of their origins and find out who is their leader. The Empire has been at peace for a long time, and we don't want to go accusing people without proof. Especially the Beta Israel. Firstly, you know of the peace treaty we have signed with the Beta Israel when the throne was passed down to me after the conflict was settled with my brother Negus Esrael. Will they dishonor the truce in this manner? And remember the oath my father made Negus Kaleb with King Justinus of Rome in Eyerusalem concerning this matter with my brother, who was given the same name as the Beta Israel people as a sign. It was an oath serious enough to cause my father to give up the throne and pass the crown on to me, so he can live an ascetic life in a

monastery for the rest of his days of Earth.[3]

Secondly, you know how my father, Negus Kaleb, feels about interfering with them after what happened to our armies across the Red Sea in Himyar."

The court became silent now as they remembered what happened about 20 years ago when the Negus's father, Ella Kaleb, reigned on the throne and uprooted the Jewish King Dhu Nuwas, who was persecuting the Krestiyans, and the plague that struck down about 6000 Aksumite warriors like it was a strange curse.[4] The Beta Israel also practiced the Jewish religion, and about 200 years ago in the 300s AD, many of them were cast out of the Kingdom of Aksum as outsiders when the kingdom accepted the Krestiyan religion while many of the Beta Israel refused to convert. It's an unfortunate, tragic

---

3 *Understanding this conflict between Negus Gabra Masqal, his brother Negus Israel and the Beta Israel people is very challenging. See Kebra Negast page 117 and other sources.*

4 I got this information about the wars with Himyarite King Dhu Nuwas from Aksum: An African Civilization of Late Antiquity, Chapter (11) by Stuart Munro-Hay.

story really since the root of Krestiyan religion is the fulfillment of the *Ayhudawi* (Jewish) prophecies written in the sacred oracles of the coming of the Krestos, the Messiah, to save mankind from sin and usher in the eternal *Mengest Egziabeher*, the Kingdom of the Almighty God. A kingdom that not of this world, but a kingdom of light, power, and glory from *Gazat Samay,* the Realms of Heaven.

The Emperor continues, "And what about my northern tributary states and provinces in Nubia? Any reports from my kinsman, Negus Amhaz[5] and his wife Kandake Amanikadetede of Alodia? Or from Makuria and Nobatia? Were these provinces also attacked as we were?"

One nobleman named Asmawi who was specialized in gathering news and tidings from neighboring provinces stepped forward, bowed and responded,

"Your Majesty, may you and the Nigist live forever. There have been no reports what so ever of any attacks or disorders in the rest of the kingdom. Not even in Himyar and Sabaea, My Lord."

"Thank you, Noble Asmawi." The Emperor replied.

Emperor Gabra Masqal turned to Mekonnen again,

"I grant your wish, Mekonnen, son of Sofaniyas, to go out with a small search party to the south while I send another party to the north where some have also fled. You shall go out tomorrow morning, bright and early. Be courageous and may *Egziabeher* grant you all success and God Speed. You are all dismissed. *Egzio Abaraq.*"

The Emperor bowed then his royal subjects bowed in unison and blessed the Negus,

"Egziabeher bless the Negus and may he live forever."

The *Qasisan,* - the priests - are there in the throne room, a score of them including deacons, and all nine *Tsadkan,* the honorable Nine Righteous Ones, sometimes called the Nine Saints. Among the holy ones was the Arch Bishop himself, the Abuna Ekklesian from Alexandria, Egypt. There he was in his brilliantly embroidered priestly regalia, a Coptic cross in his right hand and a staff in the other, he cautiously approached the Negusa Nagast, bowing with a smile and his piercing brown eyes glitter with veneration. Rumor in the halls among the court warriors and nobles is that Abuna Ekklesian is of mixed parentage, an Egyptian mother, and a Greek father.

Mekonnen, with head bowed, can see the Abuna's feet peeking under his robe as he approached from the front. The young warrior does not look up at the Abuna but kept his head bowed as he reaches for the Abuna's hands and

---

5 I made up this name for the story, but historically Gabra Masqal did have several brothers that ruled with or after him as mentioned in the previous page. Their names were Gabaz, Ioel, Hataz, Israel, Gersem and Armah. Source: Aksum: An African Civilization of Late Antuquity, Chapter 7: The Monarch by Stuart Munro-Hay.

kisses them as is customary.

It is the first time Mekonnen has had the chance to meet the revered patriarch in person; he perceived the Abuna is an older man, about 60 to 65 years old, with full gray beard, not showing signs of being decrepit of old age, but mature vitality. Abuna Ekklesian has been Arch Bishop of the Egyptian Coptic Church for almost 9 years and has ordained and sent *Ichege*, (Abbots) to Aksum and the churches in the provinces and Realms of Nubia. Now he came to pay a visit to Aksum to celebrate Timkat with the Aksumites. How awful, he must have thought, coming all the way up the great Nile River only to witness an assassination attempt on the Emperor. Yet he seemed understanding and in good spirits.

"Egziabeher Amlak bless you, my son. Yes, you are brave and courageous. How unfortunate it is that your friend was killed in the line of duty. Maybe you should yield to the Negus' first suggestion to go home and rest. Spend time to mourn with the family and bury your friend in a royal funeral with the highest honor."

The Abuna Ekklesian tried to convince Mekonnen in Ge'ez, the official language of the Aksumites. His Ge'ez is actually quite good, Mekonnen notices, considering the Abuna's native language is Egyptian, only a slight accent can be detected in his well-structured sentences.

Mekonnen replied politely with head down, "Thank you, Your Holiness, forgive me, but he was actually my kinsman on my father's side of the family. I just don't want the enemy to escape from our realms unpunished."

"Oh, I understand son, I understand. But there are other *sarawit*, regiments in the kingdom that can fill in now, are there not?"

"Uh, well, yes, your Holiness."

Abuna Ekklesian turned to the Negus and added,

"In fact, your Highness, I suggest you don't send out too many warriors to seek those vermin who attacked you. You would not want to risk losing more young warriors, wouldn't you? Why not send out small search parties instead? Might be more effective that way. Like a covert mission."

The Negus replied, "Hmm, I don't know, your Holiness I really don't want to let the 'vermin' escape into the wilderness for good. I will let the Commanders in Chief decide on details of expedition."

Then with an index finger pointing upward as if he remembered something, "Oh yes, before you leave Your Holiness, I would like you to inspect the clothing and robes the *Qataliyan* were wearing. It seems after they were killed their carcasses morphed into snakes, leaving their garments behind. But the warriors were able to remove the snakes, gather up the garments, and bring them in."

"Oh certainly, You Majesty! Let me take a look." The Abuna replied.

"The Negus adds, "I suppose the garments will be considered too accursed to keep in the palace or anywhere else, but in any case."

NIGIST SEMRET

ABUNA EKKLESIAN

His Royal Highness called aloud, "Guards! Please bring the clothing in here for the Abuna to inspect!"

At that call, two guards march in single file carrying baskets containing the garments in question and held them up to the Abuna for him to see. Abuna Ekklesian dared not touch them with his hands, so he used his staff to poke at and lift up one of the white linen robes from the basket that had a blood red jewel of sorts with that symbol in the center that does resemble a slithering snake.

"Yes, I see the symbol you were talking about. Looks like a little snake slithering on its belly. Very odd indeed."

"Have you ever seen that symbol before from your experience, your studies or your travels, Your Holiness?"

"I'm afraid I have not, Your Majesty. I've seen many symbols baring the snake, like the snake of Moses staff in the wilderness. The double snakes of Aesculapius. The snakes on the crowns of the ancient Pharoahs, and even Apep, the evil serpent of ancient Egyptian mythology. But this one does not look familiar at all."

The Negus sighs, "Okay, thank you for your insight Abuna. I suppose I should have a *Qasis* take these accursed garments away and burn them, Your Holiness?"

"Yes, as a matter of fact, Your Majesty," Abuna Ekklesian added, "I will be so obliged to relieve you of these garments and get rid of them for good in a proper manner as a High Priest should do."

"As you wish, Abuna Ekklesian. Thank you for taking care of these for us."

"You are most welcome Negusa Negast Gabra Masqal." Said the Abuna as he bowed respectfully to the Negus and two of his manakost came forward and took the baskets from the guards' hands.

"Thank you, and it was my pleasure to have you with us, Abuna despite how the Timkat festival turned out at the beginning, *Egzio Yamisgan*, God be praised."

The Negus and the Abuna bid each other goodbye with holy kisses on the hands, and other servants and warriors went to honor and minister unto them. The musicians began to strum gently on their large harps from Egypt and small *kirars*, a small local harp instrument and played a dirge. The head patron musician, Daiqon Yared, was present in throne room and began to croon a melancholy tune. In one instance he looked directly at Mekonnen and held on to his arm to stop him as he walked by to improvise a personal song for Mekonnen. Translated from classical Ge'ez, it went like this:

"Blessed be the ones that have lost loved ones
 Oh, be strong young Warrior,
Be strong and courageous
 Oh, be brave young Anbessa
Be brave and faithful.
 But let Egziabeher restore thy heart and soul
With the rivers of water that flow
 From His eternal throne."

And everyone in the Negus' court heard it and thought it was beautiful.

Before the Hade Gabra Masqal dismissed his audience, *daiqonat* were called into the throne room. Seven of them walk out in single file with small money sacks in their hands, each one positioned himself in front of Mekonnen and the scores of warriors there and handed each one of them a sack. Mekonnen looked at the sack, the contents of which clinked in his hands is puzzled for a moment as to what it was for. Then he realized it was extra payment from the Negus Gabra Masqal for their efforts and bravery that day.

The Negus slowly arose from his throne to his feet, still surrounded by male and female lions in relaxed postures making low guttural sounds. With his right hand petting the head of a full grown, male lion with dark mane that sat uprightly next to him the Negus declared,

"What you hold in your hands, my brave warriors of Aksum, is extra payment for your valiant acts and dedication today. There will be more gold for you if you catch the cloaked *qatali* for me within seven days. May Egziabeher bless you and your families to whom you return to tonight. You may all be dismissed. Selam!" The Negus Gabra Masqal turns and walks down the stairs towards the scribe, who was trying to wrap up the narrative and requests,

"Matiyas, did you get everything on paper? How many pages long is it? Let me see." The scribe Matiyas fumbled with the pages and replied, "Uh, about 6 or 7 pages, your Majesty!"

A Strange Gift

Meanwhile, everyone left the Negus' presence in single file and in order, the priests, nobles, senior warriors, commanders, and generals. As he slowly walked away, Mekonnen loosen the strings of his pouch and dipped his fingers into it, feeling around for its contents and lifting out a few minted golden coins inspects them in the palm of his right hand. Engraved on the circumference of two of the shiny coins is Gabra Masqal's royal name *"Ella Ameda"* followed by the motto *"That which is fitting for the people."* in Ge'ez script and a depiction of his facial profile with a crown on his head glittering in the lantern lights. On two more coins is the name and profile of *Ella Amida's* father, *"Ella Atsbeha, Son of Tezana"* the royal name for Negus Kaleb, followed by the motto *"May this please the city."* Mekonnen would usually be happy for the extra payment, but at this time he does not care about the money. Because no amount of gold, silver or precious stones in the Kingdom can return his cousin Afeworq from the dead.

With his head downcast and feeling a bit depressed, Mekonnen shuffles along to be the last one to exit the Kings's chambers, when he notices someone else was also lingering in the Negus' court with him. It's a young man dressed in white with a dark, speckled robe. He just blends in with the crowd of nobles, priests, and warriors, but Mekonnen noticed him at the corner of his eye while he was speaking to Abuna Ekklesian. As the others left, he lingered by the columns. As Mekonnen was about the leave and turned at a large pillar, he heard a call from behind.

"*Egzi Mekonnen!*" translated to "Lord Mekonnen!"

"Huh?" Mekonnen stopped and spins around surprised by such a calling. To be addressed as "Lord Mekonnen" was flattering but he did not feel worthy.

"Who would call me 'Lord'" he thought to himself, "I am just a young warrior."

He turned around, and it was the strange young man who lingered in the corners earlier.

Mekonnen replied, "*U-wa, Egzi?* – Yes, Sir?" As the stranger approached him with something in his hands. Mekonnen was cautious and ready to defend himself in case it was a trap, but he remains calm. The stranger approached near and proclaimed,

"Good and faithful servant, you shall be rewarded, and behold, you will be rewarded by the Nigusa Nagast, the King of Kings."

Mekonnen was a bit puzzled now by the strange salutations from the young man, whose skin is reddish-brown and a bit shinny like it was polished. His hair was full and buffed out in the style similar to Mekonnen's. He was dressed in all white from top to trousers, except for the fine robe on his back that is dark violet in color at the shoulders, speckle with fine white pearls and going downward is washed out into a rich maroon, from the center of the back down to the tips of the robe that was just a few inches shy from touching the floor. And on the palace marble floor, the stranger wore neither shoes nor sandals, but was barefooted, like many Abyssinians choose to be when they walked about. But Mekonnen lets him come closer, not really sensing danger, but still on guard.

The stranger continued,

"This is for you, your reward. Your prize for the truth" then he bows down on one knee in front of Mekonnen, holds up an item in his hands which looks like a belt of sorts with a golden buckle about the width of the palm of a man's hand and it was handsomely engraved into the shape of a cross inside a circle. Mekonnen stilled puzzled, looks at the shiny cross buckle that was just presented to him, and reluctantly lifts his hands to touch it and inquires,

"A…A reward for me? From…" Mekonnen searched for words and the stranger, still on one knee interrupted,

"From the Negusa Nagast, and Egzia Egaezt – the Lord of Lords."

Mekonnen now assumes he meant the belt is a gift from the Emperor and says,

"*Hawey*! A reward from Negus Gabra Masqal?"

The young man stands up promptly and says,

"The NEGUSA Negasts. The KING of Kings!" he emphasizes, confusing Mekonnen even more because the Emperor of Aksum is always referred to as the Negusa Nagast. The only other person who is given that title is the original Negusa Nagast, Egzi Iyesus Kristos. But how could it be?

"The Negusa Nagast wishes for you to have peace and for you to seek the truth, know the truth and bear the truth at all times. This is a symbol of his Truth."

Mekonnen accepted the gift from the strange fellow who spook a riddle about the "Truth" and replied,

"Well, I thank you, though I don't understand what you mean by…" And when Mekonnen looked up, the stranger was gone. Vanished.

"Hey, where did he go?"

Mekonnen looked around the pillar in vain, thinking he couldn't have slipped away so quickly. But apparently, he did. Just then he heard a fluttering sound, like bird's wings, coming from above. Looking upward he spotted, for sure, a bird fluttering its wings, ascending higher and higher towards the ceiling then around the other side of a column until it was out of sight.

"Strange." Mekonnen thought to himself, "That man is gone, and now a bird seems to have found its way into the palace and got trapped inside. And now that bird is gone. Maybe it found a hole in the rafters or ceiling and got out this time. As for the one that gave me this belt of fine gold? That was very strange indeed. I wish I could sprout wings right about now and fly out of this wretched world. Even better, sprout wings and use them to fly over the whole land of Habeshat to seek and find those accursed *qataliyan* and show them no mercy with my bare hands and my sharpened sword."

He looked at the golden encircled cross buckle again, then left the Emperors palace, mounted his horse and sped off to his hometown just on the outskirts of the Aksum city to the west. It was a small village called Dura near the lake *Mai Negus* translated as Water of the King.

Later, Mekonnen spent the night with his family and relatives as they mourned the passing of Afeworq. And as he perched quietly on the floor in a corner among his sorrowful relatives in the house of Afeworq's parents and siblings, the images, and sights, smells and sounds of the day replays in his mind. This day has become a turning point in his life. This day someone close to him has died in his arms, and the strange phenomenon with the hooded assassins' carcasses materializing into venomous snakes shall lingered in his mind.

One of Afeworq's little sisters, nine-year-old Meron, came near Mekonnen rubbing her right eye, crying. She dragged her feet lightly towards him as he opened his arms to her for a consoling embrace. At his gesture, she quickened her pace and fell into Mekonnen's arms sobbing more audibly.

"I am sorry, Meron." Mekonnen apologized softly with tears beginning to stream down his face as she remained weeping on his neck for a while.

But that song by Diaqon Yared stuck in his head though. Then other events of the day flashed through his mind: Afeworq's smile, priestly processions carrying the *tabots*, colorful garments, hymns in the air, the smell of incense and perfumes. Mysterious hooded strangers. Flying arrows. slithering snakes. Afeworq's blood. Rainfall. Negus' hands. Yared's song. Abuna's brown eyes. Afeworq's casket.

Mekonnen's final thought was, "Tomorrow is another day to execute justice." and he drifted off to sleep with Meron in his arms and the sound of mournful hymns permeating the cool night air.

About the Oath
In the royal chambers of His and Her Imperial Majesty, Gabra Masqal and Nigist Semret and accompanied by servants as they retired into their royal sleeping quarters.

"Your Majesty, Hade Gabra Masqal." Nigist Semret began to address her husband as one of her maid servants removed her crown while others removed her fine robes, and bejeweled sandals as she sat upon a cushioned

stood.

"My Lord, what do you suppose is happening to our kingdom? Who would want to kill us? This uprising today, with all the chaos in the streets and spears flying at us. Are we losing the love and loyalty of our subjects?"

Negus Gabra Masqal, sat on a stood across the large room as two men, and one boy servant removed his scepter from his hand and robes from his shoulders replied,

"Well, I will hardly call it an '*uprising*' my Nigist. It was just a few *Qataliyan* with spears and arrows. They may not even be citizens of the empire."

"But how do you know?" The Queen pressed.

"Well, they may not even be of mankind first and foremost." The Negus replied, as one of his men servants removed his glorious crown, to reveal white linen clothe neatly covering his head. Then another servant carefully removed the head clothe to reveal rows of meticulously braided hair, tightly secured to his light brown scalp. The black rows look like and twenty lines drawn from the top of his forehead to the back of his head, ending where it meets the neck, only to continue as twenty loose locks of hairs, extending down to the middle of his back. It is customary for the Negus of Aksum to grow long hair and have it braided in this fashion. Some adhered to this custom more or less than others.

The Negus continued, "Didn't you hear? The attacker's carcasses transformed into a pile of snakes when they fell. Even when they were alive wreaking havoc in the streets, witnesses say they didn't even have faces."

"I have heard, Your Majesty. But they may be sorcerers of the Black Arts.

Sorcerers have been known to transform into creatures, you know!" The Nigist added.

"Yes, I know that, but I am not an expert in those things, and neither are you. All we can do is make assumptions..."

The Nigist interrupted, "I am just laying out the possibilities, My Lord! Something has to be done! What will you do?! Are you not the *Niguse Negest, Seyoume Egziabeher*, 'The Kings of Kings, The Elect of God'? Will you not take charge of this burden?"

"Of course, I will take charge, My Lady! I am fully aware of my title and authority and need not be reminded! I have already given the order to dispatch regents early in the morning to sift the creatures out of the wilderness! Even the young warrior who saved my life volunteered to go..."

"The wilderness?!" The Nigist interrupted, "How about amongst our own people, within the city. They may still be among us!" The Nigist states with a worried tone in her voice.

"Sure that is possible, but my warriors and guards saw them running towards the Samen Mountains. If some are still within the city parameters, well, there are more than enough warriors among us! They are all over the city. In every palace, chapel, and alleyway."

The Nigist sighed then continued, "Sigh, I know *Egzi*, I am very worried and concerned about what happened today. I am concerned for the Empire, and our children. I just want our children to be safe and inherit a peaceful kingdom."

"I want the same for our children as well. You know this! I too I'm concerned and still shaken by what happened today. In this time of peace, I never expect to be hiding and taking cover from arrows and lances! Now everything is under control, my Nigist." The Negus attempted to ease the queen's tensions.

The Nigist, still concerned and uneasy, wanted to address another issue, so she subtly motioned with her right hand for her servants to leave the room. The Negus braced himself for whatever topic was coming his way.

The Nigist arose from her stool and took about five steps forward, slowly towards the Negus then stopped and began,

"Your Majesty, another possibility to consider. What about our relatives? What about the hundreds of *Masefint*, the Princes, locked away at Debre Damo? Could they have escaped and formed an alliance to overthrow us?"

"Hawey, if there was an escape I would have heard of it by now! I think not, Your Highness!"

"Oh, but what I'm really trying to bring up, is the Sacred Oath, in the Holy City of... Eyerusalem. Between you, your father Negus Kaleb and..." The Nigist pauses, but Gabra Masqal knows what and who she is going to mention next.

"... and your brother, Negus Esrael. Could he be responsible for this attack?"

The Negus arose from his stool and brushed off his attendants and motioned with his hands for them to leave the room, so His and Her Majesties to be in their chambers alone to discuss this private and extremely sacred matter. He seemed angry that the Queen would bring up the topic of his estranged brother. Disappointed she would accuse Negus Esrael of such a scandal, yet angry that what the Nigist just said, may be true and a justified notion to consider. Could his brother betray the Sacred Oath?

"Iyyaseh! – No! I do not believe my brother would betray the Oath. It was consecrated and binding!"

"How do you know? Mankind have been known to break covenants and sacred oaths through the ages." The Nigist was a pessimist, but her statement is correct.

"Not *this* Oath!" The Negus asserted sharply, leaned forward slightly with his right index finger pointing upwards. "This Oath was different."

"And what was the 'Oath'? You never told me explicitly what really happened in Eyerusalem! It was so vague and pedestrian."

"What more can I tell you? The Oath stipulated that my brother and I choose either Tsion, which is the Ark of the Covenant, for Aksum, or the Chariot for Nagran. And there is to be peace between the two Kingdoms and the two Neguset. I, Gabra Masqal, chose Tsion and shall rule in the open, for all to see. Negus Esrael chose the Chariot, therefore he shall rule in secret. *That* was the Oath." The Negus stated firmly.

"But, secretly where? Where is he? And what is this 'Chariot'? I just don't understand Amida!" The Nigist fretted, referring to the Emperor by his birth name.

"Some things are difficult to explain My Lady. Like I explained to you before: Emperor Justinian of Rome and the Abuna of Alexandria as witnesses. I chose Tsion for Aksum; my brother chose the Chariot for Nagran across the Erythrean Sea in Sabaea. Our father Negus Kaleb abdicate the throne for a monastic life in gesture for peace between Aksum and Beta Israel. It was a supernatural ceremony. Certain details cannot be explained or even remembered."

"But what if your brother went to the darker side of the supernatural and got involved with those savage creatures that attacked us?"

"Because he couldn't have with the Lord Iyesus Kristos as our witness!"

"And what is this Chariot? We have not seen this Chariot."

"Well, the same way you have not seen Tsion, the Ark of the Covenant and the true Tabots, but you believe they are real, and you believe where we are told they are located! Have you ever seen the True Tabots, Your Majesty? *Iyyaseh!* No! Only a chosen few have seen it. But you believe they are here with us in the Mariam Tsion Magdas!"

"Okay, My Hade Gabra Masqal. I understand your point. What you say is true. But have you seen this Chariot?"

The Negus paused and replied, "Yes! I have seen the Chariot of Nagran. Just as I have seen the true Tsion..."

Then he stopped and seemed to drift into deep thought or a mild trance-like state. The Nigist calls out, "Gabra Masqal? Ella Amida? Are you... Okay...?"

The Emperor Gabra Masqal did not respond for a little more than a minute. He just stood there, staring as if he saw right through the Nigist as if she was transparent glass. The Nigist became concerned, scared even, her heart pounded a little harder and faster each second the Negus did not respond.

"Amida! Amida!" The Nigist called out. No response.

What was he seeing? He was having a flashback, as if he was back in Eyerusalem on the very day. With his father, his brother, the Abuna and the Negus Justinian. There was much incense in the air and chanting and singing. They all fasted and had not eaten in several days. Was it five days, or seven days they fasted? Was it fourteen days? The Negus could not remember at that point. But he remembered something else. A bright light from the sky, and a streak of gold in the shape of... What was the shape and form of it? The Negus could not remember. Like a vivid dream that seemed so real as you experienced it while asleep, but when you awoke, you can barely remember the details of the dream. Yet you know you had the dream, you know it happened, but you could not describe it. Such is the matter of the Sacred Oath concerning the Ark and the Chariot. It happened, but he could not remember everything that happened. And no one spoke about it in the open and even rarely is it spoken of in secret. Just vague imagery and a few vivid scenes here and there. Seen darkly through a glass.

Suddenly he seemed to snap out of his deep trance and responded. "In the morning I shall go to my father to discuss what he thinks about this."

"You are going to Negus Kaleb at Abba Pantelowon's monastery?"

"Yes, I shall go to him in the morning. I will also send Commander Alazar and Commander Mulualem to Dabra Damo to find out of any of the Masefint escaped or anything that might be unusual to raise suspicion of a conspiracy."

The Negus walked out the room into the corridors and inquired for Commander Alazar to come to him.

"Commander Alazar! Prepare your troops in the morning to go to Dabra Damo. I want you to find out if all the Masefint are accounted for. And if anything else is stirring up there that we should know about.

"*U-wa, Girmawi*. Yes, Your Majesty." Alazar replied.

"Tomorrow I shall visit my father."

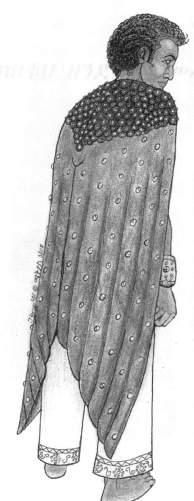

A mysterious young man.
Jerome Matiyas © 2008

Aksumite coins with engravings of Negus Kaleb.
His reign was from about 514 to 543 A.D.
Artwork by Jerome Matiyas © 2017

Mekonnen bows before Emperor Gabra Masqal.
Artwork by Jerome Matiyas © 2018

Emperor Gabra Masqal with scepter among his lions.
Artwork by Jerome Matiyas © 2018

CHAPTER 4
THE VALLEY OF DECISION

Chapter 4

Chapter 4

Valley of Decision

ATER that evening, Mekonnen spent time with his relatives and close friends as they mourned the passing of Afeworq. As he perched quietly on the floor in a corner among his sorrowful relatives in the house of Afeworq's parents and siblings, the images and sights, aromas and sounds of the day replays in his mind. This day has become a turning point in his life. This day someone close to him has died in his arms, and the horrid sight of seeing the carcasses of the hooded assassins turning into slithering, venomous snakes.

One of Afeworq's little sisters, nine-year-old Meron, came near Mekonnen, rubbing her right eye, crying. She drags her feet lightly towards him as he opens his arms to her for a consoling embrace. At his gesture, she quickens her pace and falls in him Mekonnen's arms sobbing more audibly.

"I am sorry, Meron," Mekonnen whispers in her ear with tears beginning to stream down his face as she remains weeping on his neck for a long while.

But that hymn sung by Diyaqon Yared lingers in his head, and he recalls the words and the melody. Then other events of the day flashed through his mind: Afeworq's smile, priestly processions carrying the *tabots*, colorful garments, hymns in the air, the fragrance of incense and perfumes. Mysterious hooded strangers. Flying arrows. slithering snakes. Afeworq's blood. Rainfall. Negus' hands. Yared's song. Abuna's brown eyes. Afeworq's casket.

Mekonnen's final thought was,

"Tomorrow is another day to execute justice." and he drifted off to sleep with Meron in his arms and the sound of mournful hymns permeating the cool night air.

The next day Mekonnen and his family and royal pallbearers prepared

Afeworq's body for his casket and burial. There was crying, loud wailing and beating of the chest from many of the women in his family, young and elderly, with some men. Family, friends, and strangers came by for the funeral, including his close friends Gedi, Endal, Kebi, Sammy, Bini, Moti, and Endi were there to support.

"We'll be here for you Mo'kay. Anytime, my friend. Just let us know if you need us." Said Gedi, in proxy for the other boys, rubbing Mekonnen's shoulder as he expressed his sympathies to him.

Mekonnen is sad and somber but did his best not to show emotion in public, as a warrior of the court is supposed to keep his composure as much as possible. Although he was exempted from being in uniform today, he wore it anyway, as a last homage to his fallen kinsman and fellow warrior Afeworq, son of Kidan.

Mekonnen's Family

Mekonnen, being the seventh and last born of his parents, saw most of his siblings around. Some of his siblings who were closer to him in order of birth approached him first to mourn. But his expression was stoic and almost like one who was in shock. He did not want to say anything much to anyone, but Afeworq's little sister Meron he did not push away or ignore.

Mekonnen's oldest brother Medhane was the most stoic of them all, performing his duties as a *diyaqon* in the royal house of worship. Repeating prayers and spreading incense religiously for more than 20 years. Probably before Mekonnen was even born. Medhane and Mekonnen had never been close, mainly because of the difference in age and personality, Mekonnen being more expressive, adventurous and mischievous in his youth, Medhane being more serious, studious and academic in his walk and pursuits in life. Medhane is married to Bethlehem from the Adwa region a few miles east of Aksum city. They have 5 children, all of whom Mekonnen know from family gatherings and got along with on a formal level. The oldest one's name is Atbreha and was just 2 years older than Mekonnen, but they never really become close because of different interests in life, and Mekonnen thought Atbreha was too proud and aristocratic for his own taste.

Then there is the second born, his brother Bereket, a builder and architect, married to a crafts woman from Tigre in the north-east. They have 4 children with one more on the way. The third is his oldest sister Senait, married to a peasant farmer from Mekele with 6 children. Forth is sister Hanna who is married to a merchant craftsman from Sabaea (Sheba) which is across the Reed Sea in South Arabia. Fifth is another older brother Temesgen who is engaged to a young lady from Hararege in the south-east. And the sixth, 5 years older than Mekonnen, is his sister Meseret, recently married to a musician from Gondar to the south-west.

Then there is Mekonnen, whom few took very seriously because he was the youngest in the family and was thought to be only up to mischief and play time in his youth while the rest of the siblings were growing up and moving on with their lives. Yet Mekonnen was so named because he was born at a prosperous time when his late father Sofaniyas GabraTsion, a warrior in the Aksumite Royal Army, was promoted to *Mekwannen*, a high-ranking officer for the Negus, just before Mekonnen was born. So, Abba Sofaniyas had positive hopes and aspirations for his youngest son whom he was fund of before he passed away from battle wounds when Mekonnen was just 12 years old.

But it was Afeworq who Mekonnen grew close to since they were babies, born the same year but about 3 to 4 months apart. They seemed to do everything together so much that people thought they were brothers because they resembled each other in physical appearance. Well, since their fathers were brothers, they might as well be brothers. As boys, they played games together, learned the *Mashaf Qeddus*, and the *Mezmur Dawit* together-which are the Holy Bible and Psalms of David respectively. They learned mathematics together. Slept together in the same beds and even took baths together. They even fell in love with girls in their teenage years but tried not to pursue the same girl at the same time so as not to offend each other. But now Afeworq was gone, and Mekonnen has conflicting emotions about this tragic fact. He grappled with feelings of disbelief, guilt, resentment, sadness, and anger.

"If only I were there to save Afeworq. I should have been there for him. It was all my fault!" Mekonnen thought to himself. Then he thought,

"When this funeral is done, I can't wait to get back on duty to track down those men… creatures… or whatever they are and *kill* them. I'll take a sword and a spear and skewer all of them. No mercy. Just kill them all!"

These dark thoughts of vengeance well up inside of Mekonnen's soul, and began to show outwardly as his teeth clenched, lips and cheeks tightened, and eyebrows crinkled. In the back of his mind he remembered the verse *"vengeance is mine, says the Lord…"* from reading it at some lessons of the sacred oracles, and at this time he wished to push it out of his mind and chooses to remember, *"An eye for and eye, a tooth for a tooth… and a life for a life…"* instead.

Just then he felt a soft hand inside of his, and it comforted him even just a bit. He looked down and saw Meron's smooth little face looking up at his. She was holding his hand. He had almost forgotten she was standing next to him all this time. He reached down and picks her up, and she rested her head on his right shoulder.

Moments later Medhane and his wife Bethlehem – whom they called Betty – approached Mekonnen and Meron from the crowd. Betty out-stretched her hands towards them and gave Mekonnen a hug and kiss on the right cheek and quietly said a few consoling words, "Selam, Mekonnen. I am sorry. So sorry."

Then she kisses Meron and gently took her away from Mekonnen, knowing that her husband Medhane wanted to speak to his brother Mekonnen alone. Medhane, despite being stoic most of the time, showed some compassion and hugged Mekonnen and kissed him alternately on each cheek four times, right, left, right, left. Mekonnen was still and gave little response, but his face revealed the sadness. Medhane had not spoken to his little brother Mekonnen since Afeworq's death, so he had a lot of unanswered questions on his mind so he asked:

"I am sorry, brother. This is such a sad time for all of us. We are all in mourning, but, ...What really happened out there, Mo'kay?"

Mekonnen: "We... went after the assassins. We got most of them, but some got away. Some were killed, but others were skilled with bows and arrows, spears and swords. Afeworq fought bravely and took down a few on his own, but he was pierced through with arrows, brother. That is what happened. It was all my fault. I should have been there to save him."

Medhane: "No, don't say that, Mo'kay. You were all doing your duties as good warriors and guards. This is so unfortunate, but it was probably Egzio's will. Egzio still be praised. "He giveth and He taketh away" as the *Mashaf Qeddus* says."

Mekonnen: "I know what the *Mashaf Qeddus* says, Medhane, but Afie was not supposed to die now. He was too young and too much of a good person. That is not fair, Egzio should not have taken him away from us."

Medhane: "Well we cannot blame Egzio for killing Afeworq. It is because of the world we live in Mo'kay. There is also evil in the world. The evil that kills and steals away what is good. Remember that Mekonnen."

Mekonnen: "Yeah, well I will see to it that all those evil people are dead! I will have revenge for Afeworq and all the other warriors who fell." The volume of Mekonnen's voice increased and tears began to flow from his eyes for the emotions of grief and rage that boiled up inside him.

Medhane: "Listen. You did your best, Mo'kay. It is not your fault, okay? Be not overly bitter. You and your troops can find the Qataliyan but remember *Egziabeher* says *'Vengeance is mine.'* Hrai? Please get some rest tonight." Medhane then puts his hand on Mekonnen's shoulder and guides him to the rest of the extended family who was gathered around Afeworq's body which was now in a warrior's casket. Mekonnen felt comforted to see his fellow *Sarawit* warriors – Gedi, Endalk, Kebi, Moti, Bini, Sami, and a few others – all there to be with him and see Afeworq one last time. Mekonnen walked over to Afeworq's casket to see him one last time and say a few words. Some family members and others were near the caskets crying and wailing, but Mekonnen ignored and walked pass them. He looked down at Afeworq in the casket, who looked like he was sleeping peacefully, and said,

"Rest in peace, my brother. Feel no more pain and sorrows of this world. I will find your killers, whoever they are. I owe it to you and your sister Meron. Even if it means hunting them down to the ends of the Earth."

He touched Afeworq's hands that are crosses over his chest, kissed his forehead, and walked away into a wooded area nearby. Later Afeworq's casket was closed and taken to the cemetery by royal guards. The casket was neatly draped with colorfully woven clothe and carried off in usual Abyssinian ceremonial fashion.

Afeworq's Star.

That night after Afeworq's funeral, where he was buried in an honorable grave for warriors who served the kingdom valiantly, Mekonnen went away to be alone. He found a spot in the cleft of a rock away from his relatives and friends but still within earshot where he was able to see them, but they could not see him. He strolled around, The full moon was out and bright, illuminated the paths to the forests, and the rugged Samen Mountaintops in the distance to the south. Mekonnen scanned the dark, moonlit horizons as if to search for the hooded Qataliyan moving out there. He naturally began scouting the land and thought seriously about where they would be right at this moment.

"Where would they be hiding and what would be their ultimate plan?" Mekonnen thought to himself. "Would they even try to attack us at night, out here in the towns, away from the Aksum city limits, and the royal palaces?"

These were questions Mekonnen did not have definite answers to but were valid ones to consider. He even looked up at the peeking moon and the glittering stars in the dark sky as if to find signs that may guide him. Or maybe to see Afeworq up there in *Samayat-* in the Heavens- looking down at him. He began to imagine that one of those glittering starts was actually Afeworq's soul in a new glorified state in his new home among the *Qeddusan* and *Mal'ekt* – The Saints and Angels.

He even decided which particular star was Afeworq's for sure, a single *kokab* not too far from the three stars in constellation of Orion's belt. Mekonnen laid down on the hard rock and stared at *Afeworq kokab* and reminisced about the good old days with his cousin who was more like a brother to him. Just then, as the proximity to Orion's belt came to mind, he remembered the golden belt that he received from the strange young fellow in the Negus's throne room. He touched it and decided that he must remember to hide the shining golden belt so not to attract attention, or even worst, cause it to be stolen.

Back at the house where his family and friends were gathered, it's about 2 hours since the sun set, and they realized Mekonnen was missing from among them and begin looking around the house and calling out to him. "Mekonnen! Mekonnen! Mekonnen are you with us?! Where are you?!"

Shouted his oldest sister Senait.

Mekonnen was a bit too far to hear his sister's calls, and even if he did hear her, he probably would not have responded anyway, since he really felt like being alone that moment.

As time went by and Mekonnen looks up, stared at Afeworq's star and the pleasant memories intermingled with recent tragedies he fell asleep and dreamed.

An hour, after falling into deep sleep under the moon and blanket of a starry night sky in the brisk mountain air, Mekonnen heard someone calling out to him,

"Mekonnen! Mekonnen! Mekonnen!"

It was a man's voice that sounded familiar, but he could not put a name to it. His eyes still closed and felt like he was halfway between awake and asleep, he heard the voice again, "Mekonnen! Mekonnen Hawey!" then three knocks like the knocking on the wooden door. This time he thought he recognizes the voice and he was sure it sounded like his father's, who has been dead for many years. Mekonnen tossed and turned his head, then he heard the knocking again, "Bunk! Bunk! Bunkk!"

"Mo'kay! Mekonnen get up boy ! MEKONNEN!!"

Awaken in a Valley.

At the sound of the very last loud shout, Mekonnen was startled and jumped up wide awake. Or so he thought because now he did not recognize his surroundings. He was still sitting on a hard rock ground by a mountain. He looked around quickly and saw he was between two high mountains in a deep dark valley. Had it not been for the light in the distance he would not have been able to see anything at all.

He stood to his feet quickly and said, "My goodness. Egzi Hawey! Where am I?! Am I dreaming or awake? I cannot tell."

He spun around and saw forest trees at the foot of the tall, steep mountains at his left and right. But ahead and behind him was a rocky pathway. Way ahead of him at the end of the pathway that seemed to go on forever he saw a very high mountain with a very bright light at the very top. The light engulfs half the mountain and radiated rays in concentric circles towards him. It illumined the path enough for him to see ahead but behind him, the path is dark and cold, even the sky is black, with not even a star to be seen. Just a thick black veil.

Those for, Those against.

Then he looked up at the mountain to his right, and it now looked like transparent glass, so he saw through and inside of it. To his surprise, inside the mountain, he saw people and figures of animals and other creatures, like large people dwelling inside a giant glass vase. The first person he recognized was his father, his Abba, Sofaniyas, calling out to him and pointing eagerly towards the brightly lit mountain,

"Mekonnen my boy! You're going to be alright. Just run towards that mountain over there. Come on, run. Just run!" Then next to his Abba he recognized Afeworq himself looked very much alive, also pointed towards the mountain that looked like a lighthouse on the shore of a dark ocean,

"Oh Mekonnen, my brother, I'm doing fine here. Run to the mountain, Mekonnen…" While Afeworq was spoke, another person encouraged Mekonnen to do the same thing. This time it looked like the young man who gave him the belt in the Negus' palace the other day. He beckons, "Come on Mekonnen; you can do it. You can make it to the mountain; you have a higher calling. So, go up higher!"

Mekonnen did not quite understand that last comment from the young man, but he started jogging along the path in the dark valley towards the bright mountain. Since he was being encouraged by such a recognizable and beloved crowd, he thought he should comply and wait no longer.

As he began running to his glowing target, the mountain on the left began to move, with a loud rumble and cracking of rocks like an earthquake. He looked up and saw a dark figure, only made out its silhouette, red glowing eyes and red teeth as the gigantic creature opened its mouth and said,

"Where do you think you're going? You will never make it up there. It's too far!!

The creature caused Mekonnen to be afraid, but he kept on running.

Another on the left appeared next to the first grim, dark creature, this one looked like a bearded old man with a neatly embroidered robe like that of a king, a priest, or nobleman, but Mekonnen could not tell for sure who it was that added,

"You are weak! Who do you think you are?! Just a little GNAT!! You are nothing boy! NOTHING!!"

Then another vile creature appeared next to the second, this one looked like a serpent or crocodile, or somewhat reptilian in nature with a man's body and a hand pointing accusingly at him and snarls with huge mouth and big teeth,

"SSSkkkk! You will never make it YOU SCUMM!! We will catch you and destroy you…!"

"No, Mekonnen!", shouted a pleasant voice from the right. "Don't listen to those evil, negative forces. You CAN make it! We believe in you! Egziabeher believes in you and will give you strength!"

He looked up and saw the pleasant voice was coming from a beautiful young maiden he did not recognize, but she has beautiful long Habeshinian curls, a golden jewelry shining on the her forehead and a crown that framed her pretty face. Then another person joined her who looked like a *Mal'ak* from *Samayat*, with magnificent armor and head gear like a crown, with large wings on his back and he declared,

"That is right, Mekonnen, you are going the right way if you keep on running up to that mountain, you Valiant Son of Man. You are a brave warrior. Therefore you *can* go to the *Kebur Dabr Egziabeher Amlak! - The Glorious Mountain of the Almighty Lord of All!*"

And with those last two uplifting encouragements, Mekonnen became energized and put a spring in his step, picked up the pace and ran faster to the lighted Glorious Mountain as the *Mal'ak* described it.

Mekonnen ran faster and harder along the rough stony path, in this unusual dream, wearing traditional white Aksumite linen clothing with decorations on the collar and sleeves and regular sandals. Not the same clothes he wore when he fell asleep but quite plain. The good and bad continued appearing on the right and left mountains as he ran, but he kept going. Until a landslide with rocks and stones began coming down from the vile accusers on the left, which caused Mekennen to slip and slide and fall on his back. Yet he sprang up and continued running as fast as he can, as his encouragers on the right cheered him on.

"Yeah, that's it Mekonnen warrior! You can do it! You can do it!"

The forces on the right began to help Mekonnen by revealing a great waterfall before him and sending the waters crashing down to wash away the rocks and stones from the pathway and shook the earth to open up a huge crevice on the left and washed away the debris which made the way clear for Mekonnen to run again.

The adversaries became angry and decide to put more obstacles in his way. This time in the pathway before Mekonnen appeared three of the creatures that resembled the cloaked Qataliyan who attacked the city and killed Afeworq and others a few days ago. They just materialized in the pathway in front of Mekonnen.

The Sword in the Altar.

As imposing and menacing as before with their white hooded robes, red eyes and dark bodily forms that now glitter as if they were cut out from the starry night sky, they hissed and approached Mekonnen in awkward pouncing, movements, like predatory animals in the jungle. They reminded Mekonnen of a hybrid between a hunting lion in the savannahs and a slithering snake in the grass, but viler and more threatening. They were taller than Mekonnen, about 8 to 10 feet tall, and though the warrior was frightened he was ready to take them on, one by one.

"Dream or no dream, you vile Qataliyan are not going to stop me from going to that mountain." Declared Mekonnen bravely with a lion's heart. He reached over to his left hip to grab his sword, but to his dismay there was none. He had no weapons what so ever. Still, he crouched like a cat ready to pounce and stretched his arms out ready to wrestle the dark beings, just then someone from the right Mountain with the appearance of an old monk with long white beard, very long locks of hair like ropes and brightly colored orange and yellow robes and head wrap, emerged behind the Qataliyan and signals to Mekonnen,

"Psst!" and pointed downward. And there behind the cloaked Qataliyan, just a few paces ahead in the middle of the pathway was a glowing sword. The handle and hilt stood upward resembling a letter "✝" with about a quarter of the blade stuck downward into an altar. That's exactly the weapon Mekonnen needed, but first, he had to figure out how to get past the three hooded opponents.

In a deep, raspy voice the Qataliyan in the middle and closest to Mekonnen declared, "You have come to the end of this race! You are no match for us, *Ish*! You have no weapons and no armor! And we have swords, power, and stealth!"

Mekonnen replied, "You are wrong, vile creature! I have confidence and determination. And I have courage and friends who will back me up. But most of all, I have Faith and Hope!!"

Just then the golden belt around Mekonnen's waist that was given to him in the King's palace began to glow with a bright white and golden-yellow light, blinding the creatures for a moment, causing them to groan and block their eyes.

Mekonnen saw this as his opportunity to make the first move and darted forward towards the first creature and punched him in the jaw with an uppercut. Then with a knee to the stomach, causing it the real in pain. The creature tried to grab Mekonnen, but he managed to slip away and continued stumbling towards the Sword in the altar made of white stone with fours horns at the corners.

"Almost there!" Mekonnen declared to himself. "Must… Get…the Sword!"

Somehow, he could not seem to get to it fast enough, though he scrambled and darted for it like a cheetah. A second hooded Qatali came at Mekonnen with sword drawn, swung it with aim to his head to lop it off, but Mekonnen moved with agility in his dream just as he did in the real world. He ducked and maneuvered with a flip and kicks the creature in the face with both feet, a move he learned in warrior training years ago, plus the backflips he and Afeworq already learned as young boys. In mid flip, he grabbed the sword out of the hooded one's hand, and as he came back to land on his feet again, he swiped at its left knee to chop off its leg and then stabbed the third hooded one at the end of the same move. With a sword buried deep into one creature's belly and the other one's leg cut off, they did not seem to be affected or in pain.

"It seems they cannot be hurt with their own swords." Mekonnen thought

Mekonnen uses a special Sword to battles with Qataliyan.
Jerome Matiyas © 2021

in that instant, as he ran and leapt upon the altar, grabbed the golden, ornate hilt of the Sword and yanked the metallic blade out of it. The Sword felt natural in his hand, just the right weight and balance for wielding, as it shined and flashes like newly burnished gold and steel.

A second later as Mekonnen looked back he saw not just the three Qataliyan charging at him but a whole horde of cloaked Qataliyan and other ravenous creatures—wolf-like beasts with snarling teeth and red eyes, minotaur-like beasts with huge axes and clubs; giants 20 cubits tall with horns on their heads; crocodiles, scorpions, and huge, demonic locust-like beings and other unrecognizable creatures — running and flying at full speed from a distance and rapidly got closer. And in the midst of all the hordes was a huge, most terrifying looking red dragon-like creature ever seen.

The sight almost took Mekonnen's breathe away; his quick thinking made him tackle the three Qataliyan that were just inches from him now.

One cloaked Qatali came down with a long-curved sword at Mekonnen, but the warrior held up his new Sword to brace the blow, just as quickly he swirled his arm in a circular motion and broke his first opponent's sword, shattering it into three pieces. The Sword in Mekonnen's hand was much more powerful than he thought, but he was not complaining about this fact at all. Another swift move with a spin and Mekonnen lopped off the first opponents head, both it and the body dropping to the rocky ground and decomposed into a pile of black mass like burning coal. The other two Qataliyan came at him fast. Mekonnen back flips off the altar to escape the swipe of a blade and landed onto the shoulder of his opponent and buried his Sword blade into its head, from the top of its skull to under the chin. The head popped and burned like coal and the creature crumbled to the ground.

One more opponent left: Qatali number three. Mekonnen leapt off the second one's shoulder before it fell to the ground and aimed the blade down at the third Qatali. The brightness of the belt and Sword's blade blinded the creature, so he cringed and blocked his eyes. Mekonnen brought his blade down from the creature to the top of the shoulder and sliced him in half, right down the middle. The creature split open and exploded like fiery magma from a volcano. Mekonnen's friends in the mountain on the right cheered and applauded hysterically while urging him onward,

"Yes, Mekonnen! YEEEESSS! Now RUUUUNNNN!! RUUNNNNN!!! The Armies of Darkness are coming! They are COMING! RUUUUUNNNNN!!!!

And off the warrior went, running at full speed as fast as his young legs can go as the evil hordes of darkness approached as the ground rumbled more violently as they get closer. The adversaries in the mountain on the left glowered down in anger and regret at Mekonnen's victory and gradually began to fall into the armies that were chasing after Mekonnen.

In the same way, the benevolent allies on the right slid into the valley to fight off the dark armies as best they can. Then a great battle has grown behind Mekonnen. A battle between Good and Evil. Light and Dark. The noise got loud, and all manner of lights and colors splashed behind him as he ran, and the adversaries continued chasing along the valley. Just then Mekonnen remembered a verse from the *Dawit Mezmur* (Psalms of David) about being in a dark valley of the shadow of death. This current situation was definitely the right time for the verse to return to his memory,

"*...Though I walk,–* or in this case, *run – through the valley of the shadow of death, I shall fear no evil, for You Lord, are with me. Your rod of protection and your staff of guidance, they comfort me.*" Psalm 23:4

So with that verse and a few others in his head, Mekonnen ran and ran and kept on running some more. For how long? He did not know.

The Glorious Mountain.

Ahead, Mekonnen saw the *Kebur Dabr* – The Glorious Mountain – rising up as he got closer, until he could see there are six smaller mountains at the foot of the largest one in the middle. They were all glowing each with a different color like seven various types of precious gemstones. And he saw the stream of fire flowing from the top of the mountain – where there was the likeness of a great throne with someone sitting on it – to among the ones below. He saw trees around the middle of the largest mountain and he smelled the fruits and incense and other aromas emanated from the Mountain. Then he heard a voice from the mountain in the bright light at the top in a loud voice saying,

"Come up here, my son. I have called you to a Higher Caller. A special mission I give to you."

While the voice spoke, Mekonnen felt himself lifted off the ground as he flew effortlessly, his legs moved as if he was running in midair, as if on transparent glass. When he glanced back, he still saw and felt the Hordes of Darkness advancing behind him, as close as 20 to 30 cubits away. Even with the immense light in front of them, they pressed forward toward the light that Mekonnen was about to take refuge in.

"I wonder how much closer they can run until they cannot come closer anymore?" he thought to himself.

Soon, the creatures behind him began to burst into flames as they got closer to the burning light and they began to fall back. Yet still that great red flying serpent-dragon, with its skin on fire, continued coming with mouth wide open and breathing out fire towards Mekonnen and the Mountain. This beast must be consumed with hatred to be so persistent against the warrior and the source of pure light.

A Familiar Presence.

Mekonnen kept running on the sea of glass until finally, he was close enough to the see a red carpet and Holy Ones standing on both sides of the pathway. It looked like he was entering the way into a great glorious temple with glittering lights everywhere.

Mekonnen went up twelve steps and approached the throne and saw a figure with open arms engulfed in bright light but he could not see who it is. Yet he sensed love and peace in his presence. A presence that seemed familiar. And safety from the Armies that were after him. Mekonnen knew who it is but could not say it. Mekonnen knew this figure had to be *Haraya Ahandu* – The Elect One of the Ancient of Days. The Son of Man. The Son of God. The Risen and Glorified Iyesus Krestos!

And the figure declared is a resonating tone that sounded like many voices,

"You have a Higher Calling. Abide in me, and I will show you. I will never leave you or forsake you. I will be with you always. Even till the end of this world."

Just then, Mekonnen heard a loud terrible roar behind him and looked back and saw that dragon right up on him, ready to breathe out consuming flames.

Mekonnen ran closer to the throne hoping for safety.

Suddenly, a large, fierce and fiery creature like a lion leapt out of the bright light and right onto Mekonnen with a loud roar and hot breath.

"RROOAARRR!!"

Secrets Under the Moon.

Immediately, Mekonnen was startled awake by the dream that apparently ended more like a nightmare. He could not understand the dream, but he could not forget it. But what puzzled him the most was that just when he thought he was safe at the end, he was confronted by another threat. Or was it really a threat?

He realized he was awake and back on the rock where he fell asleep while looking up at the stars. The moon was in a different position in the sky and much larger than before. In fact, it seemed to Mekonnen to be unusually large like it was magnified almost twenty times more than usual. It illuminated the sky and the earth like an orb-shaped lantern, close enough to throw a stone at. Despite this anomaly, he leapt up to his feet, determined it is late and probably not too safe to be outside near the wilderness, alone and away from civilization.

Mekonnen returned to the house where everyone was now asleep. He slipped inside and found himself a spot on the floor by the entrance. Meron saw when he came in, so she joins him like a cat trying to curl up with its owner. As Mekonnen laid down, he noticed his belt glowed in the dark like it did in his dream, so he attempted to cover it up with a *shemma* to conceal it. Gradually the glow diminished, but the fact it looked like pure gold will draw some unwanted attention. He decided he needed to hide the belt from sight, or someone may even try to steal it or ask him about it. Meron noticed the belt and inquired about it, but Mekonnen told her he got it as a gift and made her promise to keep it a secret.

"Look, you have a shiny belt, Mekonie. Where did you get it from?"

"Oh, I got it as a gift, in Hade Gabra Masqal's palace."

Meron became excited and asked,

In the Negus' palace?! From Negus Gabra Masqal? You got a present from the Negus Gabra Masqal?"

"U-wa, Shhhh! It was from the Negus Gabra Masqal. But don't tell anybody about it, *hrai*. It was a secret gift, so this will be our secret, *hrai*?"

"*Hrai*, Okay, I will not tell... anybody."

"Good girl, now get some sleep, hrai. Mekonie needs to get some sleep too, *hrai*?"

"*Hrai*." Meron whispers and drifted to sleep moments later.

In the morning Mekonnen and Meron awoke and had breakfast with the few family members who decided not to fast. Afterwards, he made a promise to Meron that he will find her brother Afeworq's killers.

Meron warned, "Please be careful, Mekonie. I don't want you to get hurt. Okay?"

He picks her up, kisses her on the cheeks four times and handed her to Liya, her and Afeworq's mother.

"I will be careful, Meron, my baby sister. I promise." He replied, knowing he could not promise between life and death in his line of work, but wanted to give his little cousin some hope.

Mekonnen packed up his belongings and left the village quietly, headed back to Aksum to reconnect with his fellow warriors to scout out the area for the mysterious cloaked Qataliyan.

Magnificent Lion with fiery mane. .
Jerome Matiyas © 2012

A furious red dragon.
Jerome Matiyas © 2011

CHAPTER 5
WILD SIMIEN

CHAPTER 5, WILD SIMIEN
JEROME MATIYAS © 9/2018

Chapter 5

Chapter 5

Wild Simien

(Erwuy Samen)

Day One: From Aksum to Inda Sellassie

The next morning, *Sarawit[1]*, were dispatched according to their regiment names and assigned to search out the region for the Qataliyan and bring them to justice. A *Sarwe* is a regiment, and *Sarawit* is plural, thus more than one *Sarwe*. The Emperor and the Commands in Chief assigned their troops according to their *sarwe* names. There were twelve *Sarawit* in all: *Halen, Hara, Hadefen, Lakenm, Mahaza, Metin, Sabarat, Sabaha, Sera, Damawa, Dakuen,* and *Falha*. Each one numbering from the 100s to 1000s.

Warriors and guards of Halen, Hara, Hadefan, Laken, Mahaza, and Metin, remained within the city of Aksum where most of the palaces and treasuries, churches and castles were located. Sabarat and Sabaha went to the cities and towns on the outskirts of Aksum city proper. Remnants of Sera, Damawa, Dakuen, and Falha were dispatched to further out pass the boundaries, east, west, north and south. Mekonnen is in *Falha* that went south-west to cross the *Tekeze* river into Gondar province on the west side of the great *Samen Adbar* – Simien Mountains. They've gathered enough food and water for about three days, and nights in case the search took longer than expected. The Negus generals supplied troops with equipment for pitching up tents with weapons of warfare included swords, shields and spears, bows, and arrows for combat. Also ropes for climbing mountains and walls, or to bound captives.

Commander Mulualem assigned Mekonnen the duty to be leader of a battalion of about 14 men, including some he consider close friends like Endal, Gedion, Kale'ab, Samuel, Motuma, Biniyam, and Nezana. The other warriors he recognized from around the barracks and royal courtyards but was not well acquainted with them. All brothers in arms, none the less.

Some *Liq Qasisan* (Arch-Priests) were sent to the warrior camps to pray for and bless the warriors before they ventured out into the wilderness, mountains, and villages, charted and uncharted to search out and capture the

---

1 *Sarawit is plural for Sarawe which is a regiment in the Aksumite army. Source: Aksum: Africa Civilization of Late Antiquity by Stuart Munro-Hay, 1991.*

The Simien Mountains, by Jerome Matiyas © 2017

hooded assassins – The *Qataliyan*. The honorable Abuna Ekklesian was also sent to bless and encourage the men and bid them Godspeed. Mekonnen was especially glad and relieved to see the Abuna here in their presence, hoping to receive some sort of extra special blessing and protection from the prayers of such a highly esteemed holy man. Mekonnen, being a newly appointed leader of his small band of Aksumite warriors, was one of the first to greet and approach the Abuna and three other *Qasisan,* namely Abba Iyeshak, Abba Filmon and Abba Ermias, and their *diyaqonat* with bowing and the kissing of hands and *masqal* crosses.

"Egziabeher yemesgan, Abuna Ekklesian. The Lord be with you and bless you greatly. Very honored to have you here with us, Abuna. Please pray for us that we will be protected and strengthen before we embark on our treacherous quest to vanquish the kingdom from evil and lawlessness and bring swift justice to the Qataliyan." Said Mekonnen in his most formal greeting that seemed to flow out of him naturally.

As Mekonnen made salutations to the Abuna, he suddenly became aware of the new belt around his waist that the mysterious young man gave to him in the King's palace. The belt grew a bit heavier, as a warm sensation began radiating from it. Mekonnen didn't understand what was going on with the belt, but it distracted him slightly, and by instinct he reached to clutch it with his right hand, and felt the warmth permeating from it. How strange indeed, but Mekonnen tried to ignore it since he was in the middle of speaking to the Abuna at the very moment. The belt was still concealed under his clothing though since he obviously still didn't want anyone prying about a precious golden belt that was obviously of great value. And that his mates will not hesitate to inquire about, and others may seek to steal it to have as their own, or even sell in the marketplace.

With a glowing smile, the Abuna looks upon Mekonnen as he bowed before him with immediate recognition. He remembered meeting the young warrior in the Negus Gabra Masqal's throne room a few days ago. He also remembered Mekonnen's loss of fellow warrior and kinsman during the attack, but saved the Negusa Negus from an assassin's spear, then received awards and recognition for his valiant acts.

"Oh, how are you, my son? *Egziabeher Yebarakih!* And how are you coping, if you do not mind that I ask?" the Abuna inquired in proper Ge'ez with a slight accent, showing concern as a rather sad expression grew on his face.

Mekonnen replied, "I am doing okay, Abuna. We buried Afeworq, my brother, yesterday. My family is in mourning, but we are coping. *Egziabeher yemesgan*, God be praised."

"All of my condolences are extended graciously from me to your family for your loss," Abuna responded, touching Mekonnen's chin with his right hand in a compassionate way. "Only Egziabeher the Almighty One and the powers that be know why tragedies occur in our lifespan but everything… happens for a reason."

"Yes Abuna, and I also believe that Afeworq is now with the Lord in the Paradise of *Samayat*. He is in a better place now, Egziabeher Yemesgan."

"Yes, Egziabeher be praised. He *is*, definitely in a better place, I am positive he is." The Abuna replied quite matter-of-factly.

One of the *qasisan* came over to the Abuna and Mekonnen while they were conversing and bowed, holding a small bottle in one hand containing a light green liquid. The liquid is called *meron,* which is olive oil that has been prayed on and blessed to become Tselot Meron – "holy oil." With the fingers of his other hand dripping with the same *meron,* the *qasis* touched Mekonnen's forehead to make the sign of the cross. Mekonnen reverently bowed slightly to receive the crux symbol. Another *qasis* or *diyaqon* was with the first *qasis* swinging a lantern of sweet-smelling incense filling the air with fragrant reverence.

Abuna Ekklesian then gestured and motions his arms around, lifted up his voice in exhortation to the crowds,

"Warriors of Aksum! Servants of the great Emperor Gabra Masqal! I pray a special blessing onto to you and all the warriors now. That you will find the lawless ones and justice will be dealt to them swiftly. The Lord's will be done. Go and return safely to your kingdom and to your families."

After this, the Abuna Ekklesian began to say a few words in a different language that Mekonnen could not understand, and he assumed his comrades could not understand it either. Mekonnen figured the Abuna was reciting words of blessing and praise in Coptic Egyptian, considering the Abuna hailed from the church headquarter in the great city of Alexandria, no doubt. Whatever the words were, they were followed by singing and chanting and ringing of *tsinatseil* (sistrums) and *melekets* (trumpets).

This went on for about an hour, but the Negus (Captains) and warriors were thankful because it gave them encouragement and the belief they were receiving supernatural strength and province with energy and insight from *Egziabeher Amlak*, the Almighty God of all gods Himself. Sometime during the blessings and singing the Abuna Ekklesian seemed to have slipped away while the other qasisan and diyaqonat remained until eventually, the regiments moved on towards the south and south-west, where the rugged and dramatic terrain of the Samen Mountain wilderness could be seen for great distances ahead.

Up and down steep mountain slopes, and high, flat and pointed zeniths. The outlines of jagged landscapes like crocodiles' teeth with the smooth, round curves of molds can all be seem together and over laying the foreground and back ground with one panoramic sweep of the eyes from east to west. The highest, greenest and most lush place of the land was the spectacular sculpture that was one of Egziabeher's masterpieces in all creation for sure. Beautiful, splendid and teeming with life. Various clans of people making a decent, simply living at the foot of mountains, in high altitudes and near rivers and lakes. Birds of many different types in trees and crags in steep cliffs. Hyenas hunting in the grasslands by pouncing on their usual prey of kudu deer, antelopes, and wild cattle. Samen wolves with their reddish brown fur pouncing on mole rats and other rodents for food. Geleda baboons who are not very large creatures but will attack to protect their territory. Poisonous and non-poisonous snakes and a much larger *Zendow* which were large serpents with venomous bites and bodies as large tree trunks that could wrap around its prey and crush every bone in a man or cattle's body before swallowing them whole. There were locusts, bees and wasps and other insects that occasionally destroyed crops and sting mankind. And many fabled and real ghosts, phantoms and demons lurking in shadows and dark places, waiting for the right person or animal to haunt or pester.

It could definitely be the wildest, and most dangerous place in the Horn of Africa. As Mekonnen leads his men on foot and horseback down a paved roadway to the town of *Inda Selassie*, he remembered being made to track through mountains and climb the highest point of Mount Samen call *Ras Dejen* (Ras Dashen) as part of his training of initiation into the Army and Royal Guard. Oh yes, he remembered how difficult and rough it was, but the Negus made them do it as the final stages of the training. But he made it, and so did most of his comrades that were with him.

Mekonnen stopped them in their track not long after leaving from the *Abuna* and the *Qassat* and gathers them around to rest. He looked around and saw his fellow warriors that were with him when the Qataliyan attacked Aksum and killed his cousin Aferworq. He walked around and looked into their alert faces. He saw Endal, Gedi, Kebi, Bini, Moti, Sami, Nabu, Desi, Nezan, Mula, Hambo, Emdi, Yazi, Zegi, and Abu. All fine young men in white garments and robes with colorfully decorative fringes that sparkled with gold and pearls in them. All with swords in sheaths at the hip and some with spears and silver shields in hand or on white Arabian horses. All armed with daggers at their hips in sheaths with the distinctive curve at the bottom tucked in and hooked into belts. Half of them wore sandals, half were bare footed. All wore warrior head gear or headbands.

"My Warriors!" Mekonnen exclaimed with pride to see his brothers in arms. "You are the brave, courageous ones of Aksum! *Anabəst!* My Lions!"

Endal cracked a smile with a glint in his eyes. Kebi and Gedi nodded their heads. Embi spat on the grassy ground, Bini took in a deep breathe.

"I'm so pleased to have all of you here with me today. We have experienced terror the past few days, and we are not sure what we are up against. But we will not back down. Some of our comrades have fallen, like my brother Afeworq, and many others were injured. We all witnessed as those evil, hooded things tried to assassinate our Negusa Negast, the King of Kings himself. Yes, there is evil out there, and we must find and destroy all of them before they return to destroy us. They want to destroy our way of living and end the way we live in peace and in harmony! They want to destroy our loved ones, our families, our wives, our children. *Selessie*, Therefore, we must stop them all!"

"*U-wa*! Yes! Yes!" The warriors shouted in agreement.

"We cannot and will not let the Qataliyan escape and get away without justice!"

Ululations began to emanate from the warriors, filling the air with sound and life, alerting the animals nearby to perk up their ears. They mounted upon their horses and rode off more excited and energized than before, feeling a sense of renewed purpose.

Soon they arrived at the town of *Inda Selassie* just half an evening's journey west of the main city metropolis of Aksum. The town was also called the *Shire,* and the inhabitants were inquisitive about the arrival of these royal fighters and guards galloping into their busy village town.

While still on his white and spotted stallion Mekonnen stated to the gatekeepers of *Inda Selassie,*

"Selamta, great people of Inda Selassie! We come in peace in the name of our Emperor Gabra Masqal as we look for men that tried to assassinate the Negusa Negast and caused disorder and confusion in Aksum during the holy festival of Timkat. Have any of you good people of *Inda Selassie*, seen any strange men or suspicious behavior in the last 4 days?"

Just then an elderly woman in front of a rounded brick house bowed and greeted the Aksumites, "Selamata, my Lords! You are all welcome! Please be at home with us." Then she addresses the people of her town is a loud voice."

"Servants of the Negusa Negus have come to our town! Bring water, bring bread, bring hay and grains for their horses! Make them feel welcomed and at home!

Just then groups of townsfolk came out of their houses like busy bees with pots and bowls of water and bread for the warriors. Among them was a young boy in his mid-teens with a basket of bread in his hands, walked up to the warriors bowed his head in respect.

"*Egzi Yeberetet*, the Lord's Blessing be upon you all. You are much welcomed. Please, can you help my wife and me?"

"How can we help you, *Egzi*?" Mekonnen enquired to the man who seemed anxious, as if he had something urgent to tell them."

"Uh, yes, please. Our son, he is missing, and we do not know where he is."

Mekonnen dismounted from his horse and accepted the water and food brought to him and his horse.

"You say your son is missing, but do you think the men we seek may have something to do with his disappearance?"

"Well, we are not sure, *Egzi*, but my wife said our son saw something when they were in Aksum the other day for the Timkat festival."

"Oh really?" Mekonnen inquired.

"Yes, please come and speak to her, Sir. Maybe she can be of help to you to catch them. My name is Zemen by the way." he said as he bowed his head to Mekonnen, stretching out his right hand for a customary handshake while touching his own right elbow with his left hand.

"*Seme Mekonnen* . Pleased to meet you, Zemen."

"Please, come this way to my home." Zemen lead the way, Mekonnen followed as he looked back to his comrades and gestures to them to be on guard until he returned.

"Take me to her then. Gedi, Kebi, Moti and Bini, Please, come with me."

Zemen pointed, "This is my house over here."

As they got closer to the two-story white bricked roundhouse, Mekonnen heard a strange sound coming from inside.

Mekonnen enquired, "I hear a woman crying from inside."

Zemen responded, "Yes, that is my wife, Eyerus. She has been very sad since..." Zemen could not finish his sentence but just kept walking to the entrance of his home where he welcomed the warriors in and introduced them to his young wife Eyerus who was being comforted by an older woman who looked like she could be about 50 years old."

"This is my wife Eyerus and her mother Wayzero Tembem. Eyerus, these are warriors from Aksum. Speak to them, please. Tell them what happened."

"Woyzeret, Selam." Mekonnen greeted the sad maiden. "May I ask what is causing you sadness?

The maiden replied, "My boy Nati. He is missing. *sniffle*. I lost him during the *Timkat* festival when the attacks happened."

"Oh, I am so sorry, but I pray he is safe and is just lost in the streets somewhere and will be found and returned home soon. When was the last time you saw your son? And where did you last see him, may I ask respectfully?"

"I was with my friends on the *Negus Way* near the palace when he came running to me saying he saw a strange man with red eyes. I did not believe him at first, thinking he was playing or making up stories. But in all the confusion, people running in all directions, we got separated. Anyway, I was holding him, then I put him down again, and a large crowd suddenly ran past us trying to get away from the runaway elephants and the rain of arrows coming down. Then I saw him no more. I keep searching and calling but cannot find Nati after two days! Please, I beg you, please find my son! Oh, *Egziabeher Hoy*, have mercy, please find my boy Nati". She begged them and sobbed with tears in her eyes and streaming down her face. Her husband Zemen tried to console his wife by holding her at the shoulders.

Mekonnen felt compassion for the woman's loss and great sadness, but he remains composed. He took note when she said her son told her the man's eyes were glowing red, recollecting the same sinister appearance of the Qataliyan he and the other warriors fought within the city proper.

"You said your son saw 'red eyes', huh, huh? What else did he see?" asked Mekonnen.

"He did not say anything else about them. He was just frightened by him." She replied tearfully.

Gedion interjected, "Well, what about appearance? Did your son, or did you see what they were wearing?

"No, there was so much madness going on. People were running around, and tripping over each other. Horses running loose. When the arrows started flying and striking people down, that's when we took shelter inside. But then, when I looked around to where I put Nati down for a moment, he was gone."

Kebi asked, "What was happening at that moment?"

"A great crowd of people was rushing by to escape the warriors chasing after the ones that tried to kill the *Hade*." She replied.

Moti asked, "I am sorry madam, but how old is your son?"

"He is 5 years old."

"I understand how you must feel. I also have a son who is 5 years old." Moti adds.

Bini asked, "Is there anything else that you can remember that can give us a clue to find your son and the Qataliyan? Or anything else out of the ordinary?"

"I am sorry… I cannot remember… anything else." She replied sobbing.

Mekonnen: "We will try our best to find your son Woyzeret."

Mekonnen responded though he knows he cannot make a definite promise that her son will be returned, but he had to say something reassuring to the poor woman and her husband.

"You are welcome to stay in our town overnight, Lords." Zemen offered to Mekonnen. "Some of you are welcome to stay in my house as well, yes."

"Thank you very much, may Egziabeher bless you for your hospitality." Mekonnen responded and took him up on his offer.

That night the warriors stayed and slept in the Shire of Inda Selassie and got some much-needed rest after a long day riding for hours.

Day Two: From Inda Sellassie to Adi Arkay

The next morning the warriors got up bright and early just after sunrise and accepted the breakfast and bunna served by the townsfolk of Inda Selassie. By the second hour of daylight, Mekonnen and his warriors bid the citizens farewell, and promised to catch the hooded villains who disrupted their lives, and off they rode southwards to cross over the guarded granite-stone bridge that arched over the *Tekeze River* and back onto the roadway to the next major towns of *Adi Arkay* and *Debarq*.

An hour and a half later the warriors finally saw Adi Arkay on the horizon.

As the warriors rode into the town Mekonnen declared the usual salutations:

"Selamta! Citizens of Adi Arkay! We come in peace in the name of our Emperor Gabra Masqal of the Kingdom of Aksum! We seek dangerous, lawless men who attempted to assassinate the Negusa Negast and caused disorder and confuse in the land!

Suddenly a middle-aged man came walking quickly from a roundhouse near the entrance towards the warriors with an irate expression on his face. They can tell he was not pleased to have the horse riders in his town and was about to let them know it.

He stormed out of his two leveled round brick house and began shouting at the warriors.

© Jerome Matiyas

"What good is it to tell you anything?! You Aksumite warriors think you can just storm into any town and village around here, don't you! You all think you own all the land and territories and don't have to abide by anybody's rules!"

Puzzled by such harsh accusations Mekonnen interrupted,

"That is not the case, *Egzi*. We are merely trying to protect this land. We enforce law and order and keep the peace throughout the land."

"*Iyyaseh*! No! You just ride in here with your damn horses to trample our roads and take our food and water like you always do!"

The irate man retorted vehemently, in a way that Mekonnen personally could not understand. He thought perhaps another *Sarawit* rode through here and abused their authority recently, so now the town elder was angry at all officials and anyone that came from Aksum. Or he may just be another Habesha citizen who was against the monarchy in general, one of those people that abhors the whole history and policies of the Aksumite Empire no matter what. He may have his own personal reasons to be disagreeable to them. Yet there was a limit to how much the warriors of the kingdom could allow being disrespected.

Gedion interjected, "Aksum is just doing its duty, *Egzi*, and we are not here to take anything from you or be disrespectful. We are seeking a group of men that attacked the city and the Emperor, and they may have passed through here or be on their way here. They are very dangerous men. Many innocents were also killed."

"I don't care!" screamed the elder, now being unreasonable in his response,

Pointing his index finger at them, he continued,

"You have no right to come here like that! You come, you disrupt our lives, and you make noise! You take our food and ravaged the land..."

Just then in mid-sentence Endal jumped off his horse in a fury, drew his sword as he charged towards the angry one. In less than 2 seconds Endal grabs his robe at the neck with his left hand and presses his sword on the elder's throat with the other to make his point clear,

"You better shut your mouth right now, old man! If you disrespect us one more time, I will cut your loud, ugly head off! *Hrai*!"

"Stand down Endal!" Said Mekonnen, "We will not spill blood of civilians here, no matter how foolish they may be. This fool is not worth it. *Enhid*! Let us go." Then he continued,

"As I said before, we are looking for dangerous murderers on the run. They have not only killed warriors but have murdered innocent civilians as well! With their swords and arrows! Therefore, we will search this town and stay here for a while. *Hrai*?"

"Let's go Endal!" said Kebi,

Endal shoved away the elder violently, causing him to stumble and almost fall over if it was not for a few younger men to catch him and hold him up.

With a scowl on his face, Endal pointed a furious finger at the elder,

"Do not ever disrespect an Aksumite warrior again! You do not know us and what we have experienced. I grew up in a town just like this not far from here, so never assume we are all some outsiders invading your country!"

The elder became quiet now, stood there staring at Endal with a scowl on his face. With all the commotion going on between the elder and the warriors more townsfolk of Adi Arkay, young and old, began to slowly creep out their homes to see what was going on. Endal pointed the blade of his sword to the elder and demands an answer.

"Now, as my scout leader was saying, old man, Speak Up! Have you seen these suspects described and have they been here to your village?"

The elder spoke, "As a matter of fact, Yes! Strange men in white robes did come here and attacked us. They killed some of our men and stole some of our children. At first, we did not know who they were. We assumed they were rogue Aksumite warriors! Aksumites has ravaged our village before you know!"

Mekonnen added, "Egzi, I am sorry and apologize for your unfortunate experience with Aksumites, supposedly. But I assure you, these villains we seek are not Aksumite warriors. Not even rogue ones. In fact, we don't even know where they are from."

Mekonnen paused, thinking of the elder's report that children were also stolen here in Adi Arkay.

"So, you say you were attacked? When did this happen?"

Elder: "A few days ago, after Timkat festival."

Mekonnen: "Did you go to Aksum for Timkat?"

Elder: "No."

Mekonnen: "Why not?"

Elder: "I had other...priorities."

Mekonnen: "Did anyone from this village go up to Aksum at all?"

Elder: "U-wa, Egzi, a few did go up. They returned with stories of the assassination attempt on the Negus, and all that."

Mekonnen: "Who are they that went up to Aksum?"

Elder motioned with his hand: "Some of them in the crowds behind you."

Mekonnen turned his horse around to face the crowd. Ten people stepped forward, indicating they went to Aksum in the past few days.

Two young ladies indicated their child was either missing or kidnapped from the town when the hooded assassins attacked the village recently.

Gedion drew closer to Mekonnen and said, "We have the information we need, but we probably shouldn't stay here. Let's ride on to the next village.

Maybe we can catch up with the Qataliyan on route."

"I agree," Mekonnen replied.

"Thank you for your information, but we will be going now. We will return your children if they are found. Egziabeher yemesgan."

The warriors rode off, leaving Adi Arkay behind.

"Come on brothers! Since we are not welcomed here, lets us ride on to the next town before it gets dark!" Mekonnen commanded and off they rode in haste, as their horses kicked up dust and gravel in the trail.

The rest of Day Two: Adi Arkay to Debarq and environs

Towards the town of Debarq, they questioned the townsfolk in which they reported confrontations with the strange men in unusual cloaks and robes with their faces shrouded in darkness. And the stories of missing children were similar: They were in Aksum for the Timkat festival and when the chaos broke out the parents could not find their child. It seemed in each town only one or two or three children were reported missing, but also a young maiden not even seventeen years old would also be missing among them. At closer examination, the boys that were missing where the firstborn sons of their families. It was a consistent pattern, but Mekonnen and the other warriors could not decipher why this was the case. They camped out in Debarq until the next day.

Day Three: From Debarq on route to Gondar province into the wilderness

As warriors continued scouting from town to town and village to village into the Gondar province, in the horizon they can see the massive Samen Mountain range and the two highest summits, *Ras Dejen (Ras Dashen)*, the highest peak in all the land of Aksum and Habeshat and *Mount Bwahit*. Indeed, it has been determined *Ras Dejen* was the highest peak for thousands upon thousands of miles. Some suspect it may be one of the highest peaks in this side of Africa, except for Mount Kilimanjaro in the land of Tanzania very far to the south which is actually the highest mountain in the whole continent.

How beautiful and enormous indeed the presence of the Samen wilderness and *Mount Dejen*, homes of many animals like the gelada baboons, hyenas, Samen wolves, walia ibexes and innumerable birds. Even rodents like larger mole rats that live in holes in the ground, they peeked out with curiosity as the warriors passed by. And tribes of people thriving in pastoral and farming livelihoods, including the *Agaw* and *Beta Israel*, among the most ancient peoples of the land, and from whom many Aksumites and Habeshat were mostly or partially extracted from, including Mekonnen himself and his family. But since the days of Negus Ezana in the 4th century A.D. when some of the Beta Israel converted to the new teachings of

Iyesus Kristos as the Son of Egziabeher and the rest refused to convert and continued in the ancient covenant law of Muse, they've been split into two kingdoms and have been in enmity with each other ever since.

But to think the Samen became the abode of evil creatures with glowing red eyes, snake venom for blood and souls blacker than the darkest night when sky are void of stars and moonlight. Shudder to think what they were doing up there and what vile schemes and devices they were conjuring up at that moment as the fourteen warriors hunted them down.

Along a chattered path the warriors went strutting on their horses, alert and a bit on edge, when the evening air became colder as the sun declined below the western horizon. Grass, trees, and shrubbery grew on the inclines at each side of the path. Patched of yellow masqal flowers decorated the verdant slopes like golden rugs.

A sense of peace and calm was just about to permeate the warriors when suddenly to their right there was frantic rustling of bushes. Then, something rushed out towards the horsemen with speed. Mekonnen and his companions were startled. Their hearts leapt in their chests and pounded hard and fast, like a musician beating on a *kabaro* drum. Adrenaline surged through them and the hairs on the back of their necks stood on end. Heads turned, and swords were instantly drawn.

"This is it! Something is approaching quickly from the side, but it is low down to the ground." was Mekonnen's first thought the moment he unsheathed his sword. Whatever was moving towards them in the grass and masqals could not be see, but I made a path towards their leader, Mekonnen. In seconds it scurried into the path in front of Mekonnen, revealing itself only to be a Habeshanian hare, they called a *tenchel*. It darted across the trodden path, barely acknowledging the men and horses it just startled them almost to death. The little critter was probably just as scared as they were. Two seconds later the same rustling noises and another hare hopped down the same slope and into the path, to follow the first one at top speed.

"Sigh!! Hawey, they were just *tenchel*!" sighed Gedi in relief. An arrow flew into the air from one of the warriors, over Mekonnen's head and struck one of the hares through the back and out the belly. The sudden impact and impalement caused the little creature to flip over several times and stopped dead in its tracks. It was Sami who shot one of his arrows with almost perfect aim. Mekonnen swung his head around to see who shot the arrow and saw it was Sami, now lowering his bow. Mekonnen glared at Sami with an expression of mild disapproval on his face.

Sami gestured with his head and replied to Mekonnen's scowl, "That could be our dinner tonight." To that idea, Mekonnen acknowledged his comrade's response with a rye one-sided smile. Kebi added, "We're going to need about ten more of those to be enough dinner for all of us. In any case, you know we don't ever eat *tenchel*."

Before they could even decide to gather up potential dinner, more noises and commotion commenced from the slopes, even noisier and more intense than before. All manner of birds fluttered out of the trees and cried out as

Hayyal = Walia Ibex

dozens of screaming gelada baboons stampeded down the hill after the hares. What were they running from? No one knew. Whatever it was, the creatures of the forest were definitely terrified. More hares and even lizards poured out from the hill into the path, then up the opposite slope. The geladas rushed down fast and straight towards them screaming and running under the horses. Some of them bumped into their horse's legs, causing them to panic and neigh, lifting front legs and threw off some of their riders.

"Steady brothers! We must move forward. Something has scared the animals!" As the warriors tried to control their steeds and get out of the way of the creatures in chaos, several hayyal – ibexes – and antelopes stormed down the slope towards the Aksumites. "This is madness! Let's move!" shouted Kebi as he remounted his white Arabian stallion. As the men took off down the path towards *Gultosh,* all kinds of terrified animals were in front of, around and behind them, running from an unknown terror on the other side of the slope. Afterwards, hyenas ran across the path ahead of Mekonnen and the warriors.

"What has scared these animals so much?" Mekonnen thought. Then he had a sudden realization.

"Wait a minute, why are we running away? These animals are probably running from the very hooded Qataliyan we are hunting down! We should be running towards the area they ran away from.

Hah! Turn around stallion! We are going up the slope to see what is causing this!"

Mekonnen stared his horse to the right and up the grassy slope, then motioned with his arm to the others,

"This way! THIS WAY!!"

The warriors were confounded by their leader's decision to go in the opposite direction without an explanation, but some of them followed anyway. They galloped upward and onward, and almost ran over some gelada, hyenas, ibexes, and rabbits, to the top of the hill. At the top, they stopped and peered down but could only see more chaos of animals, dust and a billowing, tick, dark-grey fog approaching in the forest among the trees. Whatever was causing the chaos was in that dark fog. Mekonnen made an attempt to go forward toward the fog, but his horse refused to go on. The stallion panicked and bucked as the fog accelerated into a roaring whirlwind that threw debris of tree branches at them violently. It became too dangerous for them to stay at the top of the hill, so they took flight on horseback back down the slope and into the path again. If only their horses had wings like a Pegasus, they would surely take flight far away from the Samen mountains that became a wild and dangerous wilderness to be in.

"Egziabeher help us!" whispered Mekonnen as the rushing winds spiraled behind and around them with a dreadful howl as they rode onward as fast as they could to escape the flying branches, trees, and dirt thrown at them.

Somehow, he just knew that what was in that chaos was connected to the hooded Qataliyan.

Then he had a strong feeling, almost like a faint voice telling him not to go to the village they originally planned to approach, but to go up towards the mountains.

"Do not go to *Gultosh*, go up towards the mountains, and I will show you where to go." Said the still inner voice inside Mekonnen, that was very distinct. He didn't understand how or why he got that message, but he called out to the warriors,

"We go up high into the mountains! We are NOT going to *Gultosh*!"

Zegi, stunned at Mekonnen's command disagreed and pleaded,

"Ras Mekonnen," Zegi began to address Mekonnen with the title of *Ras*, a Duke, a higher rank than his actual status, to be respectful yet sarcastic at the same time, then continued, "I beg your pardon, but I do not think that will be a good idea, *Egzi*. The sun is going down, and we can be stuck out there in the wilderness with no shelter. Wouldn't it be better for us to be inside a warm, clean house in a village instead? "

"We already have tents and enough rations for us to rest and even sleep outdoors for days, Zegi. We are prepared for this expedition. I just have a strong feeling that we should not go to *Gultosh*, so I'm sticking to this new strategy."

Zegi: "But, with all these wild animals running loose now, it is not safe! And who knows what else is out there to attack us!"

Mekonnen: "Well, of course, there are 'other creatures out there' waiting to attack us! That's why we're out here in the first place, remember? We are hunting for cloaked, dark Qataliyan that tried to murder our Negus and succeeded in kills some of our warriors! Our brothers-in-arms were killed!"

Zegi retorted, 'I understand, but maybe this is not the right time to proceed deeper into the Samen wilderness. The Qataliyan may be waiting to ambush us there…"

Desi joined Zegi in the skepticism, "Maybe Zegi is right. Going into the mountains now may not be a good idea. What if we get ambushed?"

Then Nezan, "Yeah, we should go to *Gultosh* and go up the mountain tomorrow instead."

And so, an argument ensued as the warriors rode along the path, the animals no longer in sight, now gone and scattered into the jungles among the trees. Back and forth the warriors continued shouting at Mekonnen and each other about where they should go next. To *Gultosh* or further up the Samen Mountains. Gedi, Endal, Moti, and Kebi also sided with Mekonnen to go with him, but finally, Zegi's idea prevailed with Desi, Nezan, Yazi and the like siding with him, as it seemed wiser and more comfortable to go to *Gultosh* right away. Still, Mekonnen had this strange feeling they should not be going that way. He also became more aware of the golden belt he is wearing that he received in the Negus' palace from the mysterious young man. It felt a bit warmer, and tighter in the past hour since he felt uncomfortable about going to *Gultosh*, but he tried to ignore the signs.

"Sigh! Okay, brothers! To *Gultosh* we go then!" Mekonnen complied reluctantly.

"We will stay there overnight and leave for the mountains in the morning."

Sami and Bini rode up to Mekonnen on either side and whispered to Mekonnen,

Bini first, "You know Mekonnen, what is to stop the Qataliyan from also ambushing us at Gultosh? This may not be a great idea after all. Not any wiser than going into the wilderness."

Then Sami, "In the village, we could be cornered by the Qataliyan, and innocent civilians can get caught in the crossfires. Whereas out there, we are in the open, and we can surround them and…".

Mekonnen became annoyed by the decision and interrupted, "Yes, Yes, I know there are many factors to consider! No matter where we go the chances of our fate can be anything. Egziabeher will guide and help us, hrai? There are other troops out there besides us, so maybe they will scout the mountainside before us."

"Let us just go into the village with caution and be ready for anything. Peace or war, we must be ready. Let's ride warriors!"

Mekonnen spurred on his horse with a kick and a shout, "Hiya!"

The steed accelerated and the other warriors followed suit as they hurried towards *Gultosh*.

Out of Mist

About 5 minutes later as the warriors rode along the rugged path, a tight fog descends upon them a cloud. It was natural for parts of the highlands to have the occasional fog but considering what they experienced less than an hour ago, this fog could be the precursor to another incident.

Suddenly, they heard the rumbling of galloping horses coming towards them from inside the fog. The noise grew louder as the unseen horses came closer, so Mekonnen and his men became alert and drew their weapons.

"Who goes there!" Shouted Mekonnen, as he unsheathed his glistening sword. Some of the warriors did the same, while those with bows prepared their arrows.

Galloping hooves came closer and closer. Then the familiar voice of a man called out to them.

"It is I! Mikael and the *Dakuen* company!" Just then the galloping horses and their riders emerged out the fog like phantoms. Alas, they were fellow Aksumite warriors, about eight of them lead on horseback by Mikael, known as Miki. Among them were horses rushing out of the fog without riders on them?

Mekonnen inquired, "Miki! You gave us a startle! Where are your warriors all coming from? Is this all of you?"

Miki replied, as he caught his breath, "We went to one of the Beta Israel fortresses further to the south to question their king about the Qataliyan, but when we got there, only a few of their warriors remained in the village which was already ravaged by the same Qataliyan that attacked our kingdom. They said their King Phinias was killed seven days ago by the Qataliyan and had to whisk away their women, children, priests and their king's family to another location. While we were still there, some hooded Qataliyan returned, and we ended up fighting side by side with the Beta Israel warriors against the villains."

Shocked to hear this report from Miki Mekonnen probed, "Really? So, their king was assassinated, and you fought side by side with the Beta Israel against the Qataliyan?!"

"*U-wa*! The Qataliyan ambushed us there and came at us from almost every direction. Swords were drawn, and arrows were shot at us. Some of my men didn't make it, and the Beta Israel also had casualties. They caught us by surprise, and we don't even know how many of them are out there against us. It's like they come out of the dark and the shadows."

One of Miki's men blurted out as he rode by on horseback, added to Miki's report, "Evil creatures they are! Not from this world!" and he kept on riding as if he was heading back to Aksum.

That exclamation sent a chill up Mekonnen's spine, and he could tell his warriors felt to same.

Miki continued, "My men are spooked. They have had enough for the day. Where are you going with your warriors, Mekonnen?"

"We're riding to Beta Israel village of *Gultosh* to scout the town, and possibly spend the night." Mekonnen replied.

"Egziabeher be with you. I wish what is left of my company could come with you, but that last encounter took a toll on us."

Mekonnen: "That's okay Miki, maybe you can send for more backup from Aksum. Look for Commander Mulualem and Commander Alazar and see what he can do for us!"

Miki: "I can certainly do that for you, brother. But I think we will need much more than just more warriors from Aksum. We will need lots of prayers and Armies from *Samayat* to fight those hooded demons. *Egziabeher* be with you!"

And with that cryptic statement, Miki rode off into the mist, leaving Mekonnen with a lot to worry about and to admit he was now terrified of what they may be up against.

Circle of Death and Flame

Meanwhile, deep inside the thick dark fog at another location in the Samen highlands, there was a gathering at the clearing near the top one of the highest peaks on a flat-topped *Amba*. About 30 men in white robes with hoods pulled over their heads, concealed their faces in the shadows. They encircle around a large symbol neatly etched in the ground, a five-pointed star inside a circle, an ancient symbol of the occult and black magic traced back to the Chaldeans of Babylon. Inside the spaces between the five points of the star were strange sigils/letters or hieroglyphs that were not commonly known to any of the languages in the land but mean a lot to the men gathered here. Within the center of the star and circle was the sign of the crooked serpent as seen on the clothing and imprinted on the skin of the Qataliyan who attacked Aksum. Whether these were men born of women in the Realms of Earth and given over to the dark arts, or entities from the Realms of Darkness, or a combination of both, was not revealed.

Yet that night they chanted a verse over and over, in vain repetition. They swayed and moaned as two of them walked to the edge of the symbol and ignited it with torches in their hands. Then an altar that was carved out of stone was revealed in the very center of the symbol, and beyond the altar, a large snake-like creature moved in the shadows. This altar had been used before because it was stained with dried blood. In fact, at that moment there was a young maiden squirming on the altar, bound and gagged with ropes, prepared to be the next sacrifice.

The Silver Gauntlet

At that moment lone chanter approached the maiden on the altar with a sharp nine-inch dagger in his hand fitted into an enamel handle cast in gold with finely detailed engraved patterns and bejeweled with precious gemstones, of Ruby, Emerald, and Sardinia. His robe was more decorative and elaborate than the others, suggesting he may be one of the chief sacrificial priests or a sorcerer in that diabolical gathering. His face was concealed in shadow like the rest of them, both his hands and arms were covered with a silvery material of grainy texture that glittered as it reflected the flickering orange flame that encircled them. They were gauntlets that reached all the way past his elbows It concealed his flesh completely, diminishing the ability for anyone in the gathering to determine his true identity, whether he was human, other worldly entity, or something else. The symbol of the encircled crooked serpent was also embedded in red embossed die, twice on each glove, in the palm of the hands and on the back of the hands. On his right index finger was a golden ring with an emerald jewel set in the center, which seemed conspicuous, but unknown whether or not it was essential for the ritual.

As he raised the dagger above the maiden, it was revealed the gauntlets decorated with elaborate designs and symbols. There were also unknown hieroglyphics all the way up to the elbows of the silver gauntlets. The maiden tried to scream but was unable to for the rope tied over her mouth. Before he plunged the dagger into her heart, the mysterious priest declared,

"Now with the blood sacrifice of this maiden, Great Serpent Lord, her life force shall be transferred to you, so you grow stronger until you are able to rise. Rise! Rise from the dark shadows and slumber of your spirit. You shall arise from the ashes and be alive as the days of old, *Egzi Zendow, Hawey!*, Oh Serpent Lord, WAYNABA!"

Then the shadow of a large serpent-like creature with a terrifying mouth of jagged teeth was cast on a steep mountainside nearby. It's the spirit of the snake-dragon Waynaba, the beast that terrorized Aksum more than a thousand years ago and was killed by Nigist Saba's (Queen of Sheba's) father, Prince Angabo. He demanded sacrifices then, and now he demanded sacrifices again. This gathering used the ceremonial sacrifice of innocent blood to conjure up Waynaba again from the pit of hell.

A guttural voice from the shadow answered the sorcerer,

"You have done well my sssservant. You will be greatly rewarded when I am fully ressstored to your world. With each sacrifice, I grow stronger and ssstronger! Are there more maidens and young children available for this purpose my *Gabra-Waynaba*?"

The sorcerer-priest replied boastfully, "Oh yes my Egzi Waynaba, we have been collecting young virgins and children from the Kingdom of Aksum *and* from the Kingdom of Beta Israel for sacrifice just for you and your feeding! No need to worry, Egzi Waynaba. There is enough to last us many moons and seasons. And with the two kingdoms being bitter rivals in the midst of a peace treaty, they each suspect and accuse the other of being the instigator of the attacks upon them."

"That is exxxxxxxxxxcellent!" the serpent creature acknowledged his satisfaction, "Exxxxactly what I want to hear from my servantsss! Sssoon I will be among you in the land of the living again! The Great Master will be pleased to know the territory of Habesha land, this part of Kush and Sssaba, will be under his sovereign rule again! HHISSSSSSSSSSS!!"

The sorcerer with the elaborate silver gauntlets replied,

"U-wa, Lord Waynaba, but there is one fact you must be aware of. Do not address me as your '*servant*'! For I am the one who has power over you. You and the Army Agents of Darkness have been conjured by me and the works of my disciples. I have in my possession the power and the instruments to bring you back into this world, and to return you to the ether-world and back into Tartarus, the Prison Abyss. Let us be clear on this arrangement, and that we have perfect understanding of each other, *Hrai*?

Waynaba was offended, but now cautious of the one making the bold claims, so he said, "Oh! Is that ssso?"

The sorcerer with the silver gauntlets holding the dagger above the maiden replied with confident conviction in his voice,

"Yes! This Is So!"

Then there was a scream of horror that fills the air in the mountain ranges on this dark, cold night, as a sharp pain is inflicted upon the young maiden. As her precious blood flowed a steady stream down the side of the altar.

Meanwhile, not far, in an alternate level of the mountain from this gathering for the sacrifice, there were more children chained and bound to a mountain side over heaps of skulls and bones. They were all intended for future sacrifices. Among them were three young girls between ages 9 and 14, and three boys, 5 to 9 years old. Including Natanael, the little boy from Aksum, who was just ejected from a sack that he was stuffed into, now bounded in chains to a mountain of skulls with the rest of frightened boys and girls. Despite the fear and despair, he was in, Nati remembered a little prayer his mother thought him to say every day. It was a verse from the holy oracles of *Dawit Mezmur*, also known as the Psalms of David,

"Though I walk through the valley and shadow of Death, I will fear no evil: You, Oh Lord, are with me. Your rod and your staff, they comfort me." (Psalm 23)

Mekonnen
Jerome M

124

Aksumite Warrior Comrades
Mekonnen: Warrior of Light
Jerome Matiyas 9/2018

Chapter 6

Chapter 6

Dark Simien

(Tsallim Samen)

As the sun descended below the horizon and the sky turned orange with streaks of red and purple clouds, horses ran wildly down a pathway to the south-west of the Samen mountain range which presented a spectacular view of a dramatic skyline of vast escarpments and deep chasms. Mounted upon these horses were Mekonnen and his warrior companions. Sweaty, hungry, thirsty and terrified, they approached the town settlement of Gultosh seeking shelter and answers. The warriors were in Beta Israel territory, another reason to be cautious in that region. They stormed through the gateway entrance to Gultosh which would usually be stationed with guards, but there were none. They galloped right in but slowed down after seeing how desolate and battered the town was, as if Death and Destruction personified went on a rampage. A few dead cats, dogs and chickens were in the streets. Bricks and chips of wood were scattered about. Damaged single and two-story round houses built of stones with broken doors and holes in straw roofs, some partially, others totally burnt down. Citizens of the town were seen peeking at the warriors through windows and doors.

"This town was recently attacked!" was Mekonnen's obvious observation.

"Egzio Hawey!, Looks like there was an elephants stampede through here!" Gedion exclaimed.

"This is horrible!" Kebi added, spitting on the ground.

Mekonnen raised his right hand, assumed the remaining inhabitants would be looking at them from behind their walls and announced in Ge'ez,

"*Hǝzba Gultosh! Nehna bawa'it Salam!* – People of Gultosh! We come in peace!

Gedion then translated Mekonnen's greeting into the *Agaw* language, which was the first language of Beta Israel people, in case they did not understand him in Ge'ez.

"*Eyyan Gultosh! Anandiw etey haduw!*"

No response. Only silence. The people were scared and afraid to approach the strangers, or they thought the Aksumite warriors could be Qataliyan returning to ravage them again, or simply disguising themselves as

Map showing Aksum, Beta Israel territory, Simien Mountains, Lake Tsana/T'ana and the route of Mekonnen and warriors scouting for the hooded assassins, the Qataleyan.

people coming to their aid.

Mekonnen called out again in Ge'ez, and Gedion followed by translating into Kayla as before, "We are warriors from Aksum, and we seek the same horde of savages who attacked your town. Please, we seek shelter, and information about where your attackers went. We will bring them to justice!"

Weeping Woman

Moments later, Hambo heard muffled sounds coming from one of the houses. He listened more intently and realized it was the sound of weeping.

"Mekonnen, over here! I think I hear someone crying in this house over here!" Hambo exclaimed pointing to the house just a few cubits away from him. Mekonnen stared his horse around in that direction and rides closer to the house that has several fist-sized holes in the walls and arrows on the door. He jumps off his horse and approaches the door carefully as he calls out,

"*Yikrai-ta, Wayzero!* Excuse me, Madam! Are you okay? Why are you crying? Is there anything we can help you with?"

Endal, Gedion, Samuel, Hambo, and Nezan dismount from their horses with swords drawn in case of a surprise attack. They follow Mekonnen as he touched the door, realizing it was already open, so he pushed it slowly to see who was inside.

"*Wayzero?* We are coming inside. We mean no harm."

Inside they saw a woman in a room lit by lanterns, sitting on a bed, clutching some bed sheets in her hands and rocking back and forth crying while another elderly woman sat with her trying to console her.

"They took her! They took away my daughter! They stole away my daughter!" The woman cried.

Gedion pushed forward towards the woman and asked her in Agew tongue,

"Who took your daughter? What did they look like?"

The weeping woman replied in Agew, "They... they wore white robes. And their faces were dark and covered with hoods. We could not see their faces! Was blacker than night."

Mekonnen and Gedion looked at each other after hearing that familiar bit of detail from the woman that her village was ravaged by the same creatures that attacked Aksum a few days earlier. Hambo, Nezan, and Sami also glanced at each other for the same revelation.

"I am sorry, but how old is your daughter, *Wayzero*?" Mekonnen asked in his best attempt at the Agew language that was not as sharp as Gideon's,

"She is only fourteen. Her name is Deborah. Please, bring my baby back to me."

"We will search for her if you tell us where they went after taking your daughter." Mekonnen persisted.

"It happened so fast! I do not know, Sir! I was hit and fell unconscious when they took her."

Meanwhile, outside the house where Bini, Kebi, Moti and Zegi and others were still outside mounted on their horses, more people began to slowly come out of their houses. One middle-ages man walked up to Kebi and said,

"Please, Sir. Help us. Some of our children were taken away from us. Including my son."

"Did you see where they went with your children?" Kebi asked. A young man replied. "They went east, toward the Samen Mountains."

An older woman next to him added. "A lot of our warriors were killed by these evil kidnappers. They did not even seem human."

Kebi went closer to the house where Mekonnen, Gedi, and Sami were speaking to the woman to past on the new information to them.

"Hey, there are more people out here that said several children were kidnapped, and they took them to the Samen Mountains!"

"The Samen wilderness! It's getting too dark to go up there now! Will be too dangerous!" Zegi insisted as he did before.

Bini rolls her eyes in annoyance to Zegi's apparent cowardice. Sami sighs with impatience.

An older man with three town folk brings water and bread, slowly waddling in the doorway and begins speaking to the warriors in acceptable Ge'ez dialect,

"Selam to all of you. It happened yesterday! Strange men in white robes and hoods over their faces. Stormed into Gultosh on horseback, shooting arrows at us and wounding many of our fine warriors. They snatched up five of our young children and rode off with them. We have no idea why they wanted our children!"

"Sounds like the same culprits who attacked our city and almost assassinated the Emperor. And they murdered my brother!"

Mekonnen informed the old man. "What else can you tell us about your attackers?"

"They had strange symbols on the hem of their robes, and they had *Xay-ay gezen awre-ra xay-ay jagera awre* – big savage dogs and very big baboon-beasts – with them. Like they were not from this world. I never saw anything like them before." The old man added with a wobble in his voice.

"*Xay-ay Jagera Awre!* – Very Big Baboon Beasts!? What do you mean? What did they look like?" Endal asked.

While they spoke, there was a commotion going on outside, with the sound of people screaming, and the ground shook like an earthquake as if something large was walking towards them.

The people shouted in Agew:

"Look out!"

"What is that?!"

"Get out of the way!"

"They are back! The monsters are back!"

Then there was a great noise as something crashed through the wall from outside to inside the house between Mekonnen and the old man as it let out a grizzly roar.

The Great Beast

"GRRRROOAAAWRRR!!" To everyone's shock it was a huge beast that looked like a familiar gelada baboon except it was much larger and more vicious, standing at about 10 cubits high (14.8 feet) with very dark gray fur and a red symbol in the middle of its chest where instead of the usual red, heart-shaped patch of bare skin and nipples on the chest, it has a symbol of the black, crook serpent inside a red circle.

The old man replied to Endal's question as he pointed to the creature,

"Very Big Baboon Beasts like THAT ONE!" then he and his companions ran away as fast as they can.

Before Mekonnen and the other warriors could react or even have a thought, the giant gelada beast lashed out with its long hairy arms and knocked over the warriors like sticks, sending them flying in different directions in the house, slamming them onto walls and furniture.

Mekonnen arose from the floor and shook his head, stunned by the impact and the sight of the monster, but there was no time to be paralyzed by fear. He realized he must think fast, get the women and his men out of the house and avoid getting hit and slammed into a wall again.

Outside there was another giant beast lunging at the warriors from behind, swung its arms violently, and sent Nabu and Embi tumbling back quite a distance away while still on their horses.

"Look out, there is another one!" screamed Bini while on his horse, he pulled back his bow and fired off two arrows consecutively, struck the beast only once on its left shoulder, which apparently caused no harm to the savage creature at all.

Desi aimed and threw his spear, but the baboon beast lashed it away and roared at him in anger. To make matters worse, more Qataliyan began to appear around the warriors, armed with swords, spears and bows and arrow. It appeared Mekonnen and his warriors were surrounded and doomed. This was exactly what Mekonnen, Bini, and Sami feared would happen when they were arguing with Zegi. That they would be ambushed!

The Mysterious Warrior.

"Egziabeher help us!" exclaimed Mekonnen as his belt began to vibrate and glow as if in response to his call and to urge him to think fast and get out of the house and away from the rampaging beast. He looked to his left and spotted the woman crouched and hiding in a corner under a table. Just then one of the warriors whom Mekonnen did not recognize, wielded a great long spear or lance with triple arrow heads waves his hand and shouts to Mekonnen,

"I will distract the beast while you get the woman and leave this place! Quickly!" Then the warrior thrust the beast in the back with his triple-blade at the end of a very long 7-cubit spear and shouts,

"Yah! Yah!! Look at me over here you foul abomination!"

The creature swung around violently to receive a jab to the chest from the spear while the warrior still held on to the shaft at a safe distance since it was quite long. As the beast grew angrier and preoccupied with the unknown spear-wielding warrior, Mekonnen looked around for the two women but only saw the younger one. The older one had fainted in the farther end of the room and out of reach, but out of harm's way. He ran to the young woman, grabbed her up from under the table and ran for the hole in the wall that the beast made when it crashed through. Mekonnen made one last glance at the spear-wielding warrior to see if he recognized him thank him later, but could not tell if it was Gedi, Endal, Kebi or any one of the others. He saw the warrior doing valiantly; docking, dodging and jumping over the flaying arms of the beast while he struck it repeatedly with thrusts from his unusual spear. Then, Sami, Moti, Bini, and others joined the mysterious spear warrior with the launch of arrows and spears at the beast until it became weary and stumbled to the ground and breathed its last breath.

Dark Entity

As he carried the young lady in his arms, Mekonnen jumped through the hole in the wall only to come face to face with a cloaked Qatali on the other side. About 9 feet tall, this one was draped in a dark felt type of cloak and hood decorated with the intricate but strange designs on the hem and fringes. The symbol of the red serpent inside a black circle was noticeable again. Its torso, arms, and legs literally looked like they were formed and molded from the starry night sky as if a piece of the night sky was standing in front of them in twilight of day with a curved sword drawn in its dark right hand. This confirmed to Mekonnen that they were dealing with unusual beings that were not from the Earthly realm, but diabolical creatures from another dimension.

The woman shrieked at the freakish sight, Mekonnen let her down on her feet to the side and told her to run away as he drew his sword from his side and immediately began dueling with the cloaked freak of nature. He tried to strike down his assailant but the dark being was swift and stealthy, as it ducked and bended in flexibly agile ways like a cobra and as if it predetermined every move Mekonnen was about the make. The other giant gelada type beast and more hooded beings still battled with and prevailed over some of the Aksumite warriors and local warriors of Gultosh. Suddenly there was a scream from a young girl, and to everyone's horror, they saw a cloaked Qatali riding off on a horse with a girl from one of the houses in the village.

Some of the locals screamed, "They're taking away another young maiden! It is Penuel! Save her! Stop them! Please stop them!"

In Hot Pursuit
The other Qataliyan stopped fighting the warriors and followed the one that kidnapped the maiden who could be only between 15 to 18 years old. It was as if they got what they came for. The giant beast that crashed through the house was already dead, laying on its back with mouth wide open, revealing those great fangs, and impaled in the center of the symbol on its chest by the mysterious warrior with the triple spear. He stood on top of the fallen beast's chest like it was a small hill, then quickly yanked the spear out its chest, aimed and threw it at the other beast through its right leg as it ran away with the rest of the hooded villains, causing it to trip over and tumbled to the ground in pain.

The Qataliyan became distracted and a bit fearful at the sight of the mysterious warrior who was wearing finely cut green apparel decorated with ornate gold and silver fringes at the collar, chest and sleeve cuffs under the bejeweled robe. This was odd and out of character for the cloaked villains, so Mekonnen took advantage of the situation and managed a quick maneuver with his sword and stabbed the Dark Qatali opponent on the left side of its chest. It hissed and did a swift backflip, jumped up on top a pile of the fallen rubble from the house and darted away in a flash. It was gone in a second and Mekonnen, without hesitation, ordered his warriors, "Let's pull out

Aksumites! Go after that creature and save the damsel! Let's go!"

Mekonnen grabbed the harness of one of the white Aksumite horses, mounted on its back in haste and took off after the hooded kidnapper. On his way out the gates of Gultosh, Mekonnen saw the mysterious warrior throw his spear at the giant beast through the knee then leapt upon the beast to tackle it to the ground. He grabbed the spear out of the leg to strike at it again as it tried to shield the blow with its large arms. As Mekonnen rode past the scene of the spear-wielding warrior and beast battling with each other, he thought he recognized the warrior as the same young man that gave him the golden belt in the Negus' palace the other day. He was even wearing the same type of clothing with the sparkling pearls in his blue and red robe. "Could that be him? It can't be!" Mekonnen thought to himself as he kept on riding.

"Keep going! I've got you covered!" exclaimed the spear-wielding warrior to Mekonnen as he stabbed at the beast with elaborate moves and spins of his triple-headed spear with agile skill. Mekonnen kept going with his warriors and four men of Gultosh in hot pursuit after the hooded assassins alleged to have attacked Aksum a few days earlier. Soon they were out of Gultosh and headed into the Samen wilderness and up the mountains beyond.

Moti rode up to be side by side with another hooded Qatali and looked into the darkness under the hood for a face but instead saw that dreadful dark chasm with red eyes looking back at him. Moti swiped his curved sword at its head, but it quickly docked to avoid decapitation. It raised its left leg and kicked Moti on the upper chest causing him to almost falls off his horse, but he was able to keep balance and control. Sami was behind them, so he drew his bow and fired an arrow into the creature's back. It squealed and hissed and attempted to reach for the arrow with its left hand, but it could not reach. Moti saw the opportunity and swung his sword, decapitating the Qatali, sending its black head flying off with part of the white hood. The headless creature tried to reach with its hands for the place where its head was, touching the stump of its neck, as black snakes slithered out of the wound instead of blood, just like what happened to the carcasses of the Qataliyan back in Aksum days ago. Startled by this sight, Moti kicked the headless body off its horse and rode up to the next cloaked Qatali in the chase.

They all galloped into a wooded area among unusual trees that naturally grew in twisty, uneven directions which mamde the forest have an eerie atmosphere in the moonlight and mist. Hambo and Yazi were the closest warriors behind the villain with the kidnapped girl, whose hands were now bond together at the wrists with black chains, and her body was hung over the horse's back onto her stomach in front the Qatali. Yazi attempted to be heroic to rescue the girl, so he pulled out a dagger from his belt and jumped off his horse to get on the back of the kidnapper's horse. But the cloaked kidnapper was agile and delivered a solid back kick to Yazi while he was still in mid-air, sending him crashing into a tree. Hambo tried by jumping onto the back of the kidnapper's horse successfully, but the cloaked one thrusted a blade backward and stabbed Hambo through the torso, causing him to tumble to the grassy ground from the fatal wound. The girl screamed in terror and wiggled hoping to fall off the steed rather than be held captive by the cloaked fiend but to no avail as it held her down with one hand, of which its fingers grew longer in an unnatural way to encircle her whole upper body.

Mekonnen rode up from behind and accessed the situation but became frustrated because he did not want to hurt the girl in the process. He thought,

"What should I do! Should I jump on him and send us all tumbling to the ground, including the girl, or should I throw a rope to lasso and bound him? Give me wisdom Lord!"

He decided on the latter and grabbed up a rope from the horse's saddle, swung it above his head and threw it around the cloaked kidnapper, then pulled to tighten it. The fiend just reached back with his other hand that had grown long, dark claws and swiped at the rope, and broke it like it was just thin thread for knitting clothes.

"Damn that cursed creature! Damn it to hell!" exclaimed Mekonnen in frustration.

As they rode on the terrain and mountain slope got too difficult and steep to continue pursuit on horseback, so the Qataliyan dismounted from their horses to go up higher into the mountains on foot. The Qatali with the damsel dismounted by grabbing on to an overhead branch or vine of some sort with one hand while he still held on to the girl with the other and swung off, letting the horse ride out from under them, then landed on its feet to continue running up Samen Mountain on foot towards the east and south. By then the sun was well below the horizon, so it was getting dark and harder to see but the three-quarter moon in the sky did help illumine the surrounding a bit to the warriors' advantage. The warriors also dismounted from their horses in hot pursuit up the mountain wilderness to rescue the maiden from Gultosh any way they could. Many thoughts began to race through Mekonnen's mind, so he exclaimed them out loud to Gedion who was ran alongside him,

"What could these… men… creatures… demons… Whatever they are… want with this girl? And these were the same ones that tried to assassinate our Hade?!"

Gedion added, "And remember that woman in the first village, Inda Selassie, who said her son was missing. Could her son been kidnapped by these same monsters as well?"

"I don't know Gedi. These days we've seen some evil things. And not only are we being attacked in Kingdom of Aksum but the Beta Israel in the Kingdom of Samen are also experiencing the same horror."

"Human sacrifice." Sami interjected in response.

"What?" asked Mekonnen and Gedion together at the same time.

"Human sacrifice! That was probably why they snatched the girl and why other children are missing. I heard stories like this happening. Used to be an old pagan practice, even in Habessinia before the Aihudyan (Jewish) and Krestiyan religion came to the land."

"Well whatever was the reason, we need to save that maiden soon. Let's hope she does not become a cursed victim of human sacrifice."

Suddenly they heard the sound of arrows whizzing by their ears. The Qataliyan were launching arrows at them. The warriors docked and hid behind some trees. Sami, Bini, Nezan, Abu, and Nabu drew back their bows and returned fire with arrows.

"Wait a minute! We cannot return launches with our arrows; we might hit the damsel!" Mekonnen remembered.

"Stop firing! Archers, cease firing!" Mekonnen commanded.

"We must draw nearer to confront them with swords and daggers. Only use bows and arrows if you have a clear shot on the ones that do not have the girl. *Hrai?*! Now warriors, let's move forward, with stealth! And be brave and courageous as you have always been. Let's go and rescue the damsel! Someone said her name is Penuel!"

The warriors spread out, moving forward from tree to tree, some of them crawled on the ground. Occasional arrows from the enemy whizzed by, hitting trees and the ground most of the time. Mekonnen peeked from behind a twisted tree and saw the movement of the cloaked Qataliyan among the trees under the moonlit sky, giving the forest an eerie, misty atmosphere. This made the assassins look more like ghosts in the distance with their white robes and hoods.

"Come on, let's move in closer, or we will lose them," Mekonnen whispered to Bini and Kebi who were now closest to him.

"You know what, I have a plan. I will go around from this side to the north and cut across and catch up with them from the other side by surprise." Kebi explained as he motioned with his arms to point the direction of his strategy.

"That sounds like a good idea. Go for it." Mekonnen gave his approval.

"Hawey, why don't you come with me, Desi?" Kebi asked.

"Okay." Desi replied, and off the two went with Kebi's plan.

Mekonnen affirmed, "It is a good idea we all split up like this and attempt to close in on the target from all directions so they will be surrounded. Go, Go, Go! Gedi and Endal, you come with me."

Mekonnen pointed and motioned with his arms to the others,

"Nabu, Mula… over there. Moti, Nezan… that way." Mekonnen looked at the four men from Gultosh and asked them,

I am sorry my Lords, but what are your names, Sirs?

They responded in sequence,

"Achemi."

"Bezael."

"Kariel."

"Daniab."

Okay, Achemi and Bezael, you come with me. Kariel and Daniab, you go this way to my left to close in on Penuel. Let's Go."

Off they went in various directions as planned. The Qataliyan continued going higher up the mountain. The damsel Penuel had since been bound with black chains around her wrists and ankles like a captured slave, and her mouth had been gagged with rope so she could not scream. She was being carried under the arm of one of them like a rolled-up carpet. The poor girl was terrified and had no idea where she was being taken and what her final fate would be before the night ends. She could not even understand what they were saying among themselves as they spoke and grunt in an unknown language to her. All she could do was try to remember prayers she learned from the sacred writings of the great *Nabiy Moshe* – the Prophet Moses – as inscribed in the *Orit* section of the *Meshaf Qeddus,* of which her people held as most sacred ancient writings. Somehow it seemed the Qataliyan already had a plan to escape those of the warrior's strategy. Since their senses and abilities were sharper and of a darker origin than those of Earthly skills.

Up is Down, Down is Up.

Meanwhile, in a deep dark realm, somewhere in the Samen Mountains and wilderness but not of the natural realm. But rather a dark alternate world under the mountains where the physical landscape was in reverse from the earthly dimension. Whatever was perceived as a high mountain peak in the natural world was perceived as a deep chasm in this inverted world. And what was a deep chasm in the natural world was a high mountain peak in this one. In this dark alternate realm was where young bodies and souls of boys and damsels were held in bondage and kept captive in chains, fastened to a high mountain peaks that was littered with the skulls and bones of men and beasts. These were children who were kidnapped in the natural realm by the Qataliyan and kept in this dark place for future purposes. The children could hear what was going on in the natural Earth realm above, but they could not see it. They sensed their captors were on the run and about to add another person to their prison.

In the group of children bound in chains was little Natanael. It was Nati who was taken and stuffed into a sack when Aksum was attacked, and Negus Gabra Masqal was almost assassinated. Nati was scared, but he remembered even in this dark, horrible place, to prayer to *Egziabeher Amlak*, the Almighty God of Lights, to give him peace and to rescue him from evil. He knew there was nothing else he could do but prayed and believed. Gradually he gained courage and light inside him, and he began to encourage the other scared boys and girls that were with him.

"Selam, my name is Nati, and if you pray to Egziabeher, he will save us. That was what my mommy taught me. To prayer when bad things happen. So, let us pray, okay?" Nati said plainly and innocently to the boys chained up with him.

At first, they were too frightened to heed what Nati said to them but when he began to prayer and sing a *Dawit Muzmur*— a Psalm of David— gradually their courage grew, and they joined him in song:

My refuge and my fortress,
my God, in whom I trust."
He Himself will deliver you from the hunter's net,
from the destructive plague.
He will cover you with His feathers;
you will take refuge under His wings.
His faithfulness will be a protective shield...
-Psalm of David 91:2-4

To the disgust of the dark creatures that guarded and watched the children, they demanded the singing stop immediately.

"**ROOAAAARRR! Be quiet you little worms, or we will come over there and eat your arms and legs!**" growled a dark, vile, creature with foul breathe and fouler appearance.

The children became terrified again and stopped singing because of the threat. But for the first time in many days they had a glimmer of hope.

Surrounded, Out Armed, Out Numbered

Back in the natural world in the Samen wilderness the spear-wielding warrior held his head up to the starry moonlit sky and concentrated. He heard the sound of the children singing and detected the direction from which they came from. He was alone on a special mission: Stay on the trail of the Aksumite warriors as they attempt to rescue the girl from Gultosh.

Just as he was about to head in the direction of the children singing, he was suddenly confronted and blocked by Qataliyan that appeared around him from the shadows cast by the trees. They materialized from the night sky they seem to be formed out of, first two, then four, then six of them. They surrounded him and drew out their weapons: One wielded two scimitars (curved swords), one in each hand, crisscrossing each other. Two wielded one curved sword each. One held out a lance weapon with multiple and decorative spear tips. Another drew with bow and arrows. And the last one held a length of chains in its hands. Their red eyes were fixed upon him, and they were ready to take down the lone warrior, six to one.

One of the cloaked Qatali spoke,

"So, you were sent to help these sons of Adam and disrupt our plans? All by yourself? How very brave of you. Or how very STUPID?"

"What is it to you? My Lord can send legions to accompany me on this quest. Yet he chose to send me alone for a purpose."

"Well, you are surrounds, out armed and outnumbered. You do not stand a chance. We are taking you down this hour!"

"Let's see about that!" The unknown warrior leapt into the air with spear raised over his head then quickly descends, aiming for the head of dark cloaked being who spoke. The dark being stopped the blow with his two swords and guided the blade away from himself. Another dark cloaked being fired an arrow into the unknown warrior's back and the other with the spear ran him through from his back to exit the front of his chest. A glowing cyan colored fluid spilled out of his wound. As the lone warrior screamed in pain, the chain wielder heaved back then forward, and wrapped the chains around him several times until lone warrior was tightly bound and not able to move. The warrior's arms were now fastened to his side, and his legs were also bound tightly in chains. They dragged him into the shadows, which was a doorway leading into their inverted dark realm.

"You should not have come, warrior from on high! You should not have meddled! The kingdoms of man will become the kingdoms of the shadow worlds. You and your kind cannot stop what has already been set into motion."

As the warrior reeled in pain, he attempted to speak, "Do not... be so confident of your evil... unrighteous ways, Dark one... This battle is not over. More Warriors of Light will come against you. My Lord will send them... you will see!"

"Hah ha hahh! Your Lord has made many threats and promises for ages, yet nothing happens. What makes you think he will act now! Take him away and throw in into a dark hole somewhere! Lord Waynaba will deal with this piece of trash in due time!"

As they dragged him away, the unknown warrior said. "Do not underestimate the Father of Lights!... *kakk, kaff, kaff*... And do not underestimate the Sons of Adam either... that have been redeemed by the Elect One."

"Be quiet you despicable creature!! Bind his mouth and take him away!! I do not want to hear any more of those LIES!"

Though the unknown warrior had been dealt blows that would have killed any earthly man, it was apparent that he was no mere mortal man but actually a being from another realm. Not from a realm of darkness and wickedness like that of the hooded beings that of bounded him, but from the realm of glorious Lights.

Closing In

Meanwhile, as the scattered warriors trekked higher up the mountain ridge and converged inward towards the captors of Penuel, Mekonnen, Gedi, Endal, Achemi, and Bezael spotted the group of hooded warriors in the distance among the trees about 20 yards away.

"There they are. Let's move in closer." Mekonnen whispered. They dodge behind trees under the moonlight trying not to be seen by them. As they move in closer and ready to jump out from behind trees to confront them. Instead they came face to face to their other companions: Kebi, Desi, Sami and Moti and the two other Beta Israelite men with them who approached from the other side. Each group thought they had their target in sight but lost them in a twinkle of an eye. The Qataliyan disappeared from sight and seemingly slipped away from the warriors, just like that.

"Where did they go? Kebi enquired.

"Don't know. We had them right in front of us." Achemi responded.

"I almost shot my arrow at you instead, Mula."

"This is not good, brothers," Mekonnen added with disappointment in his tone. "Okay, lets..."

Before Mekonnen could finish his sentence, suddenly the Qataliyan seemed to literally appear from out of the shadows cast by the trees in the moonlight, from every direction. From the east, west, north and south and the points in between and even from above in the trees, they jumped out in front and behind the warriors roaring and howling as they attacked them with kicks, punches, claws, swords and spears. Some even ascended from below out of the shadows on the ground. The warriors were ambushed and surrounded but still determined to fight their way out as valiantly as they could. Nabu, Kariel, and Mula screamed out in pain as they were struck down.

As Mekonnen screamed out, "*Egzi Iyesus, Hawey*!! Help us!" it was immediately followed by a great flash of light that blinded the Qataliyan, causing them to cover their eyes and mourn as if in sudden blindness. Everyone saw the flash but did not know they saw the light come from Mekonnen's midsection. It even took a few seconds for Mekonnen himself to realize the light came from his own mysterious golden belt. The flash distracted the Qataliyan and gave the warriors the opportunity to strike at them that appeared out of the shadows.

They hacked and sliced at their foes that could put up a good fight. Swords clanged together, spears thrusted and impaled Qataliyan. Warriors were cut and bruised by blades. Yet the dark ones were not as agile as they usually were, having shielded their eyes from the blinding flash of light. It then occurred to Mekonnen that they still need to save the girl.

"The damsel!" Mekonnen said out loud. He spun around, and the belt on his waist seemed to litterally light his way and focused on a cloaked creature ahead of him just a little way further up the mountain where trees merged gradually into grasslands with scattered lobelias palm trees as they went up an incline.

"Warriors! Up the slope, quickly! We must rescue the maiden!" Mekonnen commanded as he struck down two hooded opponents that were in his way. He got struck on the right thigh by one of their blades and on the left side of his stomach he was cut, but the wound was not deep. He ran relentlessly after the cloaked one who quickly ascended upwards despite having the damsel Penuel under his arm. The flash gave all the warriors a disadvantage over their attackers, so they could overcome them and ran up the mountain with Mekonnen.

Under the Mountain, In the Realm of Darkness.
Meanwhile in the realms of darkness under the mountains range, some of the Dark Qataliyan materialized back to the presence to the vile serpent Waynaba who was not fully formed into physical matter, but his head cast a shadow with red glowing eyes on a mountain side while the rest of his body was still ghostly like vapor.

"What hasss happened? Why have you returned without the sssssacrifice!" Waynaba asked with concern.

"Lord Waynaba, there was a bright, blinding light that distracted us and we were overcome." Reported one of cloaked Qataliyan.

"A bright light! What was the meaning of this bright light? Where did it come from? Anssssswer Me!!"

"It seemed to have emanated from one of the warriors from Aksum, my Lord."

"One of the warriors from Aksum!? Why is that? What is so special about him? What did he do or say? Was it some sort of magic?"

"We do not know, Lord. He exclaimed a few words. Words we are not allowed to utter here in this realm my lord. Yet still, there was something different about him that allowed such a blinding light…"

Waynaba interrupted, "Well sssend up more sssavage creaturesss to ravage them then! You know I need more virgin sacrificessss in order the rise up from the depths again! I shall hear no more exxxxcusessss!"

"Yes, my lord. One of our agents has a young maiden in his grasp right now making his way here quickly! We shall return to assist him Lord Waynaba The Great!"

Then a booming voice resonates from behind, "And we also have some good news for you Lord Waynaba." The sound of chains rings throughout the dark realm chambers and hallways of finely carved pillars and archways that support ceiling of stalagmites inhabited by bat-like creatures mingles with the sound of dragging on the tiled marble floors. It was the six Qataliyan dragging the wounded body of the lone unknown warrior they overcame on the other side of the mountains earlier.

"We have captured a filthy warrior from on high, Lord Waynaba. He was on his way to supposedly rescue the earth children from our grasp, but we stopped him."

Waynaba became anxious to see the bounded unknown warrior in his midst, glad he was in chains but still frightened, knowing what one is capable of doing to a fallen creature from the Realms of Darkness.

"Hhhsssskkk! You brought him HERE? What have you done?!"

"He was alone your majesty. There were no others around. And look, he is all chained and gagged nice and tightly."

"Hssssskk! This is risky, you FOOLS. They usually travel in at least pairs. And his friends will come here LOOKING FOR HIM! THEY CAN DESTROY US!!"

"No, Your Majesty! Not if we drop him into one of the holding pits. If we seal it tight, then they cannot find him or come after us."

"Just get rid of him quickly! And the ressst of you, go back up there and bring the virgin sssssacrifice to me!"

In the Realm of Lights

Meanwhile, in a realm much higher and much more majestic than Waynaba's dismal realm, even much more glorious than the most beautiful and amazing locations on earth, was a realm of gleaming cities reflecting a kaleidoscope of colors from magnificent structures like towers and castles made of glass and precious stones with luminous rooms and chambers.

In the midst of this glorious Realm was the life force of it all and gathered before him were beings that resembled the images of men but of greater stature and in much finer garments of brilliant colors with intricate design at the hems and fringes. Six of them bowed down on one knee with arms outstretched; reverencing one who stood within the light which was so bright only the outline of His body was seen.

The men formed a semi-circle before the Light, and one of them began to speak.

"Oh Lord Almighty, Anointed and Elect One, of Samayat and Meder. Heaven and Earth. Lord of Lights and Father of Love, Mercy, Righteousness, Redemption, Peace, Blessing, and Glory. We come to you in humility to bring word of the wellbeing of one of your creations. One of our brothers."

A voice resounded from the Light responded, "Your presences and petitions is much welcomed and accepted, my son and beloved minister. What is it do you want to report to me that you think I do not already know?"

"As you already know, my Lord, one of your ministers and valiant warriors for your cause, whom you have sent to assist the redeemed of mankind has been captured and restrained by the evil dark ones from the realms below the Samen Mountain valleys and pinnacles. What shall you have us do for our brother and fellow warrior, to rescue him from his captures, Your Majesty?"

The Almighty One within the light responded.

"What you have spoken is correct, and your request is heeded, my beloved. I am aware of the capture of your brother who was overcome because the forces of Darkness in that territory of Samen has become strong and their iniquities have grown much in the past season and come up as a stench to my Throne. Behold, I have heard the cries and prayers from the little children who have been captured and bound in the Dark realms and those that seek to resurrect the spirit and flesh of *Waynaba* the serpent, who was judged and destroyed in the past."

The figure kneeling in the front replied, "Glory be onto you Lord of Lights. Hast thou granted us access to the Realm of Samen to rescue our brother and assist mankind in rescuing their little ones?"

"Yes, thine request is granted. But your numbers and glory shall be rescinding for this season only. For I have called one of the warriors of Aksum to a higher calling, to test him and lead him into a life of great signs and wonders to defeat the Agents of Darkness with the Spiritual Weapons of the ways of uprightness and faith. It has been appointed unto him to seek, find and conquer with the articles of warfare, all seven of them, in battle against the powers and principalities in the Spiritual Realms. Behold, he has already been presented with the Belt of Truth by your brother in the palace of

Negus Gabra Masqal. And I have illumined his path to the Truth and blinded his enemies with its brightness of the Truth. Now go forth and rescue your brother and bring him back home to be rejuvenated. Afterwards, I shall tell you what next I have planned for the children of the land where the source of the Nile River springs forth."

"Thank you, Lord Almighty. We now go forth at your command."

And the six figures stood to their feet in unison, as wings slowly emerged outstretched from their back at the shoulder blades, revealed themselves to be *Mal'ekt* —Angels of The Lord of Lights. They bowed reverently one more time, slowly lifted off the translucent marble floor then took flight with great speed out the chamber, down a hallway and out the enormous pearlescent gates guarded by a pair of *kerubel* (cherubim) held great weapons in their powerful hands, then down towards Earth. In arrow head formation six more unknown warriors with various weapons unsheathed, aimed towards the Horn of Africa.

BETA ISRAEL WARRIORS AND MAIDENS
MEKONNEN: WARRIOR OF LIGHT
JEROME MATIYAS © 4/2019

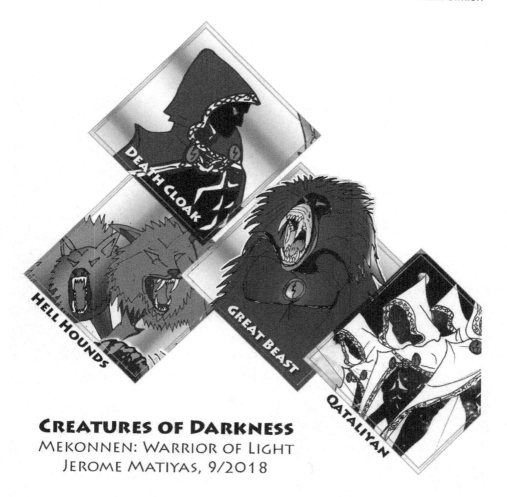

CREATURES OF DARKNESS
MEKONNEN: WARRIOR OF LIGHT
JEROME MATIYAS, 9/2018

148

CHAPTER 7
MOUNTAINS and CHASMS

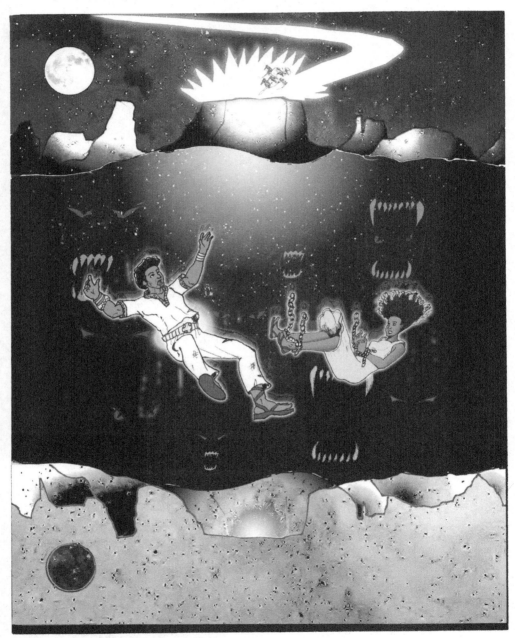

Mountains & Chasms: Falling into Inverted Realm
by Jerome Matiyas, copyright 5/8/2018

Chapter 7

Chapter 7

Mountains and Chasms

Hounds of Hell

Back on Earth, in the dark Samen mountain range, Mekonnen with sword in hand was in hot pursuit after the Dark Qatali who had Penuel under his arm. He managed to run fast enough to catch up with them, to the Qatali's surprise. The Qatali turned its head to look back to see Mekonnen's belt glowing in the dark. The creature ran and headed for an Amda in the distance, a high rising plateau about 20 cubits high with a steep, almost perpendicular slope and a flat top. Mekonnen sensed that was its destination but was determined to catch him before he got there with the girl. Was it going to climb up that amda with the girl on his back? It seemed like a difficult task, but with the sort of power and skill those Qataliyan seemed to have, anything was possible. The other warriors were still in hot pursuit behind Mekonnen, Sami and Kebi wanted to release their arrows but didn't want to risk hitting Penuel. The same went for those with spears to throw at him.

Suddenly they heard growling sounds and rapid feet coming up from behind them. Gedi, Endal, Nezana and Moti and Achemi, Bezael and Daniab looked back and saw more Qataliyan approaching them, but this time they were accompanied by more hideous beasts. Beasts that looked like black large hounds as big as leopards with large, savage teeth and red eyes glowing with rage. They could only be described as demonic hounds from hell. Now the warriors must decide if they will turn around and face the snarling beasts or keep on running towards the one that kidnapped the girl from Gultosh.

"Egziabeher Hawey! They're going to kill us!!" Screamed Zegi in terror by the sight and ran off away from the group in another direction. An unwise decision that would make him an open target.

"Zegi! Come back!! Don't run you fool! We must stick together, or they will come after you!" Endal screamed at Zegi who kept on running towards the other side of the mountain, as two evil hounds took off after him.

Up the Amba

On the steep amba slope, the kidnapper was almost at the top with Penuel still squirming, but Mekonnen was just below him about three-quarters of the way up. He grabbed on to a loose rock that caused it to fall and almost lose his grip, but he quickly regained footing to kept on climbing.

Kebi drew his bow and arrow and aimed at the kidnapper, "I have to take a chance. Must give Mo'kay more time to reach them." Achemi grabbed on to Kebi's arms to pull them down and exclaimed, "No, you will hit the girl! What are you doing!"

"No, trust me. I have great aim. You, Bezael and Kariel go closer to the amda to catch her if she falls." Achemi, Bezael, Daniab, Nabu, Moti and Sami run up to the base of the slope, looking up in anticipation, ready to catch Penuel. Kebi drew his bow again, aimed, and focused on the hooded kidnappers back, then released an arrow. The arrow flew and hit its target in the left thigh instead.

The cloaked Qatali did not seem to feel pain but the arrow did go through its leg, and pinned it to the side of the cliff. It stopped and tryed to pull itself loose to no avail. The warriors huddled together, ready to catch the girl if she was to fall with her dreaded kidnapper. Kebi pulled out another arrow from his back case, aimed and fired again. This time hitting his target in the middle of its back. It snarled and cringed in pain but was still determined to climb the rest of the way with the girl. Mekonnen continued climbing and now shortens the distance between him and the cloaked Qatali. Still more Qataliyan and hounds were came closer behind them. Nezana, Abu, and Desi drew their bows and arrows, took aim then fired. Endal, Gedi, and Moti stood their ground to face the hordes with swords and spears and braced themselves to face the hordes in close combat.

Now the hooded kidnapper pulled itself up with all its strength to reach the top and broke the arrow in its leg in the process, but Mekonnen was right at its heels, not directly below him but off to the right side. Still, the kidnapper reached the very top and hoisted Penuel to the top first, so it could use both hands to lift himself up. But to the dismay of Mekonnen and the warriors below looking up, there were more Dark Qataliyan waiting at the top to assist their friend and pulled the girl up to the top.

"Iyyaseh!" Mekonnen screamed when he saw another cloaked Qatali grabbing Penuel from above. Sami, and Kebi saw what happened and shot arrows at Qataliyan at the top, hitting three of them, causing them to reel over the edge and fall off the top to the bottom of the amba. But while Penuel, still bound at hands and feet, was being grabbed by another one from the top she managed to struggle as hard as she could and kicked her first kidnapper in the face, causing him to lose his grip from the edge and fall all the way back down to the bottom of the amba. When he hit the rocky ground at the bottom he crumbled into a dark heap. The warriors drew nearer to make sure he was dead but instead found a pile of slithering snakes scurrying into the rocks and sand to hide.

Crash Landing

Finally, Mekonnen reached the top and hoisted himself up in haste to save Penuel from her new captor who ran with her under its arm to a clearing at the top that was lit with torches around the edges. Other mountain peaks could be seen from the top as the moonlight illumined the dark horizon, including the silhouette of the top of the highest peak, Ras Dejen, could be seem to the north. With no time to admire the spectacular view, Mekonnen grabbed his sword from sheath and ran at top steed to catch up with them. Eyes blazing, teeth gritted, heart pounding, all muscles tensed! Mekonnen determined to stop at nothing to catch these creatures and save the girl. He could not accept failing now. He finally got close enough to the one holding Penuel and made a leap to grab the captor and stick his sword in its neck.

Just that moment as Mekonnen, Penuel and the cloaked Qatali was about to tumble into a heap, a bright streak of light curved across the sky. At the front of the streak of light were six objects like glowing stars, headed directly towards the top of the Amba that Mekonnen was on. It lit up the dark sky as if the sun was in the midday. Everyone saw what was happening and stopped. All the Aksumites warriors and Beta Israel warriors and the Qataliyan and hellhounds, even the animals that were awakened because of the chaos, stopped in their tracks from what they were doing, to look at the bright lights in the sky. Even back in Aksum, all the people that were outside wrapping up the Timkat festivities of eating, singing and dancing saw the light in the sky over the Simien Mountains and stopped in track to see it. The people of the Kingdom of Samen, Inda Silassie, Debarq and Gultosh as well, also stopped and wondered. Even the creatures and beasts in the Realms of Darkness tried to hide and block their eyes as they saw the light permeating their atmosphere from above.

"What is it?!" they thought and said out loud. Some people thought they were shooting stars falling to earth. They had no idea they were witnessing the rapid descent of six Mal'ekt from Samayat, the Realms of Light, coming to rescue their fellow warrior who fought with the elaborate spear in Gultosh and the little children from bondage in the Realm of Darkness. Little Natanael knew what was about to happen, so he looked up and smiled and said to the other children, "Look! They are coming to save us! We must sing!" Then he began a sing a song that was loosely based on a verse from *Dawit Mezmur* as the other children joined him in chorus:

Oh Lord, you are my refuge— no harm will befall us,
no disaster will come near us.
For He will command his Mal'ekt come to our rescue
And to guard us from danger;
They will lift us up in their hands to safety.
(Psalm 91: 9-12)

With an immense crash and flash of light like a thunder and lightning storm the six beings pierced into the mountains like meteorites but without destroying it. They caused the Earth to shake in hundreds of stadia radius. Most people thought it was an earthquake and either ran for cover or started to prayer. All the warriors lost their balance and fell to the ground. Including the Qataliyan and hell hounds that were closing in on them fell to the ground and began to run away when they sensed what fell to earth.

As for Mekonnen, the six beings from the Realms of Light crash landed right around him, Penuel and the cloaked Qatali, engulfing them all in light. With that light and blast, the mountains seemed to crack open and Mekonnen began to feel as if he was falling into a deep crevice with Penuel and her captor into the center of the Earth. They fell, and fell, and fell, with bright light all around them. The Cloaked Qatali began to burn up and glow like burning coal, then quickly disintegrated in the bright light but Mekonnen and Penuel were unsinged. Still, the sensation of falling was not very comforting, wondering when they would hit the ground. Gradually they felt like they could not tell if they were falling down or going up instead and the brightness transitioned to gray then to black. In the blackness Mekonnen could see red eyes and snarling teeth around them as they fell, growling and snapping at him and Penuel with unknown words. Only Mekonnen's mysterious golden belt illuminated the thick darkness at that moment. Finally, the fall stopped as they landed rather slowly on the ground not hitting it as hard as expected, considering the great height they fell from.

The Rescue

Now Mekonnen and Penuel were in a flat enclosure surrounded by several steep cliffs and mountain peaks near and far. Mekonnen looked around at this strange surrounding and had no idea where he was, but it looked like the amba plateau had become a low basin and what used to be high mountain peaks were deep chasms and what used to be deep chasms were now high mountain peaks. It's like they were transported to a strange inverted world. Even the sky was odd, with black dots instead of twinkling stars on a dull grayish sky and a blood red moon loomed over them like a giant, pock-marked fruit. The stench in the air was like sulphur mingled with a trash dump, and the temperature was unusual and very uncomfortable, both hot and cold at the same time. Mekonnen looked over at Penuel, laying on the ground with black chains wrapped around her body and legs, he touches her arm and asked, "Are you okay?"

All she could do was nod to say "Yes.", still stunned by her ordeal. They looked up and saw six figures like men standing around them with weapons drawn and poised in various poses, ready to fight. One of them, wore mostly blue apparel with golden fringes, a golden helmet on his head that could also pass for a crown. He held a large broad sword at the hilt in both hands with the blade pointing upwards and said to Mekonnen and the maiden in a deep resounding voice, "Do not be afraid, valiant warrior Mekonnen and Lady Penuel. We are here to protect you."

Mekonnen asked him, "Who...Who are you? Where are we?"

The one with the broad sword drawn replied,

"Do not bother with who I am. You are now in the Dark Realms of the Enemy, but we will get you out of here soon."

Then they heard small voices crying out,

"Help us! Please help us!" It was the voices of children in the distance. Up on one of the peaks the children could be seen chained to it upon heaps of skulls and bones. Up on another mountain peak littered with skulls and bones were more children. They observed the little boys and girls were kept separately from the older, teen age damsels like Penuel.

One of the six beings of Light, wore violet and wielded a long lance of impressive designs on the shaft and blade, flew over to Penuel, touched her chains and they immediately shattered into pieces like glass, setting her free. Another, wearing indigo garments and carrying a large golden axe, helped Mekonnen up to his feet. The one in violet apparel with the lance leapt into the air onto the peak where the little children were and ripped off their chains like vines. Nati smiled at him, touched his right hand and asked,

"Are you a *Mal'ak ZaEgziabeher*?" which means "Angel of God."

He answered, "*U-wa, Mal'ekt ZaEgziabeher.* We have come to rescue you. Hold on tight, little one."

Some of the vile creatures of the Dark Realm that resembled crocodiles and lizards, but much more hideous and pungent, began to emerge out of the darkness and crevices to confront the Mal'ekt that have just stormed into their domain. Another being of Light in yellow apparel with decorative violet fringes and hems and two curved swords, leapt onto the mountain with the damsels and ripped off their chains the same way while slashing off the heads and arms of vile reptilians in the process that tried to stop him. Another Mal'ak in orange apparel with a great fiery bow began firing off flaming arrows at mountains, causing them to explore and crumble. Then he aimed at individual Qataliyan and vile creatures and caused them to burst into flames

and explode into dust and ashes.

A Mal'ekt in red, wielded a beautiful crimson hammer with gold decorative fringes and wing designs on it, leapt into the air with hammer lifted high. He brought down the divine weapon to smite a mountain top with all his strength, causing a great noise and sent rocks and debris flying in all directions to reveal two Qataliyan guarding a pit that held captive the unknown spear wielding warrior in green who assisted the warriors in Gultosh. The Qataliyan tried to resist but were overcome and slain quickly with the red and gold hammer, and the warrior in green apparel was freed from his chains.

"Okay, my brother, now we leave this evil realm!"

The Mal'ak in orange launched a fiery arrow into the air to defy natural physics and pierced a hole in the murky gray sky of the dark realm to reveal the brilliant radiance of Samayat, The Realm of Light, on the other side. Two Mal'ekt, the one in violet and the other in indigo, propped up the injured green warrior to carry him.

"The Almighty One be praised! It is good to see my Mal'ekt brothers again!" The green warrior Mal'ak responded thankfully.

They spread their massive wings then jettison up into the hole in the sky with a trail of fire behind them. As the hole in the sky closed like a scroll the Green Mal'ak was carried back to a special place in the Realm of Light reserved for rejuvenation.

Three arrows were launched at the base of a mountain in this inverted Dark Realm and with an explosion opened up a wide tunnel that lead back out to the natural world on to the Samen Mountains.

The one with the broad sword said to Mekonnen,

"Mastatsabe Mekonnen, please take these little ones and maidens back to their homes in your world. We will escort you out of here, and then we must leave quickly."

Mekonnen and Penuel round up the children and lead them down through the tunnel and out to the natural world at the base of the amba on the other side. The children all held hands to make a chain as they all ran out with Mekonnen and two Mal'ekt in the front and the two others in the back of the chain of children, fending off vile creatures and Qataliyan that tried to stop them from making their escape.

The Conjurer's Escape

Meanwhile, some Qataliyan wearing white hooded cloaks and the others wearing decorative robes escaped to another end of the dark realm. The conjurer with the silvery gauntlet who used the dagger to sacrifice the maiden earlier was able to used the same gauntlets to generate power to grab hold of the serpent being, Waynaba, who had not been fully formed into a complete physical body yet, and places him into a translucent glass jar about 2 cubits high and 1 cubit in diameter with a bottle neck to a mouth and seals it with a rubber cork. Their diabolical plan to resurrect the old serpent with the sacrifice of small child and young maidens had been interrupted. So they whisked *Waynaba* away to another area of the Samen Mountains far away from where there domain was ransacked by the six warriors from the Realms of Light.

"Do not fear *Egzi Waynaba*." said the head conjurer with the silver gauntlet. "We will find another way to bring you back from the shadows of Death."

Mekonnen and Penuel with the four Mal'ekt lead the children out into the Samen wilderness under natural twinkling stars and a shining white moon. At the base of the amba, they heard the sound of familiar voices,

"Mekonnen! You're Alive! And you got Penuel!"

It was Gedion with Endal, Kebi, Moti and the rest, "Hey Mekonnen; we thought we lost you and the maiden for sure." Endal added in excitement.

Achemi, Daniab, and Bezael rush over to Penuel and the other girl from their village, "Penuel! Deborah! You are alive! We are so happy to see you two! Are you okay? Are you hurt?" Achemi exclaimed.

"It was horrible! Those monsters, they bound us in chains… inside the mountain… they, murdered one of the maidens who was with us... and..." said Deborah as she broke down crying.

Daniab reassured her, "It is okay now. We will take you all home now, okay?"

Mekonnen commanded, "Let's take these children back to their home towns. These, other fine warriors, our new friends, will help us."

"Who are they?" Gedion inquired.

Mekonnen looked at his four new warrior friends, pauses for three seconds to think of a believable and short answer, then responded,

"They are warriors from another ally kingdom. That is all I know about them right now. Come on let's go!"

Off Track

The warriors headed back down the mountain to take the rescued children back home. All the hounds and hooded creatures seemed to have gone away after seeing the flash of light. Suddenly there were loud noises in the wilderness again,

"Grooooaawwll! Aarrff!! Aarrff!!" was the distorted growl and barking of the hellish hounds.

"Help me! Aaahhhhh!" someone screamed in the distance.

"We must go back! That sounds like Zegi!" Abu screamed with concern,

"Aaahhhh! Get away from me!" another warrior bellowed in the dark.

"That sounds like Nezana! We cannot leave him out there!" Mekonnen screamed to the others. "Anyone of you feels compelled can come with me! We must save them!"

Then Mekonnen looked at the four remaining Mal'ekt warriors that helped them save the children and defeat the creatures in the inverted realm under the mountain.

"Brave Warriors! I thank you for helping us rescue the little ones, but are you coming to help us save our friends now?"

The Mal'ak with the broad sword replied,

"I am sorry, but we are not permitted to go back. We must go forward and take these children home. That was our order from the Almighty One."

Another Mal'ak in red replied. "But if you most go back, you go at your own risk. Egzaibeher Amlak be with you!"

"So be it then! Let's go!" and off went Mekonnen with six of his men, Endal, Gedi, Abu, Desi, Embi, and Nabu, ran at top speed into the moonlit wilderness and up the slopes in an attempt to save their companions. The other warriors continued down the mountain with the four Mal'ekt to take the children home, not knowing they were actually in the company of four beings from the heavenly Realm of Light.

As they ran Mekonnen thought and prayed within himself,

"Egziabeher, this has been a very strange night for me and for all of us. I have seen demons, monsters, and now I believe you have sent your Mal'ekt to save us. I was transported into that strange world that could be the very pit of hell, and you have brought me out of it with all the little children in a miraculous way. Now I ask you. I beg of you. Please save me and rest of my friends as we plunge deeper into the perilous darkness towards viscous enemies in these Samen mountains. Spear us, and I will know you are real and that you want to preserve me for your ultimate purpose. Spear me, and I will dedicate the rest of my life to serving you and your eternal kingdom."

This was the desperate vow that Mekonnen made in his heart as he continued running up the mountain with his comrades to save Nezana and Zegi.

"Over there, I see movement in the distance!" Endal said, pointing with his curved sword. The seven warriors picked up speed to catch up with the figments they saw in the distance which looked like one of the warriors being chased by cloaked Qataliyan on a high ridge. Then they heard more noises coming from another direction then a scream, "Aaahhhh!" and the sound of running and rustling trees and snapping twigs.

"You guys keep going that way," said Desi. "Abu, Embi! Come this way with me. We'll split up and take care of this one over here!" So they split up with Mekonnen, Gedion, Endal, and Nabu went southwards and Desi, Abu and Embi went east.

Endal aimed, threw his spear and struck down one of the hounds impaling it through the back. It tumbles to the ground, and the body disintegrates quickly but there were 5 or 6 more, and 3 of them turned around and ran head long into the warriors. Mekonnen, Gedion, Endal, and Nabu stop running forward although they want to run away but instead, they stand firm to confront the beasts face to face.

Each second the hounds came closer until finally, they clashed with the warriors. They fought valiantly to the best they could with swords, spears, and arrows. The hounds were almost as larger as the warriors themselves in terms of the length of their bodies as seen when they leapt into the air and onto the warriors, Mekonnen thrusts his sword upward to skewer one hell hound through the chest but still got pinned to the ground. Mekonnen was bitten on the arm. Its jaws felt like a vice grip on Mekonnen arm that will not let go. Mekonnen stabbed the beast in the neck multiple times before it finally let go and fell lifeless with Mekonnen's arm still it its mouth. Mekonnen pryed the hound's mouth open with his hand and then his sword with some difficulty but was able to get it off eventually. Just in time to saw a Qatali stood over him with a sword over his head ready to strike down on him.

With his left arm now in pain and bleeding, Mekonnen had to ignore this and lift his sword to block the blow and fight for his life. Three times the cloaked Qatali struck down at Mekonnen with his sword and Mekonnen deflected each one. Now he mustered up all his strength and roared with determination "Arrrrgghh!!" and with that roar as if to regenerate more will power he jumped up to his feet, spun around in 360 degrees with his blade out, slashing his opponent on the chest, then spun around again in the opposite direction to slash the villain at the neck, sending its right arm and head flying off. Down the body fell to the ground as snakes slithered out of the wound as before. The vipers struck at Mekonnen's feet, but he was barely able to jump away in time. Who knew what would be the dire consequences if one of those serpents injected its venom into someone?

As he jumped away to avoid being bitten, he looked up and around him to see Gedi, Endal, and Nabu clash swords and spears with the Qataliyan the best they could. He was about to help them when he noticed beyond them were dozens, almost a hundred more Qataliyan, and hell hounds coming toward him and his men from out of the forests and caves in the mountain slopes around them. Mekonnen realized there were too many for just the four of them to take on alone, so he called out to his men, "Warriors, look around you! There were too many of them! We most run. This way!"

They looked around, and it did not take them a moment to see that Mekonnen was correct. Just then Mekonnen's belt flashed a blinding light again striking the Hooded chasers and the hounds with blindness. They mourn and groan in agony with hands and paws to their faces. The warriors noticed the flash and saw their chance the escape while their pursuers were temporarily blinded.

"Mekonnen, what kind of belt is it you are wearing? That's the second time it flashed like lightning tonight." Nabu asked.

"Someone gave it to me in the Negus palace. I don't understand where its powers comes from, but it has given us another chance to escape. Let's go!"

While the Qataliyan and hounds groped around in the dark in blindness, the men ran southwards up an incline and into another forested area of lobelia plants and trees. The warriors would have favored heading northward towards Aksum, but right now they were trapped and didn't have a choice. They must find a way to make a U-turn at some point in the forest or in the mountains and head back up north, and somehow catch up with the others being escorted by the four Mal'ekt. As they ran Mekonnen turned to his warrior comrades and said, "I'm sorry for bringing you all into this predicament with me, but if we happen to get separated in this flight, please try your best too head back up north to Askum. Hrai, my friends?"

Endal replied, "No need to apologize, Mo'kay. We are all in this together, brother. We will be heading back home in no time, don't you worry!"

Nabu replied, "At some point, we may have to hide from them to let them past us then we could head up north. Does anyone of you have any water left?"

Gedi replied, "Yes, I do." and stretches out his arm to hand Nabu his flask of water while they were still running then adds,

"Let's look for tall trees or a cliff with a cave so we can hide. But we must keep on moving because I'm sure those dogs can pick up our scent."

Mekonnen adds, "I prayer Egziabeher will guide us to the right path to go back home, and that we not perish after coming all this way. If its possible then we keep going south towards *Tsana Hayk* (Lake T'ana) until we find a village or settlement that was willing to take us in."

Moments later after running for about ten minutes they find themselves on top a high ridge where they could see for great distances in every direction and also deep chasms and steep mountain ledges that were a long way down if one should fall. They have gained some distances ahead of their pursuers who have actually lost their trail now but still coming after them relentlessly.

Nabu had an idea, "Look; we can climb down the side of this cliff here and go around to the other side that will take us north. We can also hide here and let them past us by."

Gedi quickly replied, "Good idea, let's go."

"Wait!" Endal interrupted, "Since we're going to be climbing let's take off our sandals and throw them down that way and over the ridge on the other side so they will pick out scent further down south instead. Then they will pass us by!"

"*U-wa*, that's a great plan, Endal," Mekonnen replied as he immediately began unlatching his sandals. In seconds the four warriors had their sandals off, ran forward, threw them further down south and down the cliff on the other side of the ridge, then ran back and began climbing down over the steep cliff using just hands and feet without ropes. After climbing down and across for about five minutes they could hear the sound of the Qataliyan running on the mountain closer above them, and just as they planned, they kept on running southward not knowing Mekonnen, Gedi, Endal, and Nabu were climbing down the side of the cliff below them. The warriors stopped moving for a few moments to wait for the noise above to pass by to make sure they were not heard and get caught. The Qataliyan and the hounds pick up the scents of the warriors' sandals and kept running as fast as they could hoping to catch up with them, not knowing they were already climbing down below them. When the demonic hounds found sandals on the ground, they grabbed them up in their mouths and shook their head vigorously from side to side like a hyena or wolf-dog would after catching a mole rat in its jaws. They were almost certain they were on the right track and proceeded southwards with greater speed.

When the four warriors stopped hearing the movement above they sighed with relief thinking they certainly out-smarted the enemy and were now on their way home.

"Sounds like they fell for our trick. Let's keep going, brothers. Watch your step and be careful." Said Mekonnen. They continued down and sideways along a narrow ledge on the side of the mountain that was scarey to look down and hard to find a grip at certain points. The footing gave way under Nabu, and he almost fell into the dark abyss down below, but Mekonnen and Gedi were able pull him up.

Suddenly they heard a loud scream in the distance,

"Aaaaeeeehhhh!" Then some growls and guttural sounds,

"Rrrrrroooooaaghh!!"

They were blood-curdling to hear, and Mekonnen and his comrades perceive they were the sounds of the other party of Desi, Abu, and Embi that went the other way east to save Nezan and Zegi. Now they realized their other comrades were in trouble and may have been caught by the Qataliyan and their hounds. Mekonnen began to feel the pain from his bite wounds.

"Wait, my wound is bleeding." Mekonnen stopped right there on the steep, narrow ledge, took out his sword and cuts strips of cloth from his shirt, wraps his forearm near the elbow with it then continued climbing.

Suddenly stones and sands began falling on top the warriors' heads and faces. Mekonnen and his friends looked up and to their dismay saw their evil pursuers about 20 cubits above, glaring down at them with malicious red eyes.

"Oh No! They found us!" Mekonnen exclaimed.

Trapped On A Ledge

A Cloaked Qatali lowered himself down on a long rope tied to a tree above and landed onto the ledge next to Mekonnen while a hound managed the jump down nimbly onto the ledge and landed nimbly on the other side next to Nabu. The four warriors became trapped in the middle.

They needed to think fast. Trapped on both sides, should they fight and fall to their deaths or surrender? Surrendering was not an option. It didn't look like the Qataliyan took warriors as prisoners.

As the Qatali slid down the rope and stepped foot on the ledge, Mekonnen charged at him with ferocity and collided into him with an elbow to the head. This move caught the Qatali off guard and caused him to lose his grip from the rope, and sent him falling into the dark chasm below, screaming, "RRROOOOAAAaaaaaaagghhhh!"

Mekonnen was about to fall in after him but grabbed onto the robe and swung to the left. On the other side of the ledge the monstrous hound lounged viciously at Nabu, who already had his sword and dagger up, stuck his blade into the beast's neck and eye as they both fell into the chasm. Nabu and the beast bounced and roll off the side of the cliff as they fought on their way down. But no one expected any one of them to survive that great, long fall.

Two more Qataliyan swung down on ropes for Endal and Gedi as they braced themselves, with their weapons drawn. At the same time, Mekonnen came swinging back from the left to the right and kicked one of the villains in the chest and causing him to fall into the abyss with the first one. Gedi swung his sword at the other one who also had a scimitar drawn, clashed swords with Gedi while still on the rope. Gedi prevailed by slashing off the Qatali's hand and stabbing him in the torso, causing him to fall. That left two ropes for Gedi and Endal to grab on to, swing, and climb down to the far right, and jumped off onto another ledge about 30 cubits lower down, which left Mekonnen at a higher level.

Another Qatali came down quickly for Mekonnen with sword drawn towards him as Mekonnen shouted to his friends,

"Keep going! Escape while you can!"

"Mo'kay!" Endal exclaimed, as a looked up at his friend cornered on a ledge and wished he could help him but had no way of doing so.

"We can't just leave him up there, Gedi!"

"There is nothing we can do now, Endal. Let's go." Gedi added sadly.

Long Way Down

Mekonnen leapt off from his ropes and grabbed on to the Qatali's arm with the scimitar, pulled them both down into the chasm. As they free fell, Mekonnen was determined to not to let go of the creature's sword. Then that mysterious belt began to glow again as they fell into the chasm making them look like a lit torch falling into a well from the distance where Gedi and Endal stood. They were shocked to see their friend Mekonnen fall to his death, or so they thought.

"Let's go Endal, Mo'kay is in Egzio's hands now." And they kept on trekking back up north as they planned, only with just the two of them now and not the original four.

Mekonnen and the Qatali fell, and fell. Mekonnen's belt glowed while he held his opponent under him as a cushion for the impact on the side of the mountain, tree branches and eventually the ground.

"Crakkkash!" They hit a ledge of some tree branches on the way down, the Qatali took the brunt of the impact and broke their fall to stumble down a rocky slope for a while until they came to a complete stop. Mekonnen was knocked unconscious.

Four minutes later, Mekonnen awakened, bruised and battered almost everywhere but surprised to be still alive. He thought he had given up his life to save his friends. His clothes, torn and soiled with blood and dirt, but his opponent was broken beyond recognition. Just a sack of clothes and snakes hissing and slither out of them. But, to Mekonnen's horror, as he backed away from them, he witnessed the snakes wrapped themselves around each other to merge and reform the broken body of the Qatali that fell with him, to regenerate into it's previous physical man-like stature.

Still, in pain, Mekonnen struggled back his feet to get away before the creature fully reformed its body. The warrior groaned and limped in pain on his shoulders, left arm and left leg. Despite the pain from his injuries, Mekonnen was determined to keep on running, because that very moment he heard the sound of falling rocks from above. He looked up, and to his dismay, he saw not only rocks falls down, but more Qataliyan coming down the side of the cliff. Some scrambled down on ropes, others slid down the slopes with their feet. Followed by their devilish hounds, who came down vertically in a zigzag pattern as if to leapt from one mound to another on a horizontal surface.

Desperate Flight

"*Egzio Hawey!*" Mekonnen exclaimed, with no time to count how many of them came down, he dove to get out of the way of falling rocks, debris, Qataliyan, and Hell Hounds. As adrenaline kicked in allowing him to ignore the pain he took off running from his pursuers into a forested area, Mekonnen believed he could smell the presence, and hear the sound of a waterfall in the distance.

He regretted losing his sword in the fall so he was now unarmed and only had his two feet to run like a wounded gazelle fleeing from a pride of ravenous lions. His left arm that was bitten earlier pulsated with pain, but there was no time to think of it. Just run, run, and run with a limp, until he could actually ignore most of the pain. He scaled over boulders, logs and across grasslands and into another forested area.

As he ran Mekonnen remembered a desperate prayer,

"My life is in your hand, Egziabeher! Rescue me from those who hunt me down relentlessly!"

That was all he could think of at that moment. A verse from one of the beloved sections of the sacred oracles of *Dawit Mezmur* (Psalms 31:15).

Oh, how life had transformed from beauty into terror in a short space of time. Just four days ago he was fulfilling his duties as a guard in the Great City of Aksum along with his comrades. Oh, how he missed the smell of incense and spices that filled the air. The sound of church bells ringing, maidens singing and children laughing. The processions of priests and deacons in radiant robes and garments, more colorful than a rainbow. And the streets of gold he walked upon as if it was dirt and stones. How he took all that beauty and splendor for granted.

After several minutes that felt more like hours, he occasionally looked back to see how close his pursuers were behind him and the nearest ones seemed to be about 20 paces away. They fired arrows at him and even threw swords and daggers, but they missed by inches because of Mekonnen's constant movement and apparent pure fortune and luck. Soon, the sound of rushing waters could be heard and a fresh scent which meant a river or waterfall was nearby. As he ran frantically, Mekonnen grabbed on to tree branches and wood that could possibly be a weapon in case one of the fiend's gained on to him. He found one that was lean, long and strong enough and ran with it like a spear in his right hand. One of the devilish hounds caught up with him from the left and leapt at Mekonnen, but he swung the branch at its head hard enough to slow it down. He could hear rushing waters getting louder, so he knew he was getting nearer.

The creatures were getting closer; the warrior kept running through the trees to the sound and smell of the waterfall. Finally, he saw it, a beautiful clearing where he could see the sky again and below was a cliff and a waterfall rushing down from below into a deep chasm where he could barely see a river flowing in the pale moonlight. Mekonnen did not know which river this was on the map, but he knew he was about to take the risk and jump right in. He looked back one more time, saw Qataliyan and hounds getting closer from the sides as well. He turned back around and ran about 10 steps away from the edge of the cliff, then turned around and ran back to the edge, and made a great leap into the air, taking flight. Not up and away or horizontally as a bird but he formed his body straight down to make a swan drive downwards, falling alongside the waterfall. As he fell, Mekonnen felt like he was flying. He flew to freedom and safety. He hoped the wall of water would finally hide him from his demonic pursuers. He even prefered to die from the fall or by drowning than to be stabbed, impaled of torn apart by

The Hayyal
Copyright © Jerome Matiyas 2017

those creatures that have been terrorizing his Kingdom and even the people of Beta Israel.

Saved by Water

The Qataliyan and hounds remained at the top of the waterfall and watched him fall, but they didn't bother to follow him in, supposing he would not survive the plummet and would be dead soon anyway. But they lingered and looked on anyway just in case he popped up out of the river alive.

Many scenes of memories and thoughts flashed through Mekonnen's mind as his lean battered body flowed into the waterfall, feeling as if he was becoming one with the liquid. Like it was saving him, baptized him into it. He hoped his friends Gedi and Endal were able to escape and head north to make it back to Aksum. He hoped they would catch up with Desi and find Nezan and Zegi still alive, although he doubted it. He thought about the mighty warriors that appeared in a flash of light and rescued the children and maidens from the dark realm and hoped and prayed they would return them back to their towns and villages safely, though he was almost sure they would.

Then he remembered his cousin, Afeworq's sister, Meron, that he promised her that he would return to her alive. He intended to keep that promise. Finally, he plunged into the river at the end of the fall, with outstretched arms and head first. He was pushed downward then back up again by the current. Again, it seemed like time had slowed down and it took forever for him to resurface. Eventually, he swam back up and inhaled a great gasp of fresh air into his lungs. Fortunately, the evil Qataliyan were not able to see or hear him resurface for the great distance and noise from the waterfall. But they kept on looking.

Mekonnen looked around and saw many logs and branches in the river the further away he swam from the base of the falls. So he held on to one log and hid among them, keeping his head low and the rest of his body submerged in the cold water, hoping the Qataliyan could not see him. A little further down Mekonnen spotted an abandoned *tankwa,* which was a small boat made of papyrus reeds. He swam slowly and quietly towards it, just knowing *Egziabeher Amlak* prepared that boat just for him to climb into and flow down the river to safety and away from the treacherous mountains. Slowly he climbed in and covered himself with one of the many long leafy branches that were in the river. Alas, the hooded Qataliyan still could not see Mekonnen nor the tankwa he was in which looked just like all the other logs in the river. Eventually, they gave up looking and left the scene, and disappeared into the shadows and back into their dark inverted Realm to report to their master Waynaba that the warriors were gone with most of them defeated or dead. But the children they captured had escaped, being rescued by beings from the Realm of Lights. Waynaba was not happy to hear this news, neither the characters in colorful robes that seemed more human than the Qataliyan yet still sinister and unnatural in their ways.

As Mekonnen peeped through the leaves of the branches that he concealed himself with as he laid down on his back in the tankwa, he looked up at the mountain peaks above and noticed someone, or something, looking down at him from one of the peaks. He saw the silhouette of a hayyal, an ibex goat that was native to the Samen Mountains. It stared intently at Mekonnen in the tankwa for almost a minute, with its pair of impressive horns reaching up to the starry sky in a V-shape. Then it quickly turned around, leapt down from the peak and ran away.

"Was that hayyal actually looking at me?" Mekonnen thought to himself. "I hope it's not working with the cloaked Qataliyan, to go tell them where I am."

Mekonnen laid still in the boat as he drifted down the river, away from the waterfall, and waited to be out of sight and reach from the Qataliyan. After an hour, he determined they were no longer looking for him or going to find him anyway. Eventually, he drifted off into a deep sleep, passed out from exhaustion, freezing cold water, and loss of blood. He kept on flowing down the river and even through underground passageways until dawn when the warm sun was about to rise again. Three hours after the sun rose in the sky Mekonnen was still in a deep sleep, almost as if he was dead. He eventually emerged out of the secret passageways and streams, drifted down a river until he floated into a riverside village, somewhere near the legendary *Tsana Hayk* and the great *Tis Isat* Water Falls.

Escort to Safety

Meanwhile, the children were being escorted back to their homes by Sami, Moti, Kebi, Bini, Achemi, Bezael and Daniab and the four Mal'ekt. Along the way they found some of their horses roaming and grazing in the wilderness and on the mountain sides so they promptly mounted the little ones and damsels on those they could find and made good use of them. They also found about four horses dead in the forest with large bite marks on their necks, most likely they were mauled by the savage hounds from hell. Yet the hounds and Qataliyan dared not approach or launch an attack on this caravan once they saw the four powerful Mal'ekt with them now. They just lurked and follow from afar and on the peripherals beyond the warriors' sight range.

First, they arrive at Gultosh to return Penuel, Deborah and three little ones to their homes.

"We thank you so much, Lords," said Penuel and Deborah as they cried uncontrollably, and bowed and kissed the hands of the warriors.

"We cannot express to you how thankful we are for saving our lives. *Egziabeher yibarek*, The Almighty's blessings to you all forever!" Achemi, Daniab, and Bezael informed the elders of their village that they lost Kariel in battle in the wilderness but decided the go along with the other warriors from Aksum to escort the rest of children rather than stay in their hometown of Gultosh. "We shall not return home until all these children are returned to their homes. The mission was not yet complete." Achemi declared.

They continued up northwards to Debarq, Adi Arkay and finally cross the bridge back over the Tekeze River to Inda Selassie where Nati was reunited with his mother.

"Nati! Nati Hawey! Oh, my boy, my boy!" Cried the young mother Eyerus in Inda Selassie when she saw her son again, grabbing him up in her arms and kissing him all over his face profusely.

"Oh, Nati my boy! I am so happy to have you back again. I will never let you out of my sight again my darling! Never ever!"

"I am okay mommy! The Mal'ekt came and saved us, mommy. I saw them. There they are mommy. Mal'ekt!" said Nati pointed at the four mysterious warriors. But when the woman looked up, she only saw the Aksumite warriors and thought her son may be imagining things again. They were invisible to her, but Nati could still see them right there standing tall among the warriors. Yet still, his mother decided to believe her son this time by faith and said, "Ok, Nati. I believe you. I believe you."

"It is true mommy! I prayed to Egziabeher, and they came to save us from the dark mountains."

"I am so proud of you for praying Nati. I am proud you prayed like I thought you."

Kebi nodded and said, "Egziabeher be with you Wayzero. We must be returning to Aksum now." As he turned around to acknowledge the four Mal'ekt,

"And we could not get this far without assistance from these valiant warriors from... Hey... where did they go?" To his surprise, they had all vanished in the blink of an eye, transported back to the Realm of Samayat.

Return to Aksum

When the warriors arrived at the barracks in Aksum, they found Gedion and Endal already made it there. They were laying in beds exhausted, bruised and famished and being attended to by nursemaids and prayed for by *qasisan* and *daiqonat*.

"Gedi! Endal! You made it back safe!" Sami exclaimed with excitement. He looked around at the other beds and did not see Mekonnen, Nabu, or any of the other warriors. "Where is Mo'kay and Nabu? Were they not with you?"

Gedi coughed and lifted his head to speak, "They... they fell. We lost them. I don't think they could have survived." Sami sighed in dismay. Moti asked, "And Desi, Nezana, Zegi... did you see them?"

Endal answered while lying on his back with eyes still closed,

"After we split up we never saw them after that. We know not what happened to them."

Bini turned away to look outside at the panoramic view of the vast Samen Mountain range and added with hope and prayer on his breathe, "Egziabeher be with our brothers, where ever they may be. Egziabeher bless their souls and let them be at peace."

In the Spirit Realm

In the Realms of Darkness, the Cloaked Qataliyan gathered together and report to their council. One of them stepped forward, very tall in stature with his bony arms, head, arms and legs like the dark night sky with twinkling stars, switched his swords in quick stylized movements, one in each hand, and inserted them back into the sheaths that were on his back, stepped forward and bowed before the conjurer they call Lord Silver Gauntlet, who held the translucent ceramic jar that contained the spirit essence of Waynaba the Serpent. "They got away from us, Lord Waynaba. We were over powered by the Mal'ekt from on high. And one of the Aksumites carried a powerful piece of clothing that emanated brightly, my Lord."

The dark ghost of Waynaba squirmed inside the jar and clenched his jaws hard, showing jagged teeth. The Silver Gauntlet spoke to his dark audience,

"Fair enough! You all have failed this time, but we will find another way. It is not over yet." He turned and looked at Waynaba in the jar and said, "Fear not Waynaba, Lord of serpents. There is another way to get more souls for you. In the right place and the right time, we will find more blood sacrifices. And we will all become stronger. Soon I will have a new plan."

In the Realms of Light, the chief Mal'ak in the blue garments bowed to the Almighty One with the other six around him doing the same. He said,

"We have accomplished your commands, Lord Almighty, Elect One of Glorious Lights."

His face more radiant than the sun and eyes blazing like fire the Elect One, who was the Son of Egziabeher, responded, "You have done excellently, my valiant warriors, Mal'akim of Hosts. Now stand by and watch as I lead the warrior Mekonnen into a higher calling."

The Spear in the Ground.
Meanwhile back in the Samen wilderness between Gultosh and the Samen Mountains in the same spot where the six Cloaked Qataliyan surrounded the Mal'ekt in green apparel with the spear and overcame him, behold, his spear was left there, stuck blade first in the ground with the long shaft sticky up vertically at 5 cubits high. After the Hooded villains subdued the Mal'ak in green garments they dare not touch the divine spear that was forged in the fires of Samayat, for fear they would be annihilated by its power, or bringing it with them to their dark realms under the mountains will cause destruction upon themselves.

Two days later a caravan of merchants traveling from Bahar Dar to Gultosh and then to Aksum City spotted the lance jutting up vertically, with silvery glistening blade stuck in the ground and green shaft accentuated with golden decorations. One of the merchants walked up to it, ogled it from bottom to top in awe of its mastery of design. He had never seen anything like it before.

"Hawey!" he whispered, "This can be sold for a lot of Aksumite gold coins." He lifted his right hand slowly to touch the shaft then used both hands to yank it out of the hard dirt ground. It's quite heavy in his hands, but he managed to the carry it back to the camel drawn carriage by himself where three of his fellow traveling merchants waited.

"What is it you got there, Teddi?" one of them asked, sitting in the back of the carriage chewing on a reed of wheat in his mouth.

"It's a warrior's spear of sorts. Look at it! *Sannaya*! – It is beautiful! We can sell this to a rich collector or dignitary in Aksum and make a lot of money to last us a long time. Don't you think?"

"*U-wa*, it looks beautiful." replied another merchant. "Here, wrap it in this rug and hide it under the canopy where no one can see it and try to steal it from us."

They secured their new prize in the carriage and continued along the road to Aksum, not aware of the battles that took place in this region just days before.

The next day the merchants reached Debarq and stopped there to rest and try to sell some of their goods. They had ceramic pottery, incense lanterns, candles, lamps, rugs and other items suitable for lay people to dignitaries, but they had plans to hide the new lance they found and save it until they got to Aksum to try to sell it for a lot of money. There was a caravan of about eight holy men, qasisan, daiqonat and manakost passing through Debarq heading south. They saw the merchants and decided to see what type of items they could purchase from them that will be useful for their missions and worship services.

Teddi tried to entice the men of the cloth as was expected, to convince them they had many valuable items that may be of interest.

"Abuna, Egziabeher yimeskan! Please, allow me to show you what we have that will be perfect for using in the Lord's house of worship. We have lamps, lanterns, candles, you name it. We have them for you."

The holy men gathered around the carriage and looked at the items in there.

One of the elders asked,

"Do you have any rugs, Aksumite or Coptic rugs?"

Teddi responded exuberantly, "U-wa, we have some rugs over here! Barnabas, can you show the good Abuna Qass our magnificent rugs?!"

Barnabas confirmed, "Oh, look over here we have this beautiful Egyptian Coptic style rug. It came directly from Alexandria." As he showed them the rugs at another part of the carriage away from the rug that the lance was wrapped in. But one of the young manakos snuck around that side of the carriage and noticed the rugs and brought it to the attention of the elder Abuna in the group.

"Abba Libanos, look, how about this rug? There is something like a pole or staff inside of this carpet though."

Abba Libanos, who was an older man between 60 to 70 years old with his head wrapped in blue cloth/turban and long locks of gray hair like a Bahetawi, bead necklaces and a large Coptic cross hung from his neck, walked round to that side to see the rug and began to roll it out so they could get a better look at it. As they rolled it to flatten it out the rug's beautiful Coptic design was revealed, and also the great dark green spear with the

Mekonnen and Penuel Falling into the Dark Realm under the mountains.
Jerome Matiyas © 2018

shiny blade.

Abba Libanos and the young monk gasped with surprise. Abba Libanos asked, "Where did you get such a spear?"

Teddi ran around their side and began to stutter a story, "Oh, that spear, it, it was, ah, from an old warrior. An old man who, ah, was not going to fight anymore, so he sold it to us. But you will not be interested in a spear, would you, Your Holiness?"

Abba Libanos, touched the shaft and said, "Who would part with such an item? An old warrior will have pride in a spear like this, not sell it! You stole this spear, didn't you? Why are you lying?"

Teddi insisted, "Oh no, Abba, we did not steal this spear from anyone, I tell you the truth!"

Abba Libanos carefully inspected the make and design of the spear and soon realized this was no ordinary weapon. And it definitely was not fashioned in Aksum or anywhere near this part of the world.

"Is it Greek, Egyptian, Arabian, Persian or Roman origin?" he thought to himself.

"No, it is not. I perceive it is from beyond this Earthly realm."

Abba Libanos demanded a truthful answer from Teddi and Barnabas, "Where did you find this spear. The truth now."

Teddi sighed, "Hrai, we found it stuck in the ground in Gondar region. Just there by itself with no warrior nearby to claim it, so we took it and wrapped it in this rug. We were going to take it to Aksum and try to sell. Honest truth, Abba!"

Abba Libanos said, "Hrai, I believe you, son." Then looked at the spear again and made an immediate decision.

"We will purchase this spear from you and the rug it was wrapped in. For a good price."

Teddi reponded, "Oh, thank you, Abba. I do not even know how much to sell it to you, but... uh."

Abba Libanos took out a pouch of Aksumite gold coins and opened it in front of Teddi's eyes and said, "about 20 gold Aksumite coins. That should be more than enough."

Teddi and Barnabas' faces lit up, and Teddi said,

"Oh U-wa, that is more than enough Abba. Thank you so much! In fact, we will also let you have a couple of lanterns and another rug if you like!"

Abba Libanos and the manakos with him took the spear wrapped in the rug and their other purchases and strapped it to the back of one of their donkeys before they continued traveling south.

The merchants thanked the Bahetawi and manakos, bowed and nodded excessively in reverences and gratitude.

"Thank you, Abba. Thank you, manakos. Egziabeher yimeskan."

Six Warrior Mal'ekt Flying in to the Rescue.
Jerome Matiyas © 2018

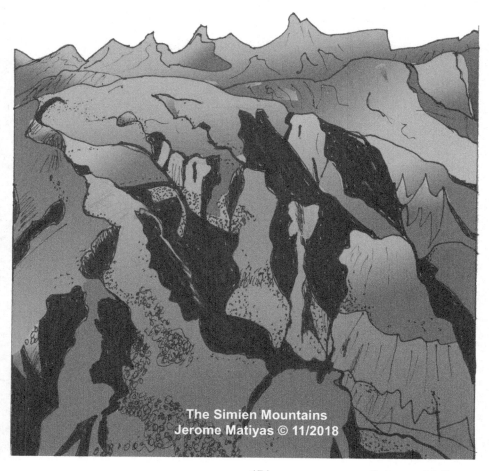

The Simien Mountains
Jerome Matiyas © 11/2018

God's Divine Weapons
Various Weapons of The Lord and His Angels

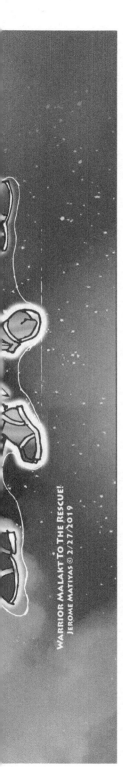

Ezekiel 9:1-2
...Cause those who are in charge of the city to draw near, every man with his **destroying weapon** in his hand.
Behold, **six men** came from the way of the upper gate, which lies toward the north, every man with his slaughter weapon in his hand...

Job 19:29
Be afraid of the **sword**, for wrath brings the punishments of the **sword**, that you may know there is a judgment.

Jeremiah 51:20-21
You are my **battle axe** and weapons of war: and with you will I break in pieces the nations; and with you will I destroy kingdoms; and with you will I break in pieces the horse and his rider;

Jeremiah 23:29
Isn't my word like fire? says Yahweh; and like a **hammer** that breaks the rock in pieces?

Zechariah 9:14
The LORD will be seen over them; and his **arrow** will go flash like lightning.

Psalm 18:14
He sent out his **arrows**, and scattered them; Yes, great lightning bolts, and routed them.

Psalm 45:3-5
3.Strap your **sword** on your thigh, mighty one: your splendor and your majesty. 4.In your majesty ride on victoriously on behalf of truth, humility, and righteousness. Let your right hand display awesome deeds. 5.Your **arrows** are sharp. The nations fall under you, with arrows in the heart of the king's enemies.

Psalm 77:17,18
The clouds poured out water. The skies resounded with thunder. Your **arrows** also flashed around. The voice of your thunder was in the whirlwind. The **lightnings** lit up the world. The earth trembled and shook.

Jeremiah 46:4
Harness the horses, and get up, you horsemen, and stand forth with your **helmets**; furbish the **spears**, put on the coats of mail.

Ezekiel 21:9
Son of man, prophesy, and say, Thus says Yahweh: Say, A **sword, a sword**, it is sharpened, and also furbished;

2 Corinthians 10:4
The **weapons of our warfare** are not the weapons of the world. Instead, they have **divine power** to demolish strongholds.

Verses from the World English Bible.
https://worldenglishbible.org/

Gihon Village: The River Man   J. Matlyas © 5/22/2018

Chapter 8

Chapter 8

Gihon Village

(Part1: The River Man)

Mamoosh! Come on Mamoosh, let's go!" the voice of an energetic young boy called out to his Samen wolf puppy. "Hey, wait for me Mamoosh! You're a fast little dog, aren't you? Ha Ha Ha!" The boy jeered at his pup who ran ahead of him in the grassy moorlands somewhere in the uncharted areas of Habeshinia in the far outskirts of the Aksumite Empire.

"Rrreff! Reff, Reff, Reff, Reff!", the cute pup replied as it bounced around through the green savannah, spinning around occasionally with its tongue hanging out his mouth to see if his boy master was still following him. The pup looked like a ball of reddish-brown fur with a bushy tail and white highlight around his mouth, under belly and feet. An animal that was very common in this part of Habeshinia, endemic to the Samen Mountains and environs, living in the wild in packs hunting mole rats, and other critters for meat, but not usually known to associate themselves with mankind. Yet somehow this boy and his wolf-cub have become best of friends.

As the two ran around in the grasslands playing fetch with each other, Mamoosh the wolf cub darts off towards a nearby river stream, which was part of the famous *Abay River*. In more ancient times this river was called the *Gihon River*, because many of the locales believed this was the very same river mentioned in the *Orit Zaladat* – The Book of Genesis – the first of the five books written by the prophet Moses, Gihon being one of the four rivers that flowed out of the Garden of Eden. Mamoosh ran off to the banks of the Gihon River, and the sight of a *tankwa* caught in some reed bushes near the bank sparks his attention. He walked up to it with tail wagging speedily from side to side and began to sniff, sniff at it, walked around it and looked it up and down then sniffed at it some more. Not that Mamoosh had never seen a tankwa boat before but he believed he could smell a person inside this one. He stood up on two hind legs to see who or what was inside but Mamoosh a too little to see over the rim.

"Where are you Mamoosh? You think you can hide from me! I will find you!!" the boy declared pretending to be serious.

Rrreff, Reff!!" the puppy barked in response, still sniffing and tried to look into the 7-foot-long boat.

"I can hear yooooou. I can hear you, and I will FIND YOU!!"

"Rrrreefffff, reff, reff, reff, reff." Mamoosh barked more rapidly to let his boy master and play friend find him quicker.

The boy reached the bank of the river and saw his pup sniffing and scratching away at a tankwa.

Hawey! Mamoosh! There you are boy. And what do you have there, my friend? You found a big *tankwa*? Too little to climb in aren't you. You're not a big boy like ME!"

The boy was about 7 years old, of medium dark brown complexion, with a round face and big brown eyes, and a tuft of curly dark brown hair on the top of his head towards the front, the rest of his hair trimmed low on the sides and back of his head. He wore modest none-descriptive beige and brown clothing, and no shoes or sandals on his feet he ran towards the dog and the boat of interest. Several little frogs jumped off into the bushes and the river to get out of his way. He approached the boat quickly and was tall enough to peer inside. To his surprise, there was a young man laying in the tankwa, unconscious and covered with tree branches. The boy had no idea if the man was asleep or dead.

He gasped, "Gasp!, OOOhh, look Mamoosh, It... It's a man." his voice lowered to a whisper, "You found a man, sleeping in the boat." The boy picked up the wolf pup to show him what he saw. Mamoosh finally saw the man in the boat and growled and sniffed some more. It's a young man who was not moving. He had bruises on his face, a cut on his left eyebrow, and his body covered with leaves and tree branches. But he appeared to still be alive, in a deep sleep. It was Mekonnen, the warrior from Aksum, who passed out in the tankwa the night before after running for miles for his life from the Qataliyan and the Hell Hounds.

"I wonder where he is from, Mamoosh. Looks like he is hurt. There is blood and bruises on his face." Said the boy with concern, then with a burst of sudden revelation, He called out to the man lying there,

"Selam, Egzeya! – Hello, My Lord! – Are you awake! Are you hurt?" The man in the boat let out a long groan as he tried to respond but could not.

"Uhhgnn."

Egzi, can you hear me? Are you well?" the boy called out again, only to get more groans from Mekonnen, who was too dehydrated from running for hours, and succumbed to the bite marks wounds on his arm from the hound that caused some loss of blood and possibly the beginning of an infection.

"Uhhgnn." was the only sound Mekonnen could summon again.

"He's trying the speak, but can't, Mamoosh. I think he is unwell."

"Reff, Reff!" Mamoosh replied in the affirmative.

"We must rescue this man in the tankwa!!! Come on Mamoosh; quick we must tell someone in the village! Let's run and tell Egzi Jallel!"
And off the two youthful creatures ran back to their village that was not very far away.

It took them less than two minutes to reach the village that was near the banks of both sides of the Abay River in an enclave. The layout of the village consisted of a unique array of round houses, back dropped at the base by trees and steep cliff sides that shaded the village from the sun for half the day, which was carved out into cozy caves inhabited by families and decorated inside just like the interior of any round house with furniture, pottery, carpets, candles and stoves for brewing *bunna* and cooking meals. Ornate rugs, ropes, and ladders hang down from these cave homes with some caves accentuated by wooden constructions of sturdy scaffolding that look more like elevated mini front porches, walkway and bridges. This commune looked somewhat familiar but unique at the same time, best described as a combination of round, thatched roofed, brick homes as in most rural villages, monastic caves often seen on the outskirts of Aksum, Asmara and most larger cities in the kingdom in the north and the classic style of Aksumite architecture but at a simplified and miniature scale.

Amidst this beautiful and concealed riverside community, the boy and the wolf pup found a dark-skinned man in his early 40s with a round, very neatly coiffed puff of hair on his head. His hair was so neat and perfectly round at the edges, with the front chiseled to a point like a triangle pointing downward on his forehead. It looked like it was carved out of wood or molded from black clay, so neat it was.

"Egzi Jallel! Excuse me for disturbing you! Please come quickly! We found a man in a tankwa by the river. Come and see him quickly!!

At first, Egzi Jallel did not move from his spot, drinking bunna in peace with his wife and two young men with him, but he realizes what the boy was saying and looked up at him slowly and asked. "What you mean a man in a tankwa? There are always men rowing down the river in tankwas?"

"No, No, this man was not moving! He is sleeping but not waking up. Mamoosh found him! Come on and see, Egzeya, my Lord!"

"Hrai, Hrai, calm down, Yonatan," he said to the boy. "I will come along with you and see for myself." Egzi Jallel summons the two other young men with him, one of them was actually his son, to come with him, accompanied with their spears and a sword just in case self-defense was needed, although this was a very peaceful village where no one has ever had to take up weapons to defend themselves from evil-doers for almost ten years.

Yonatan and Mamoosh lead the way to the man in the boat with much more urgency than Egzi Jallel and the two men within but they all got there eventually. "See, look! There he is!" said Yonatan softly as if to not awaken Mekonnen from his deep sleep but with excitement still in his facial expressions, eyes wide open and jaws slack. Pointing at the boat, he adds,

"He's sleeping in the tankwa." Jallel and the two young men peer into the tankwa cautiously, lifting the branched to see Mekonnen unconscious with the serious wound on his left arm.

"Hmm. I see his arm is wounded pretty badly." Egzi Jallel enquirers. "From his apparel, I can tell he is from Aksum. Definitely a warrior or royal guard. He sure has come a long way. Far from home indeed. Come, boys, instead of lifting him out of the boat let us just lift up and carry the boat to the village with him still in it."

Egzi Jallel and one young man each lifted the boat from opposite ends while the second young man and Yonatan heaved from the middle of it. Yonatan, of course, being shorter than the three grown men, struggle to reach the center of the boat but he tried anyway to pitch in. Mamoosh, ran around them with his four little legs, panting and wagging his tail to give moral support.

When they got to the village, there was quite a stir as people got curious as to what Egzi Jallel and company was bringing into their abode and who the person was inside the boat. They emerged out of their houses and climbed down from their caves; a few went closer, some staying afar off. Men, women, children, and toddlers. Young and old, big and small, dark, brown and lighter skin tone. Straight, curly and tightly coiled hair. They trickled out to Jallel like ants to a piece of meat.

"*Hrai*, now do not crowd him! He needs air to breath!" Egzi Jallel commanded the crowds. An older woman approached Jallel,

"You can bring him up to my home, Egzi Jallel. We can take care of him there."

"Thank you, Wayzero Ebyan," said Jallel. "And please, take care of his arm and the cut on his forehead above his eye. It looks like he was attacked by an animal of sorts."

"U-wa, Egzi Jallel."

Soon, they dragged the tankwa to a nearby round house, and the two young men lift Mekonnen's limp body from out of the tankwa and laid him on a decorative Egyptian rug on the floor, propping his head up with some sheets. They realized his clothes are wet and smelly, so the men got the women out of the house and took off his outer warrior shirt, under shirt and outer pants and replaced them with dry robes and a sheet. Mekonnen was still unconscious but groaned in his sleep as if he was dreaming or uncomfortable in some way. Then they noticed beads of sweat started forming on his face and arms and the older woman Ebyan perceived this to mean he was growing hot with a fever, most likely from an infection brought on by the animal bite on his arm, plus the shear exhaustion from running in the wilderness for hours for his life. What they did not know was that the bite was not from an ordinary creature from this world so it may not be an ordinary fever either.

"Quickly, bring some medicine, ointments and cool water for me. Ask Nuhamin, Please! She will know where my medicines are for animal bites!" Ebyan stated with urgency.

Immediately, Yonatan bolted out of the house shouting, "I and Mamoosh will go get Nuhamin!" Off he and the pup ran pass some chickens and a few sheep towards the steep mountain cliffs where the holes for the cave entrances can be seen. He ran up to the one he knew Nuhamin lived in and called out,

"Nuhaminnnnnn!!! Emm Ebyan wants you to bring the ointment and medicines. Nowwww!!!"

Inside, the one named Nuhamin was startled that Yonatan would scream out her name so loudly and embarrass her while she spoke with her friends, a girl close to Nuhamin's age named Meena and the twins Almaz and Enku, who were damsels younger than her at 12 years old. Nuhamin herself was about 18 or 19 years old, with a beautiful, oval-shaped face and dark brown, smooth skin, and a small circular nose ring in her right nostril. And long curly, black hair, flowing gloriously in waves and curls over her shoulders down to the middle of her back. It's usually styled in the traditional *shuroba* hairstyle, braided in the front, top and sides in rows, a little thicker than the way it's done in the north in Aksum and Eritrea, but now it was all loosened out, framing her lovely and intelligent face beautifully, ready to be braided later.

She sighed and said to her friends. "That little boy has such a big mouth, does he? Why does he have to scream out my name like that for the whole village to hear?" As she sprang to her feet from the bed to look outside and down to Yonatan below and replied, "Hrai, big mouth Yoni! Tell her I'm coming!" The wolf-pup Mamoosh barked as if to respond to Nuhamin. She just couldn't resist responding to the cute puppy with a wave of her hand.

"Selam, Mamoosh!"

One of the twins, Almaz, spoke, "Yoni is always up to some mischief! You know what he did to me yesterday? He..."

Her sister Enku cut her off to add, "And he's always with that smelly dog! You know what Mamoosh did yesterday...?"

Nuhamin cut them both off and said, "Come on ladies, help me get these medicines to Emm Ebyan. We will chat later, *Hrai*."

Meena, a slender girl with a smile that can light up a room, was slightly amused by the twin's complained about Yonatan and Mamoosh. She chuckles then added, "I wonder what's happening? Why would *Emm* want medicines and ointment?"

Nuhamin responsed, "Maybe someone got hurt. I guess we will find out when we get there, *Hrai*."

Nuhamin peered down to Yoni again and asked, "Yoniye! Where is Wayzero Ebyan now?"

Rubbing Mamoosh's head and neck he replied, "She's in Egzi Jallel's home. Mamoosh and I found a man in a boat in the river! We pulled him out, and he's hurt."

"Oh, really!" Nuhamin responded. Nuhamin and Meena looked at each other simultaneously with curious expressions on their faces, their interests now perked. "Is that true, Yoni? Are you just making that up?"

Yonatan replied, "Oh Yes, Numeen. That is honest to Egziabeher true!! No lie!" He points to Mamoosh, "Mamoosh found him first and then I second. Ask Mamoosh he will tell you!"

With tail wagging and tongue hanging out his mouth Mamoosh barked in response, "Reff, Reff!"

Looking at the little faces below, Nuhamin some how believed Yoni and the pup are telling the truth, despite their reputation for playful pranks. This time Yoni could be telling the truth. Nuhamin turns her head slightly to the left to look at them sideways and said, "Hrai, tell Emm I'm coming."

The four girls Nuhamin, Meena, Almaz, and Enku, climbed down the steps of rock and walk briskly towards Ebyan's house nearby. Nuhamin knows exactly where the herbal medicine and ointment shelves are and grabs up a few bottles and leaf wrappings then head over to Egzi Jallel's home.

"How odd to find a man alive in a tankwa and to pull him out of the river. Where could he be from?" she thought to herself.

As the four ladies walk towards Egzi Jallel's house at the front of the village, suddenly Yonatan and Mamoosh jumped out from behind a wall to startle the twins on purpose.

"Yaaahh!" he screamed with a scowl on his face, arms outwards with fingers curved to simulate the claw grips of a ferocious beast. The girls scream, "Eeeeaaak!" and try to hit Yoni with flaying arms as soon as they realized it was him up to his mischief again.

"Yoni, stop it! Why are so wild?!" Almaz yelled as she ran after Yonatan trying to hit him, but he dodged her swinging arms.

"You and Mamoosh are worse than, ANIMALS! You are MONSTERS" Enku screamed and also trying to hit Yoni, but he was too fast for both of them, running, dodging and twisting his body to avoid the girl's blows, while Mamoosh naps and grabs on to the hem of their dresses with his little mouth.

Usually, Nuhamin and Meena would intervene to stop the younger ones

Betty Amare as Nuhamin, © Jerome Matiyas 1/27/2012

from getting out of hand, but this time they just glance at them briefly and kept walking, considering Wayzero Ebyan's request for the medicines was more important and curious to see the new stranger that washed up on their shores.

Less than 3 minutes later they arrive at Egzi Jallel's home and gives the medicines to Ebyan. "Selam Emm. Here are the medical herbs you asked for, Wayzero Ebyan," said Nuhamin as she and Meena approached the old lady with respect. Still, the girls were curious to see the ill young warrior lay

186   © Jerome Matiyas

there with beads of sweat forming on his face, neck, and arms, groaning and moving his head slowly from side to side, not just in pain and agony but also as if he was dreaming. Most likely a bad dream, Nuhamin thought, perhaps replaying in his head the rough experiences he had that caused him to be seriously injured and far from home. Now she and Meena could not help but stare at the helpless stranger, and noticed how young he was, yet still a bit older than they were.

"Is he going to be alright, Emm Ebyan?" Nuhamin asked with genuine concern.

"Once I get the right herb on his arm and have him drink some medicinal tea then he should begin to recover."

Meena's typically happy face now became wrinkled at her eye brows as she saw the gash on Mekonnen left eye brow and bite wound on his fore arm and how it was changing to a dark purple color and spread to his biceps and wrist.

"His arm doesn't look too good, doesn't it, *Emm*." she added.

"No, it doesn't, child. Now don't just stand there staring, you two! Help me! Go boil some hot water and find strips of cloth for me to clean his wounds!"

Immediately Nuhamin and Meena hurried to fetch hot water and cloth for Ebyan, while a couple of men came in to remove Mekonnen's wet shirt as he groaned in pain. The wounded warrior's eyes were still closed as if he was wrestling with a bad dream that accompany the wound. Actually, he was. In his dreams and subconscious, he was still running for his life from the hooded Qataliyan and the wretched hounds. His pursuers seemed more elusive and menacing this time. Popping in and out of shadows to strike at him and appearing from behind trees randomly to taunt him with treats like.

"You will DIE!" "You will NEVER escape!" We will CATCH you and TEAR YOU APART!" "You are TRAPPED in darkness with US!" were the words they threw at him as he sprang through the forest and scaled the Samen mountain range like a hayyal ibex. Definitely more like a nightmare it was, as it seemed all too real as he felt and sensed everything from when it happened the day before when he was wide awake and in flight. In fact, the pain and terror felt worse now than when he was awake as there was an extra dimension that amplified sensations in this subconscious realm between dream and reality.

Immediately, Ebyan inspected the medicines the girl left with her, opening bottles to smell them and unwrapped leaves to reveal the contents. The scent of medicinal herbs and ointment begin to fill the air in the house and Ebyan begins to hum a sacred hymn from the Dawit Mezmur (Psalms of David) to anoint the atmosphere and intone herself to the Spirit of the

Almighty One who created the world and the power to heal and guide the hands of mankind to invoke healing.

While she applied the ointments on Mekonnen's arm, she passed a bottle of medicine under his nose for him to smell and wake up, Nuhamin and Meena return with the hot water and clean cloth. Ebyan thanked them and dipped the cloths in the water then wiped his arm and his forehead and neck while she still sang hymns. She cleaned the wounds on Mekonnen's arm, and eyebrow then applied more fresh ointments on them, paying special attention to the serious one on his arm. Nuhamin and Meena watched on and assisted the elderly lady when she asked for help. Almaz and Enku peeked through the doorway occasionally but felt it would be disrespectful to just walk straight in. They tried to lift Mekonnen's head to get him to drink some water from a clay cup to put up to his mouth, but it proved difficult since he was still stuck in his unconscious dream state.

Two hours later when Ebyan was done doing all she could for the ailing warrior, Mekonnen stopped groaning and fell asleep. That night he began to groan again and sweat profusely. His arm started pulsating in pain more than before, and he tossed and turned his head as he had a nightmare again. This time it was a night terror where he could see dark figures surrounding and taunting him. He had the sickening feeling he was now connected to the wretched cloaked ones and the hounds in a strange supernatural way because of the bite wound from one of the evil hounds. Like the infection from the saliva was traveling through his body, going to his heart and mind. Then a gravelly voice in his mind from one of the dark beings before him in the spirit realm said,

"We have you now. A poison has been injected into your body through the bite on your arm. It will travel through your body and take over your heart, soul, and mind. You will become like one of us!
Hah, Ha, Ha, Ha, Haaaaaaaah!"

The voice in Mekonnen head was terrifying and caused him to feel more fearful and ill. He sweated and groaned. He tried to escape from the evil dark ones but could not move. Then he looked down and saw he was bound in chained about his body and legs. Seemed like they appeared out of thin air for he did not remember being subdued and bound. Mekonnen did not know if he was just having a bad dream, or if this was happening to him for real. Or maybe he was found by the cloaked Qataliyan and hounds and pulled out of the boat from the river. He just could not pin point the moment it happened in his memory. If it ever happened as all. Whatever was the truth, what he felt at that point seemed very real. And was he really poisoned by the bite? Can they really take over his body and soul to cause him to transform into one of them? He had no way of knowing if that was the truth or a lie from the pit of Hell. Was this happening for real or was it all in his head, in his dreams? Mekonnen wished it was the latter, but he had no way finding out for certain.

Egzi Jallel, sleeping on a rug on the floor in the same room, heard struggling and pain rumbling out of his guest. He sprang off the floor and attempted to comfort the wounded warrior with water and affirming words, but to no avail. The warrior seemed to be lost and trapped in his own nightmare and pain. It was already quite late in the night, but Jallel sents for Wayzero Ebyan to return with her medicines. "Berrisa, go over to Wayzero Ebyan's home and ask her to come back and help this young man, please. Apologize to her on my behalf for awaking her this late at night." Egzi Jallel declared to his son, a young man about 5 years younger than Mekonnen.

"Yes, Abbaa! As fast as I can!" Berrisa replied and darted out the house and up the path to Ebyan's home with a touch lamp in hand to light his way in the darkness.

Awaken

Meanwhile, in the wilderness on the outskirts of the Gihon village, a mysterious figure covered in grayish robes about his body and covering over his head sat in the darkness at the base of a great tree. Suddenly, his eyes opened, as if awakened by an internal call. He remained seated, staring straight ahead into the dark, moonlit forest. He was not hindered by the darkness, for he could see clearly as if it was evening time of the day. Neither could the trees hinder his sight, for he could see the Gihon village from not too far away, but far enough to have a full panoramic view. His breathing was slow and deep; his heart beat steadily. He was focused. Focused on the sound of a young man in the village, groaning, struggling and crying out in the darkness of his own dreams, and his emotional and physical scars. A young man lost in the dark, demented parts of the spiritual realm, he senses.

"It is time." declared a deep voice inside the head of the mysterious figure in the wilderness, his eyes glowing brightly as a lantern.

"Time to wake up."

The voice spook again.

The figure, slowly and deliberately arose from the base of the tree, literally peeling himself off from it, as vines and shrubs clung to his clothes and robes as if he had been sitting there for a long time. Vines broke, twigs snapped, leaves fell off his head and shoulders, and insects scurried from underneath him as he rose uprightly with a staff in hand, almost as tall as he was at about 6 feet. He arched his back and lifts his head till his neck and back crackled from stiffness. He turned his head from side to side and moves his shoulder up and down and front and back to snap more joints and relieve more stiffness. He took in a deep breath, exhales, then took one step forward. Then another and another. Until he was walking determinedly towards his destination, Gihon Village. His purpose and motive, whether good or bad was unknown. Not even himself. He only listened to the voice inside his head.

Jerome Matiyas © 2010

Jerome Matiyas © 2010

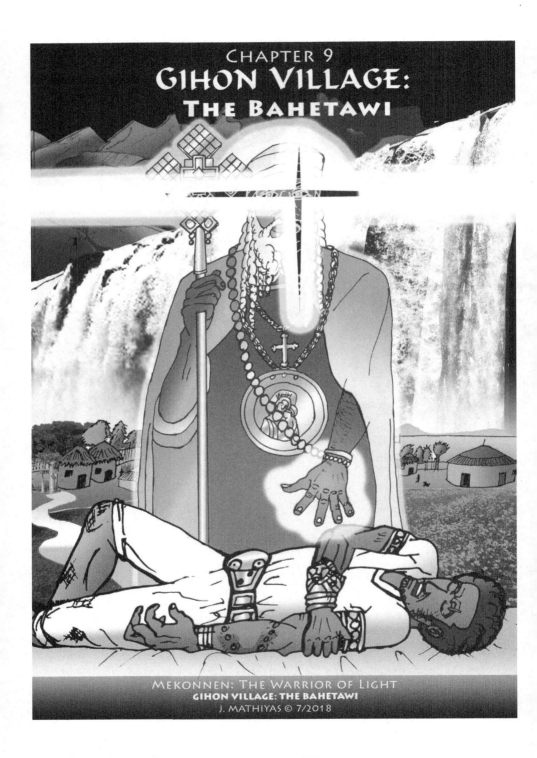

Chapter 9

Chapter 9

Gihon Village
(Part 2: The Bahetawi)

B ack at the village, Ebyan was at the bed side of the warrior, disappointed that the fever was not going away and his arm was not healing, but got worst. The dark purple mark had spread to the warrior's hand and shoulder. Egzi Jallel, his wife Lelisa and son Berissa were in the room next to the bed and look on in pity and concern.

"I don't know why the ointment did not work, Egzi Jallel." Ebyan mourned. "It seems like this wound is of some darker origins than a mere dog bite, or even a galeda baboon bite."

"Egziabeher help this young man. Try whatever you can, Wayzero Ebyan. In the mean time, we will just have to pray to Egziabeher for healing."

Ebyan cleaned Mekonnen's wounds again and applied more ointments, while Egzi Jallel, his wife, and son and another young lady from the village who helps Ebyan all prayed and sang a hymn.

While they sang, a commotion ensued outside as the dogs, chickens, sheep, goats started waking up and making noises as if it was day time. The people then start waking up to look outside to see a bright light and the figure of a man with a bright glowing lantern in his hand walking through the villages. Nuhaman woke up to the commotion and look outside herself to see. To her surprise, a man in light-colored robes and a hood over his head, concealing his face was walking quietly through the village. But more shockingly she saw the bright light was not coming from a lantern the man was holding, for his had none but a staff in his right hand, but it was has face that shone that brightly. Also, shockingly, she recognized his walk and believed she knew him. Meena awakened and walked quickly to the window next to her friend to see what was going on outside.

"Numeen, what's happening out there?"

With her eyes wide open and jaws slack she replied,

"It's him. He is back."

Back at Egzi Jallel's house as Ebyan continued to tend to him, Berissa stood by the door and heard the noises outside. He saw lamps and candles were being lit as villagers and animals awoke in the middle of the night. As he kept looking outside, he noticed a light coming up the path towards the house. As the light approached, the moonlit path became even brighter as the person came closer.

"Someone is coming up the path to the house, *Abbaa* and *Ayyoo*."

"Who is it, son? Can you see?" asked Lelisa.

Berrisa looked again, and to his shock and horror, the face of the person approaching the house was glowing like a Mal'ak. His eyes widened, and his heartbeat sped up as if the leap out his chest, with mouth opened in aghast. Yet despite the unusual glowing brightness, Berrisa recognized who it was.

"Abbaa! Ayyoo! It's... it's him! He's is back!"

"Who is back, son! Speak up!" Jallel exclaimed.

"He's back! The Bahetawi!"

"He Has Returned"

Egzi Jallel stood to his feet in excitement, mouth slightly open as if ready to say something.

"After all this time. He has returned. Just in time. Please, open the door, son, and let him in."

Berrisa opened the door, and in walked, the strange figure. his face glowed, flooding the room with immense light as if it was midday.

Ebyan stepped away from Mekonnen's bedside and bowed as was customary in respect saying, *"Egziabeher tabaraka, Egzaya– God Bless you, my Lord."* Jallel, his wife, and son and the other woman make the same gesture, stepped aside and bowed. They looked away from the light because it was so bright and blinding, and convicting. Convicting because it was not the light of the man bearing it, but they recognized it as the light of the Lord Egziabeher, Almighty Creator of the world. It was the same light that shone on the face of Moses after he returned from Mount Sinai with the Ten Commandments and the same light that shone on the face of Henok as he walked with Egziabeher for 300 years.

Without saying a word, the figure, the Bahetawi, as Berrisa revealed, walked up to the bedside of the troubled warrior Mekonnen, who was moaning and groaning in his sleep, sweating with arm infected. As the glowing figure approached the unconscious Mekonnen, the warrior's body began to shake and tremble excessively. He never opened his eyes to see who was before him, but the dark shadowing figures that taunt him in his dreams could sense something was happening on the other side. They were being challenged by the presence of Light.

"Oh, no! What is happening! What is that BRIGHT LIGHT!!" screamed one of the dark creatures with red eyes, cringing and blocking his face from the brightness illuminating from Mekonnen's own dream body and soul.

The Bahetawi lifted his staff and touched Mekonnen wounded arm with the other hand and declared,

"Be gone, dark creatures! Leave this child of Egziabeher alone!"

On the other side of the dream and spirit realm, the dark figures hissed and growled, blocking their eyes as they stepped back.

"We are LOSING HIM!" growled one of them "We must not lose him. We MUST have him!"

The Bahetawi recanted, "Oh No, you foul spirits! You will not have this one. Be gone in the name of IYESUS KRESTOS!! SON OF THE LIVNG EGZIABEHER!!"

The dark demons screamed, pulled hoods over their heads and dispersed into the darkness on the other side of the spirit realm, never being seen or heard in the house of Egzi Jallel, but only the Bahetawi, Mekonnen and the dark ones heard.

"Now I pray in the name of Iyesus Kristos, be healed."

Immediately the warrior Mekonnen's left arm healed and the purple discoloration dissolved in front of everyone's eyes that saw it in the room. His arm returned back to the natural brown color. A dark liquid oozed out of the teeth mark wounds; the bright-faced Bahetawi was able to wipe it off with a cloth before it touched the bed. The fever disappeared, and Mekonnen became silent and sound asleep.

The Bahetawi turned around, and everyone in the house lifted their heads. He spoke,

"He is well now. Give him some water to drink, then let him sleep." Then he turned around and walked out the door, back outside and down the path towards the wilderness again from whence he came, but down a different path out through the village entrance.

Jallel, Ebyan and the rest rushed to Mekonnen's side to their surprise he was asleep, and his arm was back to normal with just teeth mark prints indicating where he was bitten. His fever was gone, and he was not groaning in pain anymore. Ebyan placed a cup of water to the warrior's lips, and without even opening his eyes he gulps it down quickly. A second cup was given, and he also gulps that down in haste. Then he falls fast asleep and in three minutes he could be heard snoring quietly, as he drifts into pleasant dreamland.

"Egziabeher Amlak Temisgan! Almighty God of gods be praised! Exclaimed Ebyan and then Jallel and his wife. Berrisa was still just wide eyed, and jaw dropped at what he just saw.

Outside, a small crowd gathered to inquire about what happened and if everything was okay. A few also asked if "The Bahetawi" had returned. Even Yonatan and Mamoosh were among the curious gathering, but Nuhamin, Meena, and the twins remained inside.

"Egzi Jallel, how is the man from the river, is he feeling better? Is he Well?

Yonatan asked persistently.

"Yes, Yoni he is doing better, much better. Now go back home and back to sleep, Eshi."

Egzi Jallel, who did not want to give too much information to the crowd about what happened since it was late at night, responded,

"Everything is okay, my friends and family. Our guest is doing well now. Please, return to your homes and to your beds. Amasaganalehu!"

Yoni's Plan

The following morning, the people of Gihon village were still chattering about what happened last night. Nuhamin and Meena arose early in the morning and went over to Egzi Jallel's home to find out if the stranger was doing well before they even began their daily morning shores. It was only natural for them to be curious since they brought the medicines over for Ebyan when it was urgent. But Egzi Jallel just gave them short answers and refused to let them see the warrior as not to disturb him from sleep so that he can recover fully. Meanwhile as the able-bodied villagers were busy going about their morning duties of gathering wood for fire to cook a meal and prepare bunna over an open fire, and prepared *tef* to make injera, Yoni and Mamoosh were about to carry out their plan to sneak into Egzi Jallel's house to get a closer look at the warrior, the "River Man", who was recovering from his wounds.

"Eshi Mamoosh," said Yoni as he picked up the wolf pup, "I will lift you up to the window so you can climb through, then I will climb in after you, eshi!",

Mamoosh barked, "Reff!" in agreement.

Tiptoeing, Yoni lifted the pup to the square window sill; then he hoisted himself up to it. As he adjusted himself to sit and move his legs over from outside to inside, the pup lost his balance and fell over to the inside of the house. Fortunately, he was not hurt, because the window was not very high on the inside.

Yoni climbed in and jumped down to the floor to see the warrior Mekonnen fast asleep on a mat/bed on the floor in the middle of the room. Yoni felt excited to be this close to the warrior and Mamoosh was just as curious as he walk up to the sleeping warrior and begins to sniff his arm, then up to his shoulder and face then to the other side of the warrior's bed.

Yoni crawled closer on all fours like a dog himself to the warrior's face, gazed at his hair and face as he breathed in his sleep. But the warrior may not have been as deep in sleep and dreams anymore, as he sensed he was not alone and smelled a dog and human boy breath in his nostril, he slowly began to open his eyes. Mamoosh's tail wagged faster, and Yoni's mouth opened wider with fascination. Suddenly the awakened warrior was startled to see two faces staring at him, and he jumped up with a shout. "Hooaah!"

The boy and pup were also startled and jumped back suddenly to the floor.

Mamoosh began to bark loudly, "Rref, Ref, ref, rrreff, ref, ref!"

Mekonnen exclaimed, "Who are you... And where am I?!"

Yoni was too fascinated to answer the warrior, and Mamoosh could not stop barking.

Egzi Jallel, his son, and two other men, nearby heard the commotion and quickly realized it was coming from his house. Nuhamin and Meena were further away gathering wood and also heard the commotion, so they hastened their pace to get closer.

Jallel's Greeting

Jallel mused with a sigh to himself but loud enough for the other men to hear him, "Oh, Yoni. You just could not resist and had to sneak into my house huh?" He jumped to his feet and ran to the front door of his house. Berrisa ran to the same window Yoni and Mamoosh climbed through. Jallel opens the door to find three startled creatures in his house.

"Yoni, you had to, huh? Why won't you let the man sleep? Jallel said as Mamoosh was still barking. "Come on, get out with your dog and let the man rest! Be quiet Mamoosh!" Mamoosh heard Egzi Jallel, understood, complied, and ran out the door. But Yoni stayed on the floor, hoping to see if the River Man will speak. Jallel apologized to Mekonnen in his best Ge'ez tongue, "Yikerta, Egzi Hawey! I am sorry my Lord for waking you up! We wanted you to rest and recover from your injuries. How do you feel, Lord? Are you well?

Mekonnen paused, nodded his head and replied, "U-wa, I believe I am well?" Unsure of himself, he remembered his ordeal and injuries a few days before then raised his arm that was previously bitten by a diabolical hound and was astonished to see it was healed. He touched it with his other hand and confirmed, "I am well. My arm... it... it is healed!"

"U-wa, Thank Egziabeher. You have been healed! Egziabeher yemaskan!" Egzi Jallel replied.

"But how?" Mekonnen asked.

"Abba Shiloh prayed and interceded for you."

"Abba Sh... Shiloh. Who is that? Mekonnen asked.

"The Bahetawi. Abba Shiloh the Bahetawi was here last night then he left. He had not been seen for weeks then he suddenly appeared from the wilderness to pray for you. Who are you, *Egzi*? I mean, *Semeka man naw?*"

"*Semeya Mekonnen.*" Mekonnen responsed. "I am from Aksum."

Jallel responded then asked, "*Semeya Jallel naw. Hawey*, are you a *Masfint*, or *Negus* from the royal and holy city?"

"*Iyyaseh!*" Mekonnen replied. "*Ana Masta-tsabə. Harawi Negusawi Sarwe za-Aksum* – I am a Warrior. A Soldier of the Royal Army of Aksum. I am one of the warriors from the royal palace."

Jallel: "Oh, I see! You are very far from home, my Lord. But have no fear, you are safe here with us. Until you have recovered and ready to return."

Yoni was transfixed by the warrior's words as he let Jallel where he hailed from. He sat staring with his jaw dropped open.

Egzi Jallel continued as he gestured with his right arm to the village, "This village is called Giyhon. It is small, only about 50 of us from different regions and tribes of different languages. We all came together to live as one family. You are welcome to stay here in peace as long as like."

Mekonnen had questions to asked about his exact location in the empire at the moment but was too weak and famished even to think clearly. "Uh, do you have food? I am hungry. And *wuha,* please. Thank you."

"Oh yes, we have food for you, Lord. I shall bring for you. Come on Yoni, let us go get some injera for our guest!"

Yoni slowly stood to his dirty little feet and bows, "Egzi Mekonnen." and walked quickly out the door with Egzi Jallel, while he looked back at the tired warrior.

As Lord Jallel and Yoni left Mekonnen noticed some of the people outside through the door trying to get a look at him. But closest to the doorway entrance was Nuhamin and Meena trying to peak inside to get a closer look at the recovering warrior for few seconds. Then Egzi Jallel closed the door behind him so no one could see Mekonnen inside and he could not see outside.

Meena said, "Oh, it looks like our river man is awake now." with a broad smile as she looked at Nuhamin who nodded and calmly added, "It seems more like he has returned from the grips of *Mal'aka Mot* – the Angel of Death. It's a miracle he is still alive." Meena added, "Let us pray he does not bring the Angel of Death with him to our quiet village. Whatever chased him here from Aksum may still be looking for him, right Nuhamin?"

Nuhamin: "Egziabeher be our *galab* – our shield – to protect us from the

Angel of Death then." Meena affirms, "Amen!" Then the two girls walk away to return to Wezaro Ebyna and their morning chores.

Mekonnen, as he laid on the bed with a slight headache, thought one of the girls outside looked familiar but could not remember where he thought he saw her before. At the moment all he knew for sure was that he was hungry and wanted food, and lots of it. His growling stomach agreed.

Injera Masob

Moments later, Mekonnen smelt the aroma of *doro* and *beg*, which was stewed chicken and lamb meat, with seasoned spices, gradually permeated the air he breath. He could not see where the smell came from but sensed it come close. As he sniffed the air, the anticipation made his stomach growl louder. Then in walked Lord Jallel followed by about six more men from the village, one of them carried a colorful woven basket called a *masob*. It was about three feet high, two feet in diameter and shaped like two upside-down cone funnels stacked on top each other. The top of it was a cover that resembled a mountain with a steep peak. It reminded Mekonnen of the mountain peak of Ras Dajen. The young men placed the *masob* in front of Mekonnen, who could smell the aroma of stewed lamb meat, cabbages, goat cheese and hot spices like *meetmeeta* and *birbir* emanated from under the cover. His mouth salivated, and eyes widened. Then in walked the older, motherly woman Ebyan with a pitcher of water in her hand and a young girl with her walked towards him with an empty bucket and placed it on the floor next to him. It didn't occur to Mekonnen what was the purpose of the bucket and pitcher of water until the old lady said with a smile on her wrinkled but pleasant face, "Good morning, son! Now let us wash those filthy hands of yours before you eat. Hrai? Now hold your hands over the bucket."

Mekonnen responded with a look of confusion, mainly because he was so hungry, but then it quickly occurred they were preparing to feed him. He turned his upper body and extended both hands to the side above the tin bucket as Ebyan tilted the pitch and poured fresh rain water onto the warrior's hands. He robbed his hands together while still facing towards the masob placed in front of him. While the washing continued the men sat on small stools, they brought with them to sit around the masob with their new guest. After about half a minute Ebyan stopped pouring, the young girl dried Mekonnen's hands with a towel hung on her shoulders, picked up the bucket and left the room with mother Ebyan.

Lord Jallel sat next to Mekonnen on the left side and began, "Selamta, my friend! We thought you would like some food to eat!" Before he finished his sentence one of the men across the masob with Mekonnen removed the woven cover to reveal a platter of delicious Habeshinian delicacies. It was a large round platter carpeted with an injera with the heaps of stewed lamb, chicken, white goat cheese, spices mitmita and berbere and vegetables on top of it. It looked like a beautiful work of art to the warrior as he felt as if he had not seen or eaten food in a week. So much he did not even notice one of the men sitting with him handing him a roll of injera to begin, Mekonnen just dove right in, tearing a piece of injera that supports the food and grabbing a handful of lamb stew with it then shoving it into his mouth. As he chewed his food like a ravenous dog the men looked at each other assumed, but they dear not laugh, knowing their guest had been through some type of ordeal or trauma, and probably had not eaten in days.

Two rolls of injera were placed in front of Mekonnen, and the other men began to join their guest in the meal. The eight men ate in silence for a while then Jallel interrupted, "So, how is your arm?"

Mekonnen responded while still chewing and glancing at the healed briuses on his arm, "It is much better *chew* my Lord. *chew, chew* Thank you." Lord Jallel responded, "Hawey, Egziabeher Yamesgan! Praise be the Lord God!"

Then Mekonnen remembered, as he had almost forgotten how his arm came to be healed, "Hawey, there was an old man! He prayed for me, and he healed me! Where is he! Please thank him for me, please!"

"Hawey, that was Abba Shiloh! But do not thank him. You must thank *Egziabeher Amlak*, the Lord God of all the worlds, for healing you! Abba Shiloh is merely a servant and a vessel. He will tell you this himself!"

Mekonnen: "Oh. Oh yes of course. I meant, thank Egziabeher. That is correct." As he took a bite of lamb and mitmita roll into a piece of injera a recent memory slowly creeps into his conscious. He remembered the promise he made to Egziabeher the most high when he was running from the dark creatures in the forest before diving over the waterfall into the river. He remembered declaring he would serve Egziabeher if his life was spared, and it was. Then he remembered the golden belt that was given to him in the Negus' palace and how it flashed several times when he was in the wilderness. That was strange indeed.

He slowly took another bite and remembered the dream, or was it a vision, of running through a valley, grabbing a sword from an altar, slaying evil creatures that pursued him. Then running away from a dragon, up a sacred mountain to a bright realm. "What was that place?", Mekonnen asked himself.

"Was I in, *Samayat*?" He paused from chewing, "And, there was someone that spoke to me. Who was that? Was that, The Lord!" Mekonnen touched his waste and looked down to see if the belt was still there, and it was, but it was not glowing to be conspicuous. It's interesting how the belt could sometimes not draw attention to itself. That's when it dawn on him that everything that happened to him and his warrior companions was real and was not a dream.

Mekonnen turned to Lord Jallel and said, "Many things have happened to me these past few days. What day is it, my Lord?"

Jallel: "It is the fourth day of the week."

Mekonnen: "Oh no! It has been almost a week since I left Aksum! It cannot be!"

Jallel: "So it is true! You are from Aksum?"

Mekonnen: "U-wa!"

Jallel: "Oh! I can tell by how you speak. You have very far from home, but not very far from the Empire."

Mekonnen: "Where am I, and where is this place in the Empire."

Jallel: "This is Gihon village! You're on the south eastern end of Tsana Hayk. Tissitsat waterfall is not too far from here. So is Bahar Dar. And the Abay River, where we found you..."

Mekonnen: "On the south eastern side of Tsana Hayk?! How did I get way over here? The last thing I remember I was in Gultosh. Then the south side of Samen mountains. Then there was a waterfall I jumps into and... this cannot been! I most have ran farther than I thought."

Jallel: "Perhaps you were caught in an underground water stream, my Lord."

Mekonnen: "Perhaps. I don't know. Just seems impossible to be so far behind the lake Tsana."

Mekonnen took another mouthful of food and continued. "This village, so say, is called mandar what? Gihon?"

Jallel: "U-wa, Gihon Mandar."

One of the men interrupted, "Named after one of the rivers in the Garden of Eden like described in the *Orit* – The Octateuch!" (Consisting of the first eight book of the Bible.)

Jallel added, "U-wa, that is correct my son. Mekonnen, this is my son Berissa."

Mekonnen extended his wrist for Berissa to grab hold of it to shake.

"Awo, an honor to meet you."

Then the rest of the men around the masob followed by introducing themselves to Mekonnen one by one.

"My name is Giyorgis"

"I am Hamid."

"I am Odek."

"I am Awale."

"My name is Desta."

"I am Kuyo."

Mekonnen replied, "An honor to meet all of you. And I thank you for your kindness and this food. I owe you my services to you. How can I ever repay?"

Giyorgis responded, "You do not have to repay us. It is our honor to serve any stranger who comes to us."

Mekonnen added, "That is a righteous act you do. Egziabeher Yemesgan."

He continued, "So who is the leader of this village?"

Jallel answered "We govern ourselves not be rulers and leaders, but it was Abba Shiloh who began this little gathering."

"Who is this Abba Shiloh I keep hearing about? I should meet him." Mekonnen interjected.

"Abba Shiloh is a Bahetawi. He comes and goes wherever the Egzi leads him. But years ago, he preached the *wangel* to those people who never heard of the Son of Egziabeher before. He went around to different territories sharing the message about the Krestos Iyesus and his sacrifice in Eyerusalem to save our souls. And his power to defeat the enemy, the spiritual armies of Darkness. So, the people who heard him and accepted his message followed him and gathered here to form a new community. A new family. We forsook our ways and built a home here. We are of different clans, people and tongues have come to be as one."

Mekonnen was a bit transfixed by Jallel's little story and responded, "Hawey, that sounds amazing. I've heard the miraculous acts by the Tsadkan, but never from anyone besides them."

Jallel asked, "The who…?"

Mekonnen: "Oh, the Tsadkan. You mean you have not heard of the nine Tsad… Oh, of course, you haven't. You are not from Aksum."

"Where is Abba Shiloh? Can I speak to him? I feel like I should speak to him about what happened to me. What happened in Aksum and in the wilderness. I need a spiritual person to explain to me, help me understand what I saw."

Jallel: "I understand. I do not know where he is now, but I know the area he stays sometimes. I will take you there. Soon."

Mekonnen: "I must see him soon. Can I see him tomorrow?"

Jallel: "Perhaps, I know not. He may even come to you sometime! Abba Shiloh has a way of coming and going as he pleases."

They looked at the platter in the *masob,* and it was empty. All the injera, meat, vegetables and spices were gone, and Mekonnen ate most of it. Afterwards they brought water to wash down the hot spices.

Mekonnen caught something at the corner of his eye. He glanced over to it quickly and saw the little boy Yoni and his dog staring at him through the window. They smiled, and Mekonnen smiles back and waved at them. Jallel turned his head and saw Yoni then stood to his feet and said.

"Hrai, we will go now and let you rest. I will enquire about Abba Shiloh for you."

The men stand up, greeted Mekonnen again as they departed with the stools, masob, and pitcher of water.

Jallel exclaimed, "Eshi Yoni, stop staring and let the man rest, Okay."

Yoni and Mamoosh poke their heads down and disappeared behind the wall beneath the window.

"I thank you so much Egzi Jallel," Mekonnen said with drowsiness in his eyes and voice.

"Thank Egziabeher," Jallel added and left the room with the other men.

Blurred Figure

Mekonnen dozed off to sleep for a few hours then awakened suddenly to find Abba Shiloh sitting on the bed next to him. Was he dreaming or was this really happening? Mekonnen was not sure. Still a bit disoriented and not fully recovered. Abba Shiloh spoke, "Son, you have been recovering nicely, huh. I will have Egzi Jallel bring you to me in the wilderness, Hrai?"

Mekonnen responded to this blurred figure sitting on the bed next to him.

"Abba Shiloh, I want to speak with you. Why do you want the meet in the wilderness? The creatures might be waiting, to kill me. Can you meet me here in this village?

Abba Shiloh responded, "In the wilderness by the caves in the mountains! Egzi Jallel will know where to find me." As Abba Shiloh completed his sentence, the subtle strumming of a stringed instrument was heard coming from outside. The gentle music permeating the air and into Mekonnen's ear lobe. It was subtle and soothing, either a *begena* or a *kirar*, and then a girl's voice was heard gliding on top the musical notes as she sang a song. Mekonnen was still half awake and half asleep, and though he could not hear all the words, he can tell it was a *mezmur*, a song of praise.

As he opened his eyes, he did not see the Bahetawi Shiloh sitting beside him anymore but could hear the beautiful song being played. He slowly sat up in the bed then got up and walked towards the door to see where the angelic voice and music came from. He walked outside and walked around to the side of the house to see a small crowd of villagers sitting and standing around a young girl wearing a white *kemis*, sitting on a stool, playing a kirar and singing.

Mekonnen had found his angelic singer. But who was she? He could not see the girl's face because where he stood he could only see her full mass of curly hair blocking the side of her face. She continued to play, and her audience was mesmerized as Mekonnen walked closer to the crowd. Only a few people noticed or acknowledged him approaching. Finally, he was at an angle where he got a better view of the musician, and he saw it was the one they called Nuhamin. Yes, he remembered he got a glance of her standing outside the door with another girl yesterday, but also felt like he had seen her before. "But where was it I had seen her before?" Mekonnen thought to himself.

Girl with the Kirar

As she continued playing the *kirar* the young lady Nuhamin sang a song in Ge'ez:

Oh, Egziabeher Hawey
I sing this song to you on the kirar
You are the wonderful counselor
Almighty creator, of all the worlds

You show us your love
You gave us the Word
Sent from above
You gave us the Spirit
Sent like a dove
To sit on our head, and live in our heart
To bring light to the world
As you did from the start
In the Garden of Eden
Man's very first home
Like Earth from Heaven
Life flows from your throne

Sing glory to Egziabeher
Sing glory to Him
The Son and the Father, the Spirit within
The melakt sing Glory Halleluyah
The people sing Glory Halleluyah
The creatures sing Glory Halleluyah
The kerubel sing Glory Halleluyah
The serufel sing Glory Halleluyah
All creation sing Glory Glory Halleluyah

Then the rest of the people gathered around her joined her to repeat those last seven lines of the song two more times. Afterward, they cheered and shrilled,

"Elelelelelelelelelelelelelel!!"

Like Paradise.

This little gathering made Mekonnen feel relaxed and more at home as it reminds him of the music from choirs and the Daughters of Tsion in the chapels back in Aksum. And the happiness and ululations from the crowd reminded him of the festivals like Masqal and Timkat. That was, of course, before the attack by the dark hooded ones.

He looked around and saw men and women, boys and girls of almost all age groups and of various regional backgrounds inside and outside the Aksumite territories. He noticed people local to the region, including from his own homeland of Tigray in the north, and even further north into Eritrea near Asmara, Afar, and Bilen territories. He noticed some speaking in their dialects from the western regions like Begemeder and Gojjam and from central regions like Agew territories in Wello and Lasta where most of his forefathers were from. He saw a few features commonly originating from the east, possibly from the Harar region, to the sea coast of the Red Sea. Even ones hailing from across the Red Sea from Himyar, Hadhramaut and other regions of Sabaea. Their way of dress and accents when they spook Ge'ez mingled with their native language could confirm this. He also noticed people from Somaliland and Punt in the crowd, including the elderly Ebyan and Awale with whom he shared injera with the day before. And also, Lord Jallel and his family were most certainly of the Oromo people from Borana and surrounding areas in the lush greenery of the southern regions, he presumes. And even the one name Odek was probably from even further south from the lake areas of Kenya, a region Mekonnen only heard about from traveling merchants, and he probably spotted a few like them and other people from Kenya in Aksum passing through to do business during festivals. What a lovely mix of people living together in peace and harmony in this perfect Eden, Mekonnen thought to himself as many of the people of Gihon Village looked at him with beaming welcoming smiles on their faces.

Some of them playfully refered to and greeted him as "River Man" and said, "It's the River Man! How do you feel River Man, are you well?"

This had to be what the Garden of Eden spoken of in the Oracles of the *Orit Zaledat* – The Book of Genesis – was supposed to have been like before being marred by deceit from the serpent that caused the first parents Adam and Hawah to sin. Even the name Gihon was one of the rivers that flowed into the Garden back then. Or what the *Haddis Samayat wa-Haddis Meder*— the New Heavens and New Earth — will be like in the days after the world is judged as written by Yohannes in his Apocalypse writings.

They even had various domesticated and livestock animals and a river nearby to sustain themselves. They grew fruit trees of various kinds like oranges, bananas, ensetes, avacados and romans, and even a field where they grew *tef* to make their own injera which they probably mixed with foods from the people of other regions that do not usually eat their meal with injera. And the village was enclosed in an enclave by a forest and high steep cliffs not too far in the distance about, while the Tis Isat waterfall was just beyond the enclosure to the east. Sometimes, when the village was quiet enough, one could hear the soothing hum of the waterfall and even see the mist rising up from it.

As the young lady continued to play on her kirar the people of Gihon approached Mekonnen one by one, then two by two then three by three and more to greet and welcome him. They asked him if he had recovered and felt better, his name and where he was from. He answered openly and as honestly as he could but then got a bit tired after about half an hour of answering the same questions but still answered them politely anyway. Most of the young and small children were just as curious and fascinated by Mekonnen and wanted to know if he was a warrior or a prince and if he had a sword with him that they can touch. Including Yoni, Almaz, and Enku. Yet Mekonnen's main concern was figuring out how to get back home to Aksum and keep the promise he made to his cousin Meron, to find her brother's murderers and return home safely.

"Meron must think I died like her brother by now, the poor child." Mekonnen thought to himself.

Mekonnen's next concern was speaking with the elusive Abba Shiloh that everyone kept talking about, so he could find out how to defeat or avoid the Cloaked Ones and other creatures out there in the wilderness and get back home to Aksum.

"My name is Nuhamin"
And his third concern was to find out who was that girl, sounding so lovely, playing that beautiful sound on the kirar. Her familiarity kept nagging at his mind, and he felt like he must speak to her.

Just then the girl with the kirar ended her song and stopped playing and was about the stand up as her friend Meena approached her with that signature smile. Mekonnen excused himself from the throng of people and pressed towards her and said,

"Selam Woyzerit, your singing, and skills on the kirar is *sannaya* – beautiful! Your mezmur blessed me!"

"Amaseganalehu, Egzeya," she replied with a nod.

"Play again for me!" Mekonnen blurted out suddenly without even thinking of it.

She replied, "I would, but I must go now for I have shores to attend to, my Lord."

"Hrai! Okay, I see. No need to call me Lord. Seme Mekonnen, naw! Semesh man naw?

She replied, "Semesh Nuhamin naw. An honor to meet you, Mekonnen."

He reached for Nuhamin's hand to shake it to greet her and she did the same with her right hand while still holding the kirar in the left, and bowed slightly. Mekonnen noticed her hands were soft but strong for a young girl who kept busy using her hands. He noticed she was a bit darker in complexion than he was, maybe about two or three shades darker. His being a medium brown, while hers a deeper tone yet still even and smooth. She had soft features in her face and neck, an oval shaped face and big brown eyes framed by a full head of long curly hair like most Habesha women wore it naturally before braiding it to the scalp. Mekonnen finally got to meet this mysterious girl and immediately thought she was a beautiful young lady that looked familiar, but he still cannot remember where he saw her before.

Meena smiled and also offered to greet Mekonnen and introduced herself, "Selam, semesh Meena naw." and Mekonnen reciprocated.

He asked Nuhamin, "So, have you been to Aksum before?"

She replied, "No, I have not. That is very far from here."

Just then Jallel appeared, "Heeeyy! You are awake and alive!" Then he shook Mekonnen's hand and inspected the arm where the teeth marks were still there."

He continued,

"I see you have met Lady Nuhamin and Lady Meena!"

Mekonnen replied, "U-wa, I have, and they are very lovely, I must say. But where is Abba Shiloh? I would like to speak..."

Jallel interrupted, "Oh, Abba Shiloh, is not far, I know not where he is, but I can find him and take you to him later this evening or tomorrow."

Mekonnen insisted, "Today please! Can I see him today?"

Jallel replied, "I cannot make any promises."

Abba Shiloh Appears

Just then a voice resonated through the air, "Salamta, my friends!"

Jallel exclaimed, "There he is! Just in time, you see?"

Mekonnen sighed with relief from his minor anxiety.

The people of Gihon were also happy to see their spiritual leader return after some time.

Abba Shiloh continued, "I have returned, my children. Egziabeher bless all of you and keep you in his love and grace. I have been in his presence for a season and have now returned to tell you the Lord Egziabeher loves you and wants to guard you under the shadow of his wings."

The crowd responded, "Mezgana, Amen, Amen. Egziabeher barakat!

Bless you, Abba Shiloh!"

"Remember to walk in peace and righteousness and fear not the attacks from the enemy for our souls neither the darkness that may come over you. Remember the light of the world and you power you have within you to reflect the light and to displace the darkness."

The crowd agreed with ululations as he stepped towards the people. Some greeted and touch his hands and arms as he walked by or bow as was customary for respect and not for worship as if Abba Shiloh was a higher being nor declared himself an authority or deity over them.

This time the Bahetawi appeared as his normal, non-illuminating self. His face was not glowing as it did two days ago. It was mostly back to his true dark brown complexion, with his white beard and long locks of hair indicating his seniority to everyone in the crowd. His skin was not wrinkly and craggy like most elderly folks in the later years of life, but one can still tell he was of older years. He looked like he may be between 60 and 70 years old, though he may actually be older, and no one may really knew his exact age as most would not dear ask. And he was not obliged to reveal it.

Abba Shiloh's hairs had been locked and braided through the years as he had been living by the Nazarite vow as described in the verses in the *Orit za-Hwelq* – The Book of Numbers (Numbers 6: 1-21) from the *Mashafa Moses* which described taking a vow of devotion and purity. It included: Not letting a razor cut your hair for a lifetime or for a specified duration of time; do not drink any juices made from grape or any fermented fruits that may cause drunkenness. The Nazarite must not be near a dead body; must not live in fornication or adultery; and must devote his time, life and efforts devoted to serving and supplicating to the almighty Egziabeher.

This was the vow that the Judge Samson from the tribe of Dan (from the Book of Judges, chapters 13 to 16) only partially observed unsuccessfully but the Prophet Samuel observed successfully (First Samuel, chapter 1). By the length of his long scraggly hair reaching past his waist, Abba Shiloh had been living this life of devotion for many years, perhaps a couple of decades. Like most monks and devote men, Abba Shiloh wore a cream-colored head wrap, a royal purple under-robe and a bright orange robe on top of it. Around his neck and hanging down to his chest was an Aksumite styled *Masqal* cross, some bead necklaces of various colors, thicknesses and sizes, and a large brass or bronze disk about half a cubit in diameter that feature an engraved and embossed depiction of *Qeddus Mariam* with the *Iyesus Krestos* – Saint Mary with the Christ Jesus – as a child in her arms. At first glance, most Bahetawis usually caught the eye and one's attention in a crowd or ordinarily dressed people. Just like any active *Qasisan* or *Abunat*, Abba Shiloh was revered and respected, though he was not affiliated with a particular Beta

Krestyan. Abba Shiloh was known for bridging gaps between congregations, cultures, languages and even between followers and believers of Iyesus Kristos and the Beta Israel, followers of the teachings of Moses.

Mekonnen finally got the chance to meet Abba Shiloh and thanked him for the prayer and more, "Abba Shiloh, I thank you for your prayers that healed me and rebuked those creatures from my dream. But now I'm seeking answers as to how I got here in Gihon and how do I return safely to Aksum without getting killed by evil creatures."

Abba Shiloh replied, "Oho, U-wa, those evil creatures from the dark realm. *Urah!* I saw them, U-wa! But you must defeat them yourself, my son. You do not need me."

Mekonnen: "But I do need you. I sense what you did to them."

Abba Shiloh: "Then if I can do it then you can also. Just do what I did, Anbessa."

Mekonnen: "But I don't know what you did. You have to teach me how."

Abba Shiloh: "You have the *Qal* – the Word – don't you. Use the *Word,* and you can defeat the enemy with the *Qalat* – the words, Anbessa."

Mekonnen: "*Qalat?* What *Words* do you mean? I do not know what words to say! And I am no Anbessa!"

Abba Shiloh: "Yes you do! You have The *Qal* who can give you the *qalat!* And you can harness words of power!"

Mekonnen got a bit frustrated by the Abba Shiloh's riddles. "Why is he being difficult to understand?" he thought to himself.

Then he sighed and played along, "Hrai, I see. I can do it! But I need your help! I need your assistance, please. I need a teacher and a mentor."

Abba Shiloh: "You speak wisely, but I will think about it for I am busy."

Then he walked away, but he drew close to Jallel, spoke to him briefly for about half a minute, then kept on walking. Mekonnen was left confused by Abba Shiloh's response and seeming lack of care or interested in his plea and dire circumstances.

Jallel walked up to Mekonnen and assured him, "Do not worry Mekonnen because Abba Shiloh just told me to take you to him tomorrow."

Nuhamin playing the kirar.
Jerome Matiyas © 2018

CHAPTER 10
THE ORACLES #1:
ANCIENT SCROLLS

EPHESIANS 6: 10 - 18
FINALLY, MY BRETHREN, BE STRONG IN THE LORD AND IN THE POWER OF HIS MIGHT. 11 PUT ON THE WHOLE ARMOR OF GOD, THAT YOU MAY BE ABLE TO STAND AGAINST THE WILES OF THE DEVIL. (12) FOR WE DO NOT WRESTLE AGAINST FLESH AND BLOOD, BUT AGAINST PRINCIPALITIES, AGAINST POWERS, AGAINST THE RULERS OF [C]THE DARKNESS OF THIS AGE, AGAINST SPIRITUAL HOSTS OF WICKEDNESS IN THE HEAVENLY PLACES. (13) THEREFORE TAKE UP THE WHOLE ARMOR OF GOD, THAT YOU MAY BE ABLE TO WITHSTAND IN THE EVIL DAY, AND HAVING DONE ALL, TO STAND. (14) STAND THEREFORE, HAVING GIRDED YOUR WAIST WITH TRUTH, HAVING PUT ON THE BREASTPLATE OF RIGHTEOUSNESS, (15) AND HAVING SHOD YOUR FEET WITH THE PREPARATION OF THE GOSPEL OF PEACE; (16) ABOVE ALL, TAKING THE SHIELD OF FAITH WITH WHICH YOU WILL BE ABLE TO QUENCH ALL THE FIERY DARTS OF THE WICKED ONE. (17) AND TAKE THE HELMET OF SALVATION, AND THE SWORD OF THE SPIRIT, WHICH IS THE WORD OF GOD; (18) PRAYING ALWAYS WITH ALL PRAYER AND SUPPLICATION IN THE SPIRIT, BEING WATCHFUL TO THIS END WITH ALL PERSEVERANCE AND SUPPLICATION FOR ALL THE SAINTS

HEBREWS 4: 12 - 15
FOR THE WORD OF GOD IS LIVING AND POWERFUL, AND SHARPER THAN ANY TWO-EDGED SWORD, PIERCING, EVEN TO THE DIVISION OF SOUL AND SPIRIT, AND OF JOINTS AND MARROW, AND IS A DISCERNER OF THE THOUGHTS AND INTENTS OF THE HEART.
AND THERE IS NO CREATURE HIDDEN FROM HIS SIGHT, BUT ALL THINGS ARE NAKED AND OPEN TO THE EYES OF HIM TO WHOM WE MUST GIVE ACCOUNT.

MEKONNEN: THE WARRIOR OF LIGHT
THE ORACLES #1: ANCIENT SCROLLS
J. MATHIYAS © 6/2018

Chapter 10

Chapter 10

The Oracles
Part 1:

Ancient Scrolls

Mekonnen was startled awake by that dream of the fiery *anbessa* — a lion — leaping at him again. This time Lord Jallel was already in the room standing by Mekonnen's bedside.

"Arise and shine, Lord Mekonnen!" Jallel saluted the warrior, "I apologize for waking you this early, but it is better if we get a head start before the rest of the village awakens."

Mekonnen yawned, "Hawey, *yawwwwn*, it's okay, Hrai. You didn't wake me. It's the *anbessa* that woke me again."

Jallel was puzzled. "The *anbessa*?"

Mekonnen continued, "I keep having these dreams ever since I've been here. I don't know if it is a dream or a vision. Anyway, must we leave now? It is still early, huh?"

"*U-wa*. Abba Shiloh wants to meet you early. He may want to have breakfast with you."

"Hrai, *yawwwn*, I will go with you."

Mekonnen slid off the bed, washed his face, then together Lord Jallel, and Mekonnen left the house and quietly walked along the path towards the wilderness with the magnificent view of the mountains in the distance ahead of them. The tops of the mountains were partially covered by clouds and early morning fog.

The early hours did not prevent the Samen wolf pup Mamoosh from being awakened by the sound of footsteps, quiet chattering and the scent of two men. Mamoosh sniffed the air and perked up his ears as he sensed movement outside the room he shared with his sleeping master and friend Yoni, still snoring in slumber. The cub peeked through a small hole in the wall to see Lord Jallel and the visitor Mokennen strolling down the main path of the village. Mamoosh made a whimpering sound that awaken Yoni.

Yoni opened his eyes and lifted his head and asked the pup,

"What is it, Mamoosh? What's happening out there?" Yoni got up and pared out the window and saw what Mamoosh saw.

"Oh no! Is the River-man leaving already? But he just got here!"

Curiosity and adventure rarely left this boy, so immediately he made a decision. "We have to follow them and find out where they are going. But we follow them quietly, and not let them know we are following them. Don't let Egzi Jallel see us. Shhh!" Mamoosh whimpered and yawned in agreement.

Meanwhile, Nuhamin was already awake and looking out the window of the house she shared with Meena and the twins. Meena opened her eyes to see her friend paring out the window and asked, "Good morning my sister. What's happening out there?"

Nuhamin replied, "The warrior from Aksum, the one they found in the river. He and Egzi Jallel are just about to leave the village."

Meena opened her eyes wider in surprise. "Hawey, Really! Wonder where they're going?"

Nuhamin made a guess, "I reckon they are going to see Abba Shiloh out there in the mountains."

Meena took a gasp of air. "Why would he take him there? *yawnnnn*," she asked followed by a big yawn and stretched her arms in a V shape above her head. Then she had a thought and asked jokingly as a smile grew on her face, "Do you miss him already, Nuhamin? Is your future love leaving you?"

Nuhamin snapped back, "No, I don't! Be silent! But you know I have my ways of finding out."

Mekonnen and Jallel walked eastward on past the Tis Isat falls that was about a mile away but could still be heard in the distance. The scenery was beautiful as they walked towards the rising sun that was just about to peek above the top of the Samen mountain range. It was a bit cold, so the two men wrapped themselves in white robes over their shoulders to keep themselves warm until it was closer to mid-morning and noon when the sun was brightest and higher up in the sky.

"So, why does the Behatawi Abba Shiloh live out in the wilderness?" Mekonnen asked, "Does he actually live out there or does he live in the village?

Jallel responded, "Abba Shiloh claims he does not have a place to lay his head, but he knows he lives in the Gihon Mandar. It was he who built the foundations for the village years ago. He goes where ever the Spirit leads him. Sometimes Egziabeher leads spiritual men with a mission away from people and into the wilderness for a season to pray and fast and seek his face. Then Egziabeber will lead spiritual men back to the people to preach what he teaches him. With instructions, a prophecy, a warning, or a special word from

Egziabeher, the Almight One."

"Oh, like Iyesus Krestos in the wilderness for 40 days and 40 nights. And Moses also in the Sinai Mountain for 40 days and 40 nights. And other prophets mentioned in the Oracles?" Mekonnen stated from his memory of sacred, ancient writings.

"Correct!" Jallel affirmed.

"Iyesus said the day will come when he is not on the Earth realm that his disciples must fast and pray for the will of Abba Egziabeher to be revealed to his servants. There is a time for fasting and a time for feasting. A time for coming together and a time to come apart for a season."

Mekonnen: "U-wa, I remember those sayings from *Manfas Qedus*. What's the longest he has been gone from the village?"

Jallel: "I think the longest was about 80 days, just before you drifted into the village in that tankwa."

Mekonnen: "Hawey, Oh really!" Mekonnen exclaimed with a bit of surprise and shock at the implications that he may be pivotal in actions of some strange holy man making drastic decisions.

Jallel: "U-wa! There must have been something very significant about your presence that is part of a bigger plan. So you must be humble and try to understand what Egziabeher might be trying to accomplish through you. Listen to what Egziaheber might be trying to say to you through Abba Shiloh. But also remember Abba Shiloh is just a man like you are."

Mekonnen nodded and began to think seriously about what was happening around him that caused a holy man, hundreds of miles away from his home city of Aksum, to go into seclusion for such a long time.

"Am I that important!" he thought to himself. "Maybe I am! How? I know not, but I hope to speak with this Bahetawi and find out today!"

Then Mekonnen stated audibly, "I really need to speak with this Abba Shiloh. I have many questions."

Jallel replied, "Oh, you will have your chance to spend time with him soon enough."

Meanwhile, Yoni and his wolf-pup followed the two men but in the grasses off the path and a good distance behind them. They expected they will not be discovered, as they ducked and sometimes crawled low down in the grass and hid behind trees along the way. Sometimes Yoni picked up the wolf pup and carried him part of the way, so he did not run off and blow their cover.

Abba Shiloh's Amba

Moments later Jallel and Mekonnen approached the foot of the steep side of an amba. "Here we are, Mekonnen. Abba Shiloh's should be up there in one of those caves." Said Jallel, looking up the side of the amba, decorated with rocks, dirt, shrubs and occasional vines streaming down from the top like robes.

"Do we go up to him or will he come down to us!" Mekonnen asked.

"No, I will call him." Jallel replied as he brought both hands up to his mouth making a cup shape then formed a unique whistling sound, that to Mekonnen sounded like a strange bird or nocturnal animal. "OOOooooOOOOOOoooohh!"

At a short distance behind Mamoosh perked his ears up at the unusual sound and began to growl. Yoni whispers, "No, no, be quiet Mamoosh. Stay here."

Jallel stopped but continued looking upward with cup-shaped hands still at his mouth. Then he released the call again. "OOOooooOOOOoooohh!

Still nothing, but just then the wolf pup could not resist any longer and rushed out barking at Jallel. "Raff Raff, Reff, Reff!"

Jallel and Mekonnen turned around to see a familiar canine running towards them.

Jallel sighed, "Oh great, Yoni and Mamoosh followed us. Yoni, where are you hiding?!"

Yoni stood up from crouching behind some bushes and a tree stump and few yards away.

Jallel commanded, "Come over here and take this dog away!"
Yoni ran towards them as Jallel continued looking up for a response.

Mekonnen just smiled and chuckled at the brief interruption.

"Maybe he is not home." Mekonnen assumed.

"Wait for it." Jallel reassured.

Seconds later they noticed a glimmering light like sun rays reflecting off a mirror or glass. It was Abba Shiloh using a small mirror to peak down from a cave about 40 feet up the side of the amba before poking his head out for safety to be sure he recognized the person calling him. Then they noticed a head peeked out from the same cave then a similar sound in response, howling back down to Jallel.

"OOOAooaaOOAAooaaaOOOAAaaahh!"

"That's him. Abba Shiloh."

Mekonnen responded with a quick gasp of air.

Then they saw the figure of Abba Shiloh step out, standing in front the opening of the cave, holding on to both sides with both hands. Just then the winds began to howl and blew harder than before, causing the leaves in the trees too rustle and fly about. Then there was a loud crash in the sky like the sound of a thunder roll above the amba at that moment. Whether that was by design or coincidence, Mekonnen knew not, but it sure was an ominous moment.

Then Abba Shiloh's voice resonated down to the two men, boy, and cub in a clear baritone. "Egziabeher yemisgan my brothers. Mekonnen, climb up here to me!" Then Shiloh dropped a make-shift rope ladder with knots tired all the way up the length of it.

"Well, there is your invitation, my friend," said Jallel.
Before Mekonnen could grab it, Mamoosh ran and grabbed the dangling rope in his teeth, and growled with his body dangling from the rope, his feet not touching the ground.

Jallel shouted, "Mamoosh, No! Leave the rope alone!"
Yoni grabbed Mamoosh and tried to pull the rope out the cub's mouth, "Let go Mamoosh, come on let go."

Mekonnen held on to the rope and stated his appreciation to the wolf-cub, somewhat jokingly, "Thank you Mamoosh for grabbing the rope for me. You are a very helpful dog."

Mamoosh finally released the rope from his mouth.

Mekonnen tugged at the rope, making sure it was secure and sturdy enough to climb and up he hoists himself. He pulled himself up with his arms while supporting on the steep vertical surface of the rugged slope to climb all the way up.

As he climbed Yoni called up to him, "Lord Mekonnen! Are you coming back to the village?"

Mekonnen turned his head to look down and answered back, "Hrai, Yes, I think I will return. Just going for a little while, okay!"

Yoni: "Okay, come back soon!"
Mamoosh barked once in agreement. "Reff!"

Moments later Mekonnen reached the top of the Amba as Abba Shiloh offers his right hand to hoist the warrior up into his cave.

Jallel waved up to Abba Shiloh and Mekonnen, "Hrai, okay, may Egziabeher bless and keep you safe on your journey!" then he turned to Yoni and Mamoosh, "Okay, let's go back you the village. Why did you follow us, Yoni? You should have stayed in bed."
Yoni replied, "We saw the River-man was leaving and wanted to see where you were taking him. Is he coming back? Is he going back to his home?"

Jallel responded, "He is not returning to his home yet. His home his too far away. Abba Shiloh just wants to speak to him and show him some places for a few days; then he'll be back. Then you can ask Mekonnen more questions, Hrai? Now let's walk back and get some breakfast."

Yoni replied, "Aiy! I hope he comes back! I want to ask him if he has a big sword. And if he has a bow and arrow, and if he ever fight in a war. And if he ever chopped a man's head off!"

Jallel refuted, "No, don't ask him that! That is violence Yoni! What did we talk about violence in lessons from the *Mashaf Qedus*?"

Yoni continued, "That violence is bad! Okay, I will ask him instead if he ever saw the *Atse* – the Emperor! And if he is a *mesfin* – a prince. And if he also has a crown. And if he …he…"

So Yoni went on and on making a list in his mind about all the questions he wants to ask the warrior as they walked along the path back to Gihon Village.

Collection of Scrolls and Codices.

"Selam Mekonnen, welcome to my abode." Abba Shiloh saluted.

"Selam nachow, Abba Shiloh, Egziabeher yimesgan," Mekonnen responded with respect for his elder.

"I was just about to brew some *bunna* for us. Please have a seat over here, son," said Abba Shiloh as he guided the warrior to a modest 2 feet high, round, wooden stool in the cave. Mekonnen sat down, and his eyes began to

Many ancient scrolls and codices of the scriptures in Abba Shiloh's collection. Written in many of the languages of the earliest churches. Languages include: Hebrew, Arabic, Ge'ez, Aramaic, Syriac, Coptic, Greek, and Latin.

scan the space in the cave. He counted about four lamps in various locations lighting up the room that was mostly devoid of furniture. There are old embroidered rugs and mats, and sticks propped and tied together with strings to make racks to hang clothes and rags on. On the walls were modest to crude scribblings and drawing of religious symbols, like the masqal crosses, the fish symbol of the early disciples of Iyesus Krestos and the menorah candle sticks of the Beta Israel Jewish religion.

And many scrolls, parchments, and codices indeed are in almost every corner of the room. While Abba Shiloh was in the back of the cave in another section preparing the bunna, Mekonnen looked down at the parchments next to his stool and saw written in Geez, one of the verses from the Orit of Moses or one of the prophetic writings of the *Beluy Kidana Manfas Qeddus* – The Old Testament of the Holy Scriptures. He looked over at another scroll and with his hand nudged it slightly to see the writings inside and found it written in a language he did not understand, but recognized it may be in Hebrew or Aramaic letters. He peeked at another parchment and saw possible Greek writing. Or was it Latin? Mekonnen never considered himself to be one of the scholarly types to enjoy learning foreign languages like the scribes and *Qasisan* in Aksum. Even his oldest brother Medhane was one of those scholarly types who understood those strange writings, but Mekonnen just remained a tough, grunt warrior with a sword and a fist.

Still, the sight of one of these writings in one place, high up in a cave to boot, was impressive to Mekonnen. He knew there were many ambas and monasteries that housed old and even ancient writings from holy men, even the famous *Tsadkan*, the legendary Nine Saints who reside in Aksum now. They brought copies of scriptures and other ancient writings with them from the Holy Land of Israel. Scriptures written in Hebrew, Aramaic, Coptic, and Greek is what he was told, as reported from *Qasisan* and scribes in the churches and palaces.

Even his brother Medhane mentioned this a few times at the family dinner table. That all of these scrolls were being translated into the local Ge'ez language for all Aksumites to read and understand them. All Aksumites willing to read them anyway, and Mekonnen was not one of them, though he believed in their ancient authority and validity. He thought he may not have a choice now but to become more acquainted with these scrolls and parchments, being surrounded by them and in the company of one of the most respected Bahetawi in the land.

Abba Shiloh emerged out of the back of the cave with a small rectangular, wooden tray with a small white bunna pot in the middle of it and two empty white ceramic cups on the sides of it. He placed the tray on the ground between them then began to pour the hot, aromatic *bunna* into the two cups. One cup for himself and the other for his young guest.

"*Yekanyeley*, Thank you, Abba Shiloh," Mekonnen responded as he accepted the small, white ceramic cup of dark coffee placed in front of him.

"I have run out of honey, so if it is not sweet enough for you, you will have to drink it as it is, son." Abba Shiloh stated bluntly.

As Mekonnen took a sip of bunna to his lips, he said, "It is *Sannaya. Yekanyeley*. I like my bunna strong and hot!"

Mekonnen continued, "Abba Shiloh, I see you have a library up here. Many, many scrolls and codices. Very impressive indeed. Why so many of them? Are they all writings from the ancient scriptures and histories? Or something more?"

Abba Shiloh paused and took a sip from his hot cup of strong, bitter bunna, then responded,

"Books are the source of learning and life, my son. Hrrm. Most importantly are the writings from the *Qedus Nabiyyat* – the Holy Prophets – that make up the *Mashaf Qedus*, the Holy Scriptures. Most of them are writings of the ancient prophets, kings and wise men of old. Some are fragments of histories. All are inspired by the words of Egziabeher, which is the source of all life."

Mekonnen took a short gasp of air in agreement with the holy man's statement then took another sip, for his mind was flooded with the burning questions he would like to ask. Then he looked at Abba Shiloh and began to let it all out.

Mekonnen Tells His Story.

"So, Abba Shiloh. I have experienced some strange things in Aksum, and the in the forest, and the mountains before I came here that has been haunting me. And this belt that was given to me in the Emperor's palace, it seems to have some strange powers against... against strange creatures, I encountered with my fellow warriors. First, there were creatures that seem like men at first in white robes and hoods, but skin as black as the night sky. They were like *Qataliyan – Assassins –*, tried to assassinate the Emperor, but failed. The Qasisan and royal court argued amongst themselves them they were the Beta Israel but realized they were not. Because these Qataliyan turned to snakes when struck down. Then they had these horrendous dog-like creatures with them, as large as lions, but monstrous. One of them bit me before I slew it, as you can see by the scars on my arm. Then there was a larger creature that looked like an overgrown, giant gelada baboon, with a red symbol in the center of its chest. Looked like a serpent inside a red circle. A valiant warrior slew that one for us with a spear.

We chased the rest of them after they tried to kidnap a young maiden from Gultosh in Gondar district. Then just when I was about to rescue the maiden from one of the hooded creatures, we fell into a deep chasm to a dark realm under the mountains. Then a band of about six Mal'ekt crash-landed on the amba with us. The Mal'ekt rushed in to rescue us and some little children from the strange dark realm. After the Mel'ekt helped us return the little ones to their homes, we chased after the Qataliyan some more, but we lost them in the wilderness. Our fates were reversed, and they ended up chasing us until we were overcome and scattered in the Samen Mountains. And that's how I ended up jumping into a waterfall and woke up in your village, Abba."

Abba Shiloh nodded as he listened to the warrior. "Hrrrm, Hrai. You had a great adventure and a series of supernatural encounters. Go on. This belt, who gave it to you?"

Mekonnen: "He looked like a young Habesha man like myself. He wore a colorful robe on his back and bowed before me and said *'Egzi Mekonnen!'* and I was surprised he would call me 'Egzi,' then he handed me this golden belt that sparkled and said, *'This is your reward. Your prize for Aman – the Truth.'* So I took it, and he said it was from *'Negusa Nagast wa Egzia Aga'ezt.'* – The King of Kings and Lord of Lords. And at first I thought he meant it was from the Emperor Gabra Masqal who had just given me a pouch of gold coins for saving his life, but then I realize he might have meant the Lord Iyesus Krestos. Then the young man just disappeared, but I saw a bird flying out a window high up in the palace hall. I don't know what happened to that young man. What do you think Abba? Is this belt I'm wearing from the Almighty Egziabeher? Or is it possessed with some sort of spirit?"

Abba Shiloh, not expressing surprise by the series of events described by the young warrior, looked at Mekonnen's belt that was still on his waist and responded with a question, "What is the inscription that's engraved into the belt?"

Mekonnen remembered vaguely what was engraved on it, but he looked down at the belt on his waist and found the engraving the read "*Aman*." On the right and left side of the round buckle engraved with the cross.

"*Aman*. Truth." Mekonnen replied.

Shiloh asked, "Do you remember what the *Mashaf Qedus* says about the Truth?"

Mekonnen, stopped and thought for a second but couldn't remember any specific verses and replied, "*Iyyaseh*, I cannot remember anything right now. But I know the *Mashaf Egziabeher* is Truth."

"You are correct Anbessa, but there is an article of clothing it has been associated with." Abba Shiloh placed his cup of bunna on the tray, got up and reached over for a book, which was a copy of the *Addis Kidan*, the New Testament, written in Ge'ez language of the Aksumites of Habeshinia. He flipped through the pages to a section that was about two thirds through it and handed the codex to Mekonnen with his finger pointing to a specific line."

"Read from right here. From the Epistle to the Ephesians written by the apostle Paulos." He commanded the warrior.

Mekonnen took the book and began to read in Ge'ez,

"Stand therefore having tightened the Et'aqa Amān –Belt of Truth – around your waist, and having on the Malbasa Enged'a Tsedq – Breastplate of Righteousness..." (Eph 6:14).

Mekonnen stopped and contemplated, "So, am I wearing a belt around my waist that can literally represent Truth?"

"It could be." Abba Shiloh replied cryptically but bluntly. "Read the words before it, from the top." He said as he searched through more scrolls and codices to show the warrior.

Mekonnen read from the top of the page:

> *Finally, my brethren, be strong in the Lord and in the power of His might. Put on the whole armor of God, that you may be able to stand against the wiles of the devil.*
>
> *For we do not wrestle against flesh and blood, but against principalities, against powers, against the rulers of the darkness of this age, against spiritual hosts of wickedness in the heavenly places.*
>
> *Therefore take up the whole armor of God, that you may be able to withstand in the evil day, and having done all, to stand. Stand therefore, having <u>girded your waist with Truth</u>, having put on the <u>Breastplate of Righteousness</u>, and having <u>shod your feet with the preparation of the Gospel of Peace</u>; above all, taking the <u>Shield of Faith</u> with which you will be able to quench all the fiery darts of the wicked one.*
>
> *And take the <u>Helmet of Salvation</u>, and the <u>Sword of the Spirit</u>, which is the word of God; praying always with all prayer and supplication in the Spirit, being watchful to this end with all perseverance and supplication for all the saints— and for me, that utterance may be given to me, that I may open my mouth boldly to make known the mystery of the gospel, for which I am an ambassador in chains; that in it I may speak boldly, as I ought to speak.- (Ephesians 6: 10-20)*

Messale = Allegoria

Mekonnen stopped reading, "Hawey, this is powerful. I've heard the *Kesset* read this before, but for the first time, I'm reading it out loud for myself. What does this mean Abba? Am I wearing a physical piece of the Armor of Egzio? Does that mean I have to find more parts of this Armor? How is this possible? I thought this was just an example or what they call, *mə... məssa...*"

"*Məssale*. Or what the Greeks call an *allegoria* – an *allegory*." Abba Shiloh corrected him.

"A story that compares words and objects that share characteristic to explain an idea or mystery better, but has real implications in the Spiritual Realm. What is spiritual and invisible must become physical and visible to the eyes."

"That is strange but amazing." Mekonnen pondered.

"Strange indeed, but powerful and real as the stool you sit on and the scroll you are touching and reading!" Abba Shiloh added.

I perceive there will be more parts the armor Egziabeher want you to have."

"But which is the next one I must find Abba Shiloh?" Mekonnen asked.

"Well, I don't know, but we shall see. I can only guide you, but maybe you have to discover that by yourself. Or ask Ezgiabeher to reveal this to you personally."

Mekonnen searched the words in the sacred codex in his hand and read the item that came after the belt of Truth.

"It says here after having my waist girth with the Truth I must put on, the Breastplate of Righteousness. So obviously that is my next part to put on, hrai? But where would I find this breastplate, Abba Shiloh?"

"Ohhh, the Breastplate of Righteousness is very important, my son." Abba Shiloh said, "I do not know where you shall find it, but I must say to you that *Tsedq* which is Righteousness is very important. The holy oracles speaks very much about being righteous and following after it. But one cannot be in the presence of the Almighty without obtaining righteousness."

"Hrai, well. That young man in the palace gave this belt of Truth to me. Maybe he will suddenly appear, hundreds of stadia away from Aksum, and give the breastplate of righteousness to me also? It seems impossible that he will find me here."

"Ahh, I think if that was the case he would have given it to you in the wilderness when you needed it most. Not only that but also the Shield of Faith and the Sword of the Spirit would have been very useful, hrai?"

Mekonnen: "Oh u-wa, Abba. I could have definitely used those for sure. Why didn't he appear to me then? But those warriors who appeared in the mountains! They were fully armed and amazing in full armor and swords and bows and arrows! You should have seen these men! But I think they were actually Mal'ekt from Samayat! They slew those dark creatures that we were chasing and destroyed their domain where they had those children in chains!"

Abba Shiloh: "Oh, so you saw Mal'ekt!"

Mekonnen: "Not just saw them, but they rescued us. I don't understand why they could not stay with us, but they had some powerful weapons and armor! I thought I dreamt them, but I believe they were real!"

Abba Shiloh: "I believe you, anbessa. And they were real Mal'ekt; it sounds like. I must say that the young man in the palace was also a Mal'ak from Egziabeher's realm. He was the first Mal'ak to appear to you and handed you the belt. Whether or not you should receive the rest the same way, I cannot tell. Egziabeher has a way of doing things differently the next time."

Mekonnen paused and thought for a few seconds then said With revelation in his voice and in his eyes, "Hawey! That makes sense. He probably was a Mal'ak. That's why he disappeared around the column. And I saw a bird flying up the rafter. He changed into the bird that flew away! Egziabeher Hawey!"

Abba Shiloh remained silent to let the young warrior meditate on that little revelation he just had.

Mekonnen: "So, those dark cloaked creatures with the vicious hounds that attacked my warriors and me. And that killed my brother Afeworq. They are *aganenta si'ol* – demons from hell –for sure! Is that right Abba Shiloh?"

Abba Shiloh responded: "I perceive they are so, son. But I must say. Usually righteousness is not obtained from a Mal'ak that gives it to you from Samayat, but is obtained in the heart through the Krestos who blesses mankind with a gift from the Almighty Egziabeher. True righteousness must first come from the heart and soul when you accept His sacrifice and love, Mekonnen."

Mekonnen: "I understand. But I also don't understand all this that happened to me. Why did my brother have to die, and why did I have to get lost far away from my family and kingdom? I should have been equipped before all this happened."

Abba Shiloh: "You are right, bad things seem to happen for no good reason. But there are spiritual battles happening in the Realm of the Spirits, and when there are battles, sometimes the Mal'ekt of Egziabeher prevail and other times the Mal'ekt of Darkness prevail. I can show you the battles recorded in the Oracles of the sacred writings from even in the ancient times of Moses and before the flood in Noah's era for you to better understand what's going on around us."

Mekonnen: "So Abba Shiloh, have you seen these creatures of darkness before and how did you fight them?"

Abba Shiloh: "U-wa. I have seen and fought these creatures before and even much bigger and viler ones. I can tell you stories of my battle experiences with dark creatures, but I will not get into those now."
Mekonnen's interest peaked when the Bahetawi mentioned he had experience battling dark creatures and wanted to hear more.

Abba Shiloh continued, "One thing I can tell you that's very important is the Word of Egziabeher is very powerful and quick sharper than any two-edged Sword that can defeat the enemy, in any realm."

Mekonnen caught on to what Abba Shiloh just said, and with excitement, he read the verse in the Letter to the Ephesians again, "It's right here, '... and take *Sayfa Manfas* – the Sword of the Spirit –, which is the Word of Egziabeher.' That's it! So, I must also find the Sword of the Spirit too, right?"

Abba Shiloh: "That's right, son, but first things first. You must be ready.

One cannot just pick up a sword and run into battle without training and teaching, correct?"

Mekonnen: "U-wa, that is correct, sir. But I already know how to use a sword! I've been trained and fighting with swords for years, Abba! I am ready!"

Abba Shiloh: "But you have not used this type of Sword, my son. This is a *Sword of the Spirit*. Much different. You learn and train to use this sword differently. You learn and study this carefully. This sword of more powerful and dangerous. You use it the wrong way and don't understand it you can destroy yourself and others around you. Other innocent souls that should not be struck by it."

The Helmet Not For Lazy Lions.

Mekonnen became quiet and listened.

Abba Shiloh continued, "If you read what comes before the Sword of the Spirit, you will see what is important."

Mekonnen read, "'...take the Helmet of Salvation...'. So I need to find a helmet before I find the Sword, Abba Shiloh? These are a lot of parts that I must find! I think this will take a long time, maybe too long. I need these weapons right away, Abba Shiloh! I am sorry."

Abba Shiloh, "You see now, you are thinking too much about acquiring actually physical objects, which is thinking about it the wrong way. Before you acquire something in the natural you must first acquire it in the spiritual realm. So you may not have to get a physical helmet that is etched '*Dehnat* – Salvation' in front of it, but you must first accept Salvation in your heart from the Lord Iyesus Krestos before you can see manifestation in the physical."

Mekonnen pondered the words of Abba Shiloh for a minute. Then touched the golden belt on his waist and continued, "But, Abba Shiloh, I was not seeking after Truth before a Mal'ekt gave me this belt of Truth, and it has already saved my life without me asking. So why can't I have the breastplate of Righteousness, the Helmet of Salvation and the Sword of the Spirit handed to me the same way?"

Abba Shiloh responded, "The belt was the first article to start you off and get your attention. Start you off on your journey, and your calling. The rest you acquire in different ways. The Lord works in mysterious ways and does not do the same thing twice. Rarely He does. He may give you a first sign, maybe a second or third, but he will not give everything to you on a silver platter, like the Negus and royals in palaces, just having everything given to them with no effort at all. No growth, no strength, no learning, no discovery. Just laziness. Thus says the Lord! Is that what you want, anbessa? To be a lazy, stupid, fat lion, with no strength and no wisdom? Huh? Well?!"

Mekonnen swallowed hard as his heart began to pound harder in his chest. He knew in his heart that what the crazy Bahetawi said is correct because he has been around royalty for all his life. Though not all of them were lazy and lethargic, certainly not Hade Kaleb or his son Hade Gabra Meskel, at least he did not think so, but many were.

"*Iyyaseh*, Abba Shiloh. I do not want to be lazy, nor dumb and fat."

Abba Shiloh stepped back, took a deep breath, leaned on his staff and said, "I didn't think so. Now, do you believe that Iyesus Krestos is the Son of Egziabeher, the one true creator of all the Realms of Samayat and Meder. And that Iyesus is the son of the Virgin Mariam, that he was conceived of the Manfesawi Qedus – the Holy Spirit – which is from Egziabeher and not from a man? And that Iyesus Krestos lived and proved that he was and is the Elect One prophesied by Moses, Henok, Abraham, Dawit, Esasias, and all the prophets, and that Iyesus was crucified on the *masqal* –the cross – and resurrected from the dead on the third day as it is written in the sacred scrolls and tablets?"

Mekonnen replied without much thought because he absolutely believed everything the holy man just asked him,

"U-wa, Yes, I do believe all and everything that you said about Iyesus Krestos. He is the Son of Egziabeher. And I have met him in a vision."

Abba Shiloh smiled and replied, "*Gerum*! That is wonderful! Now you have the Helmet of Salvation!" he exclaimed pointing at Mekonnen's head then stepped back with a hand on his hip.

Mekonnen lifted his left hand slowly to touch the top of his head, and wondered if a literal golden helmet suddenly appeared upon his head, only to feel nothing but his curly hair.

Abba Shiloh chuckled with laughter, "Hahahahaha! I meant you have the helmet of salvation spiritually, in your heart. Not on top your head. Ha Ha Ha!"

Mekonnen exhaled with a bit of disappointment and dropped his hand down from his head to pick up the cup to his lips to sip his coffee.

Sharp and Dangerous.

"Patience, Anbessa! It does not mean you will not eventually find an actual, physical helmet of salvation on your journey." Abba Shiloh added, then suddenly his facial expression changed to become serious. He looked like he remembered something then began to peek outside his cave opening and looked down to see if anyone was on the ground at the base of the amba or climbing up the robes. The old man's sudden change in mood made Mekonnen a bit concerned. Then he drew closer to Mekonnen and said in a lower whispering tone of voice.

"We must be very careful not to announce too loudly or to everyone the special calling you have in your life. The enemy has his spies and minions who could be lurking in the darkness and will try to sabotage your destiny and try to stop the plan the Almighty has for you. So be careful."

Mekonnen became concerned, "You mean the Qataliyan might be out there trying to follow us?"

Abba Shiloh: "No, I don't think they know what is going on with you or about your purpose yet, but eventually they will figure out what's going on. But it's important they don't find out too early when you're not ready and equipped yet. In fact, we will have to move soon and go to another amba away from here."

Mekonnen: "Oh okay, whatever you think is best, Abba Shiloh."

Abba Shiloh: "Now before we go I want you to read these other verses in the codex here. This one is from the Letter to the Hebrews."

Mekonnen took the new codex from Abba Shiloh's hands; this one has illustrations on every other page, depicting whatever key scene is described in the Ge'ez text on the opposite page. Mekonnen read quietly:

The word of Egziabeher is alive and powerful, and sharper than any two-edged sword, piercing even to the dividing asunder of soul and spirit, and of the joints and marrow, and is a discerner of the thoughts and intents of the heart.
– Hebrews 4:12)

Abba Shiloh added, "You see, this is how I was able to speak out and rebuke the dark ones that were tormenting you in your dreams when I found you unconscious in bed with the bite mark on your arm. Remember that?"

Mekonnen: "Yes, I remember. You spoke words and told them to leave me alone. And there was a bright light, and they fled."

Abba Shiloh: "Correct! They fled because the Word of Egziabeher was the Sword that defeated them. It was not my own power, but because I know Iyesus Krestos and he knows me and my heart, and I believe in him and have faith in his light, then I was able to rebuke them in that Light.

Remember the story in the Book of the Acts of the Apostles and the seven sons of Sceva who tried to cast out demons from a man in the name of Iyesus Krestos, but the demons still overcame the brothers. Why? Because they did not know the Son of Egziabeher personally, they only heard about him. So they were not ready the fight with the Word, they were not ready to fight with the Sword of the Spirit. They did not have the Helmet of Salvation, nor the Breastplate of Righteousness, in the spirit of their souls. That could happen to you if you are not ready, Mekonnen."

Mekonnen listened intently. Abba Shiloh continued,

"Here is another one to read, from the *Ləbbunā Solomon* – Wisdom of Solomon."

Mekonenn read:

*The Lord will take his zeal as his **whole armor**,*
And will arm all creation to repeal his enemies;
*He will put on **righteousness as a breastplate**,*
*And wear impartial **justice as a helmet**;*
*He will take holiness as an **invincible shield**,*
*And **sharpen stern wrath for a sword**,*
And creation will join with him
to fight against his frenzied foes
– Wisdom of Solomon 5:17-20

Abba Shiloh: "See, even Negus Solomon wrote about the whole armor of Egziabeher before Paulos the Apostle did describe it even more valiantly. Read this one from the *Orit Zaladat* – the Book of Genesis."

Mekonnen read:

"So Egziabeher drove out the man, and he placed at the east of the Garden of Eden the kerubel and a Flaming Sword which turned every way, to guard the way to the tree of life."
– Genesis 3:24.

Abba Shiloh: "This is the first mention of the powerful Sword with flames. This is the Sword of the Spirit of the Word that existed before the creation of the world. Notice no one is said to be wielding the Sword. It moves around the garden, without the handling of the kerubel."

Mekonnen: "That is amazing! I never paid attention to that detail in that verse before."

Abba Shiloh: "Most people don't. Now read about the Sword again in the *Abu Qalamsis* – The Book of the Apocalypse of John."

Mekonnen read:

And out of his mouth goes a sharp Sword, that with it he should smite the nations: and he shall rule them with the rod of iron: and he treads the winepress of the fierceness of the wrath of the Almighty Egziabeher."
Revelation 19:15

Abba Shiloh: "With the Sword of His mouth. He shall speak the Word and destroy the evil from all the nations. But for you and I, Mekonnen, we do not slay and battle against flesh and blood and other nations and tribes, No No No! We battle against the dark spirits! The powers, principalities, thrones, and rulers of darkness in the spiritual realm. Those cloaked, Dark *Qataliyan*, the diabolical hounds and vile creatures you saw in the mountains and in your dreams, those are the powers of Darkness from the spiritual realm. And those who rule over them and dispatch them upon the kingdoms of earth to do evil deeds and cause iniquity, lawlessness, and discord among mankind, they are the dark forces of wickedness who rule in the high places of the spiritual realms."

As Abba Shiloh spoke Mekonnen was speechless as he pictured everything the holy man spook about in his mind's eye.

My Eyes Are Opened Now.

Mekonnen: "This is amazing Abba Shiloh. My eyes are open now. I understand I must be prepared first before going off on my own."
Abba Shiloh: "And you will not be alone. There will be other warriors like you, from *Samayat wa Meder* – the Heavens and Earth – to fight these battles with you."

Mekonnen: "Where can we find these other warriors!"

Abba Shiloh: "They can be found anywhere! In places scattered near and far! There are not many true warriors in the spirit realms. They can be found in places least expected. In fact, we must start our journey soon."

As Abba Shiloh spoke, he searched among his heap of scrolls and pulled out a large map and laid it on the hard floor. It showed a map of the whole land of Ethiopia, Kush and Sheba, including the territories belonging to the Empire of Aksum. Abba Shiloh kneeled over and pointed with his right index finger to the area on the map showing where they were currently located, which is the south eastern end of *Tsana Hayq* – Lake Tsana – and not far from the Tis Isat waterfalls.

Abba Shiloh: "So this is where we are now. Near the Tis Isat waterfall." Say Abba Shiloh as he pointed on the map, then he slid his finger upwards to the north of the lake as he said, "And this is where you came from, through Goltush, you said."

Then he slid his finger to the east over the Samen Mountains,

"And you mentioned you chased the Qataliyan into the Samen Mountains, where you got separated from your comrades. So we can assume and calculate the dark ones are still trekking through the mountains but to the east and south, away from the Beta Israel territory. At least for now, until they try to gather strength again."

Mekonnen: "I think they might try to enter into one of the nearby towns like Gashema, Roha or Maqdala. What do you think Abba?"

"You may be correct, anbessa!" Abba Shiloh agreed. "But they may stay and gather in the mountains for a while before picking one of the towns in that area." Abba Shiloh added.

Mekonnen continued, "It will not be good when they victimize another city. I wish I can go and warn them, but it's so far away. And as you said, I'm not equipped. I'm not ready yet."

Abba Shiloh, "Hawey, but in time you will be. I can make arrangements to send a messenger to warn them. But first, we must eat and leave this cave. I will take you to another amba with more scrolls, and then we rendezvous to a third amba to commune with more bahetawi cohorts of mine."

Abba Shiloh continued as he gathered meat, goat cheeses and potatoes on a plate of injera for their breakfast:

"We must get you ready, starting with your heart and soul. We must get your spirit prepared to get your faith strong and ready. The season of *Tsom Abiyy* – Lent – is approaching soon. We must do the 55 days praying and fasting, reading and studying the *Mashaf Qedus* and other sacred writings and history books as well. I will take you to other holy men and bahetawi, and you will learn from them as well. And you will learn, and I will show you how to fight! Fight not in the flesh but in the Spiritual Realm. Then you will be strong and equipped enough to be a warrior of Egziabeher to defeat the Agents of Darkness, travel the roads back up to your family and friends in Aksum, the glorious royal city!"

Mekonnen: "Hrai, Abba Shiloh. If you can help me be ready to defeat the creatures of Darkness, I will go with you and let you teach me the ways of being a warrior for Egziabeher. But after this, I just want to go home and be a warrior for Aksum like I did before."

Abba Shiloh: "Well, anbessa, you should know that becoming a warrior of Light for Egziabeher should be for life, or you can lapse in being ready to fight the enemy."

Mekonnen: "*Hrai*, well we will see, Abba."

Abba Shiloh: "Worry not. Once you are equipped you become more comfortable and rest in the power of the Almighty, but not your own."

Leaping Through the Shadows.

Meanwhile, in the same location in the Samen Mountains where Abba Shiloh was pointing to on the map, was the same vicinity area where the Qataliyan were converging towards in order to gather around the *Egzi Berur Gwanti* – Lord Silver Gauntlet – and Waynaba for further instructions.

The Qataliyan, still cloaked in white robes with serpentine designs on the fringes, the oversized, demonic Hell-Hounds and three giant gelada-type monsters among them, leap and sprint from shadow to shadow that were cast by the trees and rock formations in the wilderness under the rising sun. They glided and leap in acrobatic fashions, in and out of shadows as if they were stepping through doorways leading to gloomy palace corridors. Each gloomy corridor took the nefarious creatures closer to the enclosure in the mountains where the Silver Gauntlet waited, ready to speak to his vile subjects.

They grunted and murmured as they gathered in a crescent shape, facing their Lord Silver Gauntlet who stood proud with the jar that contained Waynaba's soul on the stone-slabbed ground at his right, and three more cloaked figures stood on each side to his left and right. Their faces also veiled with hoods over their heads but adorned in robes designed slightly different from the Qataliyan, yet still serpentine in nature. Whether they were men of Earthly origins or not was unknown. Standing guard on the far left is one massive gelada-type beast, breathed with its huge mouth open, and revealed its large, terrible teeth.

The Silver Gauntlet lifted his right silver-gloved hand to motion his audience to be silent. They stopped murmuring immediately.

He then began to speak.

Mekonnen and Abba Shiloh search the scriptures diligently for clues on where and how to acquire the parts of the armor of Egziabeher in order to defeat the agents of darkness in the form of Qataliyan, hell-hounds, serpents and other creatures of Darkness.

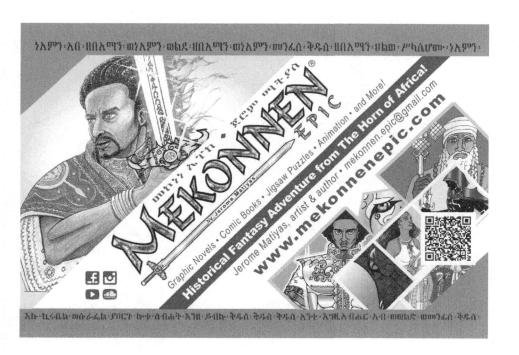

Chapter 11

Chapter 11

The Oracles
Part 2:

Quest for Righteousness

The Silver Gauntlet Speaks.

The Silver Gauntlet lifted his right silver gloved hand to motion his audience to be silent. They stopped murmuring immediately.

He then began to speak:

"Fellow comrades! We have been defeated in a battle, but we have not lost the war! We must come together and plan a new strategy, considering what we may be up against. A challenge we did not anticipate. The full resurrection of Waynaba has been interrupted and now delayed. Now we must recap to figure out what hindered our plans.

I now summon forth **Egzi Barnusa-Mot! – Lord Death Cloak!** Step forward and give me a report on what happened. What did you and your dark shadow-warriors encounter?"

The one named Barnusa-Mot, which means Death Cloak of Black Felt, stepped forward. He was the tallest cloaked Qatali among them, about 9 to 10 feet tall. This was the same Dark Qatali that faced Mekonnen in Goltush when he rescued the young maiden from the broken house. He was also responsible for other villainous acts which he shall reveal. He spoke in a deep, tonal but unnatural voice,

"In Aksum, we attacked the city, and my attempt to impale the Hade Gabra Masqal with a spear was disrupted by a warrior guard's shield. But I was successful in killing the Negus Phenias of the Beta Israel with my scimitar blades, destabilizing their kingdom in the Samen Mountains, and sparking further suspicions between the two kingdoms against each other. Then we headed south and west to the town of Goltush in the other Beta Israel region of Gondar to gather more maidens and children for sacrifice.

After we grabbed one of the maidens from Goltush and made our way through the forest to the amba, there was a flash of bright light that blinded some of us for a while. Then it happened again in the Samen mountains when we chased the Aksumite warriors."

The Silver Gauntlet: "You saw a bright light. Was it a Mal'ak with them?"

Death Cloak: "I did not perceive so, my Lord. This happened before the Mal'ekt crashed into our domain under the mountain. One of the Aksumites and the maiden fell into the dark domain when the Mal'ekt crashed down. We think he was the source on the bright flash of light."

Silver Gauntlet: "From an Aksumite warrior? You mean a man of flesh and blood, as in a son of Adam? Was there anything unusual about him?"

Death Cloak: "I confronted him face to face in Goltush before we headed for the forest to the mountain. He seemed like a common man. Yes, a son of Adam. But what he wore on his waist seemed different. Like it had glowing qualities to it that might be supernatural."

Silver Gauntlet: "Oh, is that so? The warrior may be wearing a special belt that was prayed for by one of the *Qasisan* or one of the nine *Tsadkan* – Nine Righteous Ones. They have been known to bless and pray over items and pour holy *meron* or holy water over them. Or could be a piece of clothing they actually wore and the power remained on the clothes before given to him as a present. That protective power may or may not wear off."

Death Cloak: "Whatever it is, it was powerful enough to make us blind."

Silver Gauntlet: "Fair enough. At least he is not a Mal'ak, nor wielding a sword and shield from the Mal'ekt. What about his sword, was it supernaturally powerful?"

Death Cloak: "No, My Lord. He struck me with his sword, and it barely grazed me. I recovered in minutes. If it was from the Mal'ekt, it would have wounded me more deeply. Even destroyed me."

Silver Gauntlet: "This warrior with the sanctified clothing may be the reason why the Mal'ekt came in the first place. He may be a beacon for them to follow. If you take out the beacon, we will have less Mal'ekt to deal with. Do you think you can overcome this Aksumite warrior and bring him to me so I can destroy his clothing with my own magically empowered ring?" Lord Silver Gauntlet raised his fist to show a glowing emerald ring on his index finger. This mysterious ring was the source for his power to control the dark spirits and handle the soul of Waynaba. None of the creatures knew from whence he acquired such a ring, but with it, he has some control over all of them, both to their benefit and their advantage. They would rather be free than be controlled. But without it, they would not be roaming the Earth Realms, but in chains of darkness or restraint to shadows only. That's why they will not dear challenge or retaliate because he can cast them back into dark bondage.

Silver Gauntlet: "Do you think you can overcome this mare man warrior?"

Death Cloak: "Yes! My Lord! I believe I can hunt him down. I shall find him, I shall defeat him, and I shall **kill** him!"

Silver Gauntlet: "That is good to hear. I hope you can accomplish what you boast. This will help us bring Waynaba back sooner rather than later. I command you now to take 12 dark cloaked warriors with you and find this Aksumite with the flashing garments. If you are not able to kill him, then bring him alive. If you cannot destroy him or his garments or separate him from his flashing garments, then leave him be, and return here to me with a report."

Death Cloak: "Yes my Lord. It will be my personal pleasure to take him down!"

Waynaba Speaks.

Waynaba was getting anxious in his jar and wants to speak. "Pleasssse make it fassst and remove this hindransss ssso I can have more little ones and maiden's blood for sssacrifice. I want to get out of this jar and into a new body, Now!"

Lord Silver Gauntlet: "I know you are getting impatience Lord Waynaba, but right now will not be a good idea to seek more little ones and young maidens. The Mal'ekt from on high will still be waiting and protecting the little ones and maidens in the land for a time. If the Death Cloak and his Dark warriors go out there now and lay hands on little ones, they will surely be found and destroyed. Then you will be found quickly and also destroyed, never to return to this *Medrawi Mangəst* – Earthly Realm – again."

Waynaba snarled: "Hhhhharrr! How do you know thisssss! Maybe there is a chanssssss it might work!"

Silver Gauntlet: "No, I have seen it happen before. You and the rest of your followers will be caught and destroyed if you go to the wrong place at the wrong time."

Waynaba: "Sssssoo. When can we move closer to Aksssum then? I must take back the throne from the Negusss of Aksum, and I will have revenge on the sssseed of the dreaded Nigist of Shhhheba and Negus Sssssolomon and his priestsss from Eyerusssalem!"

Silver Gauntlet: "Oh yes, you will have your revenge! But it is not the time to go up north to Aksum either. That will be a bad strategy. We are in the best region right now."

Waynaba: "What are you talking about?! I do not know thisss place! Thisss isss, not my territory! The plan wasss to return me to Aksssum and the citiesss of the north. Not on the back side of this sssstupid mountain with little towns and stinking farmers! Curse this place! You know I long to be back in Aksssum!"

Silver Gauntlet: "I am aware of your longings, Waynaba, and that is still part of the plan. And this town of Roha is not as quaint as you would think it is. But right now there are no followers of you or any snake cults in the north. Everyone goes to Beta Krestyan regularly, and there are numerous Qasisan, Qeddusan, and Mal'ekt from on high in the region. All other forms of worship are punishable by banishment, imprisonment, or death! You will not stand a chance up there. Even if there are a few secret followers of you, there will not be enough for them to rise up and willingly offer sacrifices and worship for you to grow stronger. Instead, you will grow weaker and die the second death, and slip back into the pits of *Siol* (Seoul/Hell) from whence I conjured up your spirit."

Waynaba hissed: "Hissss! Oh No! I am DOOMED!"

Silver Gauntlet: "Oh no, you are not doomed yet. You see, over here we are further away from the epicenter of Aksum, so we are more likely to find secret followers of you, Lord Waynaba, Lord of Serpents, and they will be willing to offer themselves or their daughters as sacrifices to you. There are about 15,000 inhabitants with connections to Aksum. There is a river that runs through the town, called *Roha Wehiz*, and I know you love water! There are palaces, buildings and structures built to look like those in Aksum and Yeha. There is a great palace on the south-east side where the Negus resides, and a tomb in the north they say is the burial Tomb of Adam, the first man, created by Egziabeher in the Garden of Eden! Ruling this place will be symbolic as if you are ruling over the Sons of Adam of the whole Realm of Meder! Here we can rise up an army, and when we grow in strength, in numbers, and in power, *then* we can march back up to Aksum and take back the city and kingdom for yourself, Lord Waynaba!"

Waynaba: "Hhhhhisssss! Oh, that sounds like a better plan! I like that! So what citiesss are nearby that we can take and ssseek followersss?"

Silver Gauntlet: "The nearest city is Roha. We can start there and look for loyal secret followers of you. I will send out scouts to lurk in the shadows for those with artifacts and altars in their homes. Even though they maybe religiously attending Beta Krestyan outwardly, but inwardly they may not be loyal to the belief in the one we do not name here."

Waynaba: "That sounds perfect. Their dreams! I can infiltrate their dreams and give them nightmares like old times!"

Silver Gauntlet: "Yes, I can project you into the dreams of the inhabitants. But most importantly we project you into dreams to first announce you to the loyalists that you are back and seeking new recruits. Announce you are calling all followers to come forth and reveal themselves to gather in these mountains."

Waynaba: "Yessss! And sssoon I will have my new body back."

Silver Gauntlet: "Yes, but in the meantime, we can sacrifice the body of a *Zendow*, a large python, or a crocodile to start off the essence of your reptilian-serpentine body. Then later we will get a blood sacrifice to make you even stronger to rule over the Rohanites. Any willing human sacrifice will do, it does not have to be a young maiden right now. Then you can rule over all the people of the kingdom."

Waynaba: "Perfect! But not the land of Roha, I want the land of Aksum!"

Silver Gauntlet: "You can rule from Roha to Aksum. An even larger territory than you ever had in the past. We do it by a sacrifice from every city and town you want to rule over from here to there. So for now, let us erect a slab of stone for an altar of sacrife, and I will call it *Zoheleth Meswa* – The Serpent's Altar. So this region will be called Roha-Zoheleth, as we dedicate the blood of its inhabitants to the power and majesty of you, Egzi Waynaba, Lord of Serpents!"

Waynaba acknowledged, "Oh yesss! I love the sssound of that! Yesss!"

Conjuring Nightmares

Waynaba: "Ha Ha Haa! Hhhssss! That sssounds grand! I love your plan! It is perfect! We must sssstart tonight. Conjure a spell and project me into someone's sssssssweet dreamsss tonight!"

The Silver Gauntlet immediately lifted his hands, and his emerald ring began to glow as he recited a new spell:

"A conjuring I will perform indeed. To conjure nightmares that will give them such a fright, their souls will submit without even a fight. They will see their old Lord serpent, Waynaba, and be drawn to you in spite, the presence of many holy chapels in sight."

And with those cryptic words, a billowing mist engulfed the enclosure in the presence of the malevolent gathering and also engulfed the translucent jar that contained Waynaba's ghost. The mist carried a projected image of Waynaba's frame in the form of a large, vile serpent creature with a big head that fanned out at the top with spikes or horns, menacing slanted red eyes and jagged teeth, with at least four pronounced fangs. As it rose up then billowed into the night sky above the torches, lanterns, and candlelit town of Roha.

Then the mist descended in the form of slender pillars upon the top of houses then through windows into bedrooms where most inhabitants were asleep, drifting into dreamland. Even into the rooms of royal palaces where the Negus of the town as a viceroy of Aksum, was no exception to the mist from the spell. Not even the quarters of the qasisan and diyaqons were spared. This was a test and sifting to see who would succumb to or take heed of the dream. For some who were righteous may be spared from receiving the evil vision, while others that were righteous, whether small or great, may receive the dream but should be able to discern its vile intent and not take heed of it, even rebuking it in the name of the Lord Iyesus. Others may be empty vessels and may be terrified of the vile dream of Waynaba hideous visage and threatening demands to "Follow me or die!" and threats "I will dessstroy you and eat your childrennn!"

While the last set of dreamers may take heed, listen and be welcoming of Waynaba's visage and gestures to "Rise up from the sssecret placesss, prepare your old ssserpent worshiping altarsss. For your Lord Waynaba has returned from the depths of Sssiol. He is ready for your sacrificesss, and will reward you greatly, those willing to follow the Lord of Serpentsss."

Thus was the scenario that transpired that night in Roha, as Waynaba was projected into the dreams of the guilty and the innocent. The Silver Gauntlet then ordered the rest of the Qataliyan who gathered and did not go west with Death Cloak, "Now go out, army of Darkness, into the city of Roha and observe those who respond and those who don't. Those with altars and talismans to serpents, and those without. Go out and return with your reports in two nights and let us know what you see. We will consider if the taking of Roha can ever be."

Traversing Ambas.

After breakfast, Abba Shiloh and Mekonnen carefully climbed out of the cave. Sliding his staff with an ornate Aksum styled golden cross at the head into the rope around his waist for a belt and then tightening it, Abba Shiloh tells Mekonnen, "We are not climbing down, but we go up and over this amba and into another cave on the other side."

Mekonnen exclaimed, "Oh really! Hrai. Sounds adventurous!"

Abba Shiloh explained, "We keep a low profile. Don't want to be seen by anyone. Particularly the dark Qataliyan you talked about, or their dreadful hounds."

They stepped out of the mouth of the cave onto a ledge to the right and held on to vines that looked like ropes hanging from a higher point. The footing was not too narrow but not too wide either so Abba Shiloh in the lead as they slid over, then climbed upwards. "Don't look down!" Abba Shiloh warned. "And not all of these vines are secure, so hold on to the cracks on the side."

"Uhh, *mezgana*, thank you for letting me know, Abba," Mekonnen replied sarcastically since he was solely depending on those vines up until that moment. They kept climbing until there were no more vines, just rock surface of the amba. Now they are more than 80 feet high. So high, birds were flying past them and below them. And it was becoming windier the higher they climbed.

Abba Shiloh was old, but he climbed confidently like a young man. Surely, he knew every crack and footing to hold on too because he's familiar with this amba. Mekonnen was doing okay following where every Abba Shiloh placed his hands and feet and avoiding the vines and branches he was told not to grab on to.

"We are almost at the top, hrrrm!" Abba Shiloh exclaimed. He pulled himself up to the top of the amba and reached down and gave Mekonnen a hand to pull the warrior up to the top with him. It's quite different at the top, not stack and rocky like the side but green with grass, shrubbery, and trees. And animals too, bugs, like grasshopper, butterflies with blue wings fluttering and mole rats. Even birds chirped and fluttered from tree to tree.

But surprisingly, as they walked, there were gelada baboons up there too. Many of them. Mekonnen became concerned because they were known to attack people in the wilderness if disturbed or provoked. And their red breasts in the center of their chests were very distinctive, forming a heart or triangle shape, reminded Mekonnen of the large monstrous creatures that looked like these and attacked him and his warriors in Gultosh a few days ago. Except, those had a red symbol of a serpent inside a circle in the center of their chest. Whether they were related to these rather small, but still intimidating, baboons, or perverted versions of them, Mekonnen did not know, but they do bring bad memories and cause some anxiety.

Abba Shiloh reassured the warrior, "Just keep walking straight and don't make any sudden movements. They know me, so they will let us through."

"Hrai," Mekonnen replied quietly, wishing he at least had a sword or dagger with him right now, just in case.

As the two men walked the gelada baboons just stepped out of their path, grunted and hooted slightly but not threatening.

"Good day to you all. Sorry to disturb you. This is my friend with me. We are just passing through." Abba Shiloh spoke to them as if they were familiar, friendly neighbors.

"You see, Anbessa. You just have to respect them and their territory. This can be done with almost any beast. Including anbessat, takwlat and tsebet – lions, wolves, and hyenas. You just have to know and understand your authority over all creatures in this world that Egziabeher bestowed onto us. Authority over earth, sea, air, fire and the spiritual realms."

More Scrolls.

They kept on walking pass the baboons as the creatures stared at them but did not attack or seemed ferocious. Three minutes later the two men reached the trees and Mekonnen glance behind them to see the gelada proceeded with their own business. The trees were sparse in number and not very high, so they walked past them in about two minutes. Then they got to another edge, and Abba Shiloh showed Mekonnen where they will climb down to enter another cave. After 5 minutes of climbing down, they reached another ledge the slid roughly sideways into another cave. As they entered a startled hawk squawked and flew pass the two men out the same entrance they came in, causing them to duck out of the way.

Abba Shiloh proclaimed, "See! Even the birds of the air want to come in my cave and read the Words of life!"

Mekonnen's eyes adjusted to the cave light to reveal more scrolls and books like the cave they just left and climbed out of. He commented, "Oh, another library of scrolls, Abba Shiloh? We didn't even get through reading half of the first cave!"

"Oh, I know, but this one has some other writings I wanted to show you

Mekonnen and Abba Shiloh climbing a steep mountain (amba) seeking for more ancient scrolls and codices that can lead them to the manifestation of Righteousness.
Jerome Matiyas © 2018

may believe is good in our own eyes, but we rest if the righteousness of what Iyesus Krestos did for us. Do you understand this Mekonnen?"

Mekonnen responded, "I do, Abba Shiloh. I understand plainly. More than I've ever understood before."

Abba Shiloh: "Gerum! This is the beginning of putting on the *Malbasa Enged'a Tsedq* – Breastplate of Righteousness. But when one of not living in right standing with Him it becomes easy to live to the sinful impulses of the flesh."

He reached of the Orit of Moses,

"First I will show you the first mentions of Righteousness – in the Holy Orit of Moses.

'And the Lord said to Noah, Come with all your household into the ark, for I have seen you to be righteous before Me in this generation.'

Do you know what time in history this was from, Mekonnen?"

Mekonnen responded, "Yes, the Earth was going to be destroyed by the great flood because of the evil and violence in the world. But Noah was not living in sin and violence and worshiped Egziabeher, so he was righteous. So Egziabeher warned him to build a large ship to save himself, his family and the animals too."

Abba Shiloh affirmed, "Correct! As simple as it sounds, but mankind and fallen mal'ekt cannot abide by it continuously by themselves. They need to be reminded."

Abba Shiloh and Mekonnen went through scripture after scripture and book after book, reading and comparing for hours. Time went by fast, and they did not realize it until it got dark outside as nighttime eased in. Seven hours passed but it felt like three hours.

And he saw that there was no man, and wondered that there was no intercessor: therefore his arm brought salvation unto him; and his **righteousness**, *it sustained him.*

For he put on **righteousness as a breastplate**, *and an* **helmet of salvation** *upon his head; and he put on the garments of vengeance for clothing and was clad with zeal as a cloak."*
- Isaiah 59:16-17.

This corresponded to the letter to the Ephesians about the breastplate and helmet and also the Wisdom of Solomon that was shown to Mekonnen in the first cave.

And the same prophet not only saw righteousness as breastplate and salvation as a helmet, but he saw it covering the whole body like a robe:

I will greatly rejoice in the Lord, my soul shall be joyful in my God; for he hath clothed me with the **garments of salvation**, *he hath covered me with* *the **robe of righteousness**, as a bridegroom decks himself with ornaments, and as a bride adorns herself with her jewels. - Isaiah 61:10.*

The entire Book of Yashar demonstrated the righteous and upright life of the prophets and fore-fathers from the Orit of Moses.

It read: *"And Methuselah acted **uprightly** in the sight of God, as his father Henok had taught him, and he likewise during the whole of his life taught the sons of men wisdom, knowledge and the fear of God..."* – Book of Yashar 4:3.

In the Apocalypse of Moses, also called *Mastehafa Kufāle* – the Book of Jubilees. Egziabeher spoke to Moses:

"I will build My sanctuary among them, and I will dwell with them, and I will be their God and they shall be My people in truth and righteousness." – Jubilees 1:17.

The Righteousness of the Upright was mentioned in *Mastehafa Henok* – The Book of Henok.

"The righteous and the chosen were mighty before him like fiery lights." - Henok 39:7.

They continued reading the beautiful poetry of Henok's oracles describing the righteousness in conjunction to the paths of the sun and moon:

> *"For the sun makes many revolutions for a blessing*
> *and a curse,*
> *and the course of the path of the moon*
> *is Light to the Righteous ones*
> *and Darkness to the ungodly ones,*
> *In the name of the Lord who made a separation*
> *Between Light and Darkness,*
> *And divided the spirits of men,*
> *And strengthened the spirits of the righteous*
> *In the name of His Righteousness.*
> (Henok 41:9)

As Mekonnen read this verse, it grabbed his attention and caused him to meditate and reach back into his memories of the night when his family mourned the death of his cousin Afeworq. He remembered when he wondered off into the wilderness by himself and drifting off into the dream-vision and waking up to an extra-large full moon in the sky. And how the moonlight illumined the pathway in the valley to the strong Sword in the altar, which he used to slay the dark Qataliyan beings in his vision. And how the very same moon cast dark shadows from which those same dark beings and their dreadful hounds dwelt and sprang out from to do their evil and treacherous deeds, both in the dream vision and in the real natural world when he wrestled with them in the wilderness and mountains.

How this verse rang true to the young warrior at that moment, he paused from reading and sat back for a moment, reflecting on the meaning of what had transpired in his life so far, and how the essence and meaning of righteousness played into the whole scheme of things happening in the world. Both the good and the evil.

Abba Shiloh noticed Mekonnen was staring into space, having a moment, so he did not interrupt him. Then after a few minutes, he asked the young warrior,

"I perceive the words in this version has captured your mind and spirit. Do you want to stop reading for the night? We can continue tomorrow."

Mekonnen insisted, "Iyyaseh. Let us keep on reading."

They continued reading the oracles of Henok until they got to more sacred verses on righteousness flowing from the Son of Man and his blood required with His secret name.

"And the hearts of the Qeddusan (the Holy Ones) were filled with joy,
For the number of the righteous had been heard,
And the blood of the Righteous One had been required in the presence of the Lord of Spirits"
- Henok 47:4;

And in that hour that Son of Man was named in the presence of the Egzia-Manfasat - Lord of Spirits,
And his name, before the Head of Days.
Even before the sun and the constellations were created, before the stars of heaven were made,
His name was named before the Lord of Spirits.
-Henok 48:2-3.

Mekonnen marveled at the fact that long before Noah and the flood, Henok saw the righteous Son of Egziabeher sacrificed for the souls of the Holy Ones of mankind since before the foundations of the Earth. Just as it was written in the beginning of the *Haddis Kidana Wangel Yohannes* – the New Testament book of the Gospel of John (John 1: 1-3). Even his powerful name was a secret until it was revealed when the Elect One was born in Bethlehem of Yihuda, where he was named Iyesus. In the Hebrew language he was Yahshua.

There were many more scriptures and verses from the sacred writings

The Breastplate of Righteousness
In the Spiritual Realm surrounded by the four living creatures.
(Ezek 1:10, Rev 4:7-8)
Jerome Matiyas © 2018

that Abba Shiloh showed Mekonnen to strengthen his faith. And with each reading and discovery, Mekonnen's faith grew as he saw the connections of the parts of the Armor of God to each other and how righteousness played a key part in the battle against the enemy in the strongholds of Darkness. And he became more encouraged and confident in the Spirit and in Egziabeher and began to anticipate how he must discover the Breastplate of Righteousness.

It was now three hours since the sun set, so Abba Shiloh concluded that night, "Tomorrow I will begin to show you the origins of those creatures of darkness you encountered in Aksum, in the mountains, and in your visions. Now let's get some sleep, hrrrm."

Mekonnen replied, "*Yawn*. *Hrai*, Abba. I cannot wait to hear more. Whatever it takes to grow stronger and acquire the whole armor."

Serpentine Dreams.
That night the Silver Gauntlet continued his sorcery by projecting Waynaba's vaporous spirit into dreams of some of the citizens of Roha as he did the

night before. Some people, men, women, and children woke up frightened and terrified, screaming, after tossing and turning in their sleep. When they spoke among themselves in the morning they were puzzled the learn that they all had the same or similar nightmare of a *Zendow* – a large snake or dragon-like creature –as they called it, threatening them, claiming he's returning to rule over them, and if there was no submission he will strangle them or eat their children if they did not sacrifice a virgin to him soon. And in the nightmare the Zendow would either wrap his huge snake-like body around them and squeeze tighter and tighter until they woke up gasping for air. In other night terrors he would bite them on the head and swallow them whole like a real 20 foot long Zendow would swallow an antelope or cattle, causing an equally terrifying wake from sleep.

In those night travels riding on dreams and nightmares Waynaba was able to notice a few old altars and tablet inscriptions partially covered by overgrown weeds and bushes, that pertained to him being "Lord of serpents! Negus of Aksum!" or something like that, in old Sabaean/Sheban script which was the progenitor of the Aksumite Ge'ez script.

But there was one that seemed to be a serious follower of Waynaba and the snake cults in secret. In his home, in a closet, there was an idol of a serpent-like creature wrapped around a pole or tree stump, with candles next to it and a fancy Persian-styled rug in front of it. This person was also suspiciously not very afraid or repulsed by the bad dreams but became rather curious. Despite having icons of sacred imagery pertaining to the belief in Iyesus Krestos throught the house and in his room, like masqal crosses and artwork drawings of Virgin Mariam with the Krestos Lij – the Christ Child –, this man showed signs of being a secret follower of the dark side of the spirit realms. He awakened startled and breathing heavily, sat up in his bed and glanced over to the left to see if the woman beside him, who could be his wife, concubine or mistress, was still asleep under the decorative bed covers. He slowly slipped off the bed and placed his feet on the rugged floor and walked across his dark room to light a candle. The candle lit room showed it was a rather large size space with a high ceiling, decorative drapes, and pillars of Aksumite fashion, suggesting this man was some sort of leader or Negus of the town of Roha. And this fancy room may actually be inside of a larger castle or palace. He took the candle and walked to a closet, opened it and walked in to reveal an engraved wooden sculpture vanished in dark brown polish of a Zendow coiled around a pole with its snarling mouth wide open like a crocodile. In all, it was about 2 feet in height. He knelt on the rug before it and whispered. "Lord Waynaba, is it really you? Are you really returning to us, to reveal your power and strength?"

The spirit of Waynaba could see and hear this man in front the graven image as it was able to hover over the idol in an attempt to embody it since he so yearned to be inside a physical thing or body. Waynaba only managed to make the eyes on the idol glow red. When his new worshiper saw this miraculous manifestation before his own eyes, his heart raced as his breathing deepened with excitement and anticipation. Waynaba replied hissing, "Yesss, my sssservant. I am here to take back what wasss mine. That which I lossst hundreds of years ago. Help me find a sacrificesssss!"

The man replied, shaking nervously but excited that he believed he actually heard the voice of Waynaba speaking back him in the darkness through his graven image, "Hrai, my Lord Waynaba Zendow. I, Negus Leqsem Gemalli, procurator of Roha and the province of Lasta, shall find a suitable sacrifice for you."

The Path to Righteousness

To Wereta

That anbessa with the fiery mane approached again. This time not charging aggressively but prowled up closer and closer until it came right up to Mekonnen's face. The mighty anbessa breathed in and out steadily and stared into the warrior's eyes. Mekonnen stared back into the eyes of the terrifying beast. Its pupils looked like deep blue sapphire gemstones that sparkled in the light with specks of various shades of aqua marine and sky blue. Framed by eye lids decorated with patterns of elegant spiraling designs, curving in various directions, up and down and to the sides. On this heavenly creatures forehead sat a golden crown with a red ruby gemstone in the center with an inscription on it that Mekonnen could not understand.

Gradually the anbessa's feline face began to fade to become transparent as Mekonnen slowly opened his eyes from sleep. As he opened his eyes the anbessa's mouth began to move as it spook to Mekonnen and said, "Be prepared. Your day is coming soon."

Then the lion's face disappeared, and Mekonnen woke up and sat up from the rug he slept on. He was glad for the first time the lion in his dream did not startle him awake this time. "What does that mean?", he wondered. "Does that mean the times and seasons are changing?"

Abba Shiloh was already up and sitting by the entrance of the cave, meditating with a small book in his hand, most likely it's a copy of Dawit Mezmur (Psalms of David).

Mekonnen reported, "The fiery anbessa in my dream told me to be prepared and my day is coming soon, Abba Shiloh. He did not charge at me this time."

Abba Shiloh replied, "Oh, you finally learned how to tame it to be your *qwele arwe* – domesticated animal, hrrrm." He said plainly as if he made a serious remark, without even moving from his meditative sitting and reading position.

Mekonnen said, "No, seriously. It was different this time. I think things are changing and going to be different from now on."

Abba Shiloh replied, "You are correct! You have been receiving the Word of Egziabeher into your spirit and soul and your days of revelation and manifestation in the spirit was soon approaching. Well, let's get going now and climb down this rock. We will pass through Wereta, for breakfast, then to the marketplace, and then to the next amba. Take that *meshaf qedus* with you. And we go in secret. No one must know you are a warrior and where you are from."

Mekonnen replied, "Hrai. But I think it is best I write a message and give it to one of the messengers or traveling warriors we may meet. To send to the Commanders in Aksum letting them know I'm alive and did not defect from the army guards. Don't want to get in trouble for not reporting my status."

Abba Shiloh said, "That is also risky because we do not know who to trust, but still write your letter fast and seal it. We will decide if it is safe to pass on your letter." Abba Shiloh finds some blank paper, a feathered ink pen and a bottle of ink to write with and hands them to Mekonnen.

Then Mekonnen remembered his cousin Meron, Afeworq's little sister, and the promise he made that he would return safe and sound to her and the family. She probably thought he was dead by now since he had not returned home after more than a week. He realized he wanted to also write a short letter to her letting the family know he was alive and safe, so they won't worry that another person in the family had past away. At least he was safe for now.

While Mekonnen wrote his letters, Abba Shiloh was busy gathering things for both of them to carry on the next leg of their journey. They packed them into a small sack, and down the amba they climbed without ropes or vines so no one else could climb up into the cave.

Down the road to Wereta, they walked and talked for about an hour until they came to the city bustling with people, camels, donkeys, horses, carts, carriages, and all the other trapping of a medium sized town in an empire. Many people of devout faith in the streets bow and greeted Abba Shiloh out of reverence because they could tell he was a Bahetawi by his clothing, necklaces, masqal and long white locks of hair.

"Selamta, Abba. Egziabeher yemiskan." They said to him as he walked by and he responded by bowing in return. Soon he felt they were receiving too much attention, so he motioned to Mekonnen for them to get off the main roads as much as possible. Mekonnen covered his torso and waist with a white robe that Abba Shiloh gave to him, so no one could see his Aksumite arm band and golden Belt of Truth. Most people thought he was just a monk walking in the company of the Bahetawi and did not suspect he was a warrior.

They found a tavern where travelers go to eat, drink and rest, where they bought *chechebsa* (chopped seasoned bread) with *enqulal tibs* (scrambled eggs) and *nitre kibe* (spicy butter) for breakfast; Abba Shiloh paid for it with Aksumite silver coins. Mekonnen spotted an Aksumite messenger there, and with Abba Shiloh's permission, he gave him the two letters: One for his Commander Mulualem, and the other for his family. There were some other people in the eatery of this tavern sitting around *masobs* eating and drinking and having their own private conversations.

A Mysterious One.

There was one man sitting by himself with one leg crossed over the other, not at a masob but at a table with one hand on a cup of ale. He wore a decorative wrist band on that arm, dark burgundy long sleeves and sturdy leather booths with straps and buckles around it. One could not really get a clear view of his face because he had dark green leathery hood with patterned fringes over his head that connects as one cloth to a robe over his shoulders and back.

He may have had a sword or dagger in a sheath on his waist, but it was not in plain view for anyone to see it. He sat at the far end of the eatery but has a clear view of Mekonnen and Abba Shiloh as they ate and chatted. His purpose and intent was unknown. Whether he was friend or foe, mal'ak or man, was unknown, but he had an eye on the two men as he slowly sipped his ale. Abba Shiloh did not give an indication to Mekonnen that he noticed the mysterious figure, the fact that the holy man had the gift of discernment to know if they were being followed.

On the Move.

After breakfast, they went to the busy local market to buy fruits, bread, injera and water to take on their journey to the next amba. By this time it was close to midday, and the sun was almost in the middle of the blue sky above.

As they walked eastwards down the road towards their destination Mekonnen noticed the top of a great mountain in the distance with clouds below the peak of it.

He asked, "Abba Shiloh, that mountain in the distance. What is it called? Are we going there?"

Abba Shiloh replied, "Oh, that is the great *Guna Dabr*! – Mount Guna! Too bad we are not going that far otherwise I would take you there. That's more than a 14 hours journey on foot. The amba I'm taking you to is right over there, about half a mile away."

Thirty minutes later they arrived at the base of the amba and were greeted by a Bahetawi dressed in similar garb as Abba Shiloh but in blue and green robes in contrast to Shiloh's orange and yellows, and different décor style of masqal on top his staff.

Abba Shiloh bowed to greet him and took his right hand, "Selam Abba Kiros, Egziabeher baraka. This is my friend Mekonnen, warrior from Aksum. He will be spending some time with us to learn of the Word."

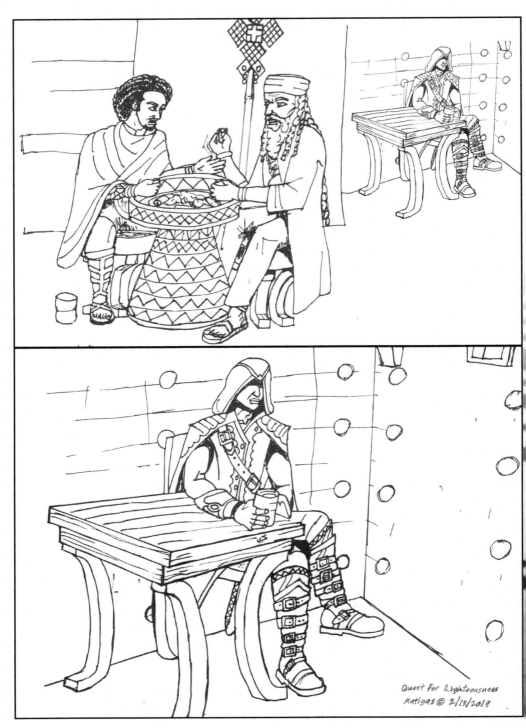

Quest for Righteousness
Matiyas © 2/15/2019

Abba Kiros responded, "Selam Mekonnen, Welcome to Amba Qedus."

There were also some young manakost there that greeted the two men, and they proceeded to assist them in climbing the two rope ladders that were just lowered down from the top. They could hear men singing hymns at the top of the amba.

Riding The Shadows.

Meanwhile, the lead Qatali, Lord Death Cloak, and his dark, cloaked warriors have been traveling through the shadows mostly by night, and at daytime they were not able to travel this way, so they tried to blend in with the people of the cities, towns, and villages wherever they happened to land before sunrise. After they left Roha, Death Cloak commanded the Qataliyan to team up in twos and fan out to the nearby towns to the west, north, and south until they reached all the way to Tsana Hayq. They were instructed to remain in a city or region for a while even if there was no sign of a warrior with a special relic or piece of clothing, and they should only have moved when they received the signal to converge unto a specific location that their target was located. So they fanned out towards Tsana Hayq, some went west towards Wereta, some went north towards Gondar, where they last encountered him, and some went south towards Bahar Dar.

Two Qataliyan land in Debre Tabor and scouts the city for anyone they might suspect but no one stood out to them. Two went to towns north of Mount Guna and found nothing. Two to east, two to south and two to west of Mount Guna, still nothing. Only regular citizens going to Beta Krestiyan on Sundays and going to work during the week. Two went to Woji, and two more to Wereta. Pairs went as far north as Addis Zemen and even as far as Goltush where they last tried to kidnap the young maiden, Penuel. And even in the Samen Mountains and forest where they encountered the flash of light that blinded them.

Then some did get as far as Bahar Dar, and the Tis Isat falls, dangerously close to the Gihon Hagar village. They did not really know what to look for, or if they should make a commotion and stir up some trouble in order to make their target reveal himself to them, but they fear putting themselves in danger of being caught by Mal'ekt from on High and cast into chains of darkness until Judgement Day.

They communicated with each other later at night, after midnight until about 2:00 am by placing their faces and mouths close to a shadow on the ground and speaking through it. When they spoke through the darkest shadows that was cast their message traveled and carried through other shadows and dark spots in the land. Even better for them would be a spot that was in spiritual darkness, not just from an absence of light from torches, lanterns, and candles, but where there was activity of idolatry or sorcery. These areas were spring boards to push their messages forward to each other and their leader Lord Death Cloak. But where there was spiritual light people living in holiness and righteousness, praying and fasting, singing mezmur in chapels or at their homes, and there was the presence of Mal'ekt, then their dark messages were hindered or diverted around those areas.

Death Cloak spoke to all his scouts through the shadows,

"Now that you are dispersed remain there until one of you gets a signal from a sure lead or from myself to move to a specific spot. Do not be distracted by other holy men like qasisan, nolawian, manakost, manakosawit or laymen who may be gifted to cast out demons. Observe them first but see if they are the warrior we are specifically hunting for. Our target may seek the sanctuary of churches or be in the company of holy men of the cloth for advice or inspiration. Next, you can consult with other agents of Darkness that are local in their territory. Ask if they noticed anyone suspicious in the region if they are willing to share with you. Some may be hostile and not willing to share, unless they understand it was also for their own benefit. I myself will begin to move westward to Dabra Tabor then to Wereta. Eventually, we will find this warrior in this region. And watch above your heads for Mal'ekt, or you may lose them."

The Circle of Righteousness

At the top of the amba the atmosphere was pleasant, and its sense of peace and joy was present, and the heart immediately felt up lifted. As the harmonious songs of manakost rang out through the air with glorious melodies from the Mezmur Dawit and traditional hymns song in the churches for years, including new ones introduced by the Tsadkan, and Diyaqon Yared, the signature musician of Aksum. On top this amba one cannot tell if you were in the presence of men or mal'ekt. It was a possibility both coexisted up there at that moment. Mal'ekt may have descended and joined these men in singing choruses and played instruments of many kinds like the krar, begena, kabaro, washintu and timbres and more played in unison and melody.

Abba Shiloh introduced Mekonnen to another Bahetawi, "This is Abba Libanos." Mekonnen shook Abba Libanos hand and bowed.

Abba Shiloh continued, "Abba Libanos, Mekonnen is on a journey on a higher calling from Egziabeher. He is here to seek righteousness. He seeks the Breastplate of Righteousness!"

Abba Libanos said with joy, "Oh, I have just the perfect apparel for you!" he turns around and enters the open door to the monastery that's in the center of the amba, then about a minute later he returned with a very well knitted *shemis* – a shirt in the Habesha style – white short sleeved shirt with beautifully decorative golden fringes on the collar, shoulders and along the front seams from top to bottom held out in full view.

He looked at the shemis, impressed but its style, but confused.

Abba Libanos declared proudly, "Behold, here is your Breastplate of

Righteousness!"

Not to be rude and ungrateful, Mekonnen smiled and accepted the shirt and said, "Oh wow, *amazgana*. This is… *sannaya* - beautiful!?"

He was confused because he expected to be handed an actual solid, hard, impenetrable breastplate, not linen clothe shirt with fancy gold fringes, that can probably be sliced to threads with a little dagger.

Abba Shiloh insisted, "You should put it on now. I know you are thinking, this is not a breastplate, but trust me. This shemis is more solid and impenetrable than it looks. Go on. Remove your robe and put it on, hrrrm."

Mekonnen obliged and removed his robe, removed his outer shirt and left on his under shirt and slipped on the new *shemis*, presumably the Breastplate of Righteousness. It fitted almost perfectly to his torso, even more than the previous clothing he wore. It also felt sturdy and not flimsy at all.

Mekonnen responded, "It actually feels quite comfortable, I must say."

Abba Shiloh added, "Hrai, and feel that." And began slapping his hands on Mekonnen's abdomen and chest to test the sturdiness. Mekonnen noticed he did not feel any pain from Abba Shiloh's lashed. Abba Shiloh then grabbed a dagger from under his clothing and said, "And how about this!" and jabs it into Mekonnen's abdomen, but the warrior felt nothing, though he flinched from seeing a blade coming to his torso. Abba Shiloh showed Mekonnen the blade, and it was bent out of shape as if it was rammed into a solid stone wall. Damaged from coming in contact with the shemis.

"Look at this. The blade is destroyed! No use anymore, hrrm! Are you satisfied now that you've found what you are looking for?"

Mekonnen replied, "Well, yes, I will have to take your word and go by what I just saw. This must be the *Malbasa Enged'a Tsedq* – Breastplate of Righteousness."

Abba Shiloh continued, "Now you're not done yet. You must now be greeted and blessed and anointed with oil by these manakost and Bahetawi. And they will prophesy over you, each one, before the end of this day."

Abba Libanos handed Abba Shiloh a bottle of *meron* - holy olive oil.

"Let me do the honors of being the first to anoint and bless you." He uncorked the bottle and began to pour the meron over Mekonnen's head at the top of his high hair do to where the forehead meets his hair. The oil continued to flow down his face, unto his shoulders, neck, and chest. Mekonnen can do or say nothing but just be humbled by what was taking place in from of dozens of manakost and hermits.

"Mekonnen, I now declare you a Son of Egziabeher and a warrior for Righteousness and Light."

In unison, all the manakos on the Amba repeated, "We declare you a Son of Egziabeher and a warrior for Righteousness and Light!"

Abba Shiloh continued, "You will walk in uprightness and holiness before Egziabeher!"

Crowd of Bahetawi in unison, "You will walk in uprightness and holiness before Egziabeher!"

Abba Shiloh: "You will seek the face of Egziabeher and flee from sin!"

Bahetawi in unison: "You will seek the face of Egziabeher and flee from sin!"

Abba Shiloh: "In the name of the Father and the Son and the Holy Spirit!"

Bahetawi in unison: "In the name of the Father and the Son and the Holy Spirit!"

Abba Shiloh rested the cross from his staff on Mekonnen's chest and said, "Now valiant warrior Mekonnen, repeat after me: I, Mekonnen, warrior from Aksum."

With eyes open, staring directly at his mentor, Mekonnen repeated, "I, Mekonnen, warrior from Aksum."

Abba Shiloh: "Do solemnly pledge to serve the Lord of the universe, Egziabeher Amlak, and his only Son, Iyesus Kristos."

Mekonnen: "Do solemnly pledge to serve the Lord of the universe, Egziabeher Amlak, and his only Son, Iyesus Kristos."

Abba Shiloh: "And continue to live uprightly and holy before you through the helper and comforter, the Holy Spirit."

Mekonnen: "And continue to live uprightly and holy before you through the helper and comforter, the Holy Spirit."

Abba Shiloh: "I shall be a warrior for your kingdom, and I shall put on and whole armor of Egziabeher to fight the spiritual battles."

Mekonnen: "I shall be a warrior for your kingdom, and I shall put on and whole armor of Egziabeher to fight the spiritual battles."

Abba Shiloh: "I battle not against flesh and blood, but against the principalities, powers, and thrones in the realms of Darkness."

Mekonnen: "I battle not against flesh and blood, but against the principalities, powers, and thrones in the realms of Darkness."

Abba Shiloh: "I shall fight the good fight of faith till the very end."

Mekonnen: "I shall fight the good fight of faith till the very end."

Abba Shiloh: "Amen."

Mekonnen: "Amen."

And the whole amba rejoiced with ululations in unison, "Elelelelelelele lelelelelelel!!"

Everyone resumed singing and dancing and playing instruments. But Mekonnen's ceremony was not complete for he was immediately led into the center of a circle of twelve Behatawi. Here he must walk around to each one as they blessed and prophesy over his life and mission from the Most High.

Mekonnen has been granted to put on
The Breastplate of Righteousness
Jerome Matiyas © 2018

He stepped over to the first one who said, "*But you, man of God, flee from all this, and pursue righteousness, godliness, faith, love, endurance and gentleness. (1 Timothy 6:11)*"

The second one: "*Like a lion, you shall rise up and slay your enemies of darkness. Abide in the Lord and the Darkness will not prevail against you. When darkness descends, a warrior must rise up to restore the light.*"

The third one: "*If you say, "The Lord is my refuge," and you make the Most High your dwelling, no harm will overtake you, no disaster will come near your tent. For he will command his angels concerning you to guard you in all your ways; they will lift you up in their hands, so that you will not strike your foot against a stone. You will tread on the lion and the cobra; you will trample the great lion and the serpent." Psalm 91:9-13*

The fourth one: "*But seek first the kingdom of God and His righteousness, and all these things shall be added to you.*" (Matthew 6:33)

The fifth one: "*The night is far spent, the day is at hand. Let us, therefore, cast off the works of darkness and let us put on the armor of Light. (Romans 13:13)*"

The sixth one: "*For he is the minister of God to thee for good. But if you do that which is evil, be afraid; for he beareth not the Sword in vain; for he is a minister of God, a revenger to execute wrath upon him that does evil."*(Romans 13:4)

The seventh one: *"You have loved righteousness and hated lawlessness; Therefore God, Your God, has anointed You With the oil of gladness more than Your companions."* (Hebrews 1:9)

The eight one: *"Iyesus Himself bore our sins in His own body on the tree, that we, having died to sins, might live for righteousness—by whose stripes you were healed."* (1 Peter 2:24)

The ninth one: *"Stand therefore, having girded your waist with truth, having put on the breastplate of righteousness,"* (Ephesians 6:14)

The tenth one: *"For He put on righteousness as a breastplate, And a helmet of salvation on His head; He put on the garments of vengeance for clothing, And was clad with zeal as a cloak."* (Isaiah 59:17)

The eleventh one: *"For the word of God is living and powerful, and sharper than any two-edged sword, piercing even to the division of soul and spirit, and of joints and marrow, and is a discerner of the thoughts and intents of the heart."* Hebrews 4:12.

The twelfth one: *"I am the door. If anyone enters by Me, he will be saved, and will go in and out and find pasture."* John 10:9.

Then there was a bright light at the last one as he made a gesture with his hands that Mekonnen should step into it. Mekonnen stepped in, and immediately he recognized it looked just like the place from his vision in the valley where the Lord spoke to him, and then the Anbessa first leapt at him.

Here the Lord Iyesus Krestos, the Elect One, approached him again in a kind way, his face brighter than the sun as before. He spoke to Mekonnen, "Well done my friend. Your faith has brought you here, and it is counted as righteousness onto you. Receive the gift of Righteousness."

The Elect One touched Mekonnen's chest with his right hand, and immediately the shemis transformed, and the white linen parts became solid hard gold. While the patterns of the golden fringes just grew and expanded into the new gold space that used to be white. It transformed to look like a real Breastplate, but like no other in the natural world, as it sparkled like the finest pure gold, so refined it reflected rays like the colors of the rainbow.

The Lord continued to speak to Mekonnen in a voice like many waters,

"You will find the Sword of the Spirit in the waters. As streaming water is the source of rivers, so is this water the source of life. Whoever drinks of the water that I shall give him will never thirst. But the water that I shall give him will become in him a fountain of water springing up into everlasting life." (John 4:14). *The Word of Egziabeher is a flaming fire, as sharp as a two-edge sword that proceeds out of my mouth to slay the enemy in the high places."*

Afterwards, the Anbessa approached Mekonnen again and came face to face again.

"Return now. I will be with you." It said. This time Mekonnen could read the engraving in the red ruby pearl that was embedded into the Anbessa's crowd, and it read *Tsion,* a symbolic name for the hill or mountain where the Spirit of Egziabeher resided.

The bright entrance closed up like a scroll and Mekonnen was back in the amba as the men continued singing mezmur and played instruments. Mekonnen joined them in celebrating, and they continued until night time without stopping until it was very later at night when gradually a few of them drifted off to sleep, but many remained awake until sunrise.

In the morning Mekonnen, Abba Shiloh, and Abba Libanos conversed about the amazing visitation from the Lord Iyesus Krestos that transpired last night. The gold in the shemis faded back to white, appearing less eye-catching compared to the way it illuminated last night.

Mekonnen said, "I am truly thankful and grateful to have come here to receive my anointing and the word and prophecies over me. And to have met the Elect One face to face again. And to receive righteousness directly from him. I am ready to accept my responsibilities for the rest of my journey."

Abba Shiloh said, "That is excellent news to hear from you, Anbessa. And now do you understand why I kept on calling you 'Anbessa' since the first time I saw you?"

"I have an idea, but why?" asked Mekonnen.

Abba Shiloh replied, "Because I know that I perceived you will have the heart of an anbessa. A conquering lion who will ravage the enemy. You must bring Light back to where Darkness has fallen."

Mekonnen responded, "I am honored that you have believed in me and brought me this far. Now, the Lord has given me a clue I believe as to where I can locate the Sword of the Spirit. He told me *'You will find the Sword of the Spirit in the waters. As streaming water is the source of rivers, so is this water the source of life.'* The only source of the rivers I can think of in this land in the Tsana Hayq, the source of Abay River. We will find the Sword of the Spirit in the Tsana Hayq."

Abba Libanos confirmed, "I also received a dream last night that you should go to one of the islands in Tsana Hayq to get the Sword. Go to Tsana Qirqos Island and one of the manakost there can lead you to it."

Abba Shiloh added, "U-wa, I also received a vision we must go to the islands in Tsana Hayq. So we all in agreement then! To Tsana Hayq we go!"

Mekonnen's Vow.

Mekonnen said, "So since we all received the same vision that I should now go to Tsana Hyaq, I would like to make a vow and pledge in front of you, Abba Shiloh and the brothers on this amba, that I will make a vow this day. My vow is to continue this journey until the end and to acquire all parts of the *Tsərura Egziabeher* – the Armor of Egziabeher – grow in the words of the ancient writings of the upright ones, and to battle against the armies of Darkness with the words and instruments of Light. With this vow, and before my mentors, I would like to go the way of the Bahetawi and take on the Nazarite vow. As it is written by Moses in *Orit Zahkwelq* (the Book of Numbers chapter 6:), I shall not have a razor touch my head, nor shall I drink strong drink from the grape vine, nor cease my dedication to my calling from my Abba up above, Egziabeher Amlak, until my assigned mission has been fulfilled. Amen."

And the men who heard what the warrior just declared and vowed in their presents all responded,

"Amen! Elelelelelelelelelelelel!"

Then Abba Libanos summoned one of the manakos to come over and braid Mekonnen high, fluffy, curly hair into seven locks of hairs. First, it was braided to his scalp in seven separate rows, then loose in the back to seven locks reaching the top of the middle of his shoulder blades. Usually, it was the Negus and Hade of the Aksumite Empire who wore their hair in this style under their crowns and not usually the common folks or warriors, but Mekonnen's calling was going to be unique.

Mekonnen remembered reading the sacred writings in one of Abba Shiloh's caves, about men who were called by Egziabeher and set apart for a special mission and lived by the vow of the Nazarite. Like the prophet Samuel, Samson the Judge, and Yakob (James) the brother of Iyesus Krestos, who was described by Eusebius the church historian as growing his hair down to his feet in dedication to the mission of preaching the *Wangel* – the good news message of the gospel – of Egziabeher in Eyerusalem then to the rest of the world. So, though not required, he saw it fitting to take on this vow upon himself as a reminder of who and what he stood for and believed in: Righteousness in Iyesus Krestos.

It took the manakos about an hour to complete the braiding, and when he was done, he got up and handed Mekonnen a mirror to show him how his new hair looked. Mekonnen touched his head and new locks and said, "It is not for vanity, but it will be suitable for my mission. And when I get the Helmet of Salvation, so it will fit upon my big head more easily, I hope."

Then he turned to Abba Shiloh and said, "I think we are ready to go on our way to the lake, but I feel like we would need some sort of weapon to defend ourselves against the Dark Qataliyan out there."

Abba Shiloh said, "Well, at this point we trust the Egzi to send his Mal'ekt to protect us from harm."

Then it came to Abba Libanos' mind right then that he bought a spear recently from some merchants, that might be a Mal'ak's weapon.

Abba Libanos said, "Wait a moment. I may have something for you Mekonnen that may be of use to you. It is not the exact Sayfa Manfas you seek, but since it is of the same origin from Samay, I think you can use it until its owner returns for it."

Abba Libanos turned around and went inside the monastery behind him and returned a minute later with a magnificent green spear. This was the same spear he bought a week earlier while he and his manakos were passing through Goltush region.

"I believe this can be of great use to you than to me or any of the manakos up here in this amba. It is a spear of one of the Mal'ekt. We bought it from a couple of traveling merchants who were planning to take it to Aksum to make a profit. I knew it was no ordinary spear when I saw it, so I traded it for the profit they sought."

Mekonnen reached out to hold the spear which has a hefty weight to it and quite long, about almost his own height of 4 cubits (6.1 feet).

"This spear is definitely not from this realm, but it is beautiful," Mekonnen said, holding up the blade part of it as it glistened in the sun light.

Abba Libanos added, "Well, it is not the Sword of the Spirit you seek, but it is from Samayat. So, it will ward off Dark spiritual beings in the meantime until you get to the Tsana Hayq. I assume eventually its owner may appear to you to claim it back."

Mekonnen said, "That will be *melkam*. If I have something that belongs to one of the Mal'ekt, then I hope that guarantees they will show up to assist us in battle in a time of need."

Abba Shiloh said, "U-wa, this spear will be useful. May it be as in Meshaf Wongel Yohannes, (The Gospel of John), when Egzi Iyesus said to the disciple Natanael, *'Hereafter you shall see samayat open and the mal'ekt of Egziabeher ascending and descending upon the Son of Man.'*"

Mekonnen stepped back and began to perform some skillful warrior battle moves and technique he learned in Aksumite warrior training sessions. He flipped and twirled it around his arms and over his shoulders and back, grabbing the attention of the rest of the manakost and bahetawit around them. The spear made a whooshing sound as he maneuvered it around and the engraving on the spear then lit up in a bright yellow-golden color, and the cubit long blade glowed like a lantern and began to look like it was lit with fire inside the blade, but not outside. It startled Mekonnen at first, but then he kept going with the techniques and moves since everyone was looking on at him.

Then he accidentally struck a nearby pot that was on a big rock, and it spilt open clean in half with a great spark and noise that startled everyone nearby. Mekonnen was also startled at what he did and apologized, "*Hazana*! I am sorry for what I did!" When he looked down for the pieces of the pot, he saw not only was the pot destroyed but the rock it sat on was also split open in two like it was a loaf of bread cut with a kitchen knife.

Abba Shiloh said, "Okay now Mekonnen. You better stop with the theatrics before you split the whole amba in two with that thing. This will give you a feel of what the true Sword of the Spirit will be like."

Mekonnen then held the green spear still with the blade pointing upward and the handle resting on the ground next to his right foot. Then he said, "This spear is powerful! Can the *Manfaswi Sayf* be as powerful as this?"

Abba Shiloh replied, "Hrrrm! It can be just as power, but even more powerful than this one, son! If a sword of a mal'ak can do this damage, imagine what the Sayf of the Almighty Egziabeher can do!"

Mekonnen paused to think for a moment the gravity of what Abba Shiloh just told him and then sat quietly on a nearby stool, rested the spear on the ground beside him.

Three hours after the noon, after they ate lunch and prayed, Abba Libanos and the manakost helped Mekonnen and Abba Shiloh gather things for the rest of their journey to Tsana Hyak. A bag with special bread and water placed on Abba Shiloh's shoulder and a special long makeshift sheath for the *mal'akawi* spear was given to Mekonnen.

Abba Libanos said to Mekonnen, "This bread is *manna* from Samay. And the water is *maya tsalot* - holy water - from Samay. They come down to us on the amba during worship to the Almighty Abba. There is also a small bottle of honey that has healing qualities if you are wounded. May you hunger not, and may you never thirst on your journey."

Mekonnen responded, "I thank you Abba for all you have done for us. Egziabeher yismeskan."

Abba Shiloh said, "I also thank you and everyone for your hospitality. Egziabeher yismeskan. I will see you again, Egzi willing."

Then the manakost helped the two men grab on to rope ladders to climb back down the amba where two Abyssinian stallions await them.

References
The Belt of Truth: Eph 6:14,
Put on the armor of Light - Romans 13:12)
The Whole Armor: Wisdom of Solomon 5:17-20, Eph 6: 12-18
He put on Righteousness as a Breastplate - Isaiah 59:16-17
Path of the moon is Light to the righteous – 1 Enoch 41:8

Iyesus Krestos
The King of Righteousness
Jerome Matiyas © 2018

Lord Death Cloak
Lead Qataliyan, Emissary of Death
Jerome Matiyas © 2018

Chapter 12

Chapter 12

Forces Collide

Fine Stallions

Abba Libanos bade farewell to Mekonnen and Abba Shiloh as the manakost assist them down to the ladder safely, back down to the base of the amba. They bought and saddled two white Abyssinian horses for their guests. The horses, white with dabs of gray shading around the nozzle and hind thighs, were well-groomed and trained.

One of the manakost said, "These steeds should get you to the lake quickly and safely. You can fasten them at the port while you use a boat to go to the island monasteries and then use them to return to your village or go where ever you need to for your journey. God Speed to you, my brothers." They thanked the manakost for their hospitality and off the two men went swiftly on horseback to Tsana Hayq.

Meanwhile, two Qataliyan were on top a hill nearby to see and hear from afar off that something was happening on the amba the night before, then they noticed the two men riding off on horseback. This seemed a bit suspicious to them, so that evening after attempting to follow them they put their heads down to the shadows on the ground to report back to *Egzi Barnusa-Mot* – Lord Death Cloak.

"Egzi Barnusa-Mot, we have suspects that just left a holy amba near Wereta. We shall track them to see if one of them is the warrior we seek."

Barnusa-Mot replied, "Good! Keep a safe distance and report back to me as soon as you have a solid confirmation."

Meanwhile, the creature with the two large, curved horns lurking in the forest among the trees is also nearby, tracking the men on horseback. It keeps up with them on its on four deer-like legs, skipping over logs and streams in the woods.

And the mysterious man with the indigo hood that was in the corner of the tavern where Mekonnen and Abba Shiloh ate breakfast has been tracking them and waiting near the base of the amba while they spent the night in the monastery at the top. He also bought himself a fine dark colored Abyssinian stallion from the same horse farmer the manakost got the two white ones for their guests.

The equine beauty had a shiny, dark brown chest and body with black head and mane, black front legs, hind legs and thighs, and black tail. The seller said the stallion was a bit wild and difficult to tame, but when the mysterious buyer approached the nervous horse, whispered reassuring words, and stroked its head and neck, the stallion became calm and submissive. He saddled and mounted the horse, and off he rode after the two men, but stayed a good distance behind not to be spotted by them.

Forces Collide.

Mekonnen and Abba Shiloh rode off towards the south on a path that will take them to the lake port town where they will take a *tankwa* and hire a boatman to row them to the islands in Tsana Hayq to the west. Their horses gallop at a steady pace, but the two Dark Qataliyan who've been secretly following them were leaping through the shadows of trees and rocks in order to keep up with them.

One of them said, "How do we know that one of them is the warrior we're looking for?"

The other replied, "The only way to find out now is to attack them. If his garments flash like lightning, then we know it's him."

The first one replied, "That's a terrible plan! If we're both blinded then who is going to keep track or tell the rest of the dark warriors that we found them?"

The other one replied, "That's easy. *You* are going to jump in from of them first. If you get blinded, *I* will tell the rest we found the target."

Before the first one could reply the other one uses both his legs to jump kick his comrade from out of a shadow into the path of Mekonnen and Abba Shiloh.

As the Qatali stumbles seemingly from nowhere into the path of Mekonnen and the Bahetawi, the two horses were startled and neighed as they raised their front hooves in the air. Abba Shiloh managed to keep his under control, but Mekonnen lost his grip and balance, and fell off his steed to the ground.

The Dark Qatali drew his long sword, poised, ready to fight. Mekonnen jumped back on his feet and draws out his new Mal'akawi spear from the sheath that was strapped onto the side of his horse. Mekonnen stood ready to fight back. Now he felt more confident and ready. Abba Shiloh remained trying to steady his horse as he held up his Masqal staff and looked around to see if any more dark cloaked Qatali like this one were about to attack.

Mekonnen declared, "Come on, demon. I am ready for you!"

The Qatali taunted, "Get ready to die!" and he lounged at Mekonnen with his scimitar above his head.

Mekonnen lifted the blade of his spear and struck his opponent's blade. The impact made a loud clang with a flash of light as sparks flew out.

The other Dark Qatali watched from the shadows and saw the signal they were looking for. A warrior with a flash of light in his apparel. He stooped to the ground and speaks into the shadow to alert the rest his dark comrades.

"We have found our target. A young warrior with flashing clothes and a great spear. Riding south with an old companion with long, white locks of hair. Both are on horseback. We need reinforcements now!"

The other Dark Qataliyan across the land received the alert. Barnusa-Mot asked, "Where are you located, shadow warrior?"

He responded, "On a path south of Wereta!"

Mekonnen and the cloaked opponent were still clashing weapons. Immediately Mekonnen's new shemis with the golden fringes transformed from white to a hardened golden breastplate, to become the Breastplate of Righteousness. Mekonnen mades a three-quarter spin with spear still up in the air and brought the hilt of it down onto the Qatali's torso. He squirmed in pain from the blow and made a return by pushing off the warrior with his scimitar blade and body force, sending Mekonnen a few feet off the path. Mekonnen maintained his footing and charged forward again with the blade pointed forward at his opponent. His opponent stepped aside and reflected the spear with his blade. Mekonnen made another quick maneuver and began to spin the spear over his arm like what he did on the amba the other day. This caught the Dark Qatali off guard and Mekonnen brought the spear blade down on its arm, slicing it off at the elbow, then spun again diagonally, slicing his opponent through from the right side of its neck down to under its left armpit.

Mekonnen stepped back and beheld his victory, his opponent in pieces. The body dropped to the ground, but there was no blood. Instead the corpse transformed into a knot of snakes that slivered away into the ground and shadows, fearing the light from Mekonnen's breastplate and belt. Its scimitar remained on the ground, but Abba Shiloh, still on his horse shouts in Ge'ez, "*Hayl ZaBirhan*! – The Power of The Light!" – waved his Masqal staff like a sword as a bolt of light and flames streamed out like in a crescent shape, striking the scimitar, burning it to ashes like it was a plank of wood.

Mekonnen looked up at Abba Shiloh quickly, not expecting to see flames shooting out of the staff then said,

"It worked Abba! The spear destroyed the Qatali! But your staff, I didn't know…"

Abba Shiloh interrupted, "You didn't know my staff could also be a weapon, hrrmm. I know. I want to look innocent. It catches the enemy by surprise, hrrm."

Abba Shiloh looked around frantically about the area and commanded, "Come on, I don't think that one was traveling alone. That may have been a decoy to sift us out of hiding. Now that you revealed your garments of light and the mal'akawi spear, they know where we are and probably sending more Qataliyan after us. Mount your horse and let us ride on!"

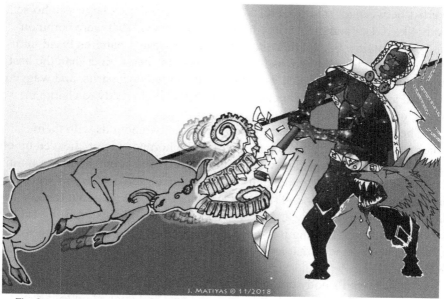

The Great Hayyal Attacks a Qatali.
By Jerome Matiyas © 9/2018

Wrath of the Great Ibex.

Mekonnen and Abba Shiloh rode on faster to the south, on the alert and ready to fight more cloaked Qataliyan that were most likely closing in on them. They came to a hill with a path going up on the side as the top of trees can be seen in a valley below.

The Qataliyan converged from the north, south, and west until they reached the location of two men on horseback. They also brought along some savage gnarling Hell-Hounds – the Kalabat-Si'ol – with them. A villainous troop of two Qataliyan and two Hell-Hounds follow the two men from the valley below and three at the top from the west while three approaching from the south to meet them head-on. The warrior and the holy man could not see that they were going to be cornered yet, but they were ready and prepared for what may transpire when the determined villains trap and surround them from all sides.

Just then, from the top of a mountain appeared a great horned creature, leaping down from mountain peak to mountain peak, and from amba to amba, towards this commotion where opposing forces intend to collide. It leapt down into the valley and sped up with curved horns pointing forward, charging headlong into the six unsuspecting Dark Qataliyan and Kalabata-Si'ol. The horned beast knocked over four out of the six off their feet, catapulting them several feet into the air. It happened so fast the other two had no idea what hit their comrades. The horned creature, which looks like a cross between an antelope and a *hayyal* – an ibex –, is a large as a horse, body like a deer and great curve horns like the hayyal that were common in the mountains. Except this one had engraved design patterns fused into its horns that glowed yellowish-gold. It was a fine beast, finer than the best horses in the land. It bucked its hooves and snorted its nostrils, and wagged its head and great horns that curves about 4 feet high, ready to charge in again, with fury.

The two Qataliyan poised for battle and the two hounds with them charged towards the horned creature first. The horned creature heaved up on its hind legs then lounged forward with a swift speed at one hound, slamming it into the ground with tremendous force. He then used his horn to scoop up the mangled Hell-Hound from the ground, flinged it up about ten feet in the air, then spun its body around and kicked the monstrous, snarling canine with its hind legs, sending it flying onto the side of the amba as it smashed onto the steep slope with a loud crash and a crumbling sound, *DOOOVVVV!!* KKRUMMBLE!!

As the hound's body crumples down to the ground into a heap of burnt ashes, the other one lounged at the horned beast and latched on to it back with its teeth. The *Abiyy Hayyal* – Great Ibex – with as much force as it could, lifted its hind legs and kicked the hound off, sending it flying up in the air. As it came back down the *Abiyy Hayyal* tossed its horns at it, sending the hound creature flying into the woods. The hound got back up on its four feet and rushed in again towards its horned opponent who heaved up again and charged its head and horns downwards onto the Hell-Hound so hard it snapped the savage canine's head clean off.

As the second hound's body disintegrates, one of the two cloaked Qatali that remained aimed and threw its spear at the horned beast, but it swirled its neck and reflected the spear away with its horns like it was just a paltry stick. The Qatali that threw the spear ran away into the shadow of the woods in fear. The last Qatali remaining has an axe in his hands. He waited first to see what his horned opponent would do, but the Great Hayyal also waited to see what its axe-wielding opponent will do. They circle each other for a minute. Then they both made their moves simultaneously. The Qatali charged forward with full speed, leaping into the air with the axe coming down from above his head. The Great Hayyal also leapt with a head on charge. Its Qatali opponent was actually pretending to make a downward move and quickly switched to a side swipe, aiming at its Hayyal opponent's broad neck. The Great Hayyal recognized the deception in time, so he lowered his horns to the left side with its horns glowing as the intricate patterns on the horns lit up like streams of gold. The axe blade struck one horn and shattered on impact like a glass mirror, sending splinters of axe blade flying in many directions. Now he was just holding the useless axe handle. Still, in midair, the Horned Hayyal creature maneuvered its body to kick the Dark Qatali in the face with its hind legs. The cloaked villain fell to the ground on its back; the Horned-creature landed on its feet with a skid. As the cloaked villain attempted to stagger to its feet the Horned one charged at it at full speed and ramed into its opponent's torso, smashing it into the side of the steep mountain slope. The impact was so hard the Dark Qatali got embedded into dirt and rocks making it seem as if it disappeared into the shadows, as it indeed fell back into the other side of Darkness.

The impact made such a loud noise that Mekonnen and Abba Shiloh heard sounds like thunder claps behind them as they were riding away from a battle they were unaware of. They did not even get to see another creature fighting against agents of Darkness on their behalf.

Mekonnen exclaimed, "What's going on back there!"

Abba Shiloh replied, "I don't know, but whatever it is, it's behind us. And we're riding away from it! Hrrrmm."

The Abiyy Hayyal creature had defeated his opponents, for now. It turns around and leapt down into the forest below and back up the amba that's adjacent to the two horseback riders he just defended. Still trying to follow them without being seen.

Meanwhile, the Dark Qatali that ran away in fear crouched down to a shadow on the ground to call for more Qatali-reinforcements. "*Egzi Barnusa-Mot* – Lord Death Cloak! Send more *Tsallim Qalatiyan* and *Kalabat-Si'ol* now! We were attacked by an *Abiyy Samayawi Qarn Arwe* – A Great Heavenly Horned Creature –, and the warrior target is riding off with an old holy man of sorts!!"

Green Warrior Dives In.

They were still not clear from danger yet because as Mekonnen and the Bahetawi continued the path while the Great Ibex covered their backs, three Qataliyan leapt from a hill above as three more were charging head on towards them with all manner of sharp, deadly weapons. One villain shot two arrows at Mekonnen and two at Abba Shiloh. Mekonnen was able to refract one arrow with his spear as the other arrow struck him on his shoulder, but it just bounces off his golden breastplate. That moment he knew and was convinced his Breastplate of Righteousness was truly impenetrable.

Abba Shiloh exclaimed those words again, "*Hayla ZaBerhan!* –Power of Light!" waved his cross staff and a crescent shaped flame flew out and above him to incinerate both arrows at once. Now Mekonnen knew the Bahetawi can defend himself without even wielding a sword or spear.

A Qatali pulled back a bow and shot off another arrow aiming at Mekonnen's chest and struck his breastplate, only to shatter into pieces on impact. Another Dark Qatali leapt at them from above to strike a blow down at Mekonnen with a sword, but the warrior was able to lift the spear in time to block the blow. He did a quick swirl and spin of the wrist to strike the creature in the neck and head. That Qatali crumbled into a knot of snakes before it hit the ground.

Abba Shiloh exclaimed, "*Sayfa ZaBerhan* – Sword of Light!" and throws a white bean of light shape like the blade of a sword at one leaping Qatali in the torso. The light-blade ran through the Qatali like linen cloth, incinerating his body into ashes.

Still, at his base in the shadowy cave near Roha where they now called *Zoheleth-Meswa* – Serpent's Altar –, Lord Death Cloak shouted commands to his dark army, "I command all Shadow Warrior Qataliyan in the region near Wereta to converge onto the target and bring them down!"

At his command thirteen more Dark Qataliyan and five more of their dreadful Hell-Hounds ran into the shadows from the north and south, intending to block the paths from the front and behind, to trap Mekonnen and Abba Shiloh in the middle.

As the two warriors of Light rode on hard, they saw in the distance a dark horde of many Qataliyan and some hounds approaching from the south. The sound of their feet could be heard rumbling in the distance. Then they noticed the same sound approaching from behind them. Abba Shiloh turned his head quickly to look behind him to see about a dozen cloaked Qataliyan approaching from the north in the road behind them.

As he rode alongside his young protégé, Abba Shiloh shouted, "Oh, Anbessa! Looks like they're trying to trap us! From in front and behind! Brace yourself! Be prepared to fight!"

Mekonnen retorted, "I see! I say bring them on! We are ready for them! We can take them on, right?!"

Abba Shiloh wanted to be in faith and positive as he's always been, but with this many of them he began to be a little concerned for Mekonnen. He wasn't sure if the young warrior was ready to take on so many of the dark evil forces at once! Despite being in possession of a Mal'akawi Spear of great power and sharpness. He spoke by faith anyway. "U-wa! We can definitely take them on! Egziabeher is with us and will give us strength! *Hayl Egziabeher Berhan*!!" Abba Shiloh's staff and cross glowed like lightning sparkling and crawling up and down the length of it. Mekonnen raised himself up high from a sitting position to a standing position on his horse and leaned forward with spear in right hand raised up above his head as he spurred on his horse, "Hiya! Hiya! Come on you demons! Come on! We come in the name and power of Egziabeher Amlak!"

The two forces rode on towards each other, head on, without stopping as if to collide with each other. The space between them became smaller and smaller. 1000 yards. 850 yards. 700 yards. Still both sides kept on charging towards each other. Mekonnen saw three Dark Qataliyan riding on the backs of three Kalabata-Si'ol, with their spears pointing forward, straight at Mekonnen, just like in a jousting match. Now 550 yards. 400 yards. Abba Shiloh glanced behind and saw more Qataliyan gaining on them from the rear, only about 750 yards behind them. A Qatali shot an arrow at them but Abba Shiloh intercepted it with his lightning imbued staff.

"Keep going Mekonnen! I'll cover the back!" the holy man shouted to the warrior, as he spun his body around to face the back while his horse kept riding forward. Several more arrows flew at them and Abba Shiloh reflected all of them expect two. One grazed his left leg at the calf and the other his arm at the elbow, but he didn't even feel them. But as Abba Shiloh looked beyond and behind the Qataliyan that pursued them, he saw another figure approaching from the north on a very fast, dark brown horse behind them. It looked like a man in a dark colored hood and a great flashing blade of a sword or a spear in his right hand. It looked like he is taking the Dark Qataliyan on a surprise attack from behind them.

Abba Shiloh exclaimed to Mekonnen, "We have company!"

Mekonnen did not understand what he meant but was focused on the oncoming collision in from of them. Only 150 yards away now, in 7 seconds.

The dark horse rider caught up with the Dark Qataliyan riders and began swiping his blade swiftly from left to right and left again, then diagonally, at their necks and torsos so swiftly and clean it took more than 3 seconds for them to fall apart like pieces burning coals on the path. The dark rider's horse leapt over the rubble of deteriorating Qataliyan, as the rider himself leapt off his horse and did a flip towards the rest of the charging horde of Qataliyan in front of them. Abba Shiloh understood now it was a Mal'ak to the rescue again, so he just smiled.

But at 0 yards ahead, Mekonnen collided with a jousting opponent causing them both to flip over their rides, as the horse and hell-hound slammed and flip over each other. They all crashed and tumble to the ground. Mekonnen's opponent's spear did impact with his Breastplate but it did not penetrate despite the great speed at which they crashed into each other. The impact did hurt and knocked some wind out of Mekonnen but he was not impaled, unlike his opponent, who was ran straight through with the Mal'akawi spear, with the blade sticking out through the Qatali's back. Mekonnen's horse still lay on the ground wounded, but his opponent's hound was still alert, snapping at Mekonnen's head. The warrior dodged the savage jaws of the foul-mouthed beast in time, rolling on the ground towards the crumbling body of the opponent, and quickly jumped up to his feet to pull out the spear and use it to stand against the Hell-Hound.

Meanwhile there were more collisions happening around Mekonnen at the same time. Abba Shiloh collided with another Hell-Hound and Cloaked Qatali rider, also falls off his horse. But the mysterious dark rider that just helped them from behind, leaps over Abba Shiloh and Mekonnen, lands on his feet with agility amid the chaos, and begins swiping his great blade at some other Dark Qataliyan and Hell-Hounds that challenge him. One Qatali opponent after another opposed him, clashing swords and spears and axes with him occasionally but eventually he overcame and swiped six of them down, one by one. He moved gracefully and valiantly, like a deadly dancer. The other two diabolical Hell-Hounds also did not stand a chance, as one got sliced through the mouth and torso.

In the midst of battle, Mekonnen observed the peculiar way the Qataliyan and Hell-Hounds' corpses decomposed as they were struck down. When the cloaked villains were struck down with the Mal'ak's spear in his hands their corpses transform into a knots of venoms snakes. Similar effect to what happens when they were struck down by regular swords and arrows in Aksum and in the mountains. But the spear in the hands of the Mal'ak cuts them down into ashes.

Also, when Abba Shiloh struck the Qataliyan with lightning or flames from his Masqal staff they burnt up into ashes, with no snakes emerging. It seemed the Bahetawi's words of declaration possessed a special power unlike the Mal'akawi weapon like the spear in Mekonnen's hands. If they survived this battle, Mekonnen wanted to remember to ask Abba Shiloh to explain the discrepancy the weapons' effectiveness.

Mekonnen managed to defeat his opponent's Hell-Hound with the spear through the chest. Then Mekonnen looked up and saw the mysterious warrior with the indigo hood and cloak, dark green apparel and buckled booths underneath cloak, standing before him and Abba Shiloh, about 9 feet tall. And immediately he recognized him as being a Mal'ak from the army hosts of Samayat, and the same green warrior who helped him and his comrades about a week ago in Gultosh. Mekonnen bowed quickly and said, "Greetings, Mal'ak. We thank you for your service to us. Egziabeher yamasgan!"

The Mal'ak responded, "Egziabeher yamasgan! My pleasure to be at your service again. I was defeated by Dark Qataliyan, as you call them, after you last saw me. I was captured, and my comrades from the army hosts of Samay came and rescued me under the Samen Mountains in the Dark Realm. When you fell into the Dark Realm with the maiden and you were rescued by the Mal'ekt, I was also rescued that same hour."

Mekonnen exclaimed, "U-wa! I remember! I did not know you were also rescued that night!"

Green Mal'ak replied, "U-wa, I was! That night I lost my spear. Now you wield it in your hands."

Mekonnen exclaimed, "Oh, your spear! I did not know. Here, it is yours. You can take it…."

The Green Mal'ak, "No, you can use it a bit longer. I will take it from

The Abiyy Hayyal   Copyright © Jerome Matiyas 2017

you when you reach your destination, at Tsana Hayq. We must move quickly; more Tsallim Qataliyan were coming out the shadows." The Mal'ak pointed in the distance about 1000 yards away where about a dozen more Dark Qataliyan running towards them.

"Quickly! I only have 7 more hours to be with you before I must return to Samay. But your horse is injured."

The Mal'ak pointed at Mekonnen's wounded horse on the ground, neighing as it bled from one of its back legs at the knee.

The Mal'ak said, "You have healing ointment in your bag."

Mekonnen was confused and did not understand want he meant that he has some medicine in his bag.

Abba Shiloh looked for the bag the manakost in the amba with Abba Libanos gave them and said the water is holy water and the honey was also blessed and had healing qualities. He gave the bottle of honey to Mekonnen.

"Mekonnen, the honey the manakost gave us has healing qualities. Quick, rub some on your horses wound!"

Mekonnen quickly opened the bottle and poured some thick honey in his right hand and robbed it on the horses wounded knee. Meanwhile, the rumbling sound of feet from the Dark Qataliyan approaching grew louder. The Mal'ak then said. "You have water in your bag, give some to you horse to drink." Abba Shiloh quickly pulled open the bottle and poured into the horse's mouth. Soon the horse began to revive as Mekonnen helps him stand up on its four legs and hooves.

Mekonnen exclaimed, "That is amazing!"

The Mal'ak immediately mounted his dark brown stallion and ordered the two men, "We must go now! I will ride with you, but we go east, to lead them off your trail."

Mekonnen said, "But Tsana Hayq is to the west!"

The Mal'ak insisted, "Trust me!"

Mekonnen argued no more and leapt on his horse since the Dark Qataliyan drew closer. Abba Shiloh also mounted on his horse and off they went. Off the trail, eastward.

The Mal'ak lead the way and said, "We have help to distract them for a while."

The two men glanced behind and saw the Abiyy Qarn Arwe – The Great Horned Beast – the Abiyy Hayyal, the one who fought for them earlier without their knowledge, had returned. They witnessed the Abiyy Hayyal running down the mountain at full speed and rammed headlong into the band of Dark Qataliyan that attempted to follow them. This bold move distracted the villains to focus their attention on fighting the Abiyy Hayyal instead.

"Oh, what is that creature with the horns?" Mekonnen exclaimed.

As they continued riding on Abba Shiloh answered, "That is another creature from the Realms of Samayat sent to fight for us against the enemy. Egziabeher has many creatures and Mal'ekt assigned to help his servants to complete their mission."

The Green Mal'ak said, "Look forward now! I will throw a stone ahead, and as it lands on the ground, you will see it open up a fiery archway in from of us. We will run through it and keep going. We will ride eastward, but it is actually a doorway to take us westward. Just follow the flow of the river. Hang on!"

The Mal'ak reached into a pouch on his waist and pulls out a smooth white stone, about 2 inches in diameter, and throws it 50 yards ahead of them. When the stone hit the ground, it caught fire, and the flames formed a fiery archway. They rode through the fiery arch as it still looked the same as if they were riding towards Guna Mountain. Even the Qataliyan behind them thought they were saw their targets rode eastwards as they fought with the

Abiyy Hayyal.

The arch of flames gradually faded until it was no more. Six of the Qataliyan escaped from the Abiyy Hayyal and took off into the shadows towards the east in pursue of their targets, but they lost them. They ended up in the Guna Mountain and found no trace of their targets Mekonnen and Abba Shiloh. When they realized they were tricked into going the wrong way, they headed back north to Roha and their altar at Zoheleth. They reported back to their Lord Death Cloak and Lord Silver Gauntlet.

"You Fools! Defeated again by a mare *Ish*! A Man!" Lord Death Cloak scolded them.

"Not so, Egzi! They had help from a Mal'ak and a Qarn Arwe! They were…"

Death Cloak interrupted, "Silence!" In anger, he grabbed a spear and threw it at the Dark Qatali who was giving his report, and pinned him to a wall, as its body disintegrated into black snakes before disappearing into the shadows."

The Silver Gauntlet interjected, "Death Cloak, be not consumed by wrath. When we have more followers from Roha ready to worship Waynaba and sacrifice to him, you will all grow stronger and more powerful than you are now. And your Dark Qataliyan will be more successful in capturing our main adversary. You just wait and see."

Standing before them was Negus Leqsem and about two dozen citizens of Roha, ready to serve Waynaba because they were promised power, prosperity, and wealth. And one of the young women actually offered herself to be a living blood sacrifice.

The Shores of Tsana Hayq.

Three hours later as the sun set at dusk, Mekonnen, Abba Shiloh, and the Green Mal'ak rode along the path that ran parallel to the Gumara River. This river flowed west until they reached the region going towards Tsana Hayq. The river flowed through a lake town and into the waters of Tsana Hayq. As they rode past two armed guards standing at each side of the gate entrance, they glanced upwards at the top of the gate's archway to read the name of the town etched in bold Ge'ez letters on acacia wood, "WANZAGAY". The three rented a tavern room to rest for the night. At the town's lake port, there were *tankwas* – papyrus canoes – that hired boatmen used to take authorized persons to the monastery islands in the lake. The Tsana Hayq could be seen in the distance just about a mile away from the tavern. That evening, for a peaceful moment, the warrior, the Bahetawi, and the Mal'ak got to witness the beauty of a sunset, as the sky became carpeted with streaks of purple, lavender and orange clouds, reflecting the sun as it glowed red and slowly dipped into the lake on the horizon.

Abba Shiloh reached into the pouch the manakos gave him and pulled out the bread that they claimed was made of manna from Samay and the *maya tsalot* which is holy water. They broke one piece of bread and split it amongst the three of them and ate it and drank some of the water from the flask. As they ate, Abba Shiloh began to thank the Mal'ak, "We were truly thankful for protecting us."

The Mal'ak replied bluntly, "Thank Egziabeher Amlak." He stood up and looks around at the horizon in all direction as a he spoke. "You will be safe in this lake town. It is called Wanzagay and the Gumara River flows through it into the Tsana Hayq. There were no Dark Warrior Qataliyan chasing you here. Tomorrow morning you shall go to the Qirqos Island. There you will find the *Manfesawai Sayf* you seek and need for the rest of your journey."

The Mal'ak stretched out his hands towards the mighty spear by Mekonnen's side and said bluntly, "You do not need that spear anymore."

Mekonnen said hesitantly, "Oh, huh, U-wa. Of course. Uh, I was getting used to it. It has been very useful. I like the way it feels in my hands. Here you go. All yours, Mal'ak."

"Amezgana. You will not be needing it when you go on the island in the lake. When you go to the island, the manakost of Beta Israel will lead you to the Sayf that was crafted and designed for you only."

Mekonnen said, "Hrai, I hope the Dark Qataliyan do not find us here. What if we need to fight them again before I reach the island and the Sayf?"

The Mal'ak replied, "If you need assistance, the Egzi in Samay will send me to you." The Mal'ak took the spear from Mekonnen's hands and attached the shaft to the hilt of his sword with a twist of the wrists and a klikity-klak sound. Now he was holding a double spear with a blade on both ends, making it look even more deadly.

"Hawey! Before you leave!" Mekonnen exclaimed with urgency in his voice, "I want to ask you about these weapons, and you, Abba Shiloh, about your Masqal!"

"Hrai." The Green Mal'ak replied, "What would you like to know, Warrior Mekonnen?"

Abba Shiloh added, "Hrrmm. Go on, Anbessa."

Mekonnen continued, "When we were fighting with the enemy I noticed when I struck down the Qataliyan and the hounds, with your spear, they transformed into snakes then slithered into the shadows. But when you struck them down with your weapon, and also when Abba Shiloh declared words of power, flames and lightnings flash out of his Masqal and struck them down into ashes!"

Mekonnen looked at both the Green Mal'ak and Abba Shiloh then continues, "So tell me, Abba Shiloh, and my friend, what is the difference between my weapon and yours, and my words and your words?"

The Green Mal'ak responded, "Egzi Mekonnen, the reason my spare in your hands cut the dark creatures down to venomous vipers is because this spear was not fashioned for you to wield in this realm of Meder. This weapon was fashioned for my use only. In Meder and Samayat. When wielded in my hands they will destroy the agents of Darkness in the way the Father, Egziabeher Amlak, intended to in my hands."

"Hrai, that is interesting." Mekonnen responded.

The Mal'ak continued, "Therefore, when you used my spear against the creatures of Darkness, their serpents slither back into the deep shadows, only to return again into another location in this Realm of Meder, to continue their evil works. As for Abba Shiloh's words of fire and lightning through his Masqal? I will let him explain it to you."

Mekonnen turned his undivided attention to his long-white-haired mentor.

"Anbessa, you see, the power is not in the Masqal, but in the *Qala Egziabeher* – the Word of The Lord of the World. The Word of Egziabeher is a mighty powerful Sword of Light that dispels all Darkness in this Meder realm and Spiritual realm. The Word of Egziabeher is a strong Sword in His mighty arm! It destroys the works of the enemy! Hrrmm! Do you understand, Anbessa?" (Psalms 89:13, Isaiah 21:1, Hebrews 4:12, Revelation 19:15)

Mekonnen was a bit overwhelmed by the deep mysteries that were just explained to him, but the eyes of his understanding had been enlightened significantly.

"U-wa." Mekonnen replied, "I understand, Abba Shiloh. So, that's why when they were cut down with earthly blades, their wounds would transform into snakes, then their limbs can grow back. Like what happened in Aksum and in the Samen Mountains. That's why we were not able to defeat the Qataliyan, the Hounds and the Great Beasts."

Abba Shiloh continued,

"That is correct. Blades and fire from natural weapons can only cut them down temporarily, but spiritual weapons can destroy their bodies and send their spirits back into the dark shadows or into the abyss where they are bound in chains until judgement day. It all depends on the weapon and the level of faith of the one wielding the weapon."

The Green Mal'ak continued, as he prepares to leave, "Correct. And also, very important to remember: One must not contend with a *ganen*, a Mal'ak, or Chief Prince (a principality) unless one recognizes the power and authority in the Elect One, Iyesus Krestos that was given to Him from Egziabeher Amlak. This power and authority is reflected into the *Manfasawi Sayf* as you stand firm against the creatures of Darkness. Now, I must leave you two, as my time has almost expired."

With a subtle bow of his head, Mekonnen acknowledged the green spear wielder, "Hrai. *Fanawa* – Farewell, Mal'ak. We thank you for your assistance."

"*Fanawa* – Farewell. I will not be far away." said the Mal'ak as he spun the double bladed spear very fast in front of him until it looked like the top of an umbrella, forming a green and silver circular pattern, and then he vanished with it, right in front of Mekonnen and Abba Shiloh in the blink of an eye.

Mekonnen sighed, "*Sigh*. I will miss that spear."

Abba Shiloh said matter of factly, "The *Manfesawi Sayf* you are about to seek is even more powerful than that spear you've been using."

Mekonnen is surprised, "How is that possible? That spear was so powerful!"

Abba Shiloh answered, "That was the *Salatina Mal'ak* – Spear/Lance of an Angel. What you seek is *Manfasawi Sayfa Egziabeher* – the Spiritual Sword of the Lord of the World. As the Mal'ak said: When Egzi Iyesus Krestos was sacrificed on the Masqal in Eyerusalem, and resurrected from Si'ol to life, then he ascended back to Samayat to sit at the right hand of His Father, Egziabeher Amlak, He was given all power and authority in the realms of *Samayat wa Meder* – Heavens and Earth – to thread upon all creatures of Darkness and their evil works. He has set us free from the bondage and unrighteousness that was inflicted upon us by force with the weapons and chains of Darkness. When you believe this Truth, you can pick up the Great Sword of the Spirit to stand firm, and battle against every principality, powers, thrones, Malekt or vile beasts that opposes the Light of Egziabeher (Luke 10:17-20; Colossians 1:16; Ephesians 6:12-18, Romans 10:15)

Abba Shiloh began to open his mouth wide to yawn from weariness. "*Yawn*! Now let us get some sleep, Anbessa. I will explain more to you tomorrow, hrrm."

Mekonnen suddenly remembered another incident from their battle with the Dark Qataliyan just before their escape through the Mal'ak's fiery gate, "Hawey! And what about that *Abiyy Awre* with the great horns who helped us by ramming into the Qataliyan? It looked like a giant deer or hayyal! Where did it come from?"

Abba Shiloh lifted his weary head off the pillow and answers, "In Egziabeher's Mangesta Samayat there are many creatures great and amazing. There are Mal'ekt, Kerubel, Surafel, Onafel and more. Some look like creatures in this earthly realm of Meder; some look more amazing, terrifying, and glorious. Some Mal'ekt and creatures are for war, and others are for ministering and singing songs. That one just happened to be a *Samayawi Arwe* – Heavenly Creature – that looks like Abiyy Hayyal – a Great Ibex. Made for war. And I believe I have seen him before around Gihon village, hrrmm. Now let us get some sleep, Anbessa."

Mekonnen and Abba Shiloh rested their heads on pillows and fell asleep to the sound of crickets and frogs singing their choruses in the brisk night air.

Before Abba Shiloh fell asleep, he had one last word for his mentee, "I must say I am proud of how you have been handling yourself and understanding spiritual things of this world and Samay now. You are learning more on how to use the Word of Egziabeher and how to fight the enemy. You have been a victorious warrior, Anbessa!"

Mekonnen laid awake for a long while after the Bahetawi fell fast asleep, staring at the ceiling, thinking of all the amazing battles he fought and won that day. Now he grew excited to discover whatever lies ahead on this perilous adventure.

He whispered a prayer before falling asleep, "Egziabeher amlak! Protect me and give me strength to seek and find your Manfasawi Sayf. Iyesus Sem. Amen."

As he laid his head on the pillow and closed his eyes, he remembered the dream-vision he had during Afeworq's funeral wake, of running down the valley with the benefactors on the right side and the adversaries on the left. It now occurred to him that the old man with the long white locks of hair and beard looked very much like his new mentor, Abba Shiloh.

Then he smiled, as he realizes he felt encouraged and liked it when Abba Shiloh called him, "Anbessa."

Forces Collide
Matiyas © 14/8/2018

Chapter 13

Chapter 13

Eyes on Tsana Hayq

(Eyes on Lake T'ana)

Mekonnen had been looking forward to this day since he was told by the Egzi Iyesus Krestos in a vision on the Abba Libanos' amba that he needed to go to the island of Tsana Qirqos on *Tsana Hayq* – Lake Tsana – to acquire the powerful *Manfasawi Sayf* – The Sword of the Spirit. This is the very sacred and legendary island where the original *Tabot* – The Holy Ark of the Covenant – from the ancient Kingdom of Israel once resided for 800 years after it was taken from the temple of King Solomon by the sons of his *kahenat* – priests – when Solomon's son Menelik left Abyssinia to visit his father more than 1400 years ago. So the legend goes.

"How does one approach such an isle with so much history and legend surrounding it? And how do I address the manakost that abide there?" Mekonnen thought to himself as he prepared, in a tavern with his new mentor and spiritual father, Abba Shiloh.

"Uhmm, Hrunn, Anbessa. This is the day." Growled Abba Shiloh as they mounted their horses. In about 10 minutes they rode through the lake town of Wanzagay to its seaport where they can hire a boat man to row them to the Holy Island of Qirqos. They left their stallions in the care of a man Abba Shiloh knew very well, then selected one of the boat men at the port, who authorized Abba Shiloh because he can see he is a Bahetawi, and Mekonnen because he showed his official Aksumite Warrior wristband, embedded with a seal engraved with a depiction of the head of a lion bracketed by two stalks of wheat, and the motto in Ge'ez language below it, "*May this please the people*".

Abba Shiloh said to Mekonnen, "Hrmm, here, Anbessa, sit in the boat and wait for me."

So Mekonnen carefully climbed into the yellowish papyrus boat that was tied to the wooden port with an old rope, and he made himself comfortable, shifting his body a bit and waited for Abba Shiloh as he conversed briefly with the boat man. He saw the old man whip out a few coins from under his clothes and gave it to the boat man to pay him, who was older than Mekonnen but still quite younger than Abba Shiloh. But to Mekonnen's surprise, after Shiloh paid the man, he walked away from them back towards the village instead of towards the tankwa he was in.

Mekonnen exclaimed, "Huh? Uh, Abba Shiloh why is he going away? Is he getting someone else to row us to the island?"

Abba Shiloh, with his staff in hand, walked towards Mekonnen and said.

"No, I paid him and sent him home. We don't need him. *You* are going to row us to the Tsana Qirqos Island."

"What, *I* am going to row us there? But I'm a warrior, Abba Shiloh, not a boatman!"

Abba Shiloh quietly eased his body into the boat in front of Mekonnen and said.

"You're a young man, fully capable of taking us there. You know how to row, right? Come on let's go!"

"But Abba, I have not rowed a reed boat in years, I..."

"All the more a reason for you to start rowing. You need the exercise anyway, hrmm. Time for you the start strengthening those arms of yours again. Ever since you've been in my village, you've been lazy."

Mekonnen recanted "But my arms are quite sore from the battles yester..."

Shiloh interrupted, "Ahhh, that is nothing, this is a different type of work. Now come on don't argue with me! Start rowing before it gets dark!"

So Mekonnen grudgingly grabbed the two ores, mumbling to himself, how the Bahetawi had the nerve to tell a warrior of the Aksumite Royal Court to row a boat.

"You will thank me for this later, my son. This is to teach you a lesson in life. You must learn the lesson of obedience and servanthood. Be a servant rather than being served, hrmm, yes that's right."

Mekonnen just kept on rowing, a little annoyed of Abba Shiloh's ranting about servanthood and lessons in life and all those wise sayings of his. He figured he better do as the Holy man said or some misfortune may come upon him for not doing what the Almighty may be saying through his Prophet. So, rowing he did, and after a good way off shore, Abba Shiloh decided to arise and stand up in the boat, propping himself up with his Masqal staff like a cane.

"Oh, Great!" Mekonnen thought to himself, "I hope a strong wind does not blow over us and knock the Bahetawi into this lake. I heard there are alligators and serpents in this lake. And only Egziaheher knows what else lurks in the deep."

About the Beta Israel

Mekonnen asked the holy man a question, "So, Abba Shiloh. The Mal'ak mentioned that the people living in Qirqos Tsana island are of Beta Israel. Is it safe for us to go there? I mean, will they welcome us?"

Still standing, he answered, "Yes, of course, they will! They know me as a friend and a brother. I have developed a relationship with the Beta Israel through the years. We have a love a respect for each other, despite our differences is belief and religion. And despite the rivalry with Aksumite Empire in previous years. As you know, they was a peace treaty, a sacred oath, made between them, which involves the *Tabot* and the *Saragalla* – the Chariot. Details of how this oath was carried about is very mysterious but this it brought about the agreement to cease warfare. I believe the exchange of wives and concubines were involves. Beta Israel maidens were given to the Nagast and Qasisat as wives. And Aksumite maidens were given to Beta Israel Nagast and Kahen as wives also. To what scale and how many were exchanged I am not sure."

Mekonnen replied, "Oh, interesting. That would explain a lot of things."

Abba Shiloh answered, "U-wa, but this conflict with the Tsallim Qataliyan attacking both kingdoms from the shadows is threatening that peace treaty. Now they are tempted to blame each other for the attacks."

Mekonnen responded, "That is true! When I was in the courts with the Nagast and Qasisan, they were arguing amongst themselves about who is really involved in the assassination attempts, and the Beta Israel came up in the conversation. But some were observant to dismiss that idea, because of the nature of the attackers: The strange symbols of their cloaks and robes, their fighting style, and the fact they transformed into snakes when struck down."

Abba Shiloh replied, "Correct! The Dark Qataliyan have absolutely no connection to the Sicarii of the Beta Israel!"

Mekonnen asked, "*Sicarii*? What is the Sacarii?"

Abba Shiloh answered, "Sicarii are the secret group of deadly warriors of the Beta Israel who used to secretly infiltrate the kingdom to kill the Nagast and leaders of the Aksumite Empire before the peace oath. This was one of their strategies to try to topple the empire. Sicarii is from the Latin word the Romans called the Jewish zealots that carried missions to kill the Roman leaders that occupied Eyerusalem before it was destroyed in 70 A.D. with daggers called *sicae*. It is basically the same as *Qataliyan* in the Ge'ez language."

Mekonnen took in a gasp of air to indicate he understood.

Abba Shiloh continued, "Only difference is that these Qataliyan are not men of flesh and blood, but as you've already seen, evil creatures from another realm."

Mekonnen added, "U-wa! I can confirm they also attacked the Beta

Israel because when I was in the Samen Mountains with my warriors, we encountered a Beta Israel warrior on horseback who told us their kingdom was also attacked. The one of their Nagast or Kahen was killed by them."

Abba Shiloh added, "That mean these creatures are out to attack and destroy all the kingdoms and people of the land, no matter what kingdom, or language, or tribe."

As Mekonnen continued rowing Abba Shiloh continues, "As I was saying, the Beta Israel have come to accept me as a brother and a friend. But also, many of my ancestors were of Beta Israel before coming to believe in Iyesus Krestos and be part of the Aksumite Empire. My family was among those who complied with Negus Ezana edict to convert the kingdom from pagan religion of the Greeks to Krestyan in 330 A.D. My ancestors were Agaw people from near the Samen Dabr that intermarried with Israelites that came from Eyerusalem after Nigist Makeda, the Nigista Saba – the Queen of Sheba – visited Negus Solomon. She brought the *Yihudawi* –Jewish – beliefs, laws and practices of Negus Solomon with her. As you know, the Beta Israel who refused to comply became outcast from the Kingdom, which was when they called them… us… *Falashas*."

Mekonnen answered, "U-wa! My family history is quite similar. They were also Agaw people that became Beta Israel. But not through Nigist Saba's visit. It was after the Israelites went into exile when the Babylonians destroyed Eyerusalem and the first temple. That is what my father told my brothers and I when he was alive."

Abba Shiloh added, "The Hebrews and Israelites came into Habeshenia at different time periods in history. They intermarried with some of the locale Agaw people to form the Beta Israel, as you know. So, our ancestors are from the same places, so we are related in a sense."

Mekonnen said, "So it is quite a contradiction for the Aksumites and Beta Israel to be fighting and hating each other since we are all of the same people."

Abba Shiloh responded, "U-wa, it is. It is almost like when Mengesha Israel split into the northern and southern kingdoms after Negus Solomon died. They fought with each other and sinned with idolatry. Provoking Egziabeher to cause both kingdoms to be destroyed and forced into exile by the invasion of the Assyrians and the Babylonians. Thus will be the fate of Aksum and Beta Israel if they turn not from their wicked ways."

Mekonnen asked, "So, what language to they speak on Qirqos and the other Islands in this Tsana hayq?"

Abba Shiloh answered, "They speak Ge'ez, but they can also speak Agawinya and Hebrew. Do not worry; we will be able to communicate with them."

Mekonnen continued rowing then he asked another question, "Now, where did the cloaked Qataliyan come from? And why do you think they wear a symbol of a serpent inside a circle on their cloaks and buckles? Why do they change into serpents when they are slain?"

Abba Shiloh began, "Ah ha! Now, as you may have heard, there was another religion that existed in the land a long time ago. They lived alongside the Beta Israel, and the Nagast who followed the Greek pantheon of gods. That was the Zendow or Sando worshippers. They worshiped snakes and sacrificed people and animals to them. I perceive our adversaries are the result of a revival of serpent worship."

Mekonnen is repulsed, "Hawey! That sounds like one of the highest forms of evil practices. Why would anyone want to sacrifice to snakes?"

Abba Shiloh responded, "You are correct! That is one of the highest forms of evil sorcery which Egziabeher hates. And remember the Devil and Saytan himself was described as a serpent. And I must also point out that most evil agents of darkest cannot enter in the Meder – Earthly Realms – unless they are summoned, or conjured by, a man, son on Adam. Egziabeher gave this Meder to mankind to have authority over all the earth, sea, wind and spirits. Whenever agents of darkness are rampaging upon the earth, they were conjured and let loose by a man or group of men. They opened the cosmic gate to the other side of under the dark mountain. I believe those dark Qataliyan, Hell Hounds, and Great Beasts are the works of a few evil men in high places of authority. That's how it usually starts, but we will wait and see and return to that topic on a later day."

Mekonnen thought and pondered the implications that a few prominent men and women may be the reason for the attacks by agents of death, perhaps even a Negus, Makwanent, or Qasis, and not necessarily the Dark Ones on their own free will. And none or very few of the regular citizens and subjects of the kingdom will ever know who is involved.

Gathering at Zoheleth

Earlier that same morning before Mekonnen and Abba Shiloh entered the tankwa, back at Zoheleth near Roha City, the young maiden is already strapped onto the slabs of rocks that make an altar for sacrifice. She volunteered herself willingly, but was in a trance, as if bewitched by the dreams of Waynaba's threats and temptations or poisoned by a portion of sorts that sorcerers and witches use to get victims to do their bidding. The new followers, led by Negus Leqsem, assisted in tying her wrists and ankles as she lay on her back on the altar of Zoheleth. The jar that contains Waynaba's soul is next to the altar, so the blood of the maiden can drip into it.

Then four Qataliyan brought in a large 20 feet long python they caught in the forest, tied to a long tree branch, and threw it in a trench they dug, 8 feet deep and 6 feet wider and filled it with water. Its mouth is bound shut with ropes and its body strapped tightly onto the long tree branch with chains. Since the Qataliyan are not natural earthly men, their unusual strength can be attributed to their unearthly origins.

They carried on with this abomination as the Silver Gauntlet leaned over the maiden's face and asked her softly, "What is your name, my daughter?"

The young maiden replied very softly into the Silver Gauntlet's ear as he turned one ear to her lips. No one else at the site of the altar heard her speak her name except The Silver Gauntlet, and he did not share it with anyone else. He believed in the ancient pagan practice that he will have control of her soul if he knows her name, even after her body has died.

The Silver Gauntlet whispered to the girl, "Now, my daughter, your name is safe with me. For your willful offering of your blood for this ritual, you shall be rewarded in the afterlife. You shall become powerful. You shall become beautiful. You shall become a Nigist – a Queen – of your own realm of paradise."

After those lying promises to the maiden, he stands upright and steps away from her to another rock where he picks up a sharp dagger. Just like the one he used to slay the first maiden on an altar in the Samen Mountains. Then he instructs his congregation of Dark Qataliyan, savage hell hounds, about 24 new snake worshiping Waynaba followers from the city of Roha and the corrupt Negus Leqsem to begin chanting, play musical instruments and dance to invoke the spirits to do their work on Waynaba when the sacrificial ceremony began.

"We are gathered here, dear Waynaba loyalists, to witness the resurrection of your old master in a new and improved form. Sing, chant and beat the kabaro drums, and play the washint flute as I perform the sweet blood sacrifice of this fair maiden!"

With that que the crowd began to ululate, "Elelelelelelelel!"

And two of the men began to beat two kabaro drums, "Boom Ba Doom! Boom Ba Doom!" repeatedly until it sounds like the beat of war drums, instilling fear and anxiety in the hearts of even the ones gathering at the altar to form this new cult of serpent worshipers. They danced in traditional *Eskista* dance, intense switching and jerking their shoulders back and forth and whipping their heads up and down and side to side. Except this time, it looked more unsettling and unnatural as they were doing it unto an evil false serpent-god and not for the usual cultural and religion festivals and celebrations. And the blazing look in their eyes and grin on their mouths also looked sinister and menacing.

And they chanted,

"Eg-zi Way-naba! Ta-le-la Way-naba!
Eg-zi Way-naba! Ta-le-la Way-naba!
– Lord Waynaba! Rise Up Waynaba!
Lord Waynaba! Rise Up Waynaba!"

Over and over again as they circled around the altar and a big fire that the Silver Gauntlet's apprentices lit up near the altar.

The Silver Gauntlet himself moved in simpler dance steps, waving the dagger around, in an almost graceful manner and may make him look a bit silly. The situation was definitely a serious one, as the young maiden bound in ropes on the altar is still unable to move or struggle, but tears welled up in her eyes and streamed down her cheeks, as if there was still a glimmer of sensible humanity deep down inside of her that realized what she volunteered for was wrong. But it was a bit too late.

Waynaba's Resurrection.

After about 10 minutes of ritualistic dancing and chanting the Silver Gauntlet finally lifted the dagger above the maiden and quickly plunges it into her chest, stabbing her beating heart. She made a deep gasp of air then gave up the ghost. Her blood dropped off the altar into the jar. Waynaba's soul jingled with delight as the jar began to glow with a mist billowed out of it, filling the area with fog. The Silver Gauntlet picked up the jar and threw it into the trench with the large *Zendow* – Python – in it. The Zendow wreathed and hissed loudly as if in pain, but the serpent worshipers all just continued to dance and chant.

A few minutes later the wreathing stopped in the trench. Suddenly another creature jumps up out of the trench, splashing water in every direction, startling the cult followers. It leapt up about 10 feet in the air and back into the watery trench. Then it arose slowly out of the water trench to reveal its new menacing form. It did not look like a python anymore as it metamorphosed into Waynaba's former self. He had a large long head with green scales over his whole body, and two short arms like a crocodile's below his head and long neck. He did not have back legs, just the long 20 feet of a serpent's body. Waynaba was back in full physical form, and ready to terrorize the world!

He hissed, "It isss good to be back! Hhsss!" Then he suddenly lunged at one of his followers and bit him on the top of his head, lifted him off the ground with feet dangling in the air and began to swallow him whole. The people ran away screaming at the sight as The Silver Gauntlet stepped forward and commanded, "Waynaba, No! You cannot eat your own followers! Then you will have no subjects to bring food and sacrifices to you."

Waynaba snapped back, "I have not eaten in more than one thousand, five hundred yearsss, what elssse do you exxxpect?!"

The Silver Gauntlet answered, "I expect you to listen to me, or you will not last long in this Realm of Meder, you foolish worm!"

Waynaba exclaimed, "Who are you calling a worm! Hsssss!" and he attempted to lunge at the Silver Gauntlet with mouth wide open to swallow him up also, but the Silver Gauntlet's ring on his right hand began to glow as he tightened his hand into a fist and swung it swiftly to land a punch to the new Waynaba in the face. The serpent to flew backwards and crashed headlong into a wall.

The Silver Gauntlet walked up to the crumpled Waynaba and pointed in his face with an index finger and said, "You must always remember who is in charge here. I am the master of you! You can be master of these people and the cloaked Qataliyan! But I have the power in my hands to destroy you all and send you all back to the Abyss! Back to Hell even!"

Waynaba quivered and said, "I sssee, you are only strong and powerful, because of that ring on your finger. I have heard of it. It is, the magic ring of Negusss Solomon isn't it! The ring that legend claimsss he used to control demonsss and spiritsss."

The Silver Gauntlet answered with a gripping jesture of his right hand where he wore the emerald ring on the index finger, as if to choke the serpent. Without physically touching the serpent, Waynaba began gagging for air as if he was being strangled.

The Silver Gauntlet responded, "The ring I bear is none of your business! As fast as I have given you a new body of flesh, blood and snake venow I can take it away from you. Do I make myself clear to you, Egzi Waynaba!"

Waynaba struggled to respond to the question, gasping for air until the Silver Gauntlet loosened his grip. "U-wa, U-wa! I will obey! I will obey, Egzi!"

The Silver Gauntlet responded, "*Gerum*! You will obey me if you want to live in this world! Now back into the water trench with you until we decide the best stratagem to catch this warrior and stop him from retrieving more holy garments and weapons to hinder our plans." The Silver Gauntlet made a quick motion, and Waynaba was slammed back into the trench. Slowly the Waynaba serpent cult followers began to return to the altar when they saw Waynaba was now under control.

The Silver Gauntlet called out, "Death Cloak! Give me a report! Where did your Qataliyan lose the warrior we seek?"

Death Cloak answered, "They chased them eastwards, but lost their trail. They may have actually ridden off in the other direction. To the west, Egzi Silver Gauntlet."

The Silver Gauntlet said, "That was exactly my thought. What is to the west of the where they lost the warrior and his manakos?"

Death Cloak answered, "Tsana Hayq is to the west, Egzi."

The Silver Gauntlet responded. "Tsana Hayq? That makes sense. There are several islands in that lake, and many holy artifacts are probably still on the islands. The Tabot was kept there, and Negus Ezana had his soldiers invade one of the islands to take the Tabot away from the Beta Israel who refused to convert to the kingdom's new belief of Krestiyanawi

– Christianity. You must take your Qataliyan there, find them and stop them before they find another weapon!"

Death Cloak replied, "The Tsallim Qataliyan cannot go into large expanses of water, Egzi. That is one of our limitations."

The Silver Gauntlet responded, "U-wa, I forgot about your limitations to land and not in the water." He thought for a minute and looked at Waynaba and sees how easily he is swimming around in the watery man-made trench.

"I have an idea." The Silver Gauntlet added, "Waynaba can enter into water with his new serpentine body. You go to the Tsana with Waynaba, let him search for them in the lake while you and the Qataliyan scout the area on land. I will give Waynaba some assistance by projecting him into the lake since he is not at full strength yet."

Death Cloak responded, "Hrai, we can travel through the shadows like we did before. This time I will go with them and confront the whelp myself."

The Silver Gauntlet asked, "Did the Tsallim Qataliyan say what was it that made the warrior special? What was he wearing, and the type of weapon he wields?"

Death Cloak replied, "They said he had on a shiny golden breastplate that their swords and arrows and spears could not penetrate. And he wielded a Mal'akawi Spear that sent many Qataliyan back into the shadows. Also, he had the advantage of having a powerful Qedus Manakos of sorts with him, also a Mal'ak warrior fighting by his side, and an Abiyy Hayyal that caught them off guard. Without all those reinforcements to his advantage, I probably could have taken him down myself."

The Silver Gauntlet said, "Well, you and your shadow warriors better come up with a better plan to catch our target."

Death Cloak added, "Fear not. I have a plan for them. His spear is nothing special. I have fought and defeated Mal'ak wielding such spears and wearing such body armor like the breastplate. He just needs a taste of my *Kele Asyeft Mot* – Two Swords of Death."

He was referring to the two swords that were sheathed crisscrossed on his back that he uses in combat. They were very strong, sharp and formidable even against high ranking warrior Mal'ekt.

Silver Gauntlet cynically added, "Your boasting better be of substance. I am growing tired of hearing about this little man getting away from your Qataliyan."

Death Cloak added, "We just need to learn his strategies and techniques. When we understand his patterns, then we can cut him and his allies down. Let us gear up and go west to Tsana Hayk now!"

Death Cloak grabbed the handles of the swords on his back and poises himself to run through the shadows.

First, he called his warriors, "Qataliyan! Kalabat Arawit! Abiyy Arawit! Attention! Fall into lines and flow into the shadows!"

Immediately dozens of Qataliyan fell into lines of army troops. The Silver Gauntlet readied Waynaba to prepare to project him through the underground channels that lead all the way to the west in unison with the Qataliyan. He gave the serpent a long, curved scimitar blade to hold in the tip of his tail as his own weapon to use in battles, and especially against the warrior and manakos they seek.

"Let's go Waynaba. Prepare yourself because you're going for a long swim. You have the advantage of being an amphibious, reptilian creature that can thrive on land and in the sea. Look for the young warrior in the Tsana Hayk and attack him with full force. Destroy him or drown him in the deep. Mankind cannot live underwater and can drown easily. They only thrive in the water of their mother's wound. After that, they forget how the swim, unless taught into adulthood. If you cannot find him, return to the shores and meet up with the Qataliyan, or return through the channels to Zoheleth to be safe from hunting Mal'ekt from on High. So off you go!"

Waynaba said, "It is about time I get to tackle and destroy this Aksssumite thorn-in-the-ssside I keep hearing everyone complain about. I will show them how it isss done!"

The Silver Gauntlet lifted his hand out with the glowing emerald ring and chanted a spell. Then they were all off into the shadows, fixed on their destination to Tsana Hayq in about 2 to 3 hours.

When some of the Qataliyan, hounds, and Waynaba disappeared into the shadows, the Negus Leqsem approached the Silver Gauntlet humbly and asked, "Egzi, please tell me how I might be able to serve you further?"

The Silver Gauntlet demanded, "Please have your subjects bring some food and drinks from the town. We will be encamped here for a while until we have Roha and environs under total control. Then we will strike at the Beta Israel in Samen Mountains and finally Aksum when we become strong enough to take them on."

Evil Eye in the Lake.

Meanwhile, Mekonnen was getting a bit tired of rowing. He was almost tempted to ask Abba Shiloh if he wanted to take over the rowing but wouldn't dear ask such a fooling question to a holy man. So, he just continued rowing, back and forth, back and forth.

Just then, to Mekonnen's horror, suddenly, a big wave rose up from his left, and which is Abba Shiloh's right. Mekonnen gasped in surprise, heart accelerated, but Abba Shiloh just stood there calmly as the boat just rose up sharply on top the wave. To Mekonnen's surprise, Abba Shiloh did not lose his balance one bit as the boat went up and down. He stood still as if he was fastened to the boat with robes and a heavy anchor. Then another wave came from the same direction with the same force, and again Abba Shiloh barely moved, while Mekonnen sat and held on to the sides of the boat to keep his balance.

"Oh, don't be scared, Anbessa, only a little wave." Abba Shiloh assured Mekonnen, "Don't lose those ores now. See, it's all calm now."

Mekonnen, looked around and expected for another wave but it remained calm. He said,

"Uh, that came out of nowhere, did it?"

"Not from *nowhere*. The sea, the winds, the currents. Thus is life, full of ups and downs. We panic and all we need to do is be still, and command the rough waters to be still like Egzi Iyesus did when he was with the disciples on the Sea of Galilee."

Mekonnen thought to himself,

"'Command the waves to be still', huh? Easier to be said than to be done. Iyesus did grant us power over the creation, I suppose."

Mekonnen looked out into the distance to see if he could spot the island close by, but to his disappointment, all he could see was water everywhere and dark gray clouds with mist under it. It looked like a rain cloud, and it was coming closer to them.

"It looks like it is going to rain Abba Shiloh, and I think I saw lightning in those clouds."

"Yes, and we must go through those storm clouds to get to the island. Come on Anbessa; you are rowing the wrong way. Come on, straighten up!"

Mekonnen thought to himself, "Are we going to attempt to go through the storm?"

It was not long before the rain came down very heavily and the lightning and rumbling thunder sure put on a show. Abba Shiloh remained standing still in the boat despite the now violently rough waters and strong winds throwing buckets of rain on his face and bright orange robes. Mekonnen kept on rowing even though the task became difficult and almost impossible to see which direction they were going. Just then Mekonnen noticed creatures, swimming near the flimsy boat. They seemed to be circling them, creatures with rough skin and large tails. Mekonnen could not make them out for certain, but they may be crocodiles or large sea serpents. Mekonnen was hoping they would be crocodiles and not the gigantic sea serpents that he read stories about the can destroy large seafaring ships. A sense a dread came over him but he looked at Abba Shiloh and saw that he was still calm, but with a serious expression on his face as if he also sensed something was not right.

Suddenly, Mekonnen was startled by the sight of a large eye glaring at him from inside a huge wave that was approaching them from the left. High and large is the wave, and hideous and menacing is a narrow, vertical pupil of a serpent's eye, glaring at him. With the snare of long fangs, blurry but visible through the treacherous waters, attesting to the type of vile creature this may be. The sight made Mekonnen's heart race with fright, and by instinct, he reaches for a sword on his waist but realizes he does not have one.

The intense stare of a serpent's eye belongs to Waynaba, who finally got a glimpse of his adversaries, the Aksumite warrior, and the Bahetawi, and said within himself,

"Ssso this is the warrior everyone is afraid of.
I have finally ssseen my adversary,
And he does not look that threatening to me.
Today I shall devour him and hisss companion in this sssea!"

Abba Shiloh also saw the creature but remained calm. Amidst the raging sea, towering waves, and evil eye, the Bahetawi slowly lifted his arms out to look like the letter 'T' with the staff in his right hand, and his wet face lifting upwards into the violent flashing dark sky. He hollered out some words that Mekonnen could not hear them clearly because just as Abba Shiloh said them, there was an extremely loud, deafening thunder clap and a streak of illuminating lightning. The sight and sound was awesome and startling as the lightning bolts zipped down from the sky and struck the wave and the creature that was in it. The creature let out a horrible, indescribable noise and its eye and fangs disappeared immediately into the watery depths of the lake. Still, the wave came crashing down upon Mekonnen and Shiloh, and for sure Mekonnen thought their boat was going to subside and dump them into the lake, but he held on, and their boat stayed afloat. To his surprise, Abba Shiloh was still standing upright, leaning on his staff.

After a few moments, the storm clouds drifted away, and the sun peeks behind rolling columbus clouds. Mekonnen was in awe. It seemed Abba Shiloh sensed that it was not a normal storm and he had to access the powers of the Creator to handle the situation. And that creature in the water was definitely not a crocodile.

Abba Shiloh's gave a mysterious warning, "The *Enemy* knows where we are and is not happy. We will be safe from now on until we get to the island. But after we leave the island, be on your guard."

Mekonnen quivered, "Th…, the enemy?"

"Remember what we spoke about back in the mountain caves and monasteries. I will explain more to you when we settle on Qirqos." Replied Abba Shiloh and Mekonnen continued to row towards the island.

On Board Qirqos Island.
"Look, we are almost there." Said Abba Shiloh, as he pointed with his staff.

To Mekonnen's surprise, there was the Qirqos Island right there about 50 rows ahead, jotting out of the waters like a large rock in the middle of the sea. There was the island surrounded by green shrubbery and trees at the foot of the shear steep rock cliffs that made the holy island look like a walled fortress. As they got closer, Mekonnen could see that there is actually a smaller island next to Qirqos. It looked like it was covered by a jungle of the same lush greenery with water birds and other flying creatures perched on and fluttering around it. He was so happy to see it so near that he began to row faster.

As they got closer, they could see dozens of human figures standing at the top of the cliffs on the larger island, staring at them as they approached. They were manakost, inhabitants and curators of the Tsana Qirqos and the other surrounding islands on the lake, like Nargadaga Deset (Dek) Island - the largest one, Daga Estefanos and Meshralia. Many of them descendants of Beta Israel and Levites that had possession of the Ark of the Covenant on this island before King Ezana took it away in 330 AD after converting to the Way of Iyesus Kristos.

About three manakost indicated to Mekonnen and Abba Shiloh by pointing to a small jetty where they can be duct and secure the boat to get onto the shore of the island. They already knew and recognized Abba Shiloh, so it was not a problem. The manakost helped their guests onto the small shore at the base of palm trees and a high cliff.

"Selamta" was the greeting and Shiloh and the manakost also greeted each other with "Shalom" and other Hebrew and Ge'ez words intermingled together.

Abba Shiloh introduced Mekonnen to the manakost in Ge'ez, "This is my friend Mekonnen, a warrior from Aksum." Then he shifted into Hebrew which Mekonnen only understood a little but didn't think much of the reason for switching languages. He was just glad to be on shore on dry, unwavering, steady land. And hopefully, there were no monsters *on* the island to be concerned about.

The manakost, dressed modestly in white and tan trousers and robes, guided them up through a narrow, winding passage way that was dug out through the rocky cliff probably hundreds of years ago. After about 14 minutes they arrived at the top where they have a beautiful view of the lake and a few of the other islands peeking out of the water and reed boats scattered on the sea in the distance. There were a lot of trees, plants and yellow Masqal flowers like the ones in Aksum and throughout the land that decorated the island like golden jewels. Red and white roses were among the flora, and there is also a monastery or shrine of sorts nearby built out of bricks and wood. Mekonnen could not help but notice the slabs of rock around the summit and had to be careful not to walk into one of the many spider web nests that were sprinkled with many spiders and the insect prey unfortunate to be entangled in them. Several solemn looking manakost were there, but they were hospitable and welcoming.

Abba Shiloh knew most of them and introduced Mekonnen to some of them as kahenat, Levites, monakost, musicians, and scribes, among other titles. The monakost and kahenat seated their guests at an old wooden table near the monastery and served them with fish, injera, bread, fruit and natural fruit juices. Mekonnen gobbled up the food really fast like a young boy while Shiloh and one of the kahen, introduced as Abba Elias, wearing a bright yellow robe and purple head wrap, talked about their journey and purpose for coming to the island.

"When we were rowing on the lake during the storm, there was a *buda* – an evil eye – that fixed itself upon young Mekonnen here, Abba Elias. Right then I knew it was not an ordinary storm and the dark forces were at work and tried to stop us from coming here." Abba Shiloh explained to Abba Elias.

Abba Elias replied, "Hmm, an EVIL EYE. That is not good, that means the enemy knows where we are, but may not know what is about to happen. But Egziabeher will protect us. He is our *gayso* – protective shield – and will shield the boy from that sinister gaze."

Mekonnen was chewing the last of his food but was getting a bit concerned being the center of attention now. He swallowed and asked, "So what is going to happen now? Should we prepare to fight? And how do we get off the island then, is it going to be safe in the waters when we leave?"

Abba Elias replied, "Oh don't worry, we must pray for you. Pray for your protection and covering. The Almighty One, Egziabeher Amlak will have HIS eyes on you from now on. And if you most fight he will give you STRENGTH! He is bigger and stronger than *Zendowu,* the dragon, so fear not, my son!

"Oh no, I'm not worried. I am a trained warrior from the Kingdom of Aksum. Trained to battle man and beast." boasted Mekonnen.

Abba Shiloh said, "Now Anbessa, courage is admirable, but don't be too boastful. The *Great Nakhach* is no regular beast to contend with; you must be well equipped with special articles of war for him and his armies."

Abba Elias whispered, "Clever, strong and experienced they are. They are ancient and know the weakness of mankind, yet, they are limited in power. No match for the Host of Samayat, they are not."

Abba Shiloh added, "Yes indeed, Miykael, Uriel, Raphael and the Chariots of fire. The Erelim, the Malakaim shall descend with a force and lay waste of the Realms of Darkness.

Abba Elias said, "Even the Elect One Himself, The Ancient of Days shall conquer with a *Hayle Sayf,* a Mighty Sword of power and light. So, we must be ready and equipped. Be strong and courageous, Anbessa! Come on, let me show you something."

Abbas Shiloh and Elias stood up immediately, Mekonnen was taken off guard and was still chewing and digesting his food, together with the exalted interplay between the two elderly men just now that sounded like enough encouragement to excite massive armies in Samayat and on Earth.

Surely, they stepped into the modest structure with two other young manakost to assist Abba Elias. Only natural light and torches lit the first room which is a sanctuary where a few of the manakost were meditating or reading hymn books, scriptures, *Dawit mezmur* (Psalms) and other sacred codices. They entered a small room and in there were ancient artifacts and relics from the old Kingdom of Sheba and Kingdom of Israel and Beta Israel. Their crowns, diadems, robes, scepters stacked neatly on shelves and hooks.

"These are old royal and noble articles from Nagast and Qasisat of old." Abba Shiloh informs Mekonnen. "At least they are the ones Hade Ezana and his armies did not confiscate when they raid these islands two hundred years ago. They could hide these from them before they came. But there used to be more artifacts than what you see here. Come on, let's keep going. Follow me."

The two men followed Abba Elias and kept walking to the other end of the room which is darkly lit.

Abba Elias dissolved into a dark corner to a steel door that looked like it had not been opened for a long time by the spider webs around it. It was pad locked and chained, so the Abba reached for keys in his hand and unlocked them slowly and carefully.

Then he turned to Mekonnen ominously and said,

"May Egziabeher be merciful and grant us worthy to enter these dark passageways. And worthy to return safely. Amen." Then he turned back into the dark room as grabbed a torch that hung by the door. Abba Shiloh helps him light it then grabbed and lights one for himself and another for Mekonnen. The young warrior looked at Abba Shiloh as if expecting some sort of response or explanation to what Abba Elias just said, but Abba Shiloh just responded with, "Amen." as he hands the lit touch to Mekonnen. They step through the creaking, open metal door.

Mekonnen's heart began bounding with anticipation and excitement. Abba Elias warned Mekonnen, "Be careful now and watch your step. We will be going through a deep, long and winding stairway, a hallway, over a bridge then another stairway. At the end is a gateway that leads to a seashore. Across from that seashore is another island. We must go to that island for the *Manfasawi Sayf.* Understood?"

Mekonnen replied in a brave manner, "U-wa. I understand, Abba. I am ready. Let's go!" Abba Shiloh pulled the clanging door shut behind them as they proceeded down a stairway.

Meanwhile, Waynaba descended into the depths of Tsana Hayk, into the shadows of the deep to communicate with the Silver Gauntlet over in Roha-Zoheleth.

"Oh, Lord Silver Gauntlet with the Emerald Ring. I have found the targetsss we ssseek. There are two of them; one is an old man, a holy man no doubt. He called down lightning to ssstrike me in the eye. The other one is a younger man. He was rowing in the boat headed for one of the islandsss. I believe he is the warrior you sssseek. I was about to ssstrike at them, but the ssstorm brought lightning down on me. As sssoon you receive my message have the Qataliyan and houndsss ready to attack them at the sssea shore if they get passst me the next time get in the lake to return to the mainland."

The Silver Gauntlet received Waynaba's message moments later, and responded, "Your message was received Waynaba. I do not like the sound of them going to the islands of Tsana Hayk. They could be retrieving another weapon and will make him even stronger. I am concerned you may not be able to defeat them, Waynaba. I advise you to return, but if you can stop them from returning to the mainland, please try the best you can. Otherwise, their new weapon may destroy you. I will inform Lord Death Cloak to have his Qataliyan, Hell Hounds and Abiyy Arawit ready to attack with full force."

MEKONNEN AND ABBA SHILOH
ROWING A TANKWA TO TSANA QIRQOS ISLAND
MATIYAS © 4/13/2019

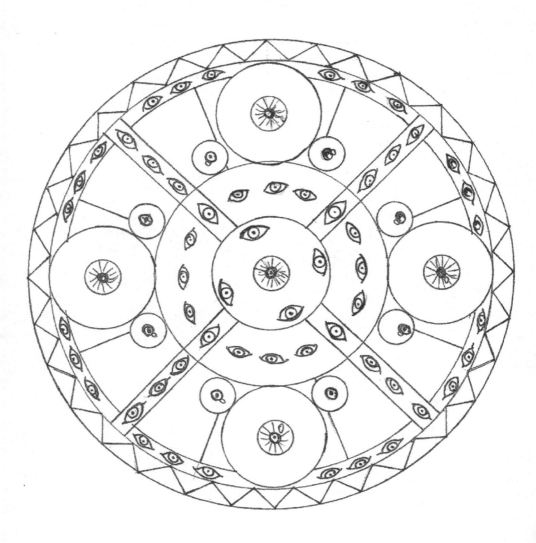

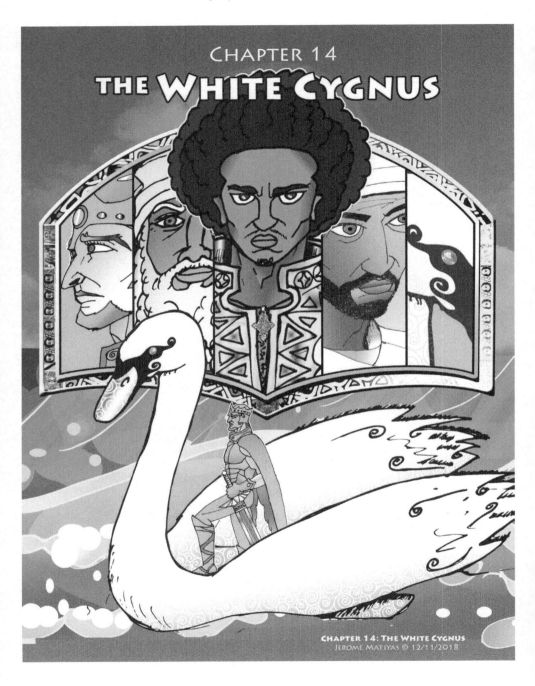

CHAPTER 14: THE WHITE CYGNUS
JEROME MATIYAS © 12/11/2018

Chapter 14

Chapter 14

The White Cygnus

The three men descended down many stairs with lanterns. Abba Elias in front, Mekonnen behind him then Abba Shiloh in the back. It was dark, but their lanterns lit the way, which was quite long. The further down the stairs they went the louder their footsteps echoed in the underground passageway. Gradually the sound of a flowing water stream could be heard below them.

Abba Elias warned, "We will be crossing a bridge now, so watch your steps."

Passageway of Murals
Soon they came to a bridge of wood planks and ropes to walk on and the hand railings to hold on to as they crossed. Below was a stream, which can be heard and smelt more than it can be seen. On the other side of the bridge, Abba Elias uses his lantern to light more lanterns on a wall, which reveals an enclosure with beautifully painted murals. Each mural tells a story or scene from the *Mashaf Qeddus* – the Holy Scriptures – and well-known ancient legends. At the top was a depiction of the *Malakot* – The Godhead. Three men standing together with white hair and beards representing The Father, The Son, and the Holy Spirit.

A depiction of Adam and Hawwah, the first man and woman, standing under the tree of the Knowledge of Good and Evil, with the Serpent wrapped around it, enticing Hawwah to eat the fruit of it. Moses and the ten commandments, Joshua at Jericho, Negus Dawit and Negus Solomon. Nigist Ester, and many more.

They walked on further and on the walls, where depictions of the legend of the Nigist Saba and her supposed seduction by Negus Solomon and the begetting of their son Negus Menelik, fabled first Solomonic Negus of the land before Aksum was even named so, but was called the Kingdom of

Da'amot.

There were rare illustrations from the Mashaf Henok – the Book of Enoch – of the prophet Henok extolling judgement on the Watchers, the Mal'ekt who sinned by leaving Samay to have intercourse with the daughters on Adam and Hawwah and begat the Giants, the Titans of ancient and recent legends.

And, of course, paintings of Mal'ekt Mikael, Gabriel, Rufael, Uriel and more, brandishing swords, trumpets, and harps. And the traditional depictions of brown heads of men with feathered Mal'ak wings at their sides.

Many illustrations from the *Beluy Kidan* – the Old Testament – of the Mashaf Qeddus, before these, were done by the Beta Israel people of old.

The three men continued walking around a larger pillar of sorts now, this time on a ledge, just steps away from a deep chasm below. Abba Elias warned, "Keep close to the pillar and don't look down. That is a very deep chasm below. If you slip, you may keep falling for days." Probably an exaggeration but still a dangerous fall anyhow. In the darkness, they could see many glittering specks of light that twinkled on and off. They realized those lights were fireflies providing a little bit of light into the darkness.

Eventually, they saw a stream of light from an opening ahead at the top of another flight of stairs that will take them out of the tunnel and to the other side. They crossed another wooden bridge swinging over a stream, up the flight of about 70 steps and then finally out through an Aksumite styled arch to a misty seashore.

Abba Shiloh was relieved, "Hrai, we are out of the tunnel. So now we figure out how to get to the other island?"

Abba Elias answered, "U-wa. It is a secret island that no one can get to unless worthy or invited. One cannot get to this concealed seashore on Qirqos Tsana unless they survive through the passageway we just journeyed through. You cannot sail or row a boat around Qirqos nor walk around the island to get here. I myself have never been here before. I only know the way because specific instructions were given to me a long time ago to only allow a certain warrior the rights of passage through the tunnel ways to retrieve the *Sayf Hayle* – the Sword of Power."

Mekonnen then asked a question, "So, now that we're out of the tunnel and on the other side, how do we get to the secret island?"

Abba Elias answered, "To be honest, I do not know the answer to that question."

White Cygnus.

Then from the distance, they saw a figure floating on the water towards them. Gradually the figure slowly emerged out of the mist. It was a boat in the shape of a giant white Cygnus – a Swan-like creature – gliding on the waters. There was a man riding in the boat; he was not staring it with ores of a navigator, as it seemed to navigate itself.

As the boat parked near the shore right in front of them, Mekonnen said, "Well, I believe this must be our ride to take us to the secret island. This is the most beautiful boat I have ever seen!"

They soon realized that the Cygnus shaped boat was actually a living, breathing creature when it blinked its eyes and slowly moved its head. Yet still, it barely moved much to be considered a living creature, although it clearly was. The Cygnus creature was about 15 feet long, 8 feet wide and the head and neck was about 10 feet high. Its wings were at its sides and propped up slightly to form an enclosure on its back like a cabin for its passengers.

The man on the back of the Cygnus stretched out his right hand to welcome them onto the Cygnus. At closer look, the man in the Cygnus was wearing aqua-marine colored garments, similar to the green appareled Mal'ak on the dark brown horse, that helped them defeat the Qataliyan the day before, and had a great sword sheathed onto his side. Then they knew this was not an ordinary man but another warrior class Mal'ak, assigned to guard and protect them and the Cygnus. The three men hopped on as the Cygnus let its wing down, turns around, and sailed back to where it came from, towards the secret island.

As they sailed on their way to the island destination, Abba Shiloh seized this moment to admonish Mekonnen some more about his next spiritual item.

Qala Egziabeher

"Now Anbessa, remember this is a very powerful weapon, and you must be ready to use it with the Qala Egziabeher – The Word of God. You may be tested and tempted by another force before you are allowed to take the Sword away from its resting place. It may be guarded by a Mal'ak, Kerubel or Watcher, I do not know exactly. Egziabeher has not shown me specifically, but I know you will be tested. Just remember reading in Orit Zaledat – Book of Genesis – when Yakob wrestled with the Mal'ak all night, then was renamed Israel. And in the Wangel – the Gospels – when Iyesus Krestos was tempted by the Adversary after he had finished fasting and praying in the wilderness for forty days. You may be tested in a unique way I am not aware of."

Mekonnen began to feel a bit concerned then asked Abba Shiloh, "So Abba Shiloh, were you ever required to seek or wield a Sayf or blade of sorts in your previous battles? I see now you have a cross on a staff that emanates powerful bolts of fire and lightning when needed. You don't even need a Manfasawi Sayf."

Abba Shiloh replied, "I do have a Manfasawi Sayf! It is the Qala Egziabeher! I speak the Word, and that is my Sayf of protection and counter-attack. But, U-wa, in my younger days I did wield a Manfasawi Sayf! I discovered it in the *Qeddus Hagar Eyerusalem* – The Holy City of Jerusalem

– a long time ago, in *Manfasawi Tsion Dabr* – Spiritual Mount Zion – and used it to slay many diabolical Daragonat, Eljo, Egregoroi, Titans, and fallen Tsallim Mal'ekt, and other fallen dark creatures! For many years I wielded it with skill, precision, and care. Then the time came Egziabeher demanded I use the Word and his power against to enemy and for his people in a different way. By speaking it instead."

Mekonnen asked, "Oh, why did he ask you to return it or give it up? Did you do something wrong or made a mistake?"

Abba Shiloh responded, "Iyyaseh! – No! I was not punished or taken away from me because of a mistake. I still have it. Although I was not always perfect and did make a few missteps, but it was just a new season came about to use the Word a different way and let other Warriors of Light, as they called them, pick up the mantle."

Mekonnen said, "Hawey! So, you found your Sayf in Eyerusalem! That is great place to make discovery."

Abba Shiloh continued, "So, for you. Remember the words of the Mashaf as written in the ancient oracles and in your heart by the Manfas Qeddus. 'Behold the Manfasawi Sayf, which is the Word of Egziabeher.' Go ahead and recite all the verses you remember right now before we reach the island."

Mekonnen paused for about 5 seconds then began, with the very first Samayawi Sayf – Heavenly Sword,

"Egziabeher drove out the man; and he placed at the east of the garden of Eden, Kerubel, and a flaming Sword which turned every way, to keep the way of the tree of life. - Genesis 3:24.

Take the helmet of salvation, and the sword of the Spirit, which is the word of God. - Ephesians 6:17.

For the word of God is quick, and powerful, and sharper than any two-edged sword, piercing even to the dividing asunder of soul and spirit, and of the joints and marrow, and is a discerner of the thoughts and intents of the heart. - Hebrews 4:12.

Balaam sees a Mal'ak with his swords drawn: Then the LORD opened the eyes of Balaam, and he saw the Mal'ak of the LORD standing in the way, and his sword drawn in his hand: and he bowed down his head, and fell flat on his face. – Numbers 22:31.

And it came to pass, when Joshua was by Jericho, that he lifted up his eyes and looked, and, behold, there stood a man over against him with his

sword drawn in his hand: and Joshua went unto him, and said unto him, Art thou for us, or for our adversaries?- Joshua 5:13.

If I whet my glittering Sword, and mine hand take hold on judgment; I will render vengeance to mine enemies, and will reward them that hate me. - Deuteronomy 32:42.

And he had in his right hand seven stars: and out of his mouth went a sharp two-edged sword: and his countenance was as the sun shineth in his strength. – Revelation 1:16.

And out of his mouth goeth a sharp sword, that with it he should smite the nations: and he shall rule them with a rod of iron: and he treadeth the winepress of the fierceness and wrath of Almighty God. – Revelation 19: 15.

After Mekonnen ended his declarations Abba Shiloh said,

"U-wa, Anbessa! Declare the Qala Egziabeher! The sharp two edge Sayf will smite the nations of the Armies of Darkness! The Realms of the *Tsallim Asf Qataliyan* – Darkness Cloaked Assassins – shall be destroyed! You shall smite the head of the Nakhach, the serpent! Waynaba! The legacy of Waynaba the Zendow shall be cut off from this kingdom!"

Mekonnen responded, "U-wa! I shall receive that declaration and agree with you, Abba Shiloh. I shall declare Light of victory over the powers and might of the Darkness! The Manfas Egziabeher will rise and conquer like the Anbessa with a mighty roar!"

Abba Shiloh prophesied, "Destruction shall come to the gates of Siol! Light shall prevail to scatter the Darkness. There will be no shadows for *ganen* – demons – to hide in! No place for fallen Mal'ekt to thread! Because the Qala Iyesus Krestos is the Spirit of the Word and the Manfasawi Qal – the Spirit of the Word – of the Power of Iyesus! By Iyesus Dem, Qal enna Manfas – Jesus' Blood, Word, and Spirit – his true people shall prevail!"

Mekonnen, Abba Shiloh, Abba Elias, the Mal'ak in aqua-marine, and the Cygnus all replied in agreement and in unison, "Amen! Amen! Eelelelelelelelelelelel Elelelelelelelel!"

On the Island.

Just as they completed that victorious exaltation, they finally arrived at the shores of the secret island. About 70 yards inland from the shore was a larger building structure like a round monastery or chapel, with pillars and arches all around it. The walls were almost 50 feet high with a dome-shaped roof at the top. It was lit ominously from the inside and by lanterns on the pillars and arches on the outside. Above the dome were several avian creatures, about seven of them, with wide wings spans circling in spiral formation like eagles over a prey. They could not tell from the distance whether these beings were eagles of the Meder Realm, or Surafel, Kerubel, or Mal'ekt of the Samayawi Realm. Still, they proceeded with confidence.

Mekonnen commented, "This is it. Truth and Righteousness has led me to enter into his sanctuary to receive the Spirit of the Word of Egziabeher."

Abba Shiloh added, "You have spoken well, Anbessa. Let us go."

The three men, Mekonnen, Abba Shiloh and Abba Elias, climbed off the Cygnus, thanked the Mal'ak and Cygnus with a bow and they walked up some stairs to an archway entrance. The Cygnus and Mal'ak remained by the sea shore until the men returned. The Mal'ak informed the men, "The Cygnus and I were given 7 hours to assist you on your journey. An hour and a half has already passed since you boarded until now, so you have about 5 and a half hours left before we must leave."

Abba Shiloh replied, "Amezgana! Thank you for informing us and for bringing us thus far. We will do our best to complete our task in time for you take us back to the Qirqos Island again."

Mekonnen offered his right hand to the Mal'ak and added "As a believer in Egzi Iyesus Krestos, who is Savior and Lord of my soul and yours, I will do my best to keep my word and return to you and Cygnus in less than five and a half hours."

The Mal'ak shook Mekonnen's hand with a bow, and the Cygnus also bowed its long "S" shaped neck in acknowledgement. And off the three men ran up the marble stairs to one of the arch-way entrances.

The arch-way was guarded on either side by two large, lion faced Kerubel, each with massive pairs of wings extending from their shoulder blades, body and tail like lions, and feet like ox hoofs. The two creatures lounged forward towards the three men, but Abba Shiloh stepped forward boldly, pushing Mekonnen and Abba Elias aside with his arms, lifted his Masqal staff as it glowed with white light in the air and declared loudly,

"We come in peace, in the name of Egziabeher and His Elect One of Samayat!". The Kerubel stopped in their tracks from attacking, then stepped back slowly to where they stood before, with low growls that gradually faded into soothing tunefully humming sounds resonating from their bodies. It happened so fast that Mekonnen and Abba Elias did not have time to be startled for long.

The Legendary Sword

As they walked pass between the two huge Kerubel and enter through an archway of the building structure, inside, they saw an amazing sight. It's the legendary sword they've been looking for. The *Sayfa Manfas Qeddus*, suspended in mid-air above a white stone altar with four pointed corners and seven steps on the right side leading to the top of it. The blade was pointing downwards with the golden hilt upwards, making the shape of a great "T."

The blade had a transparency to it, as it glowed and flashed, with the likeness of flames and lightning flowing through it, and moving up and down within the blade itself, without burning outside of it.

Mekonnen drew closer to it in awe to see many words and statements scrolling up and down inside the transparent blade. The words morphed into several different languages that Mekonnen did not understand, but he did see the Ge'ez language appear stating, *Sayfa Qala Manfes Egziabeher Amlak* – This was the Sword of the Word of the Spirit of The Lord God of gods.

Abba Shiloh proclaimed, "Behold, the *Sayfa Manfas Qeddus* – Sword of the Holy Spirit!"

Mekonnen, awestruck with mouth open, whispered, "Hawey! It is *sannaya*! More beautiful than I could ever imagined!"

Abba Elias was also awestruck at the living blade and sighed, "I agree, it is *sannaya*!"

Abba Shiloh added, "It is just as beautiful as I remember the one I possessed many years ago. *Sannaya wa Hayle*! – It is Beautiful and Powerful!"

But they did not notice the tall figure of a man of great stature, about 9 to 10 feet tall, standing with back against a wall under an arch between two pillars, ten steps behind the flashing sword blade. He seemed to be standing guard, with both hands gripping onto the handle of his own sword, with the blade pointing downward. He wore a white, flowing, textured robe covering its whole body from shoulders to feet, and a silver, crown-like helmet encircled around its head.

He opened his mouth to speak to his three guests,

"*Baha, Wəluda Egziabeher!* – Greetings, Sons of God!

Approaching the island that holds the Chapel of the Sword of the Spirit of the Word.
Artwork by Jerome Matiyas © 4/27/2019.

CHAPTER 15
THE FLASHING BLADE

CHAPTER 15: THE FLASHING BLADE
JEROME MATIYAS © 12/28/2018

Chapter 15

Chapter 15

The Flashing Blade

As Mekonnen, Abba Shiloh and Abba Elias approached the legendary *Manfasawi Sayf* – The Sword of the Spirit – with awe and wonderment of its beauty, they did not notice the tall figure of a man of great stature, about 9 to 10 feet tall, standing with back against a wall under an arch between two pillars, ten steps behind the flashing sword blade. He seemed to be standing guard, with both hands gripping onto the handle of his own sword, with the blade pointing downwards. He wore a white, flowing, textured robe covering his whole body from shoulders to feet, and a silver, crown-like helmet encircled around its head.

He opened his mouth to speak to his three guests,

"*Baha, Wəluda Egziabeher*! – Greetings, Sons of God!

Abba Shiloh nudged Mekonnen with the staff on his back and said, "Go ahead, Anbessa. Tell him you have come to claim the Manfasawi Sayf that the Egzi Iyesus Krestos sent you to retrieve."

Mekonnen stepped up seven white marble steps to draw closer to the altar and get a better look at the tall man, whom he assumes was a Mal'ak, behind it then begins,

"Uhhh, Baha! Greetings to you mighty Mal'ak. I have come with my elders to retrieve the great and powerful *Manfasawi Sayf*. Egzi Iyesus Krestos has sent me, huh, indicated, that the Sayf will be here to retrieve."

The Mal'ak responded, "Mastatsabə Mekonnen! – Warrior Mekonnen! – Why do you need this great Spiritual Sword?"

Mekonnen replied, "I need it to fight the Armies of Darkness! To defeat evil Tsallim Qataliyan – Assassins of the Dark – and the Great Serpent of the Deep. I need the *Manfasawi Sayf Qala* – Sword of Spirit of the Word – to defeat the ungodly creatures of the Spiritual Kingdom Realms that have invaded the *Medrawi Mangest* – Earthly Realm. I must defend the innocent and uphold the Truth and Righteous way of Egziabeher, which he has declared in his Manfas Qedus! I need it because my Egzi, and your Egzi, has ordered me to take it and use it!"

Mekonnen completed his statement with surprisingly passionate gusto and boldness that neither Abba Shiloh nor Abba Elias, nor Mekonnen himself expected to come out of his own mouth.

They all stood and await the great Mal'ak's response, and after a short pause the Mal'ak did respond,

"I am not convinced that you really need neither are you worthy to have and to own it. Much less use it! How do I know you are worthy?"

Mekonnen did not expect this aggressive and confrontational response from the Mal'ak, who seemed to doubt the warrior's validity. Confused, Mekonnen stuttered and looked back at Abba Shiloh and Abba Elias for some hint or clue of what he should say to the Mal'ak. All Abba Shiloh did was shrugged his shoulders in ignorance, not expecting that sort of response either.

Mekonnen turned back to the Mal'ak and looked at him for a few seconds, trying the think of the right response to give in return.

"Uhh, Well. I am, uh, quite capable of wielding this Sayf against the enemy. As I already have possession of the Breastplate of Righteousness and the Belt of Truth. And, I believe I have been justified by the blood of Iyesus Krestos. And sanctified by his sacrifice!"

Mekonnen glanced back at his mentor again for an encouraging gesture and saw Abba Shiloh nodding his head in approval.

He expected the Mal'ak to be impressed now only to hear him say cynically, "So, you believe because of all of that, you are approved to use this Sayf?! That does not prove anything to me!"

Mekonnen sighed in frustration and exclaimed, "What do you mean *'That does not prove anything'*? I am confident that I am fit to retrieve the Manfasawi Sayf! The Lord himself sent me here to retrieve it!"

The Mal'ak insisted, "You have not proven that you are fit for the Abiyy Sayf!"

Mekonnen argued, "But I have already used a Mal'ak's Spear weapon to slay some Warriors of Darkness we call Qataliyan a few days ago before coming here. Didn't your fellow Mal'ak in green apparel tell you this before we came here?"

The Mal'ak responded smugly, "I know not which Mal'ak you speak of."

Mekonnen became agitated and raises his voice, "*Hawey*, Come on!

What do you mean! Don't all you Mal'ekt know each other!!"

Abba Shiloh spoke out upwards to Mekonnen, "Mekonnen, I believe your will and your character is also being tested. Watch your temper."

Mekonnen asked the Mal'ak again, "So how do you want me to show you that I am worthy of this Sayf to you!"

The Mal'ak replied, "He who seeks possession of the Manafasawi Sayf, must first contend with me, in mortal battle, to show himself worthy of such a heavenly blade!"

Mekonnen was surprised by the Mal'ak's response, "Oh, really? How is that possible?"

He glanced back at Abba Shiloh and looked into his mentor's eyes, and remembered him saying earlier on the Cygnus, "You may be tested, like the legend written in the ancient Manfas Qeddus, when Yakob fought with the Mal'ak all night until he was blessed, and then his name was changed to Israel, Prince who struggled with Egziabeher."

Mekonnen spoke to himself softly, "So this is a test, huh."

Then he looked up at the guardian Mal'ak and said to him, "So, you want me to fight with you?"

The Magnificent Sword.

He looked at the glowing, transparent blade of the Sayf and saw words flowing from bottom to the top and top to the bottom. Then there was a sentence that stood out to him Ge'ez script, grabbing his attention,

"Take the Sword of the Spirit, which is the Word of Egziabeher."

As he looked at the complete making of the legendary Manfasawi Sayf, Mekonnen had a closer look at the hilt of the sword and beholds the magnificent design and craftsmanship of it. The hilt consisted of solid, burnished gold, with a pair of lions' heads, facing in opposite directions, at the end of the crossbars. At the center of the crossbars and the lion heads was a glowing ruby gem, almost transparent. The grip was also of fine, burnished gold with ridges engraved into it for improved handling. And finally, the pummel was like a single spherical pearl that reflected all the light and colors around them.

This was the make of the Manfasawi Sayf, the most powerful weapon in all the Realms of Samay, Meder, and Si'ol. It was a weapon that could exist here in one location and in many locations at the same time. Not fashioned in heat and flames by the skillful hands of swordsmiths among the Sons of Adam in the Realms of Meder, nor by the celestial hands of Mal'ekt in the cleansing fires that flow from under Tsion Dabr – Mount Zion –, but it was spoken into existence by the powerful Words from the very mouth of Egziabeher Amlak in his glorious Realms of Samayat.

As Mekonnen beheld the amazing beauty of this glorious Sword, his memory immediately went back to the dream he had of being in a valley with malefactors and benefactors of each side and the sword he retrieved from the altar. He remembered in that dream using the sword to defeat the encroaching Dark Qataliyan that pursued him. Now he realized that dream was a vision, foreshadowing the retrieval of this great spiritual Sword, which he may use to destroy the Armies of Darkness in this tangible world.

Prove you are Worthy!

Suddenly the Mal'ak jumped out from his place under the archway with his flashing silver sword drawn up high, speading his legs apart in a fighting pose, and his robe spread out wide to reveal them to be a pair of massive, white wing spans.

And he exclaimed, "Take the Abiyy Sayf, Mastatsabə, and prove to me that you are a warrior! Prove you are worthy to have this Sayf and wield it as your own!"

Mekonnen, startled by the Mal'ak's threatening countenance before him, quickly stepped up the seven white steps at the right side of the altar, which brought him at arm's reach with the Great Sword. He stopped to take a look at it for five seconds, then reached forward with his right hand to take hold of the grip of the swords golden hilt.

Immediately the white in Mekonnen's shemis shirt transformed into the golden breastplate as he grabbed the sword's hilt, holding the blade point upwards, as it flashed like lightning with the image of fiery flames flickered and moved within the blade. The sensation was invigorating as energy, power, and life vibrated through Mekonnen's hands, arms, shoulders to his chest and torso until it energized his whole body.

Mekonnen felt the power coursing through his veins as he lets out a shout, "Ahhhhhhhhhhhhhhh!!!! Egziabeher Yemasgan!!"

Abba Shiloh and Abba Elias looked on from below and stepped back for concern they would get in the cross fires, literally, from the Manfasawi Sayf clashing with the Mal'akawi Sayf.

Mekonnen thought to himself, "Which one is more powerful? Are they both the same? Tonight, I shall find out. Abba Shiloh did hint to me that the Sword of Egziabeher can be more powerful if used correctly."

Abba Shiloh shouted upwards to Mekonnen, "Anbessa Mekonnen! We will be right here praying for you during your battle! We will be right here when you are done! don't you worry, Hrai!"

Mekonnen replied sarcastically, "Sure! I will not worry, at all!"

First strike.

With that, the Mal'ak brought his angelic sword down onto Mekonnen but missed as the warrior jumped off to the right of the altar.

The Mal'ak's sword smashed through the stone marble altar like an axe through old wood, destroying it into many pieces, sending debris flying up

322　　　　　　　　　　　　© Jerome Matiyas

into the air then falling back down to the ground, even as far as where Abba Shiloh and Abba Elias were standing by several yards distance away.

Mekonnen exclaimed, "Hawey, this Mal'ak intends to strike me down with all his might, it seems."

The Mal'ak then swung his blade horizontally towards Mekonnen as if to slice him in half at the waist, but Mekonnen holds up his new Sayf to block it. When the two blades meet they clash loudly, and sparks fly about, but the impact sends Mekonnen flying backwards into a pillar, so hard it cracks. The air was knocked out of the warrior lungs from the impact as he drops his sword and falls forward to the ground.

Mekonnen was unconscious for about a minute before he recovered and got back on his feet. The Mal'ak said to him, "As I said before, Thou art not worthy!"

Abba Shiloh cheered on the warrior from the side, "Come on Anbessa! Get back up. You can do it!"

As Mekonnen was about to pick up his Sword again, he saw words flowing along the length of the blade in big, bold Ge'ez script letters

"*Manfas Qeddus* – The Holy Spirit –, he will teach you all things and bring to your remembrance all that I have said to you." These words were spoken by the Lord Iyesus Krestos as it was written in a verse from the Mashaf Qeddus – The Holy Scriptures, in the Yohannes Wangel (Gospel of John 14:26).

Mekonnen was reminded that the Manfas Qedus will bring the words to his remembrance. The key to understanding and using the power of the Sword. He picked up the Sword as the Mal'ak swung his sword again, but this time Mekonnen ducked as the sword passed over the locks of his head. The Mal'ak swung again from the other direction and this time Mekonnen reflected it with his Sword, keeping his balance this time.

Then Mekonnen remembered a verse, "I am victorious in Krestos who strengthens me!" (Phil 4:13)

And another, so he said it out loud, "I wield the Manfasawi Sayf – the Sword of the Spirit, which was the Qala Egziabeher! –The Word of the Lord of the whole World!"

The Mal'ak responded, "Ah, so you have a Sayf in your hands! But do you really know? Do you really believe it?!"

The great Mal'ak, brought the sword down on him again hard but this time Mekonnen was able to deflect all of them, with struggle, but without losing his footing.

The Mal'ak declared, "I still say you are not worthy and that you deserve to be destroyed!" Then he catched Mekonnen off guard and spun his body around to hit Mekonnen with one of his massive wings, sending the warrior through the air to slam into a wall between two pillars, under an arch. The warrior's body made a dent in the wall, then the Mal'ak heaved back and

Mekonnen battles with a silver Warrior Angel who guards access to the Sword of the Spirit of Light. Artwork by Jerome Matiyas © 5/2021.

swung his great sword onto the two pillars, slashing through them effortlessly, causing the pillars, arches and walls to crumble and fall on top of Mekonnen. The warrior and his Sayf got buried under rumble of bricks and mortar.

Mekonnen was stunned and bruised from the impact but not in as much pain as he could have been without the Breastplate armor he was wearing. Without it, he would have been much more injured as a regular man in such an impact. He was fortunate to cover his head with his arms to protect it from the falling debris. Slowly he climbed out of the rumble like a man climbing out of a grave.

The Mal'ak taunted him, "Oh, you are still alive? I must say you are a strong one!"

Mekonnen began to feel ambivalent about his angelic opponent. All the Mal'ekt he has encountered until now has defended him and saved his life. This one seems to be trying his best to take his life. Maybe this Mal'ak was actually a Qataliyan from the Armies of Darkness, he thought.

Mekonnen extended the point of his Sayf towards the Mal'ak and stated, "Why do you taunt me and try to harm me? I thought a true Mal'ak of Samay will try to help me. I am beginning to think you are evil, and a Dark Mal'ak like one of the Dark Qataliyan. Only you to do not wear a cloaked robe over your head and your countenance was more like a man and not as black as a deep abyss. Perhaps you are a devil masquerading as a Mal'ak of Light!"

After Mekonnen said that some words flowed through the blade of his sword again and it read, "As Yakob wrestled with the Mal'ak Egziabeher until he was bruised but blessed, so will you be. Speak no evil of my Mal'ak of Judgement and Testing."

With that message Mekonnen then knew the Mal'ak before him, though seemingly hostile towards him, was actually on the side of Egziabeher from Samayat. But somehow, he must still contend with him in battle. But can he win this battle? Or will he end up cripple and limping like his forefather Yakob?

Mekonnen continued, "So, I see you have been placed here to test me. Therefore, I shall fight you until the end. Until one of us gives up or is wounded in battle. I do not know if you are allowed to kill me, or if I am able to destroy you, but whatever happens tonight, let Egziabeher's will be done!"

The Mal'ak became excited and exclaimed loudly, "Ah Hah! Now you have spoken like a true Warrior!"

And the Mal'ak leapt into the air and came back down with the point of his sword point downwards, aiming straight for Mekonnens body as if to impale him into the ground.

Adrenaline kicked in and Mekonnen quickly leapt and rolled out of the way, barely missing the edge of his opponent's blade by an inch. The sword penetrated quite deep into the ground with a loud crashing sound, "DDOOOOOVVVVMMMKKKK!!!" the floor of the great chapel-like structure cracked and more debri flew up in many directions.

Mekonnen managed to get back up on his feet and posed with Flaming Sword upwards, prepared to clash swords some more with his Mal'akawi apponent.

He declared boldly, "The Word of God is quick, and powerful, and sharper than any two-edged sword, piercing even to the dividing asunder of soul and spirit, and of the joints and marrow. I wield the most powerful Sayf in the universe. Therefore, I will prevail!"

The Sword lit up and the image of a flame blazed inside and now outside the transparent blade. The Mal'ak, taller than Mekonnen, charged in viciously towards the warrior. Mekonnen also charged forward bravely. They clashed swords, and Mekonnen withstood the Mal'ak's swings and blows.

The two swung and swiped. They clashed blades and lit up the great chapel with sparks but also missed each other and sliced through walls and pillars, gradually destroying the structure to a demolished wreck.

Mekonnen declared more words of power and might, and each time his Sword became more inflamed and stronger.

"Behold, I come not to bring peace, but I bring a Sword."

Was one bold declaration Mekonnen made from one of the verses in the Wangel. (Book of Mathew 10:34)

"And out of his mouth goes a sharp sword, that with it he should smite the nations..." (Book of Revelation 19: 15)

The rocks, bricks and other forms of debris began to projectile so far that Abba Shiloh and Abba Elias had to retreat further back to the shore on the back of the Cygnus with the Mal'ak who helped them sail across the lake to this secret island. This secret island was now becoming an island of rubble and destruction.

Abba Shiloh said, "I hope and pray Anbessa Mekonnen will survive and come out alive after this ordeal, hrrrm."

The Mal'ak in the aqua-marine apparel said, "That Mal'ak is like unto one of the Destroyers. He has in ancient times been assigned with others like him to destroy cities, nations, and islands that have sinned against Egziabeher and the time of judgement was at hand. Jericho; Sodom and Gomorrah. He was there. Egziabeher has sent him to test Mekonnen to the maximum so he will be prepared for the Armies of Darkness."

Abba Shiloh sighed, "May Egziabeher have mercy and increase strength to Mekonnen's body and soul."

Mekonnen and the Mal'ak still battled with each other furiously, destroying the chapel structure in the process. They seemed to be fighting for about 4 hours from the perspective of Abba Shiloh and Abba Elias, by the Cygnus on the sea shore, but to Mekonnen it seems more like one hour. Time was slower inside the chapel structure where the Flaming Sword was guarded.

Decisive Strike.

Then there was a decisive move that determined the outcome of the battle. The Mal'ak swung he sword diagonally at Mekonnen, who block it with his Sayf, but the Mal'ak's sword shattered into many pieces at the impact, like glass. But then the Mal'ak tried to spin around quickly to lash the warrior man with his wings to send him flying into a wall again, but this time Mekonnen turned around quickly with the blade and swiped quickly at the Mal'ak's left wing, slicing it clean off at the shoulder.

The Mal'ak howled as his left wing fell to the ground and he cringes his back in pain. The wound where his wing was once attached sizzled like a fire inside burning coal.

Mekonnen was shocked and terrified that he has harmed one of the Mal'ak of Egziabeher and drops down on his knees and began to apologize.

"Hawey! Oh no! I am so sorry for what have done. Forgive me for my savagery."

The Mal'ak dropped to his knees and hands on the grounds amongst the rubble and said, "Fear not, valiant Warrior Mekonnen. You have fought well. You have shown yourself to be a true combatant who will not give up a good fight. And you have shown me mercy, after dealing a blow that has severed my wing."

Mekonnen inquired, "So what will happen with your wing? Will it heal or grow back?"

The Mal'ak replied, "I will return to Abba Egziabeher, and in his kingdom, there are Houses of Healing. There I will rest and rejuvenate and shall be completely healed soon."

As he said that the sky opened up and two Mal'ekt descended down from it, and onto either side on the wounded Mal'ak to pick him up and carry him back up to Samay. One of the Mal'ak picked up the severed wing and flew off as the Mal'ak said to Mekonnen,

"The island will now begin to sink into the sea, never to be seen or found again. You must now leave the island with you friends."

As they flew off the Mal'ak took off the sword sheath from his back and gave it to Mekonnen and said, "Here, you can take this sword sheath and use it to hold and carry your new Flaming Sword of Light. Also, take my gauntlets. They will give you better grip on to the Great Sayf."

Mekonnen said, "Thank you, my friend. You have been a worthy opponent and a surprisingly good teacher. I have learned a lot from you. You have taught me and pushed me into using the Sayf effectively. Farewell!"

The Mal'ak replied, "Farewell to you, and God Speed on your journey to battle against the evil forces. Use the Word against them all: the Qataliyan, Abiyy Kalabat Arawit, the Abiyy Arawit and the Serpent Waynaba, who has returned. Beware! The Dark Qataliyan are waiting for you on the shores of Tsana Hayk. So, when you return, be ready to fight. And fight to win. They must be stopped immediately."

As the Mal'ak ascends into Samay with assistance from two Mal'ekt by his side, his helmet became loose and slips off his head, falling back onto the ground. It bounces off the marble floor and rubble three times and lands next to Mekonnen, so he picked it up and waved it in the air and called out to the Mal'ak, "Hey, you dropped your helmet!"

The Mal'ak shouted back his reply, "You can keep it until you receive your own *Gera Dehnat* – Helmet of Salvation. You can wear my Mal'akawi helmet for protection in battle until then."

Mekonnen replied, "U-wa, Thank you. I will be ready for them."

Then the island began to shake as if there was an earthquake. Mekonnen put the silver, dome-shaped helmet on his head. He put on the gauntlets. He took the sheath and inserted the Sword into it. Then he ran back to the seashore where his two elders and the aqua-marine Mal'ak wait for him by the Cygnus.

They sailed off as the island sinks into the depths of the sea.

Abba Shiloh said to Mekonnen, "Congratulations Anbessa! You past the test and retrieved the Flaming Sword of Light. I was afraid you would not make it, but I prayed to Egziabeher to give you strength."

Mekonnen replied, "Thank you Abba. It was a great challenge, but I learned a lot about myself and my mission. I sure wish I already found the Helmet of Salvation or a helmet like this one the Mal'ak gave to me. I almost got my head cracked open by falling rocks and pillars!"

They returned to the seashore and on the Tsana Qirqos island and went back through the tunnel and stairways, and back out through the chapel-monastery.

Return to Tsana Qirqos.

When they returned through the secret passageway to the other side of the chapel, the manakost and kahenat on the island gathered around to see the warrior Mekonnen holding the Sword with both hands as the blade glows and reflects light with blinding glares. Mekonnen kept on walking slowly as if he was being guided until he reached a spot of evenly set stone slabs close to a ledge where he could see the lake and the horizon with the open sky above. The spot was about 20 by 20 feet area and on one side was a sort of monument or altar, about 5 feet high, made up of evenly cut cube stone bocks. Abba Elias and Abba Shiloh knew it was once the resting place of a significant sacred artifact, but Mekonnen did not. Yet he was being led to that spot.

The clouds in the sky above Tsana Qirqos Island began to open to reveal a blue opening like a great pool of water in the sky. A pattern began to form inside the blue open sky until it resembles a gigantic pupil of an eye peering down on the island. It was an amazing sight that looked like it was literally the eye of Egziabeher fixed on Tsana Qirqos island for that moment.

Mekonnen felt the Sword vibrating in his hands. He held the Sword up higher in just his right hand and declared,

"This is it!"

And immediately a bolt of lightning flashed from the eye in the sky and struck down to the Sword in Mekonnen's hand, visibly manifesting power streaming from the sky to the Sword for twenty one seconds. Abba Shiloh, Elias, and the manakost saw an illuminated Mekonnen holding aloft the Sword and electrified by the lightning, but he did not become consumes or harmed by it. At the same time, a clap of thunder boomed and engulfed the whole island in sound and a flash of light, causing many of the manakost to cover their eyes, duck for cover or fall to the ground. Then it was over, and Mekonnen brought the Sword down, and continued to stare at it in amazement and wonder.

He looked at Abba Shiloh and said,

"Things are coming together, Abba Shiloh. I assume there will be more to come, until it is all complete. It is all written in the Word, isn't it, Abba? Written in the ancient Oracles; The articles of the *Armor of Egziabeher*. Written by the Nabiyy Isayias. Negus Solomon and Qeddus Paulos. That means I still need to find the Helmet of Salvation, Sandals of Peace, and the Shield of Faith!"

Abba Shiloh walked up to Mekonnen and placed his hand on his shoulder and said gently. "You will understand fully when the time progresses, and more will be revealed to you. But remember now." Abba Shiloh leaned closer to Mekonnen and began to whisper to him,

"Do not reveal any of this to anyone. No one in the village, neither in our travels. That is very important. The Enemy has secret followers everywhere, and he must not know of your progress."

"Hrai, Hrai, I understand, Abba!" Mekonnen replied with a bow.

Abba Elias drew near to Mekonnen and said, "Mekonnen, do you know what the significance of these stone slabs and this stone altar is?"

Mekonnen replied, "No I do not know. What are these stones and altar for?"

Abba Elias said, "This is the spot where the Ark of the Covenant once rested before taken away by Negus Ezana about 200 years ago. The Ark of the Covenant was brought hear from the Kingdom of Israel by Levites who escaped the destruction of Eyerusalem by the Babylonians. It rested here under a tabernacle for about 800 years as ordinances were performed by Levites to honor the presence of the Most High."

Mekonnen stood and looked around the spot in awe; then a powerful, wise saying flows out of his mouth,

"And then the Most High sent His Son to be his divine presence on Earth. Born of the Virgin Mariam, crucified and shed His blood as the final sacrifice for our sins. The Alighty One sent His Elect One, Iyesus Krestos, who is the Word of Egziabeher, sharper than any two-edged Sword. Separating soul from spirit, and bone from marrow. Slaying the works of Darkness with the flashing blade of Light!"

The next day Mekonnen and Abba Shiloh bade farewell to Abba Elias and the rest of the manakost.

Mekonnen said to Abba Elias, "Thank you very much, Abba Elias, for your hospitality and imparting your wisdom to me. It was an honor. I shall use this gift of the Sword with care and pride." Mekonnen bowed and kissed Abba Elias's right hand then stepped into the boat and helped Abba Shiloh in after himself.

Abba Shiloh also said farewell to his friend Abba Elias, "Goodbye, my dear brother Abba Elias! I hope to see you again soon, Egziabeher Yamesgan!"

"I prayed that you will be blessed and be safe in your journey. *ZaEgziabeher Blen* – the Eyes of the Almighty will be looking after you. Have no fear, my son. Shalom!"

"Shalom, Abba Elias!"

Mekonnen felt more refreshed and enlightened and looked forward to the rest of his challenging mission.

Waynaba's Concern.
Meanwhile, that dreadful serpent, Waynaba, who glared at Mekonnen with the evil eye in the lake the day before, was lurking nearby in the deep caverns of the lake. Waynaba could sense that there was an object of great value on the boat. In fact, he could see the glow emanating from the Sword, even though it was still in its sheath. He also saw the great eye in the sky and the lightning the flashed down on the island.

Waynaba said to himself, "Well, it ssseems our warrior of concern has retrieved a weapon of great value against usss. Now he must truly be ssstopped before it isss too late!"

Waynaba maneuvered through the waters with his long scaly body fitted with pointy dorsal fins along his spine, about 20 feet long and small arms with clawed four-fingered hands at its sides, six feet below its hideous head. He descended deeper and deeper until he reached an opening in the sea floor. He poked his head into the hole in the bottom of the lake which came out in the water trench hundreds of miles away in Roha-Zoheleth.

Standing at the water trench and altar at Roha-Zoheleth was *Egzi Bərur Gwanti* – the Lord Silver Gauntlet –, accompanied by a dozen men of the serpent worshiping cult from Roha in hooded cloaks, the remaining cloaked Qataliyan, and the dreadful Hell-Hounds. The Qataliyan hummed a verse of some ungodly mantra, when one of them greeted Waynaba the Zendow,

"Greetings Oh Great Zendow, Lord WAYNABA! Your humble servants the Dark Ones are pleased to see you. How can we serve you today!"

Waynaba replied with his dreadful mouth of many teeth and long fangs in a gravely, hissing voice,

"I want as many Qataliyan and Dark Hound reinforcementsss as can be sent to line the shores of Tsana Hayk across from Qirqosss Island. I believe the warrior hasss acquired a very powerful weapon. He hasss it with him in a boat right now. I believe it is a Hayle Sssayf – A Powerful Sssword!"

The Silver Gauntlet responded, "Death Cloak and two dozen of his Qataliyan and a dozen Dark Hounds have already gone over to the shores of Tsana Hayk as your back up. The ones over here must stay to watch over and protect Zoheleth and take the rest of Roha. You should have a enough reinforcements there already."

Waynaba said, "I hope you are right, Egzi Silver Gauntlet, becaussse I sssense the warrior's new weapon is very powerful, and the 24 Qataliyan may not be enough. Can I have 36? Or 48 more?"

The Silver Gauntlet replied, "No! I cannot send you that many. Then there will not be enough of them to stand over Roha!"

Waynaba begged, "Then send me some of the big Abiyy Arawit – the Great Beasts!"

The Silver Gauntlet, "I can send you three Abiyy Arawit, and that is it! And 20 more Qataliyan only if you need them after the 24 who are already there!"

Waynaba replied, "Hrai, that will do! Just know that your failure to capture the city of Aksum and kill the Negus has ssspawned a more SSSERIOUS problem for us. Despite your Ring of Power and control over us of the ssspiritual world of the deep! I shall now ascend to the surface and strike at the warrior and the old manakos, and I will destroy them myssself!"

Sword of the Spirit of the Word, The Sword of Light.
Artwork by Jerome Matiyas © 5/2/2019.

SWORD OF THE SPIRIT OF THE WORD

The sword of the Sp
Jerome Matiyas
4/7/2018

CHAPTER 16
THE SERPENT
VERSUS
THE SWORD

In that day the LORD with his sore and great and strong sword shall punish Leviathan the piercing serpent, even Leviathan that crooked serpent; and he shall slay the dragon that is in the sea.

~ Isaiah 27:1 ~

Chapter 16

Chapter 16

The Serpent versus The Sword

With the help of a couple of manakost Mekonnen and Abba Shiloh climbed back into the boat they came in. They were given water, fruit, bread, and injera to take with them back to the mainland. Abba Shiloh placed the food in the bag pouch with the Honey, Manna bread and Holy Water they got from Abba Libanos' monastery.

Mekonnen was about to grab both ores to row, but to his surprise, Abba Shiloh took one of the ores and let Mekonnen have the other. The Bahetawi was actually going to help him row this time. The idea was that they row in unison this time, Mekonnen on the right side of the boat, Shiloh on the left. Excellent!

They sat in the boat facing each other. Mekonnen faced forward, Abba Shiloh backward. Abba Shiloh began to speak:

"Now Mekonnen, it is very important that you know the Word and remember the Oracles we talked about before. You must recite and digest the sacred oracles internally in order to use the Sword successfully."

Mekonnen in his natural mind was a bit puzzled at the holy man's riddles, but in his spirit, he understood.

"I cannot accomplish this for you. You must master it yourself. We must fight our own battles, and this is your battle to fight. The enemy hates the Word and the Sword of the Word and does not want the Sons of Adam to know the Word and the Sword. So, he will try to stop the Sons of Adam from advancing to become the Sons of Egziabeher. He wants Adam's seed to be defeated and debased and to be ignorant of Hawah's Seed. Do you understand what I am saying, Mekonnen?"

Strangely, Mekonnen did understand these cryptic sayings somehow but did not know how or why. But it all made sense. He looked down at the golden sword handle, and pearlescent pummel that's jotting out of the white linen cloth the sheath and blade was wrapped in.

"U-wa, Abba Shiloh, I do understand."

"Hrai, my boy. My Anbessa." Abba Shiloh said reassuringly then continued.

"Now tell me, what was the first Sword ever mentioned in the Sacred Oracle of Egziabeher?"

Declaring the Word.

"The first Sword ever mentioned or spoken of was the sword that flashed to and fro to guard the way to the Garden of Eden. To keep the *Nakhash*, the serpent, out of the garden after he deceived Adam and Hawah. To also keep Adam and Hawah out of the Garden and away from the Tree of Knowledge of Good and Evil, and the Tree of Everlasting Life. There were also Kerubel guarding the Garden with the Sword as it flashed to and fro. This is written in the *Orit Zalədat*, The Book of Beginnings (Genesis 3:24)."

"Yes, that is correct Anbessa. And what, who is that Sword?"

"The Sword was the Word of God, and the Word is the Sword. The Sword of the Word."

"Yes, it is a mystery only revealed to who?"

"A mystery only revealed to those who walk in The Way. The *Yashar Sodi* which is the Righteous Way."

Abba Shiloh: "Yes, but whose Righteousness, your own?"

Mekonnen: "*Iyyaseh*, No. Not mine but the Righteousness of the Word of Egziabeher. The Word of Egziabeher that became flesh and walked and taught among men."

"And who is this Word that became flesh?"

Mekonnen: "The Word is the Messiach, The Krestos, Yehshua. Iyesus Kristos."

Abba Shiloh: "Yes, that is most important of all, *Iyesus Krestos, Negusa Nagast, Egzi Hawey*. And what did the other Yehshua, the successor to Moses, see at Jericho standing before him?"

Mekonnen: "Yehshua saw a Man before him holding a drawn Sword, and the Man said he was Captain of the Armies of the Lord of Hosts."

Abba Shiloh: "And *who* is the Captain of the Armies of the Lord of Hosts!"

Mekonnen: "He is… Liq Mel'ak Mikael—The Arch Angel Michael!"

Abba Shiloh repeatd: "And who is the Captain of the Armies of the Lord of Hosts!"

Mekonnen paused and was confused for a few seconds. Was it a riddle or a mystery? Who is the true captain of the Armies of *Samayat*, he thought to himself? He knew Liq Mel'ak Mikael is a Captain of Egziabeher's Armies, but so is Iyesus Krestos, who is of much Higher rank now in the *Samayat*. Yet, Abba Shiloh did not say "'*Iyyaseh*,' which is No!" but he repeated the question. Therefore, Mekonnen was enlightened and did not hesitated any longer.

"He is, *Iyesus Kristos*! The Walda Egziabeher!"

Abba Shiloh: And who is Iyesus Kristos, the Son of Egziabeher Amlak?"

Mekonnen: "He is *Qal*, The Word. *Qala Egziabeher*. The Word of Egziabeher. In the beginning was the Word, and the Word was with Egziabeher, and the Word was Egziabeher... The Word became flesh and lived and walked among mankind. He came to his own, but they received Him not." (John 1:1, 14)

Abba Shiloh: "And where is He now? Where is the Word?"

Mekonnen: "He sits at the right hand of Egziabeher, interceding for us. But he speaks to us through the *Qedus Manfas*, the Holy Spirit. But the Son at the Father's right hand shall return."

Abba Shiloh: "And how shall He return?"

Mekonnen: "He shall return in the clouds, on a white horse. In power and might. With the Armies of Samayat behind Him. And a sharp Sword of the Word shall proceed out of his mouth to destroy the evil doers from the earth. *(Rev 19:14-15)*

The Sword of the Word of Righteousness and Judgement shall slay the evil men, Mal'ekt, Kerubel, Surafel, the creatures from the bottomless pit. The Dark Ones, and the False Meshiach." *(Rev 19: 20)*

Abba Shiloh: "Yes, that is it Mekonnen, The Sword of the Spirit of the Word, *Anbessa*. That is what you have in your possession now! It is very important that you know this and protect it. Guard it. Use it for the purpose it was created. To protect all that is good and sacred. And to destroy evil forces! Remember this, Mekonnen. You must always know this!"

All this time Mekonnen and Abba Shiloh had been rowing in unison while they talk and recite the sacred oracle of ancient text, in reference to the mysterious Sword that was just given to Mekonnen. Mekonnen realized that Abba Shiloh had been trying to instill the eternal Word of Egziabeher into his spirit and his soul so that he was connected and became one with the Sword. Until he became one with the meaning, purpose and life and power of the Sword and the Word. Still, there was more.

"Anbessa! What does the sacred oracle in the letter to the Hebrews say about the Sword of the Word?" asked Abba Shiloh, testing Mekonnen's knowledge.

Mekonnen replied, "That the Word of Egziabeher is sharper than any two-edged sword, cutting the bone from marrow. Separating the Soul from the Spirit. (Hebrews 4:12) As it said in the letter of Qedus Paulos to the Ephesians, 'The Sword of the Spirit is the Word of Egziabeher." (Ephesians 6:17)

Abba Shiloh: U-wa, U-wa, hrmm. And the Sword of the Spirit is one part of the whole Armor of Egziabeher that are more powerful when they are all united and used together as one. You must find them all, Mekonnen. Search for them, seek them, and you shall find them among the sacred Words. Among the sacred tombs, caves, and cracks in the mountains of the world. They are out there waiting to be found. You already have some of the pieces of Armor puzzle that are significant, but you must find the rest. Not to complete your journey, but to start the journey. This is just the beginning of your Higher Calling to the journey of the rest of your life. Do you understand what I mean, young *Anbessa*?"

Mekonnen: "U-wa, Abba Shiloh. I do understand. It seems I will have a long journey ahead of me."

Abba Shiloh: "We all have a long journey ahead of us in this Realm on Meder-Earth whether we choose good or bad. Yet still, it is actually a short journey on this Meder compared to the everlasting journey into the afterlife into the cosmic realms of Samayat or Gahannam-- Heaven or Hell Fire."

Mekonnen looked down at the Sword again as he rowed the paddles in unison with Abba Shiloh. The golden handle and pearlescent pummel shined and glistened in the sun. Now Mekonnen began to wonder how powerful the Sword really was, and how soon he will have to use it. In fact, now he was hoping he would get to use it very soon and test it out on the heads of some agents of Darkness. Preferably on the Dark Qataliyan that killed his cousin Afeworq in Aksum a few weeks ago.

Yet just then the waters began to stir up some more and got a bit choppy. He figured it was just the winds blowing over the surface of the lake, or could it be that creature with the evil eye returning to pick a fight.

Mekonnen noticed Abba Shiloh has his eyes fixed on him, but Mekonnen had more questions.

"So, this is the Armor that Paulos the Apostle first wrote about?"

Abba Shiloh answered, "U-wa, but Paulos was not the first the write about the full armour. He was expounding on what the prophet Isaias wrote about hundreds of years before. Isaias wrote by inspiration by the Spirit of Egziabeher, "…He put on Righteousness as a Breastplate, and an Helmet of Salvation upon his head;…" (Isaiah 59:17). And also in the Wisdom of Solomon, also wrote about all the parts of the Armor of Egziabeher.

Mekonnen was aware now that he had on the Breastplate, and the Belt and now the Sword, but not yet a Helmet of Salvation, or a Shield of Faith, and the Shoes of Peace. So, if his armor was incomplete did that mean he was not prepared to go into battle? Suddenly a still small voice spoke in his head. He did not understand where it came from, but it was clear. "He who has Faith as small as a mustard seed can accomplish anything in my name. Even cast a mountain into the sea." (Matthew 17:20; Luke 17:6).

The waters of Tsana Hayk begin to stir up and became more unstable.

Then suddenly a large wave rose up to Mekonnen's left side of the boat, and there was the large evil eye of the creature again, leering at Mekonnen and Abba Shiloh.

Instantly, Mekonnen grabs for the Sword and quickly unsheathe it, but before they know it the creature let out a loud roar with a quick jolt towards Mekonnen, which startled him greatly, causing the boat to almost turn over.

The Serpent Strikes Back.

The creature made a quick dive beneath the water's surface. Mekonnen and Abba Shiloh saw its rough, scaly back and tail. It seemed like a huge creature, but Mekonnen did not care much about its size, for he has gained more confidence in the Almighty Egziabeher. Then he remembered a verse in the prophecies of Isaias that said,

"The Lord with His sharp, great and strong Sword will punish Leviathan the swift serpent, even leviathan the crooked serpent, and he will slay the dragon that is in the sea." (Isaiah 27:1)

This made Mekonnen more excited, and then it dawned on him. This Sword in his procession may well be the Lord's great Sword, and that serpent is Leviathan, that ancient, evil, serpent of the sea. Now he knew what he must do. Slay the Leviathan!

Mekonnen grabbed up the sword and sheath and withdraws the Sword from the sheath quickly as he began to stand up in the unstable boat. Behold, the Sword glowed brightly like a lantern as power surged through it. Mekonnen felt the power vibrating in his hands as he grasped the illuminated Sword in his right hand. He looked at the blade, and it was like translucent glass with words moving up and down in it as like glowing multi-colored fish in water, but still in the midst of billowing flames inside the blade. They were some of the same words that he and Abba Shiloh were speaking, and even the thoughts in Mekonnen's mind and spirit about the Word, Sword of the Spirit, defeating the darkness with light and slaying the serpent of the sea. It was a wonder to behold the powerful weapon in his hand, but he must think and act fast. He turned to Abba Shiloh still sitting in the boat and said,

"I know what must be done now, Abba Shiloh."

Immediately while he was still speaking the creature raised it's ugly, long-fanged head from out of the water and let out a hissing roar at Mekonnen and the Sword. The creature now revealed that it was truly a class of malicious sea serpents of old. About 20 feet in length, large but not the largest of them that has been reported. It's head was large enough to fit a tall man like Mekonnen inside of it.

With sudden courage and a rush of adrenaline, Mekonnen leapstout of the boat towards the serpent with flashing Sword raised high, ready to strike down a deadly blow into the aquatic monster. The serpent dodged, dove

downwards into the depths but lashed out with its tail like a giant whip, hitting the boat in the process, causing the boat and Abba Shiloh inside it to go flying in the air for a good distance. Abba Shiloh fell out into the chaotic lake waters, but fortunately the old man knew how to swim even in these conditions. He uttered a pray for Mekonnen and himself as a waded in the water.

Brave Mekonnen was now in the water with the dreaded serpent with the evil eye, Waynaba. He swam downward after for the beast, using the flashing Sword as a torch to illumine the dark depths of the sea. Then he heard a dreadful hissing voice.

"HHHSSSSS! Little man, you are now in my domain. My rules apply, and my ssstrategies govern. Now you will never return to the sssurface. You shall remain down here with ME! Heh Heh Hehhhh HHHHSSSEEEHHH!

Mekonnen recanted, in his head. He noticed he now had the ability to communicate with the serpent underwater without opening his mouth. He sense he has now enters another realm of sorts.

"I will not listen to your lies you vile beast! I will return from whence I came. Even on that same boat."

The serpent replied. "Ohhhhh! But look up and sssee how deep down you are. And what about your companion that was in the boat with you?"

Mekonnen looked up and noticed how far away the boat seemed, a great distance than it should be because he only jumped into the water less than a minute ago. And he could see Abba Shiloh looking as if he was struggling to swim and keep afloat in the water. He began to feel a bit worried and concerned about Abba Shiloh, hoping the old man was not about to drown.

"Sssee?! You are far down, and your friend is DROWNING!! What can you do?"

Suddenly Mekonnen felt a hard blow on his back, pushing him deeper down into the sea. It was the serpent swimming up silently from behind, then lashed him on the back with his tail.

He considered that maybe the serpent was lying to him and he was not as far down as it looked, and Abba Shiloh was not drowning. Maybe the serpent was playing tricks to discourage him. That's are one of the strategies of the agents of darkness, to scare those that follow the Way of Light. But then again, what if the serpent's words said was true, and he truly was too far down, and Abba Shiloh did need help? Like when Afeworq needed help, and he died?

"No! Forget it!" Mekonnen snapped to himself, "I have the Sword of the Word, and there is a job to be done. I act by Faith and not by sight."

Mekonnen looked down ahead of him and could see the glowing red eyes of the serpent staring at him. Then the sea-beast said to him.

"Oh, you don't have Faith. All you have is a sssword. You think you can hurt me with that little thing down here, boy!"

The eyes gradually got bigger as the serpent swam closer at increasing speed. Then he could see teeth and a mouth opening wider and wider towards him. Mekonnen's heart beat accelerated with fear, but he raised the Sword, ready to strike. He swung and heard a "ping" sound as he chips off a tip of one of the serpent's teeth.

"Swwoooshhh, Paiinngg!"

The serpent hissed and quickly swerved to the left, away from the warrior as it felt the slight sting from the blade. The serpent was out of sight, Mekonnen looked around the watery battlefield with the great Sword held out in front of him. The glow from the Sword served as a source of light in the dark waters and as a source of protection, security, and reassurance as Mekonnen realized the beast feared the Sword and aware of its divine, heavenly, and sacred origins. But it bluffs and lies, as if there was no power in the blade that can cut the spirit from the soul, and bone from marrow.

Now Mekonnen noticed how long he has been under the water, longer than the average man could hold his breath, but somehow, he was not gasping for air or drowning. Very strange indeed. He presumed he has moved into a different realm from the natural one. An alternate dimension, like what Abba Shiloh spoke about in the caves and the wilderness. A realm that was not natural, but supernatural.

Immediately Mekonnen remembered that he needed to continue declaring the Word said in his spirit,

"You lie, vile beast! I do have Faith in me that is from the Egzi. Even Faith as small as a mustard seed has grown into a larger tree. And this is not a little sword as you know now. This is The Great Sword of the Spirit of the Word of Egziabeher. This Sword was forged and spoken into existence in Samayat from the beginning of time."

As Mekonnen spoke, he noticed the buckle of the golden belt that was given to him in Aksum began to glow, providing more light in the dark murky lake. It was the Belt of Truth responding to Mekonnen's spoken Words of truth.

In the depths, the serpent let out a groan and a hissing sound of agony and fear. Mekonnen could now see the serpent more clearly in the depths below him with its glowing red eyes.

What is Your Name?

Then Mekonnen pointed the tip of the flashing blade towards the creature and demanded with authority, "I command you, tell me, what is your name, creature?!"

The Serpent laughed and began uttering words that were difficult to understand.

"Waaaaaahhhh…. Ayyyyyyy!!"

Mekonnen commanded the serpent creature again, "Speak up, vile snake! What is your name, I command in the name of Yehshua!"

The serpent made a gurgling sound and continued,

"I aaaammm…… Waaahh…ayyyy……Naaahhhh….Baaaaaahhhh! WAYNABA, isss my name, Ha Hah Heeh Heeh!!

Punish Leviathan.

Mekonnen was shocked to hear the serpent declare it was Waynaba, because that was the name of the Serpent that terrorized Aksum more than a thousand years ago but was killed by Prince Angabo from Sheba across the Reed Sea, according to one legend. Angabo the Sabaean became an ancestor to Makeda, the Queen of Sheba.

"Waynaba was killed more than a thouand years ago. Stop lying! What is your real name?" Mekonnen demanded.

The serpent responded,

"It is the truth! I am the spirit of Waynaba. Returned in the flesh!! Ha Ha ha haaaaa sssssssssskkkkkkkksssssssss!!"

Mekonnen recanted, "You shall never return! You have been cast into the depths of the sea and the shadow of the abyss, and there you will remain. And there is no way you will get past my Sword, The Lord's Sword, to return to the surface."

"If I am conjured up I can. Either way, we will see about that, HHHHSSSSKKKKKKSSSSSSS!"

The serpent let out a dreadful hiss and charged upward very swiftly at Mekonnen with mouth wide open. Then it suddenly turned around to use the silver blade at the end of its tail as a whip again, and again and again. Mekonnen dodged the blows the first few times but was hit with the fifth swing. Mekonnen swung and jabbed the Sword at the swift, crooked serpent but missed 3 times, but the fourth time he dealt him a blow that sparked against the creature's body slicing off the tip of the tale that held the blade.

The serpent hissed in pain but charged at Mekonnen again with its jaws wide open and this time managed to grasp the warrior in its large jaws of many teeth. Waynaba became mad and violent as if he did not care about getting wounded by the Sword again.

Mekonnen struggled in Waynaba's jaws with the Sword still in right hand, but he was unable to move his hands as the beast dove down further to the depths of the lake and dragged Mekonnen down with him. It seemed like this was Mekonnen's doom and the end of his journey before it has even started. But Mekonnen was determined to live and whispers a pray while in the serpents jaws. Then he remembered the verse from the sacred oracle, from the prophet Isaias,

"The Lord with His sharp, great and strong Sword will punish Leviathan the swift serpent, even leviathan the crooked serpent, and he will slay the dragon that is in the sea."

And as he spoke the words, that flaming Sword of the Spirit blade becomes hot and burned the serpent's tongue. So, the serpent loosened its jaw grip and Mekonnen managed to wiggle himself loose and free his Sword arm. He could see the serpent's right eye in front of him, so he raised the Sword up high with the blade pointing downward and plunges it hard into Waynaba's large red eye. Almost one-quarter of the length of the Sword's blade was stuck into the eye. The creature began to scream in agony and anger, as sparks, flames and light erupted from where the Sword pierced the eye.

Mekonnen twisted the blade and pulled it up from the serpent, and immediately the eye exploded and was destroyed. But the rest of the serpent was not destroyed, so it continued falling downward into the depths as it hissed is agony, loosening the grip of its jaws around Mekonnen's body.

So, the victorious warrior swam freely and upward with minor bruises

on his arms, glowing golden breastplate, and flashing Sword in right hand. He looked upwards toward the surface, through the water he can see the brightness of the sun and the papyrus boat floating past it. But where was Abba Shiloh?

Mekonnen kept swimming up, up, up towards the boat. Paddling with both feet and hands for what seemed like forever, though it was only a few minutes. Then just as he was about to reach for the side of the boat with his left hand, a hand reached from inside the boat to help him into it. It was Abba Shiloh's. The old Bahetawi assisted Mekonnen into the boat and said,

"There you go, Anbessa. You did it. You defeated the sea-serpent."

"*Cough, cough*," Mekonnen coughed up some salty lake water, "It was a vicious fight, but…I thought you were drowned and gone from this earth."

"Iyyaseh! Egziabeher has more use for me here, boy. Hrrrmm! Come on, I know you are tired, but we must row back to shore before it gets dark again and that serpent returns from the depths."

Mekonnen looked at the Sword in awe and wonder now, thinking of the power it just displayed in the depths of the lake against the sea-serpent.

"The Sword, defeated the serpent, wounded its eye. He descended to the deep, but he may return."

"Oh, he may not be returning anytime soon. I think he learned a lesson today and may be afraid of the Sword."

"But, it said it was Waynaba! I was taught in school since a little boy that

© Jerome Matiyas

Waynaba was dead a long time ago, killed by Angabo the Sabaean. Is that possible, Abba?"

"Anything is possible. If it was, it is the spirit of Waynaba; he was probably conjured up into physical existence by some black magic. Remember, no Ganen or Mal'ak can enter into the Realm of Meder unless allowed by a Son of Adam, men, and women born of Earth. Because we as mankind were placed in dominion of this Realm of Meder – Earth."

So Mekonnen pondered his first real battle with the Manfasawi Sayf against an adversary as he rowed with Abba Shiloh and wondered what his next battle would be like. Abba Shiloh warned, "When we dock at the shore, keep on the alert for more attacks. They might be waiting for us at the seashore."

Mekonnen and Abba Shiloh arrived at the shore where they originally docked from. Alert with Sword drawn and staff out and eyes scanning their surroundings for possible surprise attacks from Cloaked Qataliyan or Hell-Hounds.

Lord Death Cloak and his Dark Qataliyan were originally going to attack the warrior and the Bahetawi if they got past Waynaba, but after they saw what happened to Waynaba in the lake they decided to retreat into the shadows for a meeting to discuss their next strategy to successfully take down their opponent, the warrior from Aksum, now armed with the most dangerous weapon in the universe.

Load Death Cloak spoke with his Dark Warrior Qataliyan and the hounds, "We must wait to attack them when they least expect it. Ambush them in an unexpected path. Follow me, Dark Warriors. I have a plan."

Back Into the Water Trench.

Meanwhile, the serpent Waynaba descended to the deep, wounded with only one eye. He returned to the portal at the bottom of the lake and climbed back into the water trench at Roha-Zoheleth, defeated.

The Silver Gauntlet spoke, "So, you see, Egzi Waynaba. It is not easy contending with this warrior, and his anointed weapons. Oh, my! What happened to your eye?!"

Waynaba answered, glaring at him with the other good eye, "You let him get too far! He now wieldsss a very powerful Sssword I have never ssseen before. It destroyed my eye!"

The Silver Gauntlet asked, "A sword, did this? Must be a very powerful sword."

Waynaba said, "I already said that! Sssome sssort of Mal'akawi Sssayf. But glowed and flashed with wordsss and flamesss and light in the blade!"

Lord Silver Gauntlet thought, "A sword with words inside of it. I have heard of such a sword. U-wa, but very rare. And very difficult to acquire.

Except." Then Lord Silver Gauntlet trailed off in thought and then walked away into a dark corner by himself. And then he said, "Our only hope now is for Lord Death Cloak – and his Qataliyan to confront this warrior with all the weapons they can unleash upon him! Including the Hounds and Great Beasts! After that, we will make another plan."

Waynaba asked, "And what would that entail? Thisss new plan?"

The Silver Gauntlet replied, "We still have Roha to contend with. We can conjure up a bigger and stronger army. But let's see what Death Cloak, and his Dark Qataliyan can accomplish over there first. Then I will shut off all shadow portals and gateways to the west, so the warrior cannot trace us back here until we are ready for them."

Waynaba the Terrible
Serpent
Jerome Matiyas © 10/2012

CHAPTER 17
A FORMIDABLE ADVERSARY

Be alert, be vigilant; because your adversary the devil prowls about like a roaring lion, seeking whom he may devour.
1 Peter 5:8

CHAPTER 17: A FORMIDABLE ADVERSARY
JEROME MATHIYAS © 12/7/2018

Chapter 17

Be alert, be vigilant, because your adversary the devil, prowls around like a roaring lion, seeking someone to devour. - 1 Peter 5:8

Thus said the LORD; Say, "A sword, a sword is sharpened and polished... that it may flash like lightning!" - Ezekiel 21: 9-10

Put on the Helmet of Salvation and grasp the Sword of the Spirit, which is the word of God. - Ephesians 6:17

O Death, where is your sting? O grave, where is your victory? - 1 Corinthians:55

Chapter 17

A
Formidable
Adversary

Mekonnen and Abba Shiloh quickly but carefully stepped out of the tankwa, then tied it to the dock at Wanzagay lake town and walk down the platform cautiously. Alert with Sword drawn, Masqal staff held up, and eyes scanning their surroundings for possible surprise attacks from Cloaked Qataliyan or Kalabata-Si'ol, they head towards the home of Abba Shiloh's friend whom they left their stallions in care of. As they crossed a couple of streets to get there, Mekonnen walked with his great Spirit of the Spirit drawn, drawing attention to themselves as the townspeople wondered why a warrior was walking through the streets with a sword drawn and a holy man by his side. Some wondered and whispered amongst themselves, "Is he protecting the Bahetawi, or is he holding him as a hostage?"

Abba Shiloh noticed the minor commotion they caused and spoke to Mekonnen, "Anbessa, I don't think you need the Sword drawn out now for the whole town to see, Hrai."

Mekonnen looked at the blade of the Sword and noticed it was not glowing as it did before, but looked more like a regular metallic blade, yet a message could still be seen, in Ge'ez script, scrolling along the blade, "You can put away the Sword now."

Mekonnen immediately placed The Sword back into the sheath the Mal'ak gave to him, then strapped the belt and buckle across his chest, so the Sayf hanged on his back, with the hilt of it jotted out behind his head for easy reach. The two men continued walking with faces as flints to the home of the horse keeper a few paces away.

Abba Shiloh remembered the bread and water in the bag and became concerned that the bread was now wet and no longer good for eating. He unlatched the bag to open it and reached in to touch the manna-bread. It was a bit wet but still intact. He broke off a peace and puts it into his mouth to taste it and determines it was still edible. So, he broke off another piece and puts it to Mekonnen's mouth to feed it to him as they walked and ate at the same time.

Abba Shiloh spoke, "I know we have not eaten since this morning and it is now almost 2 or 3 hours before sunset, so this bread should keep us going until night time. There is no time to sit and eat anywhere. We must make haste and get out of sight and away from the lake shore town as soon as possible, hrrm. Those dark Qataliyan can be lurking around anywhere, waiting for us."

Mekonnen replied, "Thank you Abba Shiloh. But where should we go now from here?"

Abba Shiloh responded in a lowered whispering voice, "I have not decided what a safe place for us to go now so we should ride out of here and head east. Then we will decide from there. Eventually, we must return to Gihon but we don't want to lead the Dark Qataliyan there, do we?"

Mekonnen replied sharply, "Hawey, absolutely not!"

Soon they arrived at the horse keeper's house, retrieved their stallions and mounted them quickly as they regrettably had to turn down the man's offers to go into his house for bunna and injera. Abba Shiloh insisted that it was urgent he left immediately with the warrior and promised another time he will stay for bunna. Off the two galloped eastwards in haste, away from Tsana Hayk. To a destination unknown but anticipated they will meet with their adversaries along the way.

Lurking and hiding in the shadows, Egzi Barnusa-Mot – Lord Death Cloak – and the Qataliyan emerged and began to converse amongst themselves.

Death Cloak began, "Hrai, they are riding off now. We will follow them and corner them at a place overcast by many shadows. A forested area or near a mountain. Wait for my signal to surprise attack them with deadly force. That's when you use your swords, scimitars, spears, lances, battle-axes, bows and arrows, and strike them with everything you've got! If you are not able to bring them down at first strike, restrain the old holy man. I have heard of the old man before, He is the stronger one, and his fame has echoed through the Realms of Darkness and Light for some time. He has upset our plans before, but just try to restrain him the best you can. But leave the young warrior welp to me. I will cut him down to pieces myself!"

They all answered in unison, "U-wa, Egzi Barnusa-Mot!"

As Death Cloak's commanded, "Let's go, my warriors of Darkness!"

In organized groups they presented themselves before their commander: 24 Qataliyan, 4 Kalabata-Si'ol - Hell-Hounds - and 3 hulking monsters with large teeth they call Abiyy Arawit, rushed on after the warrior and the Bahetawi, in and out of the shadows. It seems like an unfair fight with so many against two, but they anticipate the unexpected, including the intervention of Mal'ekt from the Realms of Samayat on high.

A Prayer for Strength in Battle.

Mekonnen and Abba Shiloh rode off with haste on their steeds to the east with the sun and Tsana Hayk behind them, and the wind blowing through their locks. Suddenly, Abba Shiloh had a pressing prompt in his spirit to stop and said, "Anbessa! Let us stop right now!"

Without hesitation, Mekonnen slows down his stallion with Abba Shiloh's, "Dismount your horse!" Abba Shiloh commanded as he quickly jumps off his own horse and descended upon his knees in the middle of the dusty road.

"Get down on your knees with me!" He commanded.

Mekonnen got down on his knees facing Abba Shiloh.

"Unsheathe your Sword and hold it down in front of us!"

Mekonnen obeyed, slowly unsheathes his Sword, holding on to the hilt with both hands with the tip of blade pressed into the ground.

Abba Shiloh, holding on to his staff with the Masqal cross up in the air, spoke, "It is important because we go into battle that we pray to the almighty Egziabeher for strength, wisdom, and protection. The adversary and his armies of Darkness will be wrathful and will want the attack us with full force. They will attack with all manner of weapons and obstacles. The power of prayer is one of the main parts of the Armor of Egziabeher. Do you understand what I am saying to you, Anbessa?"

Mekonnen replied, "U-wa! I do Abba. But you sound very concerned. Don't we already have the Manfasawi Sayf Qal? The most powerful weapon in the universe? In all creation? And, the *Et'aqa Aman wa Engeda Tsedaq* – The Belt of Truth and the Breastplate of Righteousness?"

Abba Shiloh responded, "Correct. But these articles will not be effective without the power of the Qala Egziabeher that connects us to the source of his power. That is our communication with Him. Otherwise, eventually, they become just like ordinary swords and shields of this Realm of Meder. Ineffective against the Spiritual beings of the principalities, and powers and thrones of the Spiritual Realm. So, I will pray for you now."

Abba Shiloh began, "Egziabeher Hawey! I pray for your son, Mekonnen, kneeling here before you. Give him strength and power and agility to stand against the savage adversaries who come against us. Invigorate the Truth, Righteousness, and Spirit of the Word he now holds. Fill in the gap where he needs the Helmet of Salvation, Shoes of Peace and the Shield of Faith."

Abba Shiloh reached out and places both hands upon the Mal'akawi helmet that Mekonnen wore on his head and declared, "This is the sign of the *Gera Dehnat* – The Helmet of Salvation – upon thine head, Anbessa Mekonnen. Thine crown will be protected."

Then he grabbed Mekonnen's wrists and crossed his arms across his chest and said, "This is the sign of the *Agre Emnat* – Shield of Faith –, which deflects the blows and fiery spears of the adversary. Anbessa, thine body is protected!"

Then he motioned for Mekonnen to bring forth his feet one at a time as he touched them with both hands, "This is the sign of you wearing *As'āna Salām* – the Shoes of Peace – ready and steady to proclaim the *Wangel* – The Good News of the Gospel – and defend the innocent and lost. Anbessa, thine feet, and legs are protected and quickened. Egziabeher, send your Mal'ekt to guard and watch over us. Amen."

Mekonnen repeated in agreement, "Amen."

Mekonnen's Sword, Breastplate, and Belt began to glow as Abba Shiloh prayed, and the likeness of a slow billowing flame moved through all of them. Abba Shiloh's Aksumite cross, and the large beaded necklace around his neck and torso, also glowed as flames flickered through them.

"Let's go, Anbessa, we go east then north, as if we are returning to Aksum, hrrmm. That's where they will expect you to go. To return home to Aksum."

Mekonnen and the Bahetawi mounted their stallions, "That is a good idea. To Aksum, we go!" This was their strategy to deflect the Qataliyan away from Gihon Village and other innocent people in their path.

A Gathering in Samay.

While the warrior and the holy man were praying a beam of light lit upon them in the spiritual realm, from the Earth up to Samay into the presence of Iyesus Krestos, the Elect One. Standing before the Elect One was the seven Mal'ekt, all together in a crescent formation as before. This is the same group of Mal'ekt who assisted Mekonnen and the maiden of Beta Israel, Penuel, in the dark realm under the Samen Mountains. With them were also other Samayawi creatures like the Abiyy Hayyal with the great horns who fought for them days ago with the green warrior Mal'ak.

Also present was the Anbessa Tsion, the Kerubel with the fiery mane, who had been appearing in Mekonnen's dreams.

Behind and encompassing this group that are involved in the matter of being guardians and protectors of Mekonnen and those involved in his assignment were hundreds of thousands of various Mal'ekt, Surafel, Kerubel, Onafel, and Qeddusan (Holy men and women who have passed from Earth and now dwell in Samayat). These heavenly creatures stood looking on as a multitude of witnesses to this dire situation involving the kingdom territory of Aksum, specifically at this moment, between the shores of Tsana Hayk and Roha City.

In a voice like the sound of many waters, The Elect One spoke to His congregation of mighty heavenly creatures, "*Samayawi Sarawit!* – My

Heavenly Army Host! Thou art great and mighty warriors. Stand by until I am ready to dispatch you to fight for my servants, Mekonnen the *mastatsabe*, and Shiloh the *manakos*."

The Anbessa Tsion approached the Elect One and asks Him a question, "Qeddus Haraya Ahandu'a Egziabeher! Is this the time when you send me down to fight for the warrior Mekonnen from Aksum?"

The Elect One answered, "No, Anbessa Tsion. Your time has not yet come, but it will soon. Now I shall go down and manifest myself inside the Sword of the Spirit as the *Hayla Qala Abba, Egziabeher* – the Power of the Word of My Father, Almighty God."

Stampede Through a Town.

The warrior and the Bahetawi rode through a small town called Wushet as they make their way to a forested area seen on the horizon. The townspeople looked on in awe and amazement at these two men on white Habeshinian horses in urgent haste. Men, women, and children enquired, "What are they running from?"

"Wow, a warrior and a Bahetawi riding together on horses?"

"Are they being chased?"

The citizens of the town looked back to see who was chasing them but saw nothing. About seven minutes later they heard the rumbling sounds of many feet and hoofs approaching in great haste. Then on the same path, stampeding through their main street they saw the horrible creatures that were chasing the warrior and holy man: Menacing Dark Qataliyan with all manner of weapons in hand, riding on black horses and running on foot with great speed and vengeful determination; Great and dreadful Si'ol-Kalabat – the Hell Hounds –with terrible growls and snarls, then three huge, monstrous Abiyy-Arawit – the Great Beasts, running like gelada baboons, shaking the ground with each thumping step.

The people screamed and gasped in horror at the terrible sight of these diabolical looking creatures stormed through their town. Mothers grabbed up their children and ran inside their homes or the nearest shelters. The men were too startled at the sudden horror parading in the streets to try to be brave. The few young Aksumite warriors that were currently assigned to watch and guard the town were also too scared the do anything significant but hide behind walls and get out of the monsters' way. Chickens, sheep, goats, and pet cats, dogs and monkeys also ran and hid in fear. Birds flew frantically from out of their nests in the trees.

"Ahh! *Aganenta Si'ol!* – Demons from Hell! Get out of the way! Ahhh!" They screamed and shouted in panic.

The Imminent Collision.

Mekonnen was now aware that the Qataliyan Armies of Darkness pursuing him and his mentor, not too far behind. This was the moment he had been waiting for. He glanced back to see how far away they were. Only about 800 yards away, he estimated. Abba Shiloh was at his left side but just a couple steps behind from their horses riding neck and neck.

Mekonnen became a little tense, but he was ready. His heart pounded in his chest, but he was courageous. His breathing was steady and not labored. Sweat dripped down from under his mal'akawi helmet, but he was cool.

Abba Shiloh rode alongside his protégé with Masqal fitted staff in his left hand, already shining with divine light.

Many Deadly Weapons.

Death Cloak was ready, riding on a jet-black horse, not of this realm of Meder but from the underworld, the abode of the Armies of Darkness. Under his dark felt cloak and hood, he was now fitted with very hard Breastplate, not of *Tsedq*, but of *Tselmut* – of Darkness. His Breastplate of Darkness was jet black with intricate silver designs and fringes on it and the engravings of serpents throughout. This Breastplate was from the supernatural realm and it was sometimes challenging even for the weapons of Chief Warrior Mal'ekt to shatter or penetrate. He wore gauntlets on his hands of similar patterns and designs. He had his double *Kele Sayfa Mot* – Double Swords of Death – sheathed to his back. He reached his right hand behind his cloaked head to unsheathes one of them then began to bark commands to his troops.

"I now command you Warriors of Darkness! Spread out into your formations as we planned. Own your titles and skills of thine weapons of death and destruction. You must embody these titles that are engraved into the blades of your weapons:

I want two more *Qataliyan Kele Sayfa Mot*- fall back with me.

Four *Zagarat-Ferhat* – Spears of Fear! Move forward, fall into the shadows!

Four *Nadafiyan Hass-Hemz* – Archers with Arrows of Venom! Fire off your arrows when I say!

Four *Maqdena Hakak* – Axes of Chaos! Get ready to hack your opponents to pieces!

Three that wield *Mafseha-Demsase*! – Hammers of Destruction! Be ready to pound their bones into shattered pieces!

Four who carry *Shotela Ma'at!* – Curved Swords/Scimitars of Wrath! Use at best judgement! Effective for stabbing around shields.

Three of you with *Qwarnena-Dugat* – Daggers of Malice! Effective for throwing at the opponents at a distance. I also possess some of these weapons.

And the Two Qataliyan with the *Mawaqeht-Gebrennat* – Chains of Bondage! Be ready to bound and subdue the old Bahetawi at my signal.

Now *Kalabata-Si'ol* –Hounds of Hell! Rush into the adversary head on!"

At Death Cloak's command six Hell Hounds ran out of the shadows from the forest ahead of Mekonnen and Abba Shiloh.

One Kalba-Si'ol rushed in with a big leap at Mekonnen. Mekonnen stared his stallion to the right and swiped the hound from its chest to the stomach, slicing it open. The beast burst into flames and disintegrated into ashes immediately as its carcass hits the ground.

Another one leaped at Abba Shiloh head on, but lightning charged out of his Masqal, burning the hound into a crisp.

Death Cloak commanded, "Launch your arrows of venom!"

The four Qataliyan Archers fired off three rounds of arrows simultaneously. A rain of twelve arrows came straight at Mekonnen and Abba Shiloh.

The holy man shouted, "Mekonnen! *Agre* – The Large Shield!" As he motioned by crossing his arms at the wrists in front his chest; Mekonnen remembered when they were prayed and made the same gesture with crossed arms to represent the *Agre Emnat* –The Shield of Faith.

The arrows rained down but ricocheted off an invisible shield that formed around Mekonnen, Abba Shiloh and both their horses. Except one venomous arrow struck Mekonnen's stallion on the front left thigh. The horse neighed

© Jerome Matiyas

and grunted but continued riding on. "That's it, boy! You can do it, keep going boy!" Mekonnen urged his steed.

Abba Shiloh and his horse did not seem to be struck at all by any arrows. Mekonnen looked down and realized he was also struck in the left thigh. He was shocked to see it at first even though he did not feel any pain yet. Just the sight of it. He kept on going. Abba Shiloh saw Mekonnen's predicament and remarked, "You've been hit, Anbessa, don't worry! Remember, the bite of snakes and scorpions, and the fiery arrows of the enemy will not harm you. Thus says the Word. The Qala Egziabeher!"

"U-wa! I remember the Word." Mekonnen affirmed.

Just then the arrow became soft and began to wiggle as it transformed into a little snake and worked its way deeper into Mekonnen's thigh. Mekonnen grabbed the snake by the tale and pulls it out quickly and exclaimed, "Oh no you don't!"

He threw it up in the air and cut it in half with his great Sword. Then he considered the arrow in his horse was probably also transforming into a snake, but he could not reach to pull it out. It's only a matter of time before his stallion succumbed to the snake arrows venom.

They were now amongst the trees in the forest as more Hounds and Qataliyan wielding spears, axes, and swords charged at them for a head on collision. Also coming up from the rear was the Qataliyan's leader, Lord Death Cloak, followed by ten Qataliyan, armed and ready, six more Hell Hounds and three Abiyy-Arawit.

The Righteous Warriors, Mekonnen and Abba Shiloh, seemed to be grossly outnumbered. Abba Shiloh reminded Mekonnen, "Remember the Word, Anbessa, *'One can put a hundred to flight, and two can put ten thousand to flight!'" (Deuteronomy 32:30, Joshua 23: 10).*

Mekonnen exclaimed, "U-wa! Thank you for reminding me Abba Shiloh!"

Mekonnen then began to climb and positioned himself to stand on top his fine stallion's back, to balance himself as steadily as he can, as they continued to gallop at full speed. The warrior held up his Sword in the air in his right hand as he stretched out his left arm to balance himself, poised and ready to leap with his Sword of Light blazing to victory, no matter how brutal the collision was going to be.

He screamed, "Come on, you diabolical beasts! I will whet my flashing Sword into you dark souls! The Manfasawi Sayf is more power than any two-edged Sword. Cutting through flesh, bone, and spirit from soul!" (Hebrews 4:11)

Seconds later a Hell Hounds collided with Mekonnen's and Abba Shiloh's horses, catapulted both warrior and holy man into the air, both poised in battle formation, ready to strike down and through any creature they landed upon.

The horses were not as fortunate, as two Hell Hounds pounced upon them and locked onto their necks and shoulders like a vice-grip in the jaws of these diabolical canines, savagely shaken and torn up like an animal predator would attack its prey.

Two Qataliyan wielding *Maqdenata Hakak* – Axes of Chaos – leapt to meet Mekonnen in midair. One brought his axe down from the top while the other swiped from the side. Mekonnen managed to block the axe from the top with his Sword, but the one from the right-side landed the axe on Mekonnen's golden Breastplate of Righteousness. The Axe did not cut through the Breastplate, but the impact shifted the warrior's body to the left. Still, Mekonnen manages to maneuver his Sword to swipe and cut the first Qatali across and through the torso, cutting it clean in half. Its upper and lower body flew in different directions, falling to the ground and burnt up into ashes. As Mekonnen fell back to the ground, he managed to swing his Sayf again and lopped off the head of another Qatali, before colliding with a body slam into a Hell-Hound and two Scimitar wielding Qataliyan.

Abba Shiloh, as he landed back on his feet, he waved his Masqal staff at a Hell Hound and blasted a hole through its torso with a bolt of lightning, then burned through a Dark Qatali, wielding a Shotel, a sword with a blade curved like a letter "C." Abba Shiloh came down with a knee upon another Qatali while he blocked its Axe with his Masqal staff. The cloaked opponent went down to the ground as Abba Shiloh shouted, "*Hayla Berhan*! – The Power of Light!" and struck him through the torso with lightning.

Next came the rushing horde from behind as one of the three Qataliyan with a *Mafaseha-Demase* – Hammer of Destruction – threw his hammer from behind Abba Shiloh and hit him hard in the top center of his back. The Holy Man was caught off guard and fell forward face down into the dusty ground and lost grip of his Masqal staff as it flew out his hand several yards away.

Mekonnen noticed his mentor going down and shouted, "Abba Shiloh!" as he ran to his aid. But two Qataliyan wielding the *Maqdena-Hakak* – the Axes of Chaos, and one of the *Mafseha-Demsase* – Hammers of Destruction! These three now blocked Mekonnen from helping his white-bearded mentor.

Still a bit disoriented and dizzy, Abba Shiloh attempted to get up slowly, but one of the Qataliyan threw a great *Mawaqeht-Gebrennat* – Chains of Bondage, around his body and arms, preventing him from reaching his staff. Then the four Zagarata-Ferhat – the Spears of Fear, were thrown at Abba Shiloh, but not piercing him. Instead, one spear pins him to the ground through his clothes and the other three encircled around the Bahetawi to cage him into a makeshift prison of spears. Four more spears landed as stakes into the ground around Abba Shiloh to restrain him even tighter, then another Chain of Bondage was thrown and tightened around those eight spears. Now the holy man was bound, unable to move and separated from his trusted Masqal staff, leaving Mekonnen to fight by on his own.

The Hammer wielding Qatali was quite tall and brought down the hammer to smash Mekonnen's skull, but the warrior dove off to the left and rolled away on the ground just in time. As he rolled, another brought down a great axe, and the warrior rolled, and again, the axe missed his head by less than an inch. The second axe wielder brought down his weapon and Mekonnen could not roll away in time, but with back still to the ground, lifted his flashing Sword now blazing from within, clashing blades with the axe, cutting through it by almost 6 inches deep. He maneuvered his body from under the axe, so it hit the ground, jumped up to his feet, and pulled his Sword from out of the axe blade in one a quick move. With the axe blade still in the ground, he ran up the axe handle all the way up to the Qatali's arm to get up close to its face. Quickly Mekonnen thrusts his blade into his opponent's heart, then pulls it out and swiped at its neck, lopping its head off.

The other axe wielding Qatali tried to cut down Mekonnen as he still stood on his comrades' arm, but the warrior did a back flip from off it and landed onto the ground, causing the axe wielder to chop off his fellow headless Qatali's arm at its shoulder instead.

The Qatali still pursued after Mekonnen, as he swiped his axe again and again, but the warrior deflected them each time. Then in one quick move, Mekonnen rolls under his opponent and cut off its right leg at the upper thigh. The Qatali wreathed in pain as its leg burned up in flames and he fell to the ground. Mekonnen ran and cut off its head from it body, terminating him from this Earth for good as his head and body caught fire. The rest of the Qataliyan became a bit hesitant to attack the warrior, as they noticed how powerful his fiery Sword was. It's just as powerful or maybe more so than the Swords of the Warrior Mal'ekt from Samayat.

Battling the Great Beast!

Death Cloak sat on his horse with four of his Qataliyan around him, studying Mekonnen's moves as he took down his Dark Warriors one by one. He laughed and commented, "Hah ha, hah! You have acquired a powerful weapon and sound skills. Now you appear to be winning. Let's see how you fair against a creature of truly great size now!"

One of the large Abiyy Arwe – Great Beasts – about 13 feet tall and as broad as a cedar tree trunk, approached Mekonnen, roared with its mouth wide open. "Rooooaaaarrrrr!!"

It was huge and hairy with long fangs, and that red symbol with the crooked black serpent inside the ruby disc fitted into its broad chest. All the Qataliyan have the same circular red brooch with this same serpent symbol on their cloaks, Mekonnen noticed.

Then the arm that was cut off from the Qatali transformed into a 10-foot-long snake, like a great python, as it slithered towards Mekonnen, and got ready to strike at him unknowingly from behind.

Abba Shiloh saw it and shouted to warn Mekonnen, "Mekonnen, look

out behind you!"

Mekonnen spun his head around and saw the snake approaching him from behind at the same time the giant hairy beast charged from the front. He was cornered.

Abba Shiloh stretched his hand out towards his staff which is yards away and spoke to it, "As Moses rod transformed, so shall you become as a great wise serpent!"

Immediately, the Masqal rod transformed into a golden-headed serpent like a cobra, with the pattern of the Masqal cross on its head. It slithered towards the other snake that threatened Mekonnen.

Meanwhile, the Great Beast rushes at Mekonnen and pounded its fists into the ground, causing the earth around them to shake and Mekonnen to lose his balance, falling to the ground. Just then the serpent attempted to strike at Mekonnen, but he pulled away in time. He swung his Sword to cut off the serpent's head, but it dodged the blade quickly and hissed,

"Hssssssssss!".

Mekonnen had to turn around again as the Great Beast tried to pound him into the ground with two huge fists. The warrior rolled away just in time. The beast attempted to pound the warrior again and this time succeeded in striking Mekonnen, but the warrior had the tip of the blade pointing upward, caused the blade to run deep up into its massive fist. The creature roared in pain from the blade that stung and burned like a hot knife into flesh.

Then the serpent that was once the arm of a Qatali came again coming to strike at Mekonnen's head as he lay on the ground. But Abba Shiloh's spoke to his Masqal staff that transformed into a Golden Serpent and commanded it,

"Now swallow up that other serpent, now!"

Abba Shiloh's Masqal Serpent struck and bit the Qatali serpent by the head and began to the swallow it up whole. Now that the serpent was gone so Mekonnen was able to focus on bringing down the huge and horrible Great Beast.

The giant Beast lashed out at Mekonnen again from side to side, this time the warrior swung he blade and cuts off its left hand at the wrist. The Beast roared in pain as its hand flew off and rolls on the ground. Mekonnen declared a Word for his flashing Sword of the Spirit before his next move,

"With this Sayfa Berhan – Sword of Light – I shall strike down the creatures of the Darkness and crush the head of the Nakhash! I shall slay the giant as Dawit slew Goliat!"

Mekonnen ran up to the Great Beast, leapt towards it with Sword held back then he thrust the point of the blade swiftly, running it through the center of the red circle with the black serpent symbol in the middle of the creature's chest. The Sword glowed with a golden flame inside the transparent blade and sparked like lightning. When Mekonnen pulls the blade out of the Beast's chest a stream of fire flowed from the blade to the serpentine symbol. The beast slowly fell backwards as Mekonnen balanced himself on its chest. Then the shattered serpent symbol exploded, leaving a huge cavity in the beast's torso. The blast pushed Mekonnen backwards onto the ground onto his back. The Great Beast fell to the ground with a thud. THOOOMM!!

As the remainder of its corpse was consumed in flames, the other two Great Beasts ran away at the sight of one of their companions destroyed. They disappeared into a great shadow cast by the trees, returning to Roha-Zoheleth.

Death Cloak shouted at them, "You cowards! Why do you run away? So big yet so weak and stupid! Running from one little man!" He insulted his comrades as if to speak boldly and seem braver, but deep down in his dark soul he knew he should be a bit fearful of their opponent's powerful new weapon of Light. Somehow, he believed he may still have a fair chance to bring down the warrior with a few tricks up his malicious sleeves.

The rest of the Hell Hounds and Qataliyan began to surround Mekonnen,

as they growled and jeered at him. Mekonnen held his great and mighty Sword up ready to take them on. Suddenly flaming arrows landed on the ground between Mekonnen and the vile creatures, keeping them at bay and away from getting too close to the warrior.

They all looked up to see where the arrows were fired from and saw Mal'ekt from Samay. The same ones who were before the Elect One and rescued Mekonnen, Penuel and the children from the Dark Realm under the Samen Mountains. They stood on the edge of a steep sloped amba overseeing where the battle took place at the other end of the forest.

The seven of them, stood with various weapons drawn, in their color-coded apparel of Red, Orange, Yellow, Green, Blue, Indigo, and Violet, with gold and silver fringe patterns.

The leader in blue with the broadsword declared with echoing, baritone voice, "By the authority of the *Heruy* – The Elect One, Iyesus Krestos, we come to bring order and ensure a fair battle between you and the valiant warrior, Mekonnen, and the righteous Bahetawi, called Shiloh."

Death-Cloak's Proposition.

Death Cloak spoke, "Oho, great Mal'ekt from the Realms on High! Thou hast come just in time to see me battle your valiant warrior. Now I know his name: Mekonnen!"

The Dark Qatali leader dismounted from his horse and leapt into the air then landed in the middle of the circle where Mekonnen stood with his Sword drawn. The translucent blade was alive with flames and Words of power and victory flowing inside and outside of it that only Mekonnen can see and understand, though in plain Ge'ez language.

Death Cloak addressed the Mal'ak with the broadsword, "And how may I address you, *Egzia Samay* – Lord from Heaven? For I have a proposition to make."

The Mal'ak responded, "I am known as *Liq Rəhub Sayyafi'El* – Arch Broad Sword-bearer of God! I am a chief emissary in *Liq-Mal'ak Miykael's* Army – The Arch-Angel Michael's Army! You may call me *Liq Sayyafi'El*. State your proposition!"

Death Cloak declared, "I would like to take on this warrior with the *Esatawi Sayf* – The Fiery Sword – and challenge him to a dual! To the Death! And there must be no intervention from you or any of the Mal'ekt with you to assist or to save him!"

The Mal'ekt murmured amongst each other, but the Qataliyan and Hell Hounds chuckled and jeered at each other in approval.

Sayyafi'El responded, "You ask us to go against the will of the Elect One. Our purpose is to protect the lives of those Righteous Ones when He has sent us."

The Dark leader added, "U-wa, but you are also allowed to let the precious ones be tested and tried in the fires of battle. To test their strength, U-wa! I demand a fair fight with no interruptions! I am *Barnusa-Mot* – Death-Cloak! An emissary of The Great Death Master himself. I demand to challenge this Mekonnen, as I see this warrior as a most formidable adversary!

If I defeat him, his soul goes to you in the glorious Realms of Samayat. And I will gain some rank in this Meder Realm.

If he defeats me, I go down to the pits of darkness. And your warrior will gain some power and authority in this Meder Realm, if he perseveres.

We both have mixed feelings about if we want to leave this realm of Meder before finishing our assignments. It's a win-win I say, and a worthy challenge! So, what do you say?!"

Sayyafi'El glanced at his comrades and thought in silence for a minute, to analyze the situation. He did not want to disobey the instructions of the Lord in Samay but was aware of the willingness for the Lord to test his Sons and those he considered his Holy Righteous Ones.

He glanced at the green-clad Mal'ak, who had been with the warrior Mekonnen for a significant amount of time and had grown to care for him more than the rest. His facial expression and eyes seemed to suggest he thought Mekonnen may actually be ready to take on the diabolical, powerful dark entity that is Death Cloak, who was once a Mal'ak of Samayat, eons ago, before the Great War, when he was cast out from Samayat with the Nakhash, in the Great Fall. Mekonnen himself looked spry and poised, ready to take down the Death Angel. Having gained confidence after using the powerful Manfasawi Sayf to cut down and destroy so many Qataliyan, Si-ol-Kalabat, and Abiyy Arawit. But was he ready to take on a Mal'ak of Death himself?

Green Mal'ak gave a wink and a nod. He communicated with Sayyafi'El telepathically without moving his lips, "If the dual gets out of hand, and Death Cloak is about the kill the warrior, we will intervene, and stop the battle."

Sayyafi'El answered telepathically, "Agreed. And if he does kill the warrior, by the power of the Almighty Giver of Life, we will bring him back to life!"

Sayyafi'El turned to Death Cloak and Mekonnen in the circle below and stated, "Very well! We agree on the challenge. Let the dual begin!"

A Dual with Death-Cloak.

Death Cloak wielded his two swords and spun them around with skillful circular motions. Then he tightened his arms suddenly with a quick up-and-down movement, and immediately sharp blades and spikes protruded out of his shoulders, upper back, elbows, and wrists. This immediately gave Death-Cloak a more intimidating façade to all creatures looking at him, including his warrior opponent, who heart began to accelerate at that moment.

Then he said to Mekonnen,

"Alas! I come face to face with the puny warrior with the Malakawi Sayf! They keep speaking about you as if you are such a great danger and a treat to our Kingdom of Darkness! As if they are afraid of you! Well, I had to see you and challenge you for myself. For all Sons of Adam must face Death in their life time. At least once. Finally, a formidable adversary! Someone worth fighting that is of mankind, a Son of Adam. Well, tonight I am cutting you down for good. There shall be no more talk of you after this dual!"

366

Mekonnen held aloft his great Sword of Light with the flashing blade and declared, *"No weapon formed against me shall prosper!"* (Isaiah 54: 17).

The entity of Death spun and swiped both his swords at Mekonnen, who successfully deflected them, then spun around himself to swipe at Death Cloak's leg.

He missed. Death Cloak spun around again in the opposite direction and swiped again, and this time swiped and sliced Mekonnen's right thigh, drawing blood. He felt the sting of the blade but continued being on the alert for his opponent's advances.

Death Cloak taunted Mekonnen, "Ah, you thought you could grin and bear the pain, but you forgot a poisoned arrow was shot into your other thigh earlier."

As soon as he said that Mekonnen felt dizzy and weak. He looked down at his left thigh and saw the tail of a little snake wiggling inside his wound. He tried to grab it but missed it as in slips deeper inside. Why would he suddenly feel weak just because the fallen Mal'ak of Death mentioned the arrow that he already recovered from? And he thought he already pulled out the little snake when he was still riding his horse earlier.

Abba Shiloh was still imprisoned inside the spears with chains around him but saw what the Qatali of Death was trying to do.

"Oh no, Mekonnen! Anbessa, do not listen to him! It is not true. The venom has no effect on you. *Ba-Emnat* – By Faith, remember!"

Mekonnen vaguely remembered. The Dark Qatali was playing tricks with his mind and affecting his faith. He remembered now.

"*Iyyaseh!* I shall drink poison and will not die. Serpents shall strike at me, and I will not die. Scorpions shall sting me…"

Before Mekonnen could finish his sentence, Death Cloak did a diagonal flip and kicked Mekonnen across the neck where it met the right shoulder and as he made this move he declared,

"I *am* a scorpion!"

Mekonnen flew backward with the impact and dragged and rolled on the stony ground. He lost grip of the Fiery Sword, as it clattered to the ground.

The rest of the Qataliyan laughed and the Hell Hounds howled in delight to see one of their worst enemies succumb the Death Cloak's blows.

The Mal'ekt became concerned and were about to lounge forward but remembered the promise they made to stay out of the battle and not to interfere with the dual.

Abba Shiloh exclaimed, "Come on Anbessa, Come on! Get up!"

Death Cloak interjected, "This anbessa is more like a little whelp to me!"

Mekonnen tried to pick himself up slowly and shook his head for clarity. He looked around for the Sword but it was a few yards away. He must get to it. Death Cloak approached, 9 feet tall, he towered above the warrior. With two swords drawn he came down fast upon Mekonnen.

Mekonnen rolled away quickly towards his Sword as his opponent's blade stabbed into the rocky ground. Mekonnen reached for his Sword and grabs the hilt quickly.

Just as he had it, suddenly a dagger flew towards him and knocks the great Sword out of his hand. It was Death Cloak throwing daggers at him. More daggers flew at Mekonnen, so he spun around to protect his face from them. About three of them hit his Breastplate of Righteousness on the back, and one hit him on the helmet, and they all ricocheted off his armor.

The Death Mal'ak chuckled and said, "Those are the *Qwarnena-Dugat* – the Daggers of Malice! Aiming directly at you, Whelp!" The rest of the Qataliyan laughed hysterically at their leader's remarks. Death Cloak reached for more daggers from his belt and boots and threw them rapidly at Mekonnen as the warrior stumbled and leaped for his Great Sword. He grabbed it up and deflected the daggers while still on his back on the ground.

Mekonnen felt a sharp pain in his left upper arm. He reached over with his right hand and feels a dagger pierced into his flesh. He stuck the Sword in the ground to get a good grip of the dagger in him and pulled it out quickly. The pain was sharp and stinging; probably a venom-tipped blade like the arrow.

Mekonnen dropped on his knees as he leaned on the hilt of his Sword, feeling weak and breathing heavily, with blade stuck in the ground. He realized he needed to recover fast or he will be defeated by this nemesis.

As he looked down at the blade of the Sword of the Spirit of the Word, it was not glowing as much as before, but there was a word, a short sentence flowing in it, "*With faith as small as a mustard seed.*"

Then another verse, "*These signs will follow them that believe. In my name shall they cast out devils, they shall speak in new languages. They shall take up serpents, and if they drink any deadly thing, it shall not hurt them. They shall lay hands on the sick, and they shall recover.*" (Mark 16: 17-18)

Gradually the strength returned to Mekonnen and the Sword began to glow again. Mekonnen lifted the Sword from out the ground and swung it with precision to knock away more daggers thrown at him until Death Cloak ran out of daggers.

More words flowed through Mekonnen's mouth and the blade at the same time, "*I can do all things through Iyesus Krestos who strengthens me. (Phil 4:13)*

He is the Word and the living water which gives me strength, power, and life. (John 7:37)

The Word is Egziabeher, and the Word was with Egziabeher from the very beginning! (John 1:1)

And the Word was a great flashing Sword that protected the way of the Tree of Life." (Gen 3:24)

Now all the evil dark creatures cringed and hated the sound of the words

Mekonnen was declaring and retreated further into the forest and shadows.

They yelled out, "Oh no! Stop saying that! Stop saying those dreadful words!"

Abba Shiloh encourages him, "Hawey, that's it! Keep talking. The Manfas will give you the right Words to say at the right time! Come over here for some *Wuha Tselot* – Holy Water."

Mekonnen ran over to Abba Shiloh who was still trapped inside the spears and chains where fortunately he still had the bag with the holy water, and honey and manna bread.

Death Cloak shouted "No!" and threw one of his curved swords at Mekonnen's head to cut it off but Mekonnen managed to duck down to the ground quickly and skidded to the rest of the way towards Abba Shiloh. He reached inside the holy man's cage and opened the bag and grabbed the bottle, opened it quickly and drank some on the water in one gulp. He was about to free Abba Shiloh from the Chains of Bondage, but just then Death Cloak threw another sword he grabbed from another Qataliyan aiming for the spear cage and Mekonnen, attempted to swipe both at once. Mekonnen shouted, "Watch out!"

Abba Shiloh and Mekonnen ducked, just a second in time as the sword, mowed the spears that cages Shiloh in half.

Mekonnen was now fully revived and the Sword fully charged with life and flames.

Mekonnen exclaimed, "Hrai, you fallen Mal'ak! You had me down and defeated, but now I'm back and ready for you!"

Death Cloak exclaimed, "Impossible! How can it be!"

Mekonnen replied, "Anything is possible, with the Elect One!"

Mekonnen ran up to charge at the giant 9 feet tall Death Cloak and clashed swords with him for a good while. For about 7 minutes they dealt blows and clanshed Manfasawi Sayf to Tsallim Sayf. Both powerful and supernatural weapons, not of this Meder Realm.

Death Cloak thought Mekonnen's Sword was one from the Mal'ak all this time, not knowing it was more powerful than expected, from the mouth of Egziabeher himself! And the Breastplate and Belt he also did not know their origin. Only Mekonnen's gauntlet and helmet were formally belonged to a Mal'ak. Now Death Cloak was confounded.

Mekonnen dealt some blows to his opponent's breastplate, but it was very strong and solid. He figured it would take some time and more blows and striking at to get it cracked open.

The Mal'ekt from Samay were now happy at the outcome of the dual between Death Cloak and the warrior they came to protect, seeing him bounce back from near defeat to now relentlessly clashing swords with the

Qatali of Death.

The Abiyy Hayyal was also still present watching on from a nearby Amba but was also ordered not to intervene.

Death Cloak Revealed.

Now Death Cloak found his second curved Sword of Death and swiped at his opponent but missed and cut down six trees in the forest instead as they battle in and out the edge of the forested area. He swiped at Mekonnen's legs, but the warrior was alert and agile enough to do a backflip. Death Cloak thought he could catch Mekonnen off guard with his other sword, but he was able to block it with his Sword of the Spirit. This time the Demon's second sword brook and shattered into many pieces when it clashed with Mekonnen's Sword.

Then Mekonnen reached back with his fist and punched Death Cloak in the face, catching him by surprise. The Dark Qatali's hood began to slip off his head, to reveal part of his face and head.

Mekonnen then declared, *"Oh, Death, where is your sting. Oh Grave, where is your victory?"* (1 Corinthians 15:55, Hosea 13:14) And reaches back with a fist and punches the Dark Qatali in the face again. This time the hood slipped all the way back behind his head, revealing a hideous face as he stumbled backward. Death Cloak's head is shaped partly like a snake, and partly like that of a man. His head a jet black with scraggily gray hair reaching his shoulders. His mouth and nose resemble that of a snake or a lizard, with a scaly nozzle and two slits for nostrils. His red eyes have narrow pupils exactly like that of a serpent or lizard. He has no eyebrows, nor ears that resemble that of a man, only small holes on the side of its head for hearing, but no ear lopes. Then a long skinny tongue stuck out his mouth like a true reptilian creature.

Mekonnen gasped in shock naturally for 7 seconds, at the sight of the unnatural, ungodly creature, then he just boiled up in his spirit and soul with a righteous indignation and says,

"Your face is as ugly as your soul!"

Then Mekonnen ran and took a leap at his opponent and came down with his Sword, and shattered the other sword as he tried to block impact of the warrior's blade. A trail of flames follows the path of Mekonnen's swinging Sayf. The tip of the Sword's blade cuts through Death-Cloaks breastplate, making a big, long gash diagonally on the chest, smashing one of the two red serpent symbol brooches he wore to clip on his cloak to his breastplate. The dark cloak fell off and blows away in the wind into the forest, and got caught in a tree branch, but the gash in the breastplate was not deep enough to do damage to the Dark Qatali leader.

Lord Death Cloak had something to say, "You have done well in battle. You have been a worthy opponent."

Mekonnen exclaimed, "Shut your mouth, you *Ganen*! I will have no more conversations with you! I will now let the FIERY SWORD OF THE WORD do the talking!"

With that, Mekonnen ran up towards the Dark Qatali and leapt from a tree stump for a good height. He kicked Lord Death Cloak in the chest with both feet, causing him to fall backward and bounce off a tree then as he bounces forward again Mekonnen reached his Sword from all the way back then accelerated it forward. In that split second, time seems the slow down for Lord Death Cloak, to his terror, he caught a glimpse of *who* embodies the fiery Sword. It is the outline of a man as bright as the mid-day sun, in the midst of billowing flames. With a crown of burnished gold on his head, robes as bright as flashes of lightning, and eyes of fire, the figure was instantly recognized as the Elect One. The Lord Iyesus Krestos himself. The Elect One pointed at Death Cloak with his right index finger and victoriously declared,

"FINISHED!!"

The blade swiftly sliced through Death Cloak's breastplate and torso from the left of his neck where it met the shoulder all the way through diagonally to the right side of his chest.

The flame in the Sword made it cut through Death-Cloak like a hot knife through butter. It happened so fast Death-Cloak remained in one piece for a few seconds, he even tried to speak his last words, "No, it... Cannot... be..."

Then his severed head, shoulder, part of his torso and right arm slipped down to the dusty ground, and the rest of his body followed, before both pieces caught fire and quickly engulfed into flames.

Egzi Barnusa-Mot – Lord Death Cloak – was no more. Terminated from this Realm of Meder - Earth. At least for now.

At the sight of their slain leader the rest of the Dark Qataliyan and Hell Hounds retreated back into the shadows and returned to Roha-Zoheleth to report to *Egzi Bɔrur Gwanti* – Lord Silver Gauntlet.

Mekonnen cut Abba Shiloh free from the Chains of Bondage with the fiery Sword of the Spirit.

"You did it, Anbessa. You have defeated the Lord Death Cloak. The rest on the *ganen* and Dark Mal'ekt will now be afraid of you and the Sword because of this."

Mekonnen said, "Praises be to Egziabeher! I thank you for teaching me Abba Shiloh."

Mal'akawi Meetings.
The Mal'ekt floated down from the height of the cliff like eagles landing from the sky and begin to praise Mekonnen for his brilliant performance in battle and come back from seemingly losing the dual in the beginning.

Sayyafi'El spoke, "You have done well, Valiant Warrior Mekonnen.

But your assignment is not complete. There is still a threat of the agents of Darkness. There is much terror and bloodshed in Roha, and a sorcerer is the cause of this evil. It is this sorcerer who opened the forbidden gates to the Dark Realms for the Dark Qataliyan and other evil creatures to come through to this Meder Realm and attack the kingdoms of the land. And he has also resurrected Waynaba; you already fought him in Tsana Hayk. Waynaba is wounded and weak for a season, but he is still a threat."

"Thank you for telling us what is happening Liq Sayyafi'El." Mekonnen added.

Abba Shiloh enquired, "So, from whence has the sorcerer acquired this power?"

Sayyafi'El answered, "The sorcerer has acquired some sort of accursed Ring of Power, possessing dark magic. We do not know how or where he acquired the ring, for the powers around him were too dark and thick to see. It is from a realm, entity, or principality of Darkness. But this is for you to find out, and stop him!"

Sayyafi'El continued, "You two must go through this fiery gateway now which I will open for you."

The Mal'ak threw a white stone like the one Green Mal'ak had days ago. It landed on the ground and immediately opened an archway of fire facing north.

Sayyafi'El commanded them, "Go through this gate. It will take you southwards, back to Gihon Village. Rest there for a while and stay out of sight from the adversary. After that, prepare yourself with the 50 days of *Tsoma Arbe'a* – Lenten Fast – and be ready to battle in the Manfasawi realm again to rescue the people of Roha, then Beta Israel, and then Aksum. Stop the works of the Darkness with the Light."

Before Mekonnen rode off into the fiery arch-way with Abba Shiloh, he realized he didn't get a chance to thank the Mal'ak in green apparel properly. So, he walked up to the Green Mal'ak, grabbed his right hand and said, "My fellow warrior! I must thank you more, a thousand times for saving our lives earlier. Please, may I ask, what is your name?"

The Green Mal'ak replied, "I am *Hamalmil Zagar'El Sarwe Rufael.* – Green Long-Spear of God. A chief soldier in the Army of Raphael. Call me *Zagar'El* – Spear-bearer of God."

Mekonnen held the hand of Zagar'El and bowed but did not worship the Mal'ak, for he knew from the Mashaf Qedus that doing so was prohibited. "It is a pleasure meeting you, fellow warrior and servant of Egziabeher."

The Mal'ekt presented two new stallions for the men because the first two were viciously attacked and terribly wounded by the Hell Hounds. But they were revived by the Mal'ekt and retired from this Realm of Meder and transported into the Celestial Realm of Samay. The two stallions' assignment in the Earthly realm was complete.

Mekonnen and Abba Shiloh mount the new white horses as Sayyafi'El granted them farewell, *"Egziabeher Baraka* – May the Almighty One bless you. And God-speed to you."

Off they rode through the fiery arch-way that secretly took them southwards, back towards Gihon Village. They estimated arrival in about two days with periods of rest.

Mekonnen and Abba Shiloh were not able to speak to anyone in the towns and villages they pass through about the amazing yet harrowing adventures they have shared. And as they valiantly rode on with pride and quietly celebrated recent victories, the reality set in that the mission had just begun, and they must prepare themselves for more fierce battles to come.

Thus said the LORD; Say, "A sword, a sword is sharpened and polished...
that it may flash like lightning!" - Ezekiel 21: 9-10

And take the helmet of salvation, and the sword of the Spirit, which is the word
of God. - Ephesians 6:17

Be alert, be vigilant, because your adversary the devil, prowls around like a roaring lion, seeking someone to devour. - 1 Peter 5:8

Oh, Death, where is your sting. Oh Grave, where is your victory? - 1 Corinthians 15:55

Chapter 18

Chapter 18

Epilogue

Back in Roha-Zoheleth, the remaining Qataliyan reported on what happened after Tsana Hayk and the demise of Lord Death Cloak. Lord Silver Gauntlet spoke, "I will devise a new plan. Waynaba will be revived, nurtured and improved. The Qataliyan will be improved with new, better armor and weapons, now that they know what they are dealing with."

Silver Gauntlet retreated into a secret location in the mountains to consult with his mysterious emerald ring and conjure up the presence of an unknown entity of Darkness.

"Oh, ancient Great Supreme Lord. Lord of the remnant of *aganent*. I come before you, with humility. I seek your strategic counsel concerning the takeover of the Empire of Aksum for your ultimate sovereign rule, and the setting of your throne for this territory.

The silhouette of a dark principality emerged from the shadows, revealing great horns protruding from the sides of its head, accentuated by a blazing inferno behind it. The entity donned a jet-black flowing cloak over its shoulders with two red discs pinned at the top below its dark head, linked by a short, thick, silver chain. Inside the ruby red discs is that symbol again of the black, crooked serpent. And out of the darkness, creatures like black ravens with red eyes that seem to flutter out of the fabric of the entity's cloak.

The Dark Entity spoke in a terrifying, guttural voice, "Speak to me! What is the status on the Aksumite Empire?"

Lord Silver Gauntlet replied, "We seem to have a problem, with a certain Aksumite warrior. Wielding a certain powerful, supernatural Sword. We must devise a plan to stop and destroy him. Immediately!"

About a week and half earlier, in the morning after parting from the discussion with his wife Nigist Semret about the Sacred Oath that took place in Eyerusalem, Hade Gabra Masqal arrived at Abba Pantelowon's monastery with a small entourage of about twelve warriors, led by Commander Alazar.

His Holiness Abba Pantalewon greeted the Emperor at the entrance himself with salutations and a bow and kiss of the royal ring.

"Selamta, Your Imperial Majesty. It is an honor to have you grace the house of Egziabeher with your presence. Please, come inside and be comfortable."

Hade Gabra Masqal responded, "It is my honor and my pleasure, most Holy Abba. May I ask to speak to my father, the Negus Kaleb, please?"

"Oh, most certainly! I shall bring him to you."

Moments later, an old man with a white beard and a staff in his right hand walked from under an archways and slowly towards Gabra Masqal. It was Negus Kaleb, also known as Ella Atsbeha, wearing an off white robe and a turban wrapped around his head. Selam, my son, Egziabeher mezana! I am so happy to see you, my son."

Negus Kaleb greeted Gabra Masqal with the traditional side to side kissed on the left and right cheeks.

"Selamta, my Abba. Egziabeher mezana. My father, you may have heard that Aksum was attacked days ago during Timkat celebrations. But my suspicion has risen. Abba. Do to think my brother Negus Esrael may have been responsible for the attack?"

Negus Kaleb remained silent for a moment, stared at his son, in deep thought at the implications of such a situation if it were true at all. Egziabeher forbid if it was true to the slightest degree.

"Please, son. Come inside and let us talk about this and pray for wisdom and understanding of what is happening in the realm of the spirit and the realm of the flesh."

Meron has been silent and aloof for days. She has not spoken of eaten much since Mekonnen left to track down the cloaked Qataliyan that attacked Aksum, attempted to assassinate the Emperor, and murdered her brother Afeworq. No matter how much her mother tried to comfort her and encourage her to eat the child will not be comforted. "First Afeworq, now Mekonnie." She thought to herself. "Both gone."

Then one morning a messenger with two warrior guards accompanying him entered the town of Dura and into their home and spoke with Meron's mother and uncles. She saw a small scroll handed over to Medhane, Mekonnen's brother. He broke the seal and read it.

"Mekonnen is alive." He said with a sigh, paused, then continued. "He continued:

"Selam, my dear family. Egziabeher yemiskan. I am alive and well. I am in the southern regions of the kingdom, but it is unsafe for me to tell you exactly where I am. My Sarwe army troop was attacked and scattered in the wilderness. Some returned to Aksum. Others did not. I am on a quest to hunt

down the Qataliyan who attacked the Timkat festival. They are vile creatures. That is all I can say to you now until I return, my beloved family. Please tell Meron I am well and shall return. I promised her I will return soon, but it will be longer, but not to worry. Egziabeher be praised. ~ Mekonnen."

Meron began to be encouraged by the letter Medhane just read and happiness wells up in her slowly. She had been sad for so long it is almost as if she did not know how to react. Her mother clapped her hands and turned to Meron and sighed. "Hawey, you see Meron baby, Mekonnie is okay and will return." She scooped up Meron in her arms, and her daughter wrapped her arms around her mother's neck as tears welled up in both their eyes at the sound of good news in this season of sadness for the family. Medhane thanked the messenger and warriors for the message as they left. As Meron hugged her weeping mother, a butterfly with blue and white patterns softly landed upon her little thumb, as if to reassure her that Mekonnen and her whole family is in Egziabeher's hands now.

Meanwhile Mekonnen and Abba Shiloh were passing through the great lake town of Bahar Dar at the southern tip of Tsana Hayk, just a few miles away from Gihon Village to the east just before the Tis Isat Waterfalls. They had been traveling on horseback for about a day since the last battle with the Dark Qataliyan, stopping only for food along the way. Bahar Dar was meant to be the last stop before reaching Gihon village.

They left Bahar Dar and stop for a minute on a high ridge where they could see Gihon village from a distance about 2 miles away. Mekonnen stood on a large stone with the great Sword, the Manfasawi Sayf, sheathed on his back, and the Breastplate of Righteousness reverted to regular white linen with gold fringe patterns and the golden Belt of Truth just naturally reflecting the rays of the sun. The warrior looked down at the village and spoke his thoughts.

"I truly pray that I am not bringing trouble to your village, Abba Shiloh. Whatever happens, I will do everything in my power to protect your village and its people. I have not been there very long, but they are my family now." Mekonnen said.

Abba Shiloh responded to Mekonnen's concerns, "Anbessa, you do not bring trouble to the village or the kingdom. You bring hope."

Meanwhile, that Great Hayyal creature with the mighty horns, the same one that fought for Mekonnen and Abba Shiloh, and defeated the Qataliyan and Kalabata-Si'ol on the path to Tsana Hayk, was on the run through the Samen mountain range. He galloped, leapt and skipped over, ambas, mountains, and streams, towards the mesmerizing sound of a maiden singing beautiful notes to a tune that floated upon the gentle strums of kirar strings.

He drew closer to the young maiden crafting this mezmur tune as she sat upon a tree stump, next to a pail of water freshly drawn from the Abay River that flowed by Gihon Village. The Hayyal slowly walked through the stream towards her. Her face lit up with a subtle smile indicating that she recognized the fine horned creature. The young maiden was Nuhamin from the village. She drew closer to the Abiyy Hayyal, reaching forward with her right hand to touch his head and nose.

"Selam, Kebur." She whispered, "You have returned after many days. I assume you have been on a long journey. So, Kebur, what have you learned about our new friend, the River-man?"

The Abiyy Hayyal, speaking clearly through its deer-like mouth, responded to the maiden,

"He is a mighty warrior of Egziabeher."

~~~~~~~ End of Book One, Part 1 ~~~~~~~

Next:
Mekonnen: The Warrior of Light, Part 2
Publishing date to be announced.

Back Stories and Legends

The Legend of Angabo the Sabaean
Queen of Sheba's Father (1500-1000 BC)

In the history of the Ethiopian monarch, there is a legend that gives account of **Angabo the Sabaean** (Sheban) who sailed across the Red Sea to Habeshat /Abyssinia and saved the land from a great snake dragon named **Waynaba**.

As it was recorded, a great Zendow—a Snake-Dragon—ruled the land of Abyssinia in tyranny between Aksum and Temben, and demanded a regular sacrifice of a young virgin in exchange for a season of peace and security. Angabo, who was probably a Prince in his homeland, sailed across the Red Sea from Sabaea and after settling in Aksum for a while, he heard the outcry of the people who were terrorized by the wicked Waynaba and wished to be free from bondage and fear. Angabo harkened to the outcry and attempted to rid the land of the evil dragon.

At a time when new maiden was due to be sacrificed, Angabo mixes a special poison, feeds it to a goat, then feeds the goat to Waynaba, who in turn eats it and dies as the poison worked its way into his bowels.

The people rejoiced when news spread abroad that the Sabaean killed Waynaba the Snake Dragon and they rewarded him by making him King of Habeshat and give him the young maiden whom he rescued to become his wife. It is said that either his daughter or one of his descendants from this marriage, was **Makeda**, who became the legendary Queen of Sheba that traveled three thousand miles to meet King Solomon of the Kindgom of Israel.

Sources list the names and reign of five of Queen Makeda's ancestors as follows: Kawnasya (1 year) > Siebado (50 years) > Giebur (100 years) > Angabo 200 years) > Makeda (? years) > **Menelik** (? years).

Note: > = begat.

References:
Kebra Negast; trans. E.A. Wallis Budge; Introduction page xliii.
Aksum: An African Civilization of Late Antiquity, by Stuart Munro-Hay
Biblical Archaeology Society Online Archive Search: http://members.bib-arch.org/

Prince Angabo sails from Sabaea to Aksum, Abyssinia and resues a young maiden from being sacrifed to Waynaba the Serpent-King. Artwork by Jerome Matiyas, © 4/2018, 2021. www.mekonnenepic.com.

The Queen of Sheba, King Solomon, and their son Menelik
The ancestors of the Kings of Aksum (c. 960-930 BC)

The events surrounding the well-known legend of the **Nigist Saba/Sheba**, **Negus Solomon** and their son **Menelik** is probably one of the greatest mysteries in the world. As it involves the perceived disappearance and final resting place of the **Holy Ark of the Covenant** has stirred up even greater mystery and intrigue for all realms in the universe.

As recorded in the annals of the Kings of Israel and the Kebra Negast, the virgin **Queen Makeda,** The Queen of Sheba, heard of the great wisdom and riches of King Solomon from **Tamrin**, her chief of caravans. Queen Makeda traveled thousands of miles to the Kingdom of Israel to meet King Solomon, and they both grew impressed of each other's wealth, wisdom and beauty. The King eventually tricks the Queen to sleep with her and they produce a son named Bayna Lehkem or **Menelik**, which mean "Son of the Wise Man." When Menelik grows up, he travels to Eyerusalem to meet his father Solomon who acknowledges him and wants to make him King of Abyssinia/Ethiopia and send the firstborn sons of his priests, Levites and nobles and a copy of the Ark of the Covenant with his son to set up a Kingdom there.

Eventually, **Azaryas**, the son of **Zadok,** the High Priest, conspired a successful heist to switch the real Ark with the duplicate and take it to Abyssinia with the caravan. Menelik was unaware of the conspiracy and switch, and by the time he and his mother Makeda found out, it was too late and already on their land. They came to the conclusion that if Egziabeher (The Almighty God) allowed the removal of the Ark to happen, then it must be his will to have the Glory of Tsiyon (Zion) to move from Eyerusalem to Aksum.

Some skeptics say this story is a myth and never happened; others say the Ark was taken to Abyssinia at a later period in a different way. Either way, there are lots of evidence to indicate that the Ark (or a copy) did make its way up the Nile River from Elephantine Island to Lake Tana and finally to Aksum. Only Egziabeher knows the truth.

References:
1 Kings 10: 1-13;
2 Chronicle 9:1-12;
Kebra Negast; trans. E.A. Wallis Budge.

The Queen of Sheba and her Son King Menelik 1. Artwork by Jerome Matiyas, © 4/2018.
www.mekonnenepic.com.

Qeddus Yared Diaqon

Musical genius of the Aksumite Empire (c. 501-571 AD)

Saint Yared became known as one of the first musical geniuses to emerge after the days that **Iyesus Kristos** walked the earth. During the reign of **Negus Gebre Meskel** and the ministry of the **Tzadkan**, the Nine Saints, he revolutionized the composition of liturgical Beta Krestyan Mezmur, Church music, to more melodic beauty and lyrical devotion.

As it has been recorded, when Yared was a young boy he had difficulty memorizing the **Dawit Muzmur**- the Psalms of David- under the tutelage of **Za-Mikael Aragari**, one of the Tzadkan. One evening while young Yared sat under a tree sulking about his failures, he noticed a caterpillar struggling to climb the tree, falling back a few times, but it still tried each time again. Eventually, the catepillar did reach the top of the tree, and Yared saw this as a sign from **Egziabeher Amlak** (Egzio) to never give up. Young Yared became encouraged to return to his tutors, and miraculously he was able to memorize the Psalms in a short space of time. The boy then grew to be a well-accomplished musician of several instruments and a singer with a beautiful voice that captivated all that heard it.

There is a story concerning Qeddus Yared about an occasion when Negus Gebre Meskel summoned Yared and his musicians to the royal court to minister in music. The Negus was so captivated by Yared's voice as he sang that he did not realize that he had pierced Yared's foot with the end of his royal spear. At the same time, Qeddus Yared was so enraptured while singing the songs that he did not even feel the Negus' spear pierced his foot and con-tinued singing until the end when they both realized what had happened, the Negus hastily pulls out the spear and only then Yared's foot started bleeding. Of course, eventually Yared's foot was healed, and all was well.

In his collection of hymns, Mezgeba Degwa, Qeddus Yared stated that he learned the music from **Egzio** himself, influenced by His Qeddus Manfes, the Holy Spirit.

References:

DACB; www.dacd.org/stories/ethiopia/yared_.html

Saint Yared the Deacon. Artwork by Jerome Matiyas, © 2021.

Traditional painting of Saint Yared on goat skin.
From Lalibela, Ethiopia, January 2021.
Artist unknown.
Used by permission from Dn. Setegn Mekonnen.

Henok the Prophet

Antedelugian Prophet that walked with Egziabeher (c. 5000 BC)

One of the first and most ancient of the writing prophets of **Egziabeher** was **Henok**, the one who walked and communed with the Almighty One for 300 years on the Earth then was taken up to **Mengistu Semayat**– The Kingdom of Heaven–out of the sight of mankind.

As written in the oracles that bare his name, Henok was the first prophet to write of the coming of the Elect One of Egziabeher, the holy Meshiach, which is Iyesus Krestos, the one who shall come to Earth in the last days with his Yasemay Mel'akt–His Heavenly Host of Angels and Saints–to execute judgement on the wicked and purge the Earth with fire.

As confirmed in the short oracle of **Yihuda** (Jude 14-15), Henok wrote, "Behold the Lord comes with ten thousand of his saints, to execute judgement upon all, and to convince all that are ungodly among them of all their ungodly deeds which they have ungodly committed, and of all their hard speeches which ungodly sinners have spoken against Him." - (Enoch 1:9).

The oracles of Henok tells of many accounts of awesome visions and heavenly journeys the prophet experienced while in the presence of Egzio, including trips to Semayat where he saw magnificent mountains of precious stones, the Tree of Life, pillars of fire, the seven Liq Mel'akt (Arch Angels) of antiquity and even the dark abyss and fires of punishment.

It was during the days of his father **Yared** that about 200 Mel'akt – later called **The Watchers** – led by **Shemihazah** broke the commands of Egzio by leaving Semayat to have malevolent offspring with women of Earth and teach mankind evil deeds. It was Henok that first testified against the Watchers and prophesied that their offspring must be destroyed, the Watchers must be imprisoned in the abyss until judgement day and that Egzio will destroy the world with a deluge of water, saving only his grandson **Noah** and his family with the animals in the great Ark.

According to the **Book of Yashar**, Henok was made a King among the people of Earth and reigned in wisdom and righteousness, teaching the holy and Upright Way to those that will listen. Because he walked so close in the presence of Egziabeher his face and body glowed with brightness and the people were reverent and convicted of their trespasses in his presence. When it was time for him to be taken up "Henok ascended into Semayat in a whirlwind, with horses and chariots of fire." in the presence of many witnesses. - (Jasher 3:1-38)

References
Genesis 5:21-23;
1 Enoch, A New Translation by W. E. Nickelsburg and J. C. VanderKam;
Book of Jasher (1840);
Book of Jubilees;
Jude 14-15

The Seven Mountains of Magnificent Stones as shown to Henok by the Arch Angel Uriel in the Heavenly Realms. Artwork by Jerome Matiyas, © 11/2008. www.mekonnenepic.com.

1 Enoch, chapter 18: 6 - 16:

6. And I proceeded and saw a place which burns day and night, where there are seven mountains of magnificent stones, three towards the east, and three towards the south.

7. And as for those towards the east, (one) was of coloured stone, and one of pearl, and one of jacinth, and those towards the south of red stone.

8. But the middle one reached to heaven like the throne of God, of alabaster, and the summit of the throne was of sapphire. (9. And I saw a flaming fire. And beyond these mountains (10. is a region the end of the great earth: there the heavens were completed.

11. And I saw a deep abyss, with columns of heavenly fire, and among them I saw columns of fire fall, which were beyond measure alike towards the height and towards the depth.

12. And beyond that abyss I saw a place which had no firmament of the heaven above, and no firmly founded earth beneath it: there was no water upon it, and no birds, but it was a waste and horrible place.

13. I saw there seven stars like great burning mountains, and to me, when I inquired regarding them,

14. The angel said: 'This place is the end of heaven and earth: this has become a prison for the stars and the host of heaven. (15. And the stars which roll over the fire are they which have transgressed the commandment of the Lord in the beginning of their rising, because they did not come forth at their appointed times.

16. And He was wroth with them, and bound them till the time when their guilt should be consummated (even) for ten thousand years.

The Queen of Sheba and Her Son Menelik

Mural Depicting the history, legend and legacy of the Queen of Sheba

Jerome Matiyas © 2017
The Queen of Sheba modeled by Saba Fassil with permission.
www.MekonnenEpic.com

References:
1 Kings 10:1-13 | 2 Chronicles 9:1-12 | Matthew 12:42
Kebra Negast translated by EA. Wallis Budge, 1922.

The Ark of the Covenant

Jerome Matiyas © 2013

Glossary
Mekonnen: The Warrior of Light

Note: Most of the non-English words used in book one are of Ge'ez/Ethiopic origin unless otherwise mentioned. Most of the non-English words in the Prologue are of Hebrew or ancient Semitic origin. Ge'ez was the South Semitic language spoken in the Aksumite kingdom by the monarch and local inhabitants who became, and still are, known as Habesha people. Most scholars believe Ge'ez is the root/mother language from which Amhara, Tigrinya, Tigre, Gurage, and Harari evolved from. Sometimes I may use the terms Ge'ez and Ethiopic interchangeably. There were also many people whose native language was not Ge'ez but Kushite languages like Agew, Afar, Beja, Bilen, Oromiyya, Somali and Nubian to name a few. Hebrew, Arabic, Greek and Sabaean/Sheban were also spoken, written and understood by some and influenced the culture in varying degrees.

Abba – (Semitic/Ge'ez/Ethiopic) Father. A biological father, father figure, a priest or monk.

Abbaa – (Oromiya) Father, Daddy.

Abiyy – (Ge'ez) – Great, Large.

Abuna – (Ge'ez/Ethiopic) Title of the Arch bishop of the Ethiopian Orthodox Church. In ancient and medieval time, the Arch bishop was always ordained and sent from the Orthodox head quarters in Alexandria, Egypt.

Abyssinia (Ge'ez/Ethiopic) – Northern Ethiopia and Eritrea. From "Habeshinya" meaning "Land of Hashesha," an ancient word for the land of northern Ethiopia and Eritrea when it was one kingdom ruled by the kings of Aksum, and the Kingdom of D'mot before that.

Adam (Hebrew) – The first man mentioned in the Bible, who was made in the image and likeness of the Almighty Creator yet formed from the dust of the Earth. The root meaning for Adam or Edom means "red," suggesting the first man could have been red is appearance.

Afeworq – *Ah-fay-wor-k (Ge'ez, Ethiopic)*, – A boy's name of Ethiopia and Eritrea, literally meaning "mouth of gold." Also spelled **Afeworqi, Afewerk** (Ah-fay-wor-k).

Agaw/Agew – *Ah-gow* (Kushitic) – One of the most ancient people in the land of Abyssinia, descendant from Kush, son of Ham, son of Noah. Many had intermingled with ancient Hebrews that migrated into the land, forming the Beta Israel people and adopting the Jewish religion and culture. They spoke Agew, Hebrew and Ge'ez. It is also believed they were the first to either adopt or speak the Semitic Ge'ez language, the word *ge'ez* being a variation of the word *Agew*. Some modern anthropologists and researchers believe some of the various people groups in Ethiopia and Eritrea are off shoots of the Agew people, namely the Amhara, Tigrinya, Tigre, Harari and Gurage people.

Aksum – *Ak-soom* (Kushitic-Semitic/Ge'ez) – "Water of the Chief." From "Ak" a Kushitic word for "Water," and "Sum/Shum" a Semitic word for "Chief" (Ethiopia Bradt, PhillipBriggs, 2002). An ancient, holy city in northern Ethiopia that was once the center of the great Kingdom and Empire of Aksum that flourished from about 400 BC to 10th century AD. The Kingdom of Aksum was once one of the first nations in Africa and the world the accept Christianity as a state religion around 330 A.D. during King Ezana's reign. Before this time some of the kings followed pagan religions, and some were of the Jewish religion. Many that converted to Christianity were Ethiopian Jews, but the ones who did not convert became bitter rivals since then, now almost 1700 years later. At its peak, Aksum ruled over most of northern Ethiopia, Eritrea, Djibouti, Nubia/Sudan, Southern Arabia and Western Yemen. It is believed that the legendary Ark of the Covenant that Moses and the people of Israel made in the Sinai wilderness is in a chapel in Aksum. It is disputed if it is really there and how long it has been there, whether it was since the time of King Solomon and Queen of Sheba (950 BC) or later after the Babylonian invasion of Jerusalem when the priests kept it in Egypt before moving it again up the Nile to Abyssinia. Today Aksum is a small town of many churches, monasteries, stele and historical museums and is now a UNESCO World Heritage Site.

Almaz (Ge'ez/Ethiopic) Diamond.

Amba (Ge'ez) – A flat-topped hill or mountain. Used as a fortress, a place of refuse, or to build monasteries and churches.

Amin/Aman (Ge'ez) – Truth. Truly.

Amlak (Ge'ez/Ethiopic) god (small "g"). The expression "Egziabeher Amlak" means Almighty God of gods.

Anbessa – *Ahn-bih-sah* (Ge'ez/Ethiopic) – Lion. Also used to refer to a brave and courageous person, particularly a male.

Angabo (Sabaean/Sheban) – A prince from Sabaea/Sheba and ancestor of Mekeda the Queen of Sheba, probably her father or grandfather. According to legend, Angabo slayed a terrible serpent-snake named Wainaba who terrorized Aksum for a long time. Afterward the people appointment him ruler of the land. See **Wainaba**.

Arwe (Ge'ez) – Beast, wild animal. Plural **Arawit**.

Ayyoo – (Oromiya) Mother, Mommy.

Bahetawi (Ge'ez/Ethiopic) – "One who lives in the wilderness." A hermit monk in Abyssinia/Ethiopia, not affiliated with one particular church but lives a life dedicated the fasting, praying, performing miracles, reading the holy scriptures, preaching and prophesying. They are revered, sometimes feared, and considered holy men by common people and clergy. They usually grow long locks of hair and refrain from certain foods and live by all the rules of the Nazarite vow. The vow is described in detail in the Book of Numbers 6:1-21. Notable Biblical figures who lived by the Nazarite vow were Samson and Samuel. In Eusebius' book of early church history, it describes James the brother of Jesus Christ grew his hair very long after accepting his brother in the flesh as the Messiah/Christ. The Rastafarian movement also adopted their "Dreadlocks" hairstyle and other ordinances from this Nazarite vow.

Benai/Bene Elohim – (Hebrew) The Sons of God. Bene = Sons; Elohim = God. Another expression for the Angels. See **Mal'ak**.

Beta Krestiyan – (Ge'ez/Ethiopic) – Church. Literally "House of Christians."

Beta Israel – (Ge'ez/Ethiopic) – House of Israel, the Ethiopian/Habesha Jews. The official name for Ethiopian Jews whose history and origins can be traced back to the Israelites from Egypt during the time of Moses, The Babylonian invasion and captivity of Israel and King Solomon and the Queen of Sheba. During the time of the Kingdom of Aksum's conversion to Christianity in 330 AD, the Beta Israel established their Kingdom to the south of the Tekeze River and in the Simien Mountains building fortresses and palaces alongside villages, extending further south to around Lake Tsana/T'ana and west to Gondar province. According to their histories, the first king of Beta Israel was King Phineas, a descendant of the Jewish High Priest Tzadok from the temple in Jerusalem during the time of King Solomon of Israel.

Cherub/Kherub *(Hebrew/Semitic/Chaldean)*: A class of heavenly creature that usually has the physical characteristic of a combination of two or more earthly animals usually having multiple pairs of wings (usually 1 to 3 pairs as described throughout the Bible). Plural is **Cherubim**. They guard, protect and/or worship God continuously. First mentioned in Genesis 3:24 as one of the creatures who guarded the Tree of Life after Adam and Eve sinned. See description of Cherubim/Kerubel in Ezekiel 1:5-11, Ezekiel 10:1, and Revelation 4:7.

Chayot HaKodesh *(Hebrew):* The Living Creatures. The Four heavenly creatures that are described in the scriptures as worshiping God, the Almighty Creator, around his throne. They are described as having 4 different faces: a Man, a Lion, an Ox, and an Eagle.

Cubit *(Latin):* A Biblical cubit in approximately 18 inches or 1.5 feet. A 6 feet tall man will be about 4 cubits.

Dabr (Ge'ez), Mountain. Also related to holy mountains and monasteries which are usually up on mountains in Ethiopia and Eritrea. Plural **Adbar**, Mountains. In Amharic it is **Terara**.

Dəhnat (Ge'ez) – Salvation.

Diyaqon/Deaqon (Ge'ez), Deacon.

Egzi – *Eg-zee* (Ge'ez). Lord. The title given to an official, leader, elderly man or to anyone in authority.

Egziabeher/Egziabher – Eg-zee-ah-bih-hayr *(Ge'ez/Ethiopic)*, The meaning of this word, describes the almighty God as being the Lord of All Nations or Lord Father of Nations. *Egzi* = Lord, *a* = of, *Beher* = Nations.

El/Elohim *(Semitic/Hebrew),* One of the most ancient Hebrew names for the God and creator of the whole universe including heavens and earth. **El** is singular; **Elohim** is plural but still refers to one united entity.

Emm / əmm (Ge'ez) Mother. A biological mother or mother figure.

Emnat (Ge'ez) – Faith, **Agre Emnat** - Shield of Faith.

Enku – En-k'oo (Ge'ez/Ethiopic) Pearl or Jewel.

Erelim *(Hebrew):* A class of heavenly angels meaning The Valiant or Courageous Ones. Also spelled Arel, Ar'el, and Er'el.

Eritrea *(Greek/Italian):* Red Land. From the Greek word, *Erythraiā* then translated into Italian as *Eritrea*. The Kingdom of Aksum included the land of modern-day Eritrea with the main seaport at Adulis/Zula. Eritrea shares a lot of ancient and medieval history, culture, food, language (Ge'ez) and alphabet/writing systems in common with Ethiopia. After centuries of tension and wars with Ethiopia, Eritrea has established its own country and government. The sea between the Somalian coast and Sabaea/Himyar (modern-day Yemen) was known to the Greek and Roman sea traders as the Erythraean Sea, and they used a popular ancient map known as *The Periplus of the Erythraean Sea*.

Ethiopia *(Greek):* Burned Face. A general term used by the ancient Greeks to refer to any land south of Egypt beyond the 3rd cataract, including Nubia (modern day Sudan), Abyssinia (modern day Ethiopia) and Eritrea. In the origin Hebrew Tanakh/Old Testament, the word "Kush" was used. Later it was translated into Greek then English to Ethiopia, usually referring to land of Kushites in Nubia/Sudan first. Other sources, like the *Book of Aksum*, claim the word originated from a descendent of Ham and Kush named *Itiopp'is* who settled in ancient Ethiopia and founded the city of Aksum.

Falasha (Ge'ez) – "Outsider" or "Outcast." A sort of derogatory reference for Ethiopian Jews. See **Beta Israel** for details.

Gānen (Ge'ez) – A demon. An evil spirit or fallen angel. Plural – *Agānənt.*

Gabra Masqal – (Ge'ez/Ethiopic) Servant of the Cross. The royal/throne name of one of the most well known Emperors of Aksum in the 6th century AD. Also known as *Ella Ameda II*, reigned circa 543 to 560 AD. There was mostly peace during his reign in contrast to the reign of his father **Kaleb** (*Ella Atzebeha, reigned circa 514 to 543 AD*) before him. After making a sacred oath in Jerusalem concerning the Ark of the Covenant, and settling a conflict for the throne between his two sons **Esrael/Israel** and **Gabra Masqal**, (see Kebra Nagast 117) King Kaleb abdicated the throne to become a monk and live in monasteries for the rest of his life.

Gerum – *G-room* (Ge'ez) Excellent, Wonderful.

Habesha/Abesha – *Hah-bih-sha* (Ethiopic/South Arabic) Mixed people. The people of Ethiopia and Eritrea became known as "Habesha People" since ancient times, into the Aksumite period until today they still refer to themselves by this unique term. Most scholars say it is a South Arabic word that means "Mixed people" or "Crowd of people," suggesting the many ethnic groups that lived and intermingle with each other, including Semitic and Hamitic peoples. Research has proved (including DNA tests) that people from the Mediterranean and Near East have also intermingled into the bloodline of many Habesha people.

Haddis Kidan – *Hah-dees Kee-dahn* (Ge'ez/Ethiopic) – New Testament, of the Holy Bible. In Amharic, it is **Addis Kidan**.

Hade – *Hah-day* (Ge'ez) – Emperor. The Emperor of Aksum, also titled "King of Kings." The Emperors of Abyssinia (Ethiopia and Eritrea) reigned from the throne in the city of Aksum and assumed sovereign rule over the Nubian Kingdoms, Sheba, Himyar, South Arabia, and at times, the Kingdom of Beta Israel. In Amharic this word is **Atse**.

Hawwah/ Hawa (Hebrew): Eve. The first woman mentioned in the Bible, formed from Adam's rib. The very first prophecy in the Bible is centered around the "Seed of the Woman" that will defeat the "Seed of the Serpent," a prophecy of the coming savior and virgin birth of the Messiah.

Ham/Kham (Semitic/Hebrew) – Meaning *warm* or *hot*. One of the three sons of Noah said to be the principal ancestor of most people of Africa. There is a Tomb of Ham located near Aksum since ancient times.

Hashmallim *(Hebrew):* Electrum. A class of heavenly angels. The name suggests they look like the Electrum which is an alloy of gold and silver, that range in color from pale yellow to white. It was sometimes called White Gold or Green Gold in the ancient world.

Hawəy (Ethiopic/Amharic) – An exclamation similar to "Oh!" In Amharic it is **Hoy!**

Hayyal (Ge'ez) – The Ibex mountain goat of Ethiopia. Mostly found in the Simien/Samen Mountains. In Amharic, they are called **Walia**.

Helel – *Heh-lehl* (Hebrew) – *Brightness, Bringer of Light, Morning Star.* Supposedly the name of the Nakhash before he rebelled and became *Satan.* This name suggests his shining, luminous glory as the covering Cherub in heaven before his pride and rebellion to overthrow the Almighty Creator. Helel is translated into the Greek word *Lucifer* in the Old Testament of the Bible/The Torah meaning "Light Bringing" from Isaiah 14: 12.

Henock/Henok (Ge'ez/Ethiopic) – Enoch. Means "Teaching." The great-grand father of Noah, who walked with God for 300 years and was translated/taken to heaven without dying. The books of Enoch are attributed to him and his experiences in the multiple levels of heaven, hell, abyss, and judgments against the fallen angels/Watchers and their evil offspring the giants/titans or "Nephilim." The Books of Enoch were thought to be lost for hundreds of years until they were found in Ethiopia in the Ethiopia Orthodox Church Bible as one of the 81 canonical books, and among the Dead Sea Scrolls in the Qumran caves in Israel. The writings of Enoch are also included of the scriptures/canon of the Eritrean Orthodox Church and the Beta Israel.

Hrai (Tigrinya/Ge'ez) – Okay.

Ish / Isha *(Hebrew)* – Man / Woman. An angelic being that looks like a man; A human of mankind. A descendant of the first man and woman, Adam and Eve. Plural: **Ishim**

Iyesus Kristos (Ethiopic/Greek) – Jesus Christ. Derived from the Greek spelling of the name and title of the Jewish Messiah worshiped by Christians. In Hebrew and Aramaic, his name is Yehshua HaMashiach. Believed to be the Son of God, born of the Virgin Mary. Also called the Son of Man and the Elect One.

Iyaseh/Iyyaseh – *Ee-yah-seh (Ge'ez)* – No.

Kalb (Ge'ez) – Dog. Plural **Kalabat**. Corresponds with the Hebrew **Kaleb/**

Caleb, meaning "Like the heart" as a boy's name or "a faithful dog" depending on context.

Kahen *(Ge'ez/Semitic)* – Priest of the Beta Israel/ Ethiopian Jews.

Kerubel – (Ge'ez) From the Hebrew/Semitic word "Cherub," a creature from the realms of heaven.
See **Cherub/Kherub**.

Kush/Cush (Semitic/Hebrew) – Black. One of the sons of Ham/Kham, son of Noah. One of the earliest and largest groups of people to inhabit Nubia (Sudan), Ethiopia, Eritrea, and Somalia. According to the Bible, the Book of Jubilees and Book of Jashar, the descendants of Kush, including King Nimrod, also first settled in the Mesopotamian area and ruled over large portions of the known world. (Genesis 10: 6 to 12)

Makeda *(Ge'ez/Ethiopic)* – The traditional name for the Queen of Sheba in Ethiopia. The Arabians and Sabaeans/Shebans called her **Bilqis**.

Mal'ak/Mal'akim *(Hebrew/Semitic)*: Messenger or an Angel from heaven or hell, whether good or bad. *Plural: Mal'akim* . See **Mal'ak** below for more details.

Mal'ak/Mal'ekt *(Ge'ez/Ethiopic)* – Angel(s). A powerful being from the realms of Heaven. Sometimes they interact with humans and look like regular men, other times they appear with armor as warriors. They are usually not described as having wings, but in medieval and modern art they are depicted as having one or more pairs of wings. By contrast, kerubel/ cherubim and surafel/seraphim are always described in the Bible as having wings. Sometimes angels are described as wearing white apparel. They vary in appearance and sizes. According to Biblical text and legends around the world, some angels have left their ranks in the realms of heaven to intermingle with humans and produce offspring known as giants, Nephilim, Rephaim, Anakim, etc. In other cultures, they correspond with titans, gods, elves, trolls, and more.

Manakos *(Ge'ez/Greek)* – Monk. From the Greek Monakhos. Plural **Manakost**.

Manfas *(Ge'ez)* – The Spirit of God. **Manfasawi** – Spiritual.

Mastatsabe *(Ge'ez/Ethiopic)* – Warrior.

Mastema/Mastemo *(Hebrew)*: Hatred, Adversary. A fallen angel mentions several times as the main adversary of the apocryphal writing of The Book of Jubilees (Also known as the Apocalypse of Moses). Also mentioned in the Zadokite Fragments and the Dead Sea Scrolls, he is the angel of disaster. The true origins of Mastema is a mystery. In this story, I spell his name with an "**o**" at the end.

Mashaf Qedus *(Ge'ez/Ethiopic)* – The Holy Bible, literally translates as "Words Holy." The canon of the Ethiopian and Eritrean Orthodox Church from the Aksumite period until today include the 27 books of the New Testament, the Jewish Tanakh (Christian Old Testament), the Apocryphal Books (Esdras 1 and 2, Maccabees, Tobit, Baruch, etc.) and the Book of Enoch, Jubilees, etc., adding up to a total of 81 books.

Meder (Ge'ez/Ethiopic) – The Earth

Mekonnen/Makonnen *(Ge'ez/Ethiopic)* – Elite, Lifted Up. An aristocratic title of the royal court for a Governor, Noble or General. It is a common boy's name in Ethiopia and Eritrea. The given name of Haile Selassie I, the last Emperor of Ethiopia, was Tafari Makonnen at his birth. His father's name was Makonnen Woldemikael. Ethiopians and Eritreans carry over the father's first name of the child's last name. The hero of this story, **Mekonnen**, is a fictional character I created in a historical setting and is not of the royal family but one of many warriors in the Kingdom of Aksum. When I chose the name, I was not aware it was Haile Selassie I's father's name at the time because I only knew him by his throne name and as Ras Tafari. Pronounced *Mo-kay* as a short nickname.

Menelik *(Ge'ez)* – Son of the Wise Man - from Ethiopian Legend, Menelik was the son of King Solomon and the Queen of Sheba and the ancestor of the kings of Aksum and Ethiopian Solomonic Dynasty. See section in **Back Stories and Legends** for details.

Mengist (Ge'ez/Ethiopic) – Government. An organized establishment of rulership in Heaven or Earth or the Spiritual Realm whether good or evil.

Meshiach *(Hebrew)* – Messiah. In Jewish and Christian legend and beliefs, the Messiah will be sent to earth by God to save/rescue his followers from the evil forces of the world and the spiritual realm at an appointed time. Christians believe Iyesus Kristos/Jesus Christ is the Messiah prophesied in Jewish scriptures.

Nachash/Nakhash *(Hebrew)* – Snake, Serpent, Shiny/Fiery Serpent. This is the word used to refer the serpent who deceived Adam and Eve in the Garden of Eden in the Book of Genesis, chapter 3:1.

Negus (Ge'ez/Ethiopic) – King. Also refers to a secondary king or a general of an army or brigade.

Nigist (Ge'ez) – Queen.

Negusa Nagast (Ge'ez/Ethiopic) – King of Kings, official title given to the King/Emperor of Aksum and Abyssinia.

Nephilim (Hebrew) – Fallen Ones. The product/offspring of an angel/

Watcher with a human woman. As first mentioned in Genesis 6:1-4, and all through the Bible particularly in Numbers 13: 33, Deuteronomy, Books of 1 and 2 Kings, 1 and 2 Chronicles. Also mention in Jude, and 1 and 2 Peter, the Book of Enoch and Book of Jubilees. Also mentions together with Rephaim, Anakim, Emim, Zim Zumim, etc. Giants, titans, trolls, cyclops, and ogres of ancient myths and legends from all over the world are in this category. Goliath and his brothers of Gath were also Nephilim (1 Samuel 17). Og the King of Bashan (Deut 3:11). The children of Israel were afraid to enter the promise land because of the giants, "children of Anak" that lived in the land of Canaan. (Numbers 13-14).

Onaphel/Onafel (Ge'ez/Ethiopic) – The Wheels of Gods with eyes all over. From the Hebrew word Onaphim.

Onaphim/Onafim *(Hebrew)* – Same definition as above.

Orit (Ge'ez/Ethiopic) – From the Greek Octateuch, referring to the first eight books of the Old Testament. Including the Pentateuch, the five books of Muse/Moses: which are Genesis, Exodus, Leviticus, Numbers, Deuteronomy, plus the Book of Joshua, the Book of Judges and the Book of Ruth.

Qal *K'al* (Ge'ez) – Word. **Qala** – Of the Word. Example: *Qala Egziabeher* – The Word of God.

Qasis/Qas *K'a-sis/K'as* (Ge'ez/Ethiopic) – A Priest of the Ethiopian Orthodox Church. Plural **Qasisan, Qasawest**.

Qataliyan/Qataləyan – *K'a-ta-lih-yan* (Ge'ez) – (plural) Assassins, Murderers; Singular **Qatali**. – an assassin, murderer.

Qedus/Qeddus – *K'uh-doos* (Ge'ez/Ethiopic) – Holy. Saint. Plural: **Qeddusan, Qeddusat** – Holy Ones.

Ruach *(Hebrew):* The Spirit/Wind of God.

Sabaea(n)/Saba / Sheba (Semitic) – The ancient region of Southern Arabia, modern-day country of Yemen. From a root word meaning "An Oath." Once part of the extended Empire of Aksum that was centered in northern Abyssinia (Ethiopia and Eritrea).

Samen (Ge'ez) – South. Referring to the **Samen Adbar** – the Simien Mountains – which are south of the city of Aksum which was the center of the kingdom and empire. In Amharic, it is *Simien/ Semien Terara*.

Sannaya (Ge'ez) – Beautiful.

Sar (Hebrew/Semitic) A Prince or Chief. Example: *Sar Malak Miykael* means Arch Angel or Chief Angel Michael. (Daniel 10:13-21)

Sayf (Ge'ez/Arabic) – Sword.

Serufel (Ethiopic/Ge'ez) – Seraph. A heavenly being, based on the Hebrew root meaning of the word and descriptions in the Bible, "Seraph" is an angel with six wings and look like a flaming torch, or the whole body is on fire without being destroyed.

Serafim/Seraphim *(Hebrew)* – Same definition as above.

Samay/Samayat – (Ge'ez/Ethiopic) Heaven. Similar to the Hebrew word *Shamay*. The sky or the celestial home of The Almighty One, God the creator the universe and the angels.

Shamayim *(Hebrew)* – Heavens. Same definition as above.

Shem – (Semitic/Hebrew) Honor or Name. One of the sons of Noah. The father of all Semitic peoples and languages, who mostly inhabit the Middle East and parts of north and east Africa.

Si'ol – The grave of the dead. Similar to the Hebrew word "Seoul." A waiting place for the should of the dead. Translated as "Hell" in most English/ Western Bibles. Not to be confused with the lake of fire which is "Gehenna"

Sodi (Ancient Semitic): The Way; The root for the word *Zodiac*.

Stadia (Latin): 1 stadia = 600 feet.

Stele/Stelae (Latin) – An Obelisk. In locale Ethiopic/Semitic languages it is ***Hawelt***. One of Aksum's distinctive historical land marks, hundreds of stelae of varying sizes and heights are erected in Aksum. Most of them stand tall in the "stele fields" to the north east of Aksum city. The tallest one stood at 33 meters and was one of the largest stele in the world until it collapsed and broke into 5 pieces a long time ago. Currently, the tallest one stand at 24 meters. The oldest and smaller stelae are said to have been erected about 4,000 years ago. Archeologist believe the earliest ones were erected by Sabaeans (Shebans) from southern Arabian in pre-Christian time for their sun worship religion. Similar stelae were also erected in Sabaea, and some still stand to the present day in the old city of Marib in the country of Yemen.

Tabot (Ge'ez/Ethiopic) – The tablets carried by the priests above their heads in processions. The tabots represent the tablets that the Ten Commandments were written on and placed in the Ark of the Covenant by Moses. Also refers to the actual Ark of the Covenant which is never shown to the public.

Timkat (Ge'ez/Ethiopic) – An annual three-day holy festival held in early January to celebrate the baptizer of Jesus Christ by John the Baptist. It includes colorful processions of Orthodox priests carrying Tabots followed by Arch-Bishops, musicians, monks, incense bearers, dancers and crowds of lay people.

Tsedq (Ge'ez) – Righteousness. A state of being morally upright and just.

Being truthful, holy, moral and upright before God and mankind. Trusting in the pure, righteous standards of the Almighty Egziabeher and His Son Iyesus Krestos and not in the flawed standards of men.

Tsadqan, *T-sad-kan* (Ge'ez/Ethiopic) – The Righteous Ones, referring to the nine "Syrian" monks who came to Aksum in the 5th century AD and inspired the building of many churches and monasteries. They also encouraged the Bible to be translated from Greek to the Aksumite's native and official language of Ge'ez. The origins and nationalities of the Nine Righteous Ones were from regions around the Mediterranean, including Syria, Turkey (Anatolia), Rome, Israel.

Tsion /Tsiyon (Semitic/Hebrew/Ge'ez) – Zion. The supernatural mountain of God or the location of Jerusalem in Israel.

U-wa/Owa (Ge'ez) *Uh-wah,* – Yes.

Wainaba/Waynaba *(Ethiopic)* – Based on ancient Ethiopian legend, the serpent-snake Waynaba terrorized the people of Aksum and nearby towns, including the demand for an annual sacrifice of a young virgin. A prince named Angabo from Sheba/Sabaea (Modern day Yemen) killed the serpent and was made king of the land. Angabo is said to be an ancestor of the Queen of Sheba who visited King Solomon of Israel as recorded in the Bible and legends. Historically, some people did practice a religion of worshiping snakes and snake gods in certain parts of Ethiopia and surrounding areas.

Wayzerit (Ge'ez) – Miss, an unmarried woman or young woman. A royal title for "Lady."

Wezaro (Ge'ez) – Mrs. or Madam, a married or older woman. A royal title for "Dame."

Yashar Sodi *(Hebrew/Semitic)* – Upright Way. The phrase is used a lot in the Book of Jashar/Yashar, meaning the Book of the Upright. The ancient biblical characters: Enoch, Noah, Abraham, Moses, Joseph, etc., were described as living the *upright and righteous way before God and mankind.* This will become a sort of catch phrase for the Warriors of Light in the Mekonnen Epic story.

Yaphet/Japhet *(Hebrew)* – Beautiful, Expansion. One of the sons of Noah. According to the Bible, Book of Jubilee, Book of Jashar, after the great flood the descendants of Yaphet settled in all Europe, parts of the Iran and Turkey (Anatolia). From Russia and Scandinavia in the north, British Isles and Iberian Peninsula to the west, Greek isles to Cyprus to the south to Armenia and northern Persia in the East.

Yohannes *(Hebrew/Ge'ez)* – John, as in John the Baptist or John the Apostle of Jesus and the writer of The Apocalypse or Book of Revelation.

Zendow (Ge'ez/Ethiopic) – A large snake, python or dragon.

References:

African Names (1993) by Julia Stewart

Aksum: An African Civilization of Late Antiquity (1991), by Stuart Munro-Hay

A Rasta's Pilgrimage, 1998, by Neville Garrick

Amharic Bibles (KJV), 1980 by Bible Society of Ethiopia

Comparative Dictionary of the Agaw Languages, 2006, by David L. Appleyard

Comparative Dictionary of Ge'ez, 2006, by Wolf Leslau

Concise Amharic Dictionary, 2004, Wolf Leslau

Cosmic Codes, 2004 by Chuck Missler

Ethiopia, The Bradt Travel Guide, (2002) by Philip Briggs

Ethiopic Grammar, 2nd ed (1855), by August Dillman and Carl Bezold

Ethiopia & Eritrea, 2nd ed, 2003, (Lonely Planet)

Eusebius: The Church History, Trans. and Commentary by Paul L. Maier

Good News Bible with Deuterocanonicals/Apocrypha, 1979 by American Bible Society

Josephus, The Antiquities of the Jews, by Josephus Flavius, trans. by William Whiston

1 Enoch, 2004, by G.W.E. Nickelsburg, James C. VanderKam

The Lost Book of Enoch, Trans. by Joseph B. Lumpkin

The Book of Jasher, 1840 edition, by unknown ancient authors

The Histories by Herodotus (490-420(?) BC), 2003, Penguin Books

The Lost Civilization of Petra, 1999, Floris Books, by Udi Levy

Petra and the Lost Kingdom of the Nabataeans, 2001, by Jane Taylor

Kebra Nagast (1922), English translation by E.A. Wallis Budge

The Book of Jubilees (The Apocalypse of Moses), 2006, Trans. by Joseph B. Lumpkin

The Sign of The Seal, 1992, by Graham Hancock

The Book of Angels, 2006, by Ruth Thompson, Williams and Taylor

The New Strong's Exhaustive Concordance, by James Strong

The New Testament in Amharic and English, Copyright 1962, 1994 by United Bible Societies

Warfare in the Classical World, 1995, by John Warry

The Witness of the Stars (1893) by E.W. Bullinger

The Interlinear NIV Hebrew-English Old Testament, 1987, by J.R. Kohnlenberger III

Acknowledgments:

Special Thank You to:
Seifu Haile Selassie
Kamau Sennaar
Claire Dorsey
Israel Endalkachew
Betty Amare
Gedion Mulat
Kaleab B. Megersa
Hawani Tessema
Yerusalem Work
Samuel Getahun
Awale Abdi
Pastor Paul Hanfere
Yared Tadase
The Ethiopian and
  Eritrean Communities
of Baltimore, DC and Virginia, USA.
Thank you all for your support,
encouragement and inspiration.

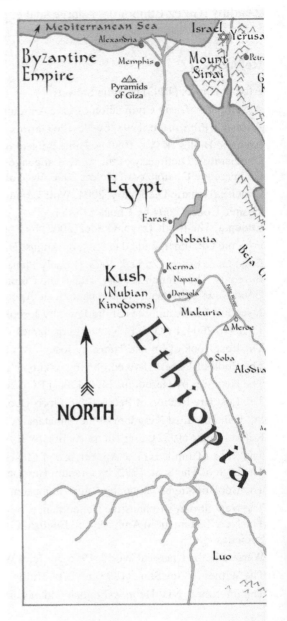

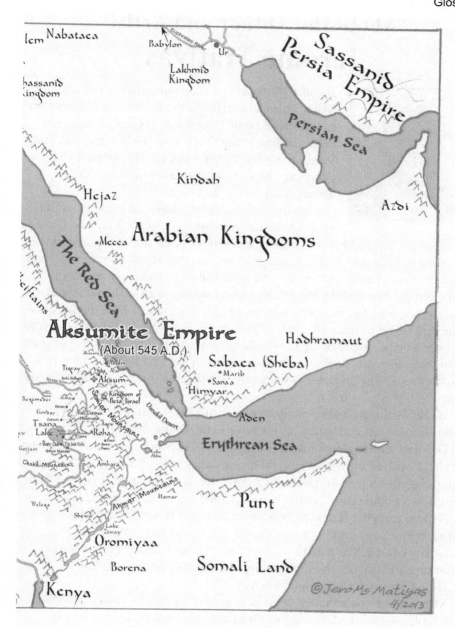

About the Author and Artist

Jerome Matiyas

Jerome Matiyas is a visual designer, artist, and writer. Born and raised in the festive Caribbean twin island Republic of Trinidad & Tobago, Jerome has been residing in the DMV area (DC, Maryland, and Virginia tri-states), USA since 1998. From a very young age he has had a love and passion for art, history, film, music and cultures.

Jerome has a special interest in Biblical studies in scripture and archeology, lost books of the Bible and other ancient Hebrew writings, and has developed a growing love for Ethiopian & Eritrean culture, history, art and people. He also loves sci-fi and fantasy movies, books, American and Japanese animation (anime), comic books and graphic novels. He enjoys getting wrapped up in the worlds of great stories, whether fact or fiction, and reflecting on how they might relate to the real world of the past, present and future. He dives into the research to discover whether a tale or legend could have developed from kernels of truth. All of these interests combined in the making of the first book in the series of historical, Christian fantasy-adventure novels, *Mekonnen: The Warrior of Light*.

While working on his Epic Adventures of Mekonnen in his small home studio, Jerome has conducted art displays in the Baltimore, Silver Spring and DC area with more planned for the future. The story is set in an alternate historical earth in the 6th century AD, as a young warrior name Mekonnen from the great Empire of Aksum in the highlands of Ethiopia & Eritrea finds himself in a grand cosmic battle between good and evil, Light and Darkness.

Jerome earned a Bachelor of Science in Information Technology - Software Emphasis from Western Governors University (WGU), Salt Lake City, Utah, USA in 2016, and an Associates of Arts degree in Visual Communications from the Community College of Baltimore County (CCBC), Catonsville, Maryland USA in 2001.

Many of Jerome's family, friends, fans and supporters say they would really love to see his Mekonnen sagas made into exciting feature length movies on the big screen, a television series or an animated feature sometime in the near future. Jerome is open for his work to be revealed to the world in any type of medium possible, including as comic books and graphic novels.

Follow Jerome's art and story at www.mekonnenepic.com, also on facebook, and instagram.

!~~~~ End of Book One, Part 1 ~~~~

Next:
MEKONNEN: The Warrior of Light, Part 2
Publishing date to be announced.